# Too Many Cooks

## Dana Bate

CORSAIR

First published in Great Britain in 2015 by Corsair

1 3 5 7 9 10 8 6 4 2

Copyright © Dana Bate, 2015

The moral right of the author has been asserted.

A CIP catalogue record for this book
is available from the British Library.

ISBN 978-1-47211-462-4 (paperback)
ISBN: 978-1-47211-463-1 (ebook)

Typeset by SX Composing DTP, Rayleigh, Essex
Printed and bound in Great Britain by Clays Ltd, St Ives plc

Corsair
An imprint of
Little, Brown Book Group
Carmelite House
50 Victoria Embankment
London EC4Y 0DZ

An Hachette UK Company
www.hachette.co.uk

www.littlebrown.co.uk

For Harriet and Sam, in loving memory

# Chapter 1

Twenty minutes after the pallbearers lower my mother's casket into the ground, I am back at her house, surrounded by friends, family and thirty-two salads. Everywhere I look, everywhere I turn: salad. Potato salad. Pasta salad. Tuna salad. Ham salad. There aren't any leafy ones, although some, like my aunt's beloved cottage-cheese lime-Jell-O salad, are decidedly green. No, the bowls lining the tables and windowsills are filled with the kinds of salads I grew up with in Michigan, most containing some combination of proteins and carbs, the ingredients bound up with a spoonful of mayonnaise or its zesty cousin, Miracle Whip, my mother's all-time favourite condiment. She told me she'd never met a recipe that couldn't be improved with a spoonful of Miracle Whip. That, and maybe a dash of rum.

As I rearrange the dining-room table to make room for a bowl of macaroni tuna salad, I feel a tap on my shoulder and whirl around to find Meg, my best friend for the past twenty years, holding a large glass casserole dish covered with aluminium foil.

'Another casserole,' she says. 'This one from the McCrays.'

'Let me guess: chicken, broccoli and rice?'

She peeks beneath the foil. 'Yep. Although I think this one has carrots in it, too.' She takes another look. 'Or maybe that's just cheese. I can't tell. Where do you want it?'

I scan the table, which, in the two minutes I've spent talking to Meg, has given birth to three more creamy white salads. 'In the kitchen, I guess. With the others.'

'You got it.' She re-covers the dish. 'How are you holding up?'

'Okay. Not great. It's been a rough week.'

'I'm so sorry.'

'I'm just exhausted, you know? Physically, emotionally – I'm drained.'

She glances over my shoulder. 'How's Sam?'

'My rock, as usual.'

'What a trouper. Most guys I know would have been on a plane back to Chicago after one night on your dad's pull-out couch. How old is that thing, anyway?'

'Ancient. And filled with equally ancient crumbs.'

'Gross.'

'Very. But we've been together six years now. If he were offended by my family or my humble roots, he would have been out the door a long time ago.'

'Rest assured, there's still plenty of honky-tonk Michigan he hasn't seen.' She looks down at her watch. 'If he isn't busy later, I'd be happy to give him a tour…'

I chuckle for the first time in a week. 'Thanks but no thanks. Dealing with my dad for three days has been painful enough.'

'Speaking of which...' Her eyes drift over my other shoulder.

I turn around and spot my dad charging towards me, his floppy greying hair falling into his puffy eyes. He's dressed in a faded black suit and tie, the only suit he has owned in the twenty-eight years I've known him. He buried both his parents in that suit, his brother, and now, after thirty-three years of marriage, his wife.

'I'd better put this in the kitchen...' Meg says, backing away slowly to avoid having to converse with my dad. He's a loose cannon on a good day, and the past three have been worse than most.

'Dammit, Kelly,' he says, adjusting his tie, which looks as uncomfortable at being around his neck as he looks wearing it. 'Where the hell is your mother's spaghetti salad?'

It seems weird calling it *her* spaghetti salad, as if she might walk out of the kitchen at any moment, dressed in her oversized powder-blue sweatshirt with a big bowl of spaghetti salad resting on her arms. My mom was never much of a cook – her style of cookery mostly involved cream-based canned soup and processed cheese – but her spaghetti salad was something of a delicacy in my town when I was growing up. The combination of spaghetti, ham, shredded cheese and Miracle Whip doesn't sound as if it should go together, but somehow, when combined, the result is downright delicious. Maybe it's the fact that every bite reminds me of my mom, but when I crave something comforting and familiar, it's the first thing that comes to mind. Just thinking about it causes a lump to form in my throat.

'Crap! I made it last night and forgot to put it out,' I say. 'It's in the fridge.'

'Well, could you go get it? Everyone is asking.'

'Sure. Of course.'

'Good.' He runs his fingers through his hair and looks as if he might say something more, but instead he stares at me. '*Today*, please?'

'Sorry – I'm on it.'

'Thirty minutes too late…'

I hurry into the kitchen, telling myself through deep breaths that my father isn't a jerk: it's just his grief talking. Realistically, he is a bit of a jerk, but not a mean spirited one. Expressing emotion has never been one of his strengths, and since my mom's heart attack, his feelings have come bursting out in fits and starts, like water from a punctured hose. Last night he kicked his couch and yelled at it for being 'lazy'.

I push past a few old neighbours and head for the refrigerator, where I find the bowl of spaghetti salad I made last night. Preparing it seemed like a fitting tribute to my mom, using my professional cooking skills to recreate the one dish for which she was known. While I'd boiled the spaghetti and diced the ham, I'd blasted ABBA's 'Dancing Queen', my mom's personal anthem, which she'd play on repeat as she danced around the house, often after a Rum Runner or two. I don't think I'll ever be able to hear that song again without picturing her twirling in the family room, her feathered blonde waves bouncing off her shoulders, a boozy grin on her face.

4

'Need help?'

Sam is standing behind the refrigerator door, looking handsome and decidedly out of place in his tailored Hugo Boss suit. His honey-coloured hair is styled with a bit of pomade and his deep dimples make him seem as if he's smiling, even though he's not. When Meg first met him during my senior year at University of Michigan, she called him 'Ken' behind his back because he bears such a striking resemblance to a Ken doll. By extension, I guess that would make me Barbie, which, given my long flaxen hair, might work if I weren't a slight and flat-chested five foot three. I'm also pretty sure there was never a 'Cookbook Ghostwriter Barbie' or an 'Art History Major Barbie' or, at least, if there was, she certainly never made it to Ypsilanti, Michigan.

'No, I'm okay. Just need to put this on the table.'

Sam glances down at the bowl. 'So that's the infamous spaghetti salad?'

'The one and only.'

'Ever try making that for François?' he asks, referring to François Bardon, one of Chicago's most famous chefs, whose cookbook I've just finished ghostwriting.

'I don't think he'd know what to do with it. I can hear him now: "What ees zees...spa-gay-tee salade?"'

Sam laughs. 'His wife would probably assume it was some sort of Midwestern aphrodisiac.'

'The way people fight over it, maybe it is...'

Sam raises his eyebrows suggestively, then catches himself. 'Sorry – bad timing.'

'It's okay. My mom wouldn't have wanted a big weepy scene.'

'No?'

'Are you kidding? She hated being around sad people. She'd want us to be laughing. Laughing and drinking.'

Even though my mom never told me this explicitly, I know it's true. At my grandpa's funeral, when I was ten, she'd started singing the theme song to *Cheers* while some old guy played piano, so that she could, in her words, 'lighten the mood'. Granted, she was on her third rum and Coke and had a long history of breaking into song at inappropriate times, including at several of my birthday parties, but I know she'd have preferred a veiled sex joke to tears at her own funeral. Part of me is surprised she didn't demand an ABBA-themed graveside song-and-dance in her will.

I'm about to ask Sam to restock the bar when my dad bursts into the kitchen, his face flushed. 'Jesus, Mary and Joseph,' he says. 'Where is the damn spaghetti salad?'

'I was just bringing it out,' I say, lifting the bowl in my hands.

'Oh, really? Looks to me like you were talking to Dr Cock.'

I let out a protracted sigh. 'Dad, we've been over this a zillion times. It's pronounced "Coke". And you don't have to keep calling him "Doctor".'

'Well, he is a doctor, isn't he?'

'I am. But, please, call me Sam.'

My dad clenches his jaw as his eyes shoot from me to Sam and back to me again. 'I just buried my wife. I can call him whatever I want.'

I take a deep breath and look at Sam, but he just shrugs and stares back because, really, how can anyone argue with that?

In what is surely a Madigan family record, we blow through two litres of vodka, two bottles of rum, a bottle of Jim Beam, two cases of beer and thirty-six salads in less than two hours. By the time most of the guests have left, only a humble bowl of ham salad and a trickle of whiskey remain.

'I'm going to take off,' Meg says, leaning in for a hug as she slings her purse over her shoulder. 'You'll be okay?'

'I've got things under control.'

'If you need anything, you know where to find me. When do you drive back to Chicago?'

'Tomorrow afternoon. Sam is flying back tonight because he's on call tomorrow.'

She sighs. 'Dr Dreamy. What a catch.'

My eyes wander over her shoulder, where I see Sam drying a big salad bowl with a tea-towel. 'He's a good one.'

'Good? Try great. Although I can't believe he hasn't popped the question yet. What is he waiting for?'

I pick at a ball of fuzz on my black cardigan. 'We're not in any rush.'

'Obviously. It's been six years.'

'He was finishing med school when we met, and then there was residency, and—'

'And now he's doing his fellowship. I know. Those are excuses, not reasons.'

'Those aren't excuses. We've both had a lot on our plates. You know how precarious my job is – I'm always chasing the next project.'

'I still don't fully understand why you're writing other people's books. When are you finally going to get your own gig?'

'Writing about what? Spaghetti salad?'

'Hey – don't kid yourself. Not everyone can afford truffles and *filet mignon*. Some of us might like to hear from someone on our level.'

'And if a big fat pay cheque falls out of the sky for me to do that, I will. Until then…things are a little in flux.'

'That may be, but it still doesn't explain why Sam hasn't made an honest woman of you. What – is he afraid you'd say no?' She chuckles to herself but stops abruptly when I don't join in. 'Wait – you'd say no?'

My stomach curdles. 'What? No. Of course I wouldn't say no. He's great. He's…perfect.'

'You're damn right he's perfect. A cardiologist who looks like a Ken doll? Who lives and works in Chicago? You're living the dream, my friend. The *dream*.'

'I know,' I say. 'I know', even though I'm no longer sure if that dream belongs to me, or the me Sam met six years ago.

Thirty minutes before I'm supposed to take Sam to the airport, I wander past my brother's old bedroom and find him sitting on the bed in the dark. His twin bed still bears the Detroit Tigers comforter my parents bought him when he was ten, above which hangs a dated poster of Britney Spears in a pair of denim cut-offs and a fluorescent crop top.

'Stevie? What are you doing in here?'

'Don't call me Stevie,' he says. 'I'm twenty-five. People call me Steve.'

'I don't care how old you are. You'll always be Stevie to me.' I notice a folded-up letter sitting on the edge of his bed. 'What's that?'

8

'A letter from Mom.'

'From Mom? From when?'

'Not sure. Dad found the letters when he was looking for something in one of her drawers.'

'What do you mean "the letters"? There was more than one?'

He scratches the light brown stubble on his chin. 'I think she left one for both of us. Yours is probably in your room.'

My head feels light. 'But…she dropped dead of a heart attack…'

'Which, apparently, was a surprise to everyone but her.'

I nod, conceding his point. A few hours after she died, my dad got a phone call from her doctor, who was effusively apologetic. Evidently my mom had visited him six months ago, thinking she had a cold, but she was troublingly short of breath so he ordered a few tests, including an echocardiogram. It turned out she had cardiomyopathy, a heart-muscle disease. He'd put her on medication and told her to follow up in three months, and if the drugs didn't work, he recommended she get an implantable defibrillator. But she never showed up for her follow-up appointments and didn't return any of his calls, so he wasn't sure if she'd even filled her prescription.

This was the first any of us had heard about a heart problem, including my dad, and it made me so angry. Why would she keep her condition a secret? So we wouldn't worry? Surely we had a right to know, a right to worry. Maybe Sam could have helped her – he's a cardiologist, after all. But what bothered me most of all was the question I'd never be able to answer: if I'd known about her condition, would our relationship have been any different?

Or would it have remained the same: loving, complicated and admittedly dysfunctional?

'But I mean…a letter? Mom didn't even write Christmas cards. Why would she write us a letter?'

Stevie hunches his shoulders. 'Do I have an explanation for half the things Mom did? Maybe this was her way of saying goodbye, on her own terms.'

I concede his point once again. For a guy who, at twenty-five, technically still hasn't finished college, Stevie often surprises me with his perspicacity. I sometimes wonder where he'd be if he'd been born into a different family, with parents who took a genuine interest in his intellectual development and didn't delegate most parental duties to his big sister. Maybe he would have made more of himself.

'So what did it say?'

'That's between me and Mom.'

'Stevie, I'm your sister. You can tell me.'

'Go read your own letter.'

'Stevie…'

'Kelly…' he whines back.

I let out a huff. 'Fine.'

I march across the hall to my old bedroom, which, like Stevie's, looks almost exactly as it did nearly twenty years ago: hot pink comforter with brown and green polka dots, a two-foot-tall piggy bank shaped like a crayon in the corner of the room, and a small white desk and chair below the window. I creep towards the desk, on top of which sits an old blotter studded with hot-pink hearts. A white envelope rests to the left of the blotter: 'To Kelly. From Mom.'

My hands shake as I tear open the envelope and read the letter inside, which is written in my mom's swooping cursive, the slanted lines indicating the involvement of a blackberry brandy or two:

*My dear little Kelly Belly,*
*If you're reading this, I've finally kicked the bucket.*
*I hope it was quick and relatively painless and didn't*
*cause the rest of you too much trouble. Lord knows,*
*I gave you enough trouble when I was living, so I*
*hope I went out on a high note.*

*I have a few parting requests for you, so I thought*
*I'd put them all together in a list. That's right – a list!*
*I bet you're liking me better in death than in life*
*already. (Kidding.) Unlike you, I'm not much of a*
*writer, so I hope you'll* ~~*bear bare*~~ *bear with me.*
*OK, here we go.*

1. *First of all, keep Irene O'Malley away from your*
   *father. She always had her eye on him, and even*
   *though I'm dead, I do NOT want her getting her*
   *hands on him. Frankly, I don't want him dating any*
   *of my friends, but especially not Irene.*
2. *Speaking of Irene, if I had to guess, she still has my*
   *square Tupperware container with the maroon lid.*
   *Now that I'm dead, she'll think it's hers, but it is not.*
   *Make sure you get it from her and explain that I*
   *hadn't forgotten she never returned it – even though*
   *I reminded her <u>seven times</u>. (You can mention the part*
   *about seven times; I bet she'll be impressed I remem-*
   *bered that.)*

3.  *If anyone asks about the rest of my Tupperware collection, it is not up for grabs. It's for you, your dad and Stevie. (You're welcome.)*

4.  *As for your dad, don't let him get too kooky. He never liked to feel a lot of feelings, so he's probably acting all sorts of strange, and that's okay, but don't let him get too weird. I'd say a good gauge would be: if he's shouting at the newscasters on TV, that's fine, but if he starts talking to the bushes, you might want to encourage him to get a dog.*

5.  *Look after your brother. I don't mean move back to Ypsilanti (please, don't do that, I'll explain why below), but check in on him once in a while and make sure he isn't doing something stupid, like growing pot or dating that floozy Catherine Gornicki. I know you've always looked out for him, but now that I'm not around, it's extra important that you're there for one another.*

6.  *That brings me to you. I know, I know, I can see you rolling your eyes: 'Here goes Mom with her kooky ideas!' But a person only gets one chance to make a dying wish, so listen up! Here's what I want: I want you to walk away from the beaten path and, for once in your life, do something unpredictable and a little crazy. Not crazy by Kelly standards. Crazy by my standards, which, as you know, are pretty darn crazy. You've spent your whole life following the rules, and it's time for you to make a change. I've always seen you as my star, the Madigan who would go on an adventure – a real honest-to-goodness adventure – maybe in Hollywood or New York or some place*

*really exotic like Switzerland. I'm so proud of all you've accomplished so far, but you haven't managed to leave the Midwest, and I feel like you were destined for so much more. You're probably thinking, What does Mom know? She's never lived anywhere but Ypsilanti! And that's true. But that's also why I know what I'm talking about. I'd hate for you to turn forty and never have lived anywhere outside the Midwest. If you decide to come back here some day after all that travel, so much the better, but as Dr Phil would say: 'Make an informed decision.'*

7. *Finally, a word about this Sam guy. Really, Kelly? I get that he's a doctor and looks like a Ken doll and is steady and reliable, etc., but I have to be honest with you: he is a little boring. Is this what you want for yourself? A fifty-year snoozefest with some fuddy-duddy who eats the same bowl of cereal for breakfast every single morning? Zzzzz ... Oh, sorry, I fell asleep just thinking about it. I'm not saying you have to marry Crocodile Dundee, but I think your life will be a lot more exciting and interesting if you find some-one a little more spontaneous.*

*So there you have it. My wish list. I'm sure there are plenty of other things I'll think of before my time comes but, knowing me, I'll forget to add them. I wasn't always the most reliable mom along the way, and I know that, but I loved you and your brother more than anything in this world, even if I made a hash of showing it at times. You, especially, have made me so proud, even if I still don't fully understand what you do for a living. Whatever it is, you can be sure I'm bragging about it in Heaven.*

*Love you so very much.*

*xoxo*

*Mom*

*PS You don't have to do everything on this list, but if you don't, I'll haunt you for the rest of your days. (Kidding. Or am I?)*

'You ready?'

I jump as I look up and see Sam standing in the doorway. 'Sorry,' I say, clutching my chest. 'You scared me.'

His eyes land on the letter in my hand. 'What's that?'

I glance down at the piece of paper, the words inside still spinning in my head. I consider telling him about my mom's laundry list of dying wishes, about Irene O'Malley and the Tupperware and her desire for me to see the world. About the shock I feel that she actually wrote a letter. That she was worried about my brother and my dad. That she had the gall to call Sam *boring*. But instead I fold the letter into a small square, hold it tightly in my hand and rise from the bed.

'Nothing,' I say. 'Just my mother, torturing me from beyond the grave.'

Because, as both of us know, there's nothing shocking about that.

## Chapter 2

I should probably clarify something: Sam *is* boring.

He is. But that's part of what I fell in love with – his boringness. After twenty-two years of dealing with an eccentric and unreliable mother and an inept and crotchety father, I felt blessed to have found someone so normal. Someone who didn't break into 'Dancing Queen' randomly and without warning. Someone who actually kept stamps and light bulbs in the house. Someone who showed up.

We met during my senior year at the University of Michigan, while I was working an afternoon shift at Zingerman's, a gourmet deli in Ann Arbor. I was running the sandwich counter that day, and he came in wearing a big U of M sweatshirt and blue scrubs, his honey-blond hair sticking up in every direction. He sauntered over to the counter and ordered the Zingerman's Reuben – a sandwich consisting of house-made corned beef, nutty Swiss cheese, pungent sauerkraut and Russian dressing, all piled together on fluffy slices of house-made rye and grilled – except he asked me to hold the sauerkraut.

'Then you don't want a Reuben,' I said.

He furrowed his brow. 'Yes, I do.'

'If you don't have sauerkraut, then it isn't a Reuben. It's a perfectly fine sandwich, but it isn't a Reuben.'

'Okay, then. I want a grilled corned-beef sandwich with Swiss cheese and Russian dressing on rye.'

'Do you have something against sauerkraut?'

'And what if I do?'

'Have you tried our sauerkraut?'

He blushed. 'No.'

'Then how do you know you don't like it?'

'Because I've never liked sauerkraut. Our cafeteria used to serve it with hot dogs on Wednesdays when I was a kid, and it smelt terrible.'

'Did you ever try it?'

He blushed again. 'No.'

I put my hands on my hips. 'Okay, here's what we're going to do. I'm going to make you a Zingerman's Reuben *with* sauerkraut and you're going to try it. If you don't like it, the sandwich is on me. Sound like a plan?'

He smirked, his eyes sparkling. 'Sounds like a plan.'

Long story short: he liked the sandwich.

But, more than the sandwich, he liked me. And I liked him. He had a gentle touch and an easy smile, and he was studying to become a doctor. Some of my friends heard the word 'doctor' and saw dollar signs, but that wasn't the main attraction for me. What I saw was someone with discipline, diligence and drive, three attributes neither of my parents had ever had. Anyone who could study hard enough to get into medical school and then survive four years of exams and overnight shifts – not to mention cut open a living person and sew her back up – was probably someone who wouldn't flake out and leave me standing on the side of the road.

And I was right. Sam is as steady as a metronome. He pays his bills on time. He never runs out of toilet paper. He does his own laundry and stacks his T-shirts with the folds facing out. I never have to worry that I'll come home, like I did in the fifth grade, and find a lake-size puddle in the middle of the living room because there was a thunder-storm and he left all of the windows open. He is dependable. Consistent. Predictable.

That also means he has never booked a last-minute trip to Barbados or played hooky from work so that we could catch a movie or have a picnic in the park. We've never dropped everything because we were suddenly craving tacos from a Mexican joint in Chicago's South Side or bought a new TV on a whim. We never have sex on a Tuesday. Everything in our lives is planned and steady and … well, after six years, a little boring. Boring, just like my mother said, which is why her words gnaw at me the entire three-and-a-half-hour drive back to Chicago, stirring up doubts I've tried to silence.

I shake off those doubts as I park the car beneath our apartment building, a twenty-six-storey tower of glass and steel perched on Chicago's famed Lake Shore Drive. The building was designed by Mies van der Rohe, which had appealed to my inner art-history nerd when Sam showed me the apartment two summers ago. We'd been living in

Chicago since he'd started his residency three years earlier, but he planned to start a fellowship at Northwestern the following year and wanted something closer to the hospital. I couldn't believe I was seeing the work of one of the architects I'd studied in college and, improbably, might also call that building my home. The lease was only for two years, but Sam said that was fine because in two years we might be ready to buy a place of our own. The idea scared me a little, but I told myself I had more than 730 days to get comfortable with it. Well, here we are, two years later, and I still haven't set up a time to meet with an estate agent. Buying seems so…permanent. Technically we have until July to find a place but, given that it's already mid-April, I'm not sure how much longer I can stall.

I take the elevator to the eighth floor, and when the doors open, I toddle with my suitcase towards our apartment at the end of the hallway and let myself inside, knowing Sam will still be at work until at least eight o'clock tonight.

As soon as I open the door, I take a whiff: Pine-Sol. Sam must have cleaned the apartment last night before going to bed. Because he knew I would be emotionally drained when I got home and wouldn't want to do it myself. Because he thinks of things like that. Because he's perfect.

I dump my suitcase in our bedroom and make my way to the kitchen, a small galley lined with grey-and-white granite countertops, espresso-coloured cabinets and stainless-steel appliances. As much as I was attracted to a building designed by a famous architect, the kitchen is what sold me on the apartment. It isn't big – with only one bedroom and a small living room, neither is the apartment

– but all of the appliances are new, meaning I can test recipes at home and not worry my efforts will be foiled by a forty-year-old oven.

As I open the refrigerator to deposit some containers of macaroni tuna salad, my cell phone rings. It's Sam.

'Welcome back,' he says. 'How was the drive?'

'Not bad. How was your flight last night?'

'Mercifully brief. Which is less than I can say for this day.'

'Bad?'

'Bad. Don't expect me home before nine.'

'Ugh, I'm sorry. Will you have a chance to eat? I could bring you something.'

'Nah, I'll be fine. Thanks, though. Speaking of food, I left some for you in the fridge – for dinner or a snack or whatever.'

My eyes land on the middle shelf, where he has left a container of chicken noodle soup, an apple and two chocolate cupcakes. 'Aw, thank you,' I say, wedging the macaroni tuna salad between the soup and the cupcakes. 'That was sweet of you.'

'My pleasure. After everything you've gone through the past week, I figured you might not feel like cooking.'

I twitch. Cooking is *exactly* what I feel like doing, what I always feel like doing when I'm overrun with emotions I don't know how to process. I'm not sure Sam fully understands that or if he ever will. In his efforts to be supportive and helpful, he often overlooks my need to 'do', and instead does for me. Part of that is probably my own fault. After taking care of everyone else for so many years, I liked having someone take care of me. But some days I feel as if I've created a monster – though if I ever said that to Meg, she'd probably punch me in the face.

'Thanks,' I say. 'I brought back some leftover macaroni tuna salad, so you're welcome to have some when you get home, if you have any interest. Which, I realize, you very well may not.'

'Are you kidding? That stuff was delicious. Consider me a convert. Did you bring some leftover spaghetti salad as well?'

'Sorry, no. Everything went the day of the funeral, except a little ham salad. The macaroni tuna came from an old neighbour who dropped it off this morning.'

'Ah, well. Another time, then.' He clears his throat. 'So, I emailed a realtor today about potentially seeing some properties. I'm on call this weekend, but she said she could take us to see a few places next Saturday.'

My chest tightens. 'Oh. Wow. So soon?'

'Soon? Our lease runs out June thirtieth. It's the middle of April.'

'I know, I just…After everything that's happened with my mom, it feels sort of sudden.'

'We've been talking about this for almost two years.'

I gulp. 'I know.'

'Do you not want to live with me or something?'

'Don't be ridiculous – of course I want to live with you. I'm living with you now.'

'I mean live with me…permanently. As in for ever.'

The word lands with a thud, sitting in the empty space between his phone and my ear, like a steaming hot turd. *For ever*. For ever? As in this-is-a-proposal for ever? No. No, proposals involve rings and romance and face-to-face

20

interaction. Proposals don't happen over the phone – at least, not proposals from guys like Sam. He is a planner. He is not the kind of guy who, while watching TV in his pyjama pants, would say, 'Hey, could you pass the remote, and by the way I think we should get married.' Everything involves planning. Everything is a production. When I mentioned wanting a new couch, we had a 'house meeting' to discuss whether it fitted into the budget.

So, no. This can't be a proposal. And even if it is, I refuse to accept it.

'Fine, we can meet with a realtor Saturday,' I say. 'Set it up.'

'Yeah?'

'Yeah,' I say. I just hope he can't hear the hesitation in my voice.


I should want to marry Sam. And part of me does. But another part of me thinks back to the letter my mom wrote, the way she articulated the fears and doubts that have been nagging at me for the past year or so, and wonders if marrying him would be a huge mistake. And then I hate myself for being so selfish and stupid, and proceed to eat the two chocolate cupcakes Sam left in the refrigerator.

After licking the buttercream from my fingers and scraping every last chocolaty crumb from the cupcake liner, I flip open my laptop and check my email, something I haven't done in a record-breaking twenty-four hours. I scan and delete the usual junk – flash sales on at least a dozen websites, news alerts from CNN, recipe digests from Serious Eats and Food52 – until my eyes land on an email from someone named Poppy Tricklebank with the subject

'Setting up a call'. I open the email, which is a mere two sentences long:

Dear Ms Madigan,
   My employer is interested in collaborating with you. When are you available to speak?
All best,
Poppy xx

I scroll down to see if the email bears a signature or any indication of who her employer might be, but I find nothing. I pull up Google and run a search for 'Poppy Tricklebank'. I find a profile for a twenty-six-year-old woman living in London, who works as a personal assistant. But a personal assistant to whom? I scroll through a few more entries, when I come across an article mentioning Poppy's name: '…TMZ reached out to Poppy Tricklebank, Natasha Spencer's assistant…'

I freeze. Natasha Spencer? *The* Natasha Spencer? The raven-haired American actress who won an Oscar three years ago and now lives in London with her husband, a well-known British politician? Why would that Natasha Spencer want to work with *me*?

Before I can contemplate what this means and what I should write to Poppy, my phone buzzes on the table next to me. Meg's name is on the screen.

'Hey,' she says, when I pick up. 'Made it back in one piece?'

'Yep…' I say, my attention still focused on my computer.

'Are you okay? I know the past week has been really hard on you.'

'Sorry – yeah, I'm okay. Or, you know, trying to be. I just got a weird email, that's all.'

'From whom?'

'Someone named Poppy Tricklebank.'

Meg snickers. 'Poppy what? Who is she?'

'I'm not sure. I think…I think she might be Natasha Spencer's personal assistant.'

'Natasha *Spencer*? As in the actress?'

'I think so.'

'Whoa, whoa, whoa. Hang on a sec. Why is Natasha Spencer's assistant emailing you?'

'She says her employer is interested in collaborating with me.'

'Natasha wants to write a cookbook?'

'I guess. She didn't elaborate in the email. She wants to set up a call.'

Meg squeals excitedly into the phone. I should have known not to tell Meg about anything possibly involving movie stars or pop culture unless it was a sure thing. She works in public radio, covering the wonkiest news imaginable, but in her free time she reads celebrity websites obsessively and never lets a week pass without buying *Us Weekly* or *People*, usually both. The prospect of me working for a Hollywood superstar is like catnip.

When it comes to celebrities, Meg has always been this way, from our earliest days at Carpenter Elementary, where she and I met in third grade. Our school district was sort of an Ann Arbor/Ypsilanti hybrid, a no man's land called Pittsfield Township that straddled the two cities. For families like mine, the draw was decent Ann Arbor schools, without having to paying Ann Arbor property taxes. It was a great deal for my parents, and in terms of getting a moderate education, it was for me, too. But, socially, I never felt I fitted in. Since my mailing address was Ypsilanti, my classmates who lived in wealthier sections of Ann Arbor thought I was some poor hick (or their moms did, which made play dates a little awkward). But then the people I knew in Ypsilanti who lived a few blocks away in a less-good-school district thought I was too fancy for them because I went to school in Ann Arbor.

Obviously there were other kids in my exact situation, but the problem was…I didn't like any of them. Jennifer Slattery lived three doors down but was still occasionally peeing her pants in the third grade, and Melanie Doyle liked to play games that involved trying to throw her cat out of various windows in her house. They weren't my people.

Then Meg moved into my neighbourhood, and finally I had someone who not only seemed normal, but who also felt like the sister I never had. We loved the same books and movies – *Beezus and Ramona*, *The Babysitters Club*, *Beauty and the Beast*, *Beethoven*. We preferred tea parties to baseball, vanilla to chocolate, and we didn't mind swimming against the current if we didn't feel like going with the crowd. Not all of our interests intersected, but that only made our friendship stronger. I'd introduce her to a new food or recipe I'd discovered, and she'd update me on the latest Hollywood teen gossip. I was never nearly as interested as she was in Jonathan Taylor Thomas or the latest issue of *Tiger Beat*, and I watched with some bemusement as she founded the Ypsilanti chapter of the Leonardo DiCaprio Fan Club when we were thirteen. But her infectious enthusiasm only made her dearer to me than she already was. Even when she went to Eastern and I went to U of M, we'd talk on the phone multiple times a week and, more often than not, she'd brief me on the current celebrity headlines. Our calls became less frequent once I moved to Chicago and we both became busy with adult life, but I can always count on her to tell it to me straight – whether she's talking about my personal life or the lives of the rich and famous.

'Oh, my God, this is so cool,' she says, still on her star-induced high. 'When are you guys going to talk? Are you going to speak to Natasha directly?'

'I don't know. I haven't replied yet.'

'You haven't replied? What are you waiting for?'

'Meg, I opened this email approximately thirty seconds before you called.'

'Okay, okay! Then reply right now, while I'm on the phone. That way I can feel connected to Hollywood fame by association.'

I click reply and begin to type a response.

'What are you saying?' Meg asks.

'So far I've written, "Happy to talk."'

'That's it?'

'Geez Louise – give me a sec. What day is it? Tuesday?'

'Yeah.'

'Okay. "Happy to talk. I'm around the rest of this week, pretty much any time. Let me know what works best for you. My cell number is below. Best, Kelly."'

'Did you use any exclamation points?'

'No.'

'Good. You don't want to seem overly eager, but at the

same time you want to seem interested. Interested, yet professional.'

'Considering this pertains to my professional life and not yours, I think you need to take a few deep breaths.'

'Easy to say from your fancy perch on Lake Shore Drive. Some of us are still living in Michigan, twenty minutes from the house where we grew up.'

'You produce a radio show in one of the coolest college towns in America. Cry me a freaking river.'

Meg huffs. '*Anyway*, the point is, you are going to work for one of the most famous movie stars on the planet, and this is amazing.'

'First of all, I'm not even a hundred per cent sure Natasha Spencer is the employer Poppy is talking about. And second of all, I have neither been offered nor accepted a job of any kind.'

'But you will, right? You have to.'

'I don't have to do anything. Working with celebrities can be a nightmare. I've heard horror stories – you have no idea.'

'So you'll have to deal with some Hollywood nonsense – so what? You can put it in your tell-all some day.'

'Let's not get ahead of ourselves. For all we know, this could have nothing to do with Natasha Spencer.'

'I know,' Meg says. Then she lets out another enthusiastic yelp. 'But I really hope it does.'

I lean back in my chair and glance at my response to Poppy's email one last time before I hit send. 'I know you do,' I say, even though, for reasons I don't want to admit to myself, what I really want to say is, *I really hope so, too.*

## Chapter 3

The next morning, I awake to the sound of my cell phone humming and buzzing on the nightstand next to me. I rub the sleep from my eyes and grab the phone, whose display bears a long series of numbers beginning with '44020…'

'Hello?' I say, my voice scratchy with sleep.

'Hello,' replies a young woman's voice. 'Is that Kelly?'

'It is.'

'This is Poppy Tricklebank. Have I…caught you at a bad time?' Her voice resonates with a plummy English accent.

I sit up in bed, stretching out my shoulders. 'No, this is fine. How can I help?'

'I have Natasha Spencer on the line. She'd like to discuss collaborating with you on a project.'

My heart nearly stops. 'Now?'

'Is that a problem? You said in your email you were free any time.'

'I know, but I thought…' *I thought you'd give me a little notice. I thought I'd have time to prepare. I thought I'd be talking to* you. I run my hand across my forehead. 'Now is fine,' I say.

'Excellent. I'll put her through.'

I hold my breath as the line goes silent, in disbelief that I'm about to speak to one of the most beautiful and famous actresses in the world. Being a cookbook ghost-writer, I often work with renowned cooks and chefs, translating their celebrated dishes into recipes an average home cook can understand and follow. I like to think of myself as one of those translators at the United Nations, only instead of working for heads of state, speaking Russian and Farsi, I work for chefs who use jargon like 'robot poix' (pulse vegetables in a food processor) and 'five min – salamander' (broil for five minutes). But even the biggest celebrity chefs are celebrities only to a specific subset of the population. Movie stars cross borders, both cultural and physical. Over the course of her career so far, Natasha Spencer has starred in action flicks and serious dramas, high-brow art films and low-brow comedies. A lot of people know who Jamie Oliver is. *Everyone* knows who Natasha Spencer is.

'Hello, is this Kelly?' says a velvety voice, at the other end.

'It is,' I say, my palms sweating.

'Hi, Kelly, this is Natasha,' she says. 'I'm so glad Poppy tracked you down. I've heard great things about your work.'

I try not to sound surprised. 'You have?'

'You worked on François's book, yes?' Her American accent bears a *faux*-English lilt.

'I did.'

'François is a dear friend. He recommended you highly.'

'That's nice to hear.'

She takes a sip of something. 'Yes, well, anyway, before we talk about my project, why don't you tell me a little more about your background? Are you professionally trained?'

'Not exactly. I never went to culinary school, if that's what you mean. But working closely with so many chefs, I've had a lot of on-the-job training.'

'Ah,' she says. 'Hmm.'

I bristle, feeling the need to defend my reputation. 'For what it's worth, I actually think my lack of professional training has been an asset.'

'And how is that?'

'I write recipes for home cooks, who don't have professional training either. So if a chef gives me a recipe, and I screw it up, chances are a home cook will screw it up, too. I streamline the process to make sure a dodo like me could follow it.'

'Ah. I see. How did you get into this line of work?'

'It's kind of a long story.'

'Is it interesting?'

'Sorry?'

'The story. Is it interesting? If it's interesting, I'd love to hear it.'

I hesitate. 'I mean...I'm sure some people find it interesting.'

An uncomfortable silence hangs between us. 'Well?' she finally says. 'What's the story, then?'

I gnaw at my thumbnail, wondering how to condense a long story involving Sam, an art-history degree, a cake book and a mom who loved fake cheese into a story that might interest one of Hollywood's most famous stars. I'm pretty sure this is impossible.

Nevertheless, I give Natasha an abbreviated version of my bizarre career track. As I talk, the panic I felt as I approached college graduation returns, pulsing through my veins as if I'm twenty-two again. By then, all of my other friends had jobs or acceptances to law or medical school, but I had nothing – not even a request for an interview. Why had I majored in art history? Why hadn't I done something practical, like economics or accounting? The choice was so unlike me. Every decision I'd made before that one had been cautious and pragmatic – holding down multiple jobs, living with my parents for longer than necessary, learning Spanish. But when I attended my first art-history lecture with Professor Lawrence Davis, an authority on modern art, I found myself hanging on his every word. Who knew learning could be such fun, that not everything in life had to feel like a chore? When I was growing up, my favourite books and TV shows had depicted college as a liberating rite of passage, four years of exploration, freedom and fun. Now I was experiencing that high for myself, and no one could stop me.

The problem, I discovered, was that my decision to throw caution to the wind might have been better served if I'd majored in accounting and just taken up a crazy hobby. The job market for art-history majors was bleak, and I cursed myself for following my heart and not my head. I was moments away from applying for a job as an insurance sales representative, when, to my infinite relief, Professor Davis emailed me, saying he had a job lead. His friend's daughter was a pastry chef in Chicago and she needed help writing a cookbook about how to bake cakes that looked like famous pieces of modern art: a Mondrian-inspired Battenberg, a Rothko wedding cake. Since he knew I loved to cook – I was regularly bringing homemade treats to our afternoon seminars – and was writing my thesis on Roy Lichtenstein, he passed my name along, and a week later I had a job offer. Sometimes I wonder what would have happened if Professor Davis hadn't sent that email – if I'd be in Michigan, selling insurance, or if I would have found my way to this job eventually, through many years of trial and error.

I give Natasha an edited version of this story, skipping the parts about the insurance job and my self-doubt, as well as the unfortunate incident in the Chicago bakery involving Andy Warhol and an oven fire.

'So…that's pretty much it,' I say, once I've finished my spiel.

Silence.

'That wasn't very interesting,' Natasha says eventually.

As expected: professional suicide.

'But,' she continues, 'I like what I've seen of your work, and François tells me you're professional and…shall we say discreet?'

'Yes,' I say, wondering if she knows about his sous-chef's drug habit. 'Absolutely.'

31

'Good. That's really important to me. For obvious reasons.'

Obvious because she is who she is. But also because, aside from being a famous movie star who is married to a British MP, Natasha was once involved with another famous star named Matthew Rush, and the tabloids ran their relationship into the ground. 'Mattasha', as they were known, became such fixtures in gossip columns and magazines that they were stalked constantly by the paparazzi, appearing every day on Perez Hilton's blog and People.com. Even someone like me, who doesn't follow celebrity news, knew the ins and outs of their courtship, mostly thanks to Meg, who would regale me weekly with their ongoing saga. When Natasha's maid eventually sold a story to *Star* about how Matthew was carrying on an affair with Natasha's trainer, they broke up, and Natasha fired half her staff and went into hiding for six months. I can see why she would be careful about hiring new people.

'So let me tell you a bit about my project,' she says, after taking another sip of her drink. 'I have a contract with a major publisher to write a cookbook. My editor said she could find me a ghostwriter, but I haven't been impressed with any of the names she has given me. Some serious attitudes. You know what they say – too many cooks…'

'. . . spoil the broth,' I say.

'What?'

'Too many cooks spoil the broth. That's the expression.'

Silence.

'*Anyway*,' she continues, 'the point is, none of these other writers share my vision. I don't want this to be any cookbook. I want it to be a landmark cookbook. A cookbook that will sit on people's bookshelves, sandwiched between Martha Stewart and Julia Child. Can you help me write that kind of book?'

I hesitate. 'Sure.'

'Great. Because that's the book I want to write.'

'Okay…So what's the hook? What's the story tying everything together?'

'*Exactly*,' Natasha says.

Apparently she doesn't realize those were actual questions. 'I'd…need to know those things before we start testing recipes,' I say, 'especially given that we'd be working on a lot of this long distance.'

'Long distance?'

'Well…yeah. You're in London, and I'm in Chicago.'

'Oh, no. No, no – if we were to work together, you would obviously live here.'

My eyes widen. 'In London?'

'Of course. Where else would you live?'

'Chicago.'

'No, that won't work at all. You have to be here. How else would you be able to write as me?' She makes a valid point. Normally, when I ghostwrite for a chef, I spend hours with that person in and out of the kitchen, so that I can capture in writing how he or she speaks, cooks and thinks. When the cook lives in Chicago – as most of my clients do – that isn't a problem. When I've ghostwritten for a personality who lives elsewhere – Nashville, say, or St Louis – I'll chat with that person on the phone extensively or even visit to ensure I get the voice just right. But moving? To another country? That has never happened before. I've never left the country, period.

'I see what you're saying, but…London isn't exactly next door. How long do we have to write the book?'

'We'd have about five months until our deadline. But then I'd want you to stick around for another five or six months to help me prepare for the launch – media appearances, guest columns, things like that.'

'You'd want me to move to London for almost a year?'

'At *least*. Would that be a problem?'

My eyes land on a framed photo of Sam and me, which a friend took on a boating trip on Lake Michigan last summer. 'It might be a little…complicated, that's all. And, financially, I'm not sure I can manage an apartment in London.'

'Oh, well, obviously you would be well compensated. Do you have representation?'

'No. Not at the moment.' In truth, I've never had an agent, but for most of my gigs so far that hasn't been a problem. With someone like Natasha, well, part of me wishes I had one.

'Ah,' Natasha says. 'Interesting. Well, my business manager deals with all of the finances but, given the advance from my publisher, you'd be paid somewhere around two hundred thousand dollars. And we would take care of your accommodation as part of the package.'

I choke on the air. 'I'm sorry, did you say two hundred thousand dollars?'

'We can't go any higher, I'm afraid. Is that a problem?'

A problem? For my first job, working on the modern-art cake book, I made twelve dollars an hour, after a probationary period of three weeks when my hourly rate was ten. As my experience and reputation have grown, I've drastically increased my take-home pay, but even working for François – my best-paying project so far – I only made seventy thousand dollars, and that was for twelve months of work. My last project before that paid a hundred dollars per recipe.

'No, that isn't a problem at all,' I say. 'That would be just fine.'

'Good.' She takes a deep breath and lets it out slowly into the receiver. 'Okay, I've decided. I like you, Kelly. I like your vibe. And, given what François has told me, I can see us working very well together. I'd like to offer you the position.'

The phone slips out of my hand onto the bed, and I scramble to pick it up. 'Oh. Wow. Thank you. I…I don't know what to say.'

'The word "yes" comes to mind.'

'It's just…I need to talk to my boyfriend before I commit to anything.'

'Ah. I see.' She pauses. 'If there's one bit of advice I can give you, from one woman to another, it's never to let a man stand in the way of your career. It'll only come back to haunt you later.'

'The London thing makes the job a little complicated. That's all.'

'You can make it work. Trust me. The distance is just a small hitch.'

But as my eyes wander back to the photo of Sam and me – his arm around my waist, my head on his shoulder, his smile bigger than Lake Michigan – I know this so-called hitch is anything but small.

## Chapter 4

I can't move to London. Can I? My entire life is in Chicago. Or I guess Chicago and Michigan. But I've spent all of my life in the Midwest. I belong here. This is where I fit in.

Then I think back to my mom's letter. She wanted me to get out of the Midwest, to see the world, to make something of myself. This would be the perfect opportunity to do all of those things. If I produce the sort of cookbook Natasha wants – a landmark cookbook that will be used by home cooks all over the world – it could make my career. In a few years, I could be the go-to ghostwriter for chefs and celebrities alike. I could finally afford a new set of knives. Hell, maybe I could even write my own cookbook, like I've always wanted to. This could be my springboard.

That is, if it weren't for Sam. There is no way he'll want me to take this job. He still has two years of his fellowship left, plus an extra year after that for his training in heart transplants. He certainly can't fly to London all the time to visit me, and even with a nice salary, I can't afford to visit him often either. Taking this job would mean putting our relationship on ice for at least a year, possibly closer to two.

But maybe that's exactly what I need. A break. A break from Sam, a break from Chicago, a break from the comfortable and the familiar. Maybe it's time for me to do something crazy, like my mom said. Maybe writing that list of dying wishes was the sanest thing she ever did.

Or maybe I'm about to alienate the one person in my entire life I've been able to rely on. The person who has encouraged my career and picked up my dry cleaning, the person who spends three days with my crazy family and still manages to stock the refrigerator with chicken soup and cupcakes. Could I really leave him? Could I really break his heart?

No. No, I can't do any of it. Which means that, no matter how wonderful this job might be, no matter how great an opportunity, no matter how much I really, really want to, I can't move to London.

'I'm moving to London.'

The words burst out of my mouth as Sam walks through the door later that night, his briefcase in his hand, his tie loosened around his neck.

'What?' His brow furrows as he drops his briefcase by the front door. 'What are you talking about?'

'Natasha Spencer. She's working on a cookbook, and she wants me to ghostwrite it.'

'Whoa, whoa, whoa – back up the bus. Natasha Spencer? As in *the* Natasha Spencer?'

I nod. 'I spoke to her today.'

'You *spoke* to her? Like, on the phone?'

'She called me. Well, her assistant did. And then I talked to her for twenty minutes.'

He stares at me, wide-eyed. He seems to be holding his breath.

'Sam?'

He lets out a gust of air. 'Sorry. It's just ... Wow. Natasha Spencer. I kind of had a thing for her in college after I saw her in *The Devil's Kiss*. She's ... Wow. What was she like on the phone?'

'I don't know. Business-like.'

'Wow,' he says again. He shakes the stars out of his eyes. 'So what does this have to do with moving to London?'

'Natasha lives in London.'

'She does?'

I smirk. 'And I thought I was out of touch. Haven't you seen the photos of her with that British MP, Hugh something?'

He shrugs. 'Maybe?'

'Well, he's her husband. And they live in London, and she wants me to move there to help her with her cookbook.'

'For how long?'

'Close to a year.'

His expression darkens. 'Close to a *year*?'

'Yes.'

'But I still have two years of fellowship left. Three, really.'

38

'I know.'

'Then how would we see each other?'

'We wouldn't.'

'We wouldn't see each other? How would that work?'

'It probably wouldn't.'

He stares at me for a long while. 'I don't understand. I thought we were looking at properties together next weekend. I thought...' He shakes his head. 'Are you breaking up with me?'

'No. I'm...It isn't...' I take a deep breath. 'I need to take this job. For me. And for my mom.'

'Your mom?'

I consider telling him about her letter, but since that will inevitably involve mentioning her request for me to ditch the 'fuddy-duddy', I decide not to.

'She wanted me to see the world,' I say.

'So? As I recall, she also wanted you to take up the accordion.'

'Yeah, and she wanted me to get a perm, too. That's beside the point.'

'Then what is the point?'

'That *I* want to see the world.'

'Okay. Then let's see the world. Together.'

'I don't think you understand...'

'No, I understand,' he says, his voice rising. 'You want to see the world? Let's see the fucking world. Let's go to London and Paris and, I don't know, some place with drug-resistant TB, like India or Kazakhstan. And, hey, while we're at it, why don't we visit Nigeria or the Congo, where maybe we can pick up malaria?'

'Sam, you're being ridiculous.'

39

'I'm being ridiculous? *Me?*' He lets out a frantic laugh. 'You're the one who, after six years, is making a unilateral decision to pack up and move to London without me. After all I've done for you, after everything we've been through, don't I deserve a vote in this?'

The obvious answer is yes. Of course he does. There are two people in this relationship, and we both deserve to have our voices heard. But over the past six years, I've felt my voice slipping away, yielding to what Sam wanted, what Sam needed, what Sam thought was best for us both. Sam made it easy to lose sight of 'me' in the context of 'us' because he has only the best intentions. He wants to take care of me, to worry about even the most trivial matters so that I don't have to. And as much as I love that about him, I worry that five or ten or fifteen years from now, I won't even know what I want or need any more because Sam has taken care of everything for me.

'I didn't come to this decision lightly,' I say. 'I've given it a lot of thought.'

Sam sneers as he glances at his watch. 'What – two whole hours?'

'Sam…'

'Don't "Sam" me! Have the past six years meant nothing to you? How can you do this to me?'

'I'm not doing it to hurt you. I'm doing it for me.'

'A little selfish, don't you think? After everything I've done for you?'

My cheeks flush. He's right: this is the most selfish thing I've ever done. With every decision I've made throughout my life, I've taken others into account. I took my first job at fourteen, washing dishes at Abe's Coney Island, because

I knew my family could use the extra cash. I lived at home in my freshman year of college so that I could help my parents around the house. I followed Sam to Chicago and limited my ghostwriting jobs to those that wouldn't take me away from him for long. I've always been the friend that people call in an emergency because they know I'll drop everything and rush to their aid. Other than majoring in art history, I've never done something for the simple reason that I wanted to. But I want to take this job in London and, as much as I hate myself for acting so selfishly, I feel I've earned the right to put my needs first, just this once.

'I think I'll always regret it if I turn down this opportunity.'

Sam huffs. 'What about ruining our relationship? Don't you think you might regret that?'

'Yes,' I say. 'I do.'

'Then why are you taking this job? Do you not love me any more?'

'Of course I love you.'

'Then what is it?'

I fidget with the sleeve of my sweatshirt and consider how to respond, how to tell Sam that as much as I love him – as much as I will always love him – I'm not sure I'm 'in love' with him any more. How do you tell someone something like that? Something so harsh and undeniably hurtful? How do you tell the truth without cementing yourself in the top tier of Biggest Jerks of All Time?

'I need a change,' I say, which is also true.

'A change from what? Aren't you happy here?'

Again, I grasp for a response. The truth is, when I search

my soul and really think about it, no, I'm not happy. Or, at least, not as happy as I think I could be. But I've never admitted that to myself until now, mostly because I didn't think I had the right to feel that way. I grew up in a house with two wackadoodle parents who could barely pay their mortgage and often forgot to pick me up from school. Now I live in a great apartment in one of the best cities in the world with one of the most handsome and thoughtful boyfriends on the planet. How could I not be happy? And if I'm not, what kind of fucked-up creature am I?

'I guess I'm not as happy as I'd like to be,' I say.

Sam's expression sours. 'What does that even mean?'

'It means…I have to take this job.'

Sam's eyes grow moist. 'And what am I supposed to do, huh? Sit here with my thumb up my butt for a year while you "find yourself" in London?'

'First of all, whatever you do, please don't sit with your thumb up your butt.' I attempt a smile, but Sam remains stone-faced, unmoved by my admittedly lame joke. 'But second of all, I don't expect you to wait for me. That isn't fair. I can't ask you to put your life on hold while I figure out mine.'

'How considerate of you.'

I reach out to touch Sam's shoulder, but he jerks it away. 'I'm sorry,' I say. 'Really I am. I'm not doing this to hurt you. But I'll never be able to make you happy if I'm not happy with myself. I hope you understand.'

He rips off his tie. 'So this is it, then? It's over?'

The word rattles in my ears: *over*. Is that what I really want? And if it isn't…what *do* I want?

'For now, I guess…'

'If it's for now, then it's for ever.' He grabs his suitcase off the floor and heads towards the bedroom. 'You'd better find somewhere else to sleep tonight. And I want you out of this apartment by the end of the week.'

He marches into the bedroom and slams the door behind him.

With a lump in my throat, I creep over to my laptop, where Poppy's email stares back at me. Am I ready to do this? Is this really what I want? If I officially tell Poppy yes, that's it: Sam will be gone from my life for ever. We've been together six years – *six years*. I can barely remember what my life was like before I met him. Leaving him will be like losing one of my limbs.

I stare at the bedroom door and listen as Sam crashes around, slamming drawers, throwing open closets, banging lids. It's too late. I've already told Sam I'm going. If I back out now – if I tell him I've changed my mind – things will be even worse. He'll know I was willing to leave him, and I'll always curse myself for chickening out. For his sake and mine, I have to follow through.

I look back at my computer screen, and my hand wanders to the keyboard. I press 'reply':

Poppy,
I'm in. How soon can I start?
Best,
Kelly

Then I click 'send' and sink down in my chair, hoping I haven't just made the biggest mistake of my entire life.

# Chapter 5

'Here we are, miss. Miss?'

I startle awake in the back seat of the car, the jetlag already taking its toll less than two hours after landing in London. 'Sorry – I must have fallen asleep.'

'Quite all right, miss.'

The driver, an Indian man in a smart black suit and aviator sunglasses, steps out of the sleek black Mercedes and opens my door, gesturing at the six-storey Victorian building behind him. 'Please,' he says. 'After you.'

My eyes crawl up the building's façade, which is pale grey limestone adorned with ornate balusters, corbels and carved stone wreaths. A large wrought-iron gate covers the front entryway, its black spindles ornamented with shimmering gold leaves. A window box filled with petunias sits above a gold plaque that reads 'Hampden House', part of the address Poppy sent me when she confirmed all of my arrangements.

I grab my carry-on and step out of the car, making my way to the front gate as the driver removes my two suit-cases from the trunk. I press the bell for the building manager and take a deep breath as I look around, sizing up my new neighbourhood. Hampden House takes up the entire block on this stretch of Weymouth Street, in a section of London called Marylebone, a name I'm still not entirely sure how to pronounce. (Maree-le-bone? Mar-le-bone? Marill-bone? I have no idea.) Across the street, a cherry-red wine shop called Nicolas advertises a special on cabernet sauvignon, the deal scrawled in swooping cursive on a big black chalkboard. On the street perpendicular to Weymouth, smartly dressed people bustle in and out of a chic grocery-cum-restaurant named Villandry, whose sage-coloured awnings stretch across the sidewalk. On this crisp May morning, a few men and women sit at small tables outside, sipping coffee and nibbling bits of flaky croissant and slices of buttered toast.

'Hello?' says a man's voice, through the intercom.

'Hi, this is Kelly Madigan. Poppy Tricklebank sent me?'

'Ah, yes. Just a moment.'

He hangs up as the driver wheels my suitcases up behind me, and a second later, a stocky man with wild brown hair and stubbly jowls opens the front gate.

'Hello,' he says, reaching out to shake my hand. 'I'm Tom, the building manager.'

'Nice to meet you.'

'Your flat was serviced this morning. The keys are in my office, so if you'll follow me...'

I reach for my suitcases and notice the driver standing behind them. Crap – a tip. I forgot to get money from the ATM and have nothing to give him.

'I'm so sorry,' I say, fumbling for my wallet. 'I only have dollars.'

The driver raises his hand. 'Miss Tricklebank has taken care of everything. Have a lovely stay.'

He heads back to his car, and I follow Tom into Hampden House, whose foyer is lined with thick ruby carpeting, the walls stark white. Tom grabs one of my suitcases and leads me into his office on the ground floor. The small room is stuffed with books, magazines and, as far as I can tell, junk – empty boxes, candy wrappers, torn sheets of bubble wrap, a bicycle wheel. A scuffed desk sits in the back corner, crammed between the wall and a bookcase, the surface covered with papers, a desktop computer and a clunky black telephone.

He grabs a small key ring off his desk. 'Right. This is the key to the front gate, which locks automatically behind you. If you forget your key, you can call my office between the hours of eight and five during the week, and I will let you in. On Saturdays, you can reach me between nine and noon. Outside those hours…well, you're buggered, I'm afraid. But sometimes if you ring one of the other flats, someone will let you in.'

His words come at me fast and furious, with a husky English accent, many of the terms – 'serviced', 'buggered' – foreign to my American ears.

He holds up the second key. 'This is the key to your flat, which is just down the hall. If you lose either of these keys, the replacement fee is forty-five pounds and a bottle of wine.' He smirks. 'Kidding about the wine.' Then he winks and cups his hand to his mouth conspiratorially. 'But not really.'

He hands me the set of keys. 'I have an extra key if you plan to have visitors. A boyfriend, perhaps? Or a family member?'

'Nope. Just me.'

'In that case, one will do. Please don't make copies. For security reasons, anything to do with keys must go through me.'

'Got it.'

He wheels one of my suitcases towards the door. 'Right. Off we go.'

I follow Tom down the hallway, passing a wooden console lined with unopened mail, above which hangs a large gilded mirror. Tom slows his step as we reach the door to flat two.

'Here we are,' he says. He sticks the key in the lock and jiggles it back and forth. 'The lock can be a bit sticky. Ah. There we go.' He gestures inside. 'After you.'

I walk through the doorway into a small, carpeted entry area. To the left lies a small living room, with parquet flooring, a black vinyl couch, a red armchair, a wooden coffee table, and a small wooden dining table surrounded by four chairs. The entryway to the kitchen sits just beyond the dining table, the door propped open with a wooden wedge.

Tom wheels my case into the living room and deposits it next to the couch. 'Right. Living room here. Kitchen there. Washing machine in the kitchen. And if you'll follow me this way...' He heads back towards the front door and continues along the carpeting down a small hallway.

'Bedroom here. Bathroom there. Water heater can be a bit dodgy so it's best to keep showers brief. I don't recommend using the bath.'

I inch along the carpet and peek into the bathroom, which features a black-and-white tiled floor, a pedestal sink and a claw-foot tub-and-shower combination.

'What's that cord hanging from the ceiling?' I ask, pointing above the toilet.

'The loo flush.' He yanks on the cord, and there's a loud *whoosh*.

'Ah. Got it.'

Tom turns back towards the front door, and I follow him into the entryway. 'The flat is serviced on Thursdays between nine and eleven, unless you say otherwise. If you require any more cleaning, please let me know, and I can arrange it for an additional fee. Oh, and Miss Tricklebank sent over a hamper, which I've left in the kitchen.'

'A hamper? Like for laundry?'

Tom looks at me quizzically. 'No. For eating.'

I quickly realize this is yet another linguistic Britishism with which I am unfamiliar so, instead of pressing the issue, I simply nod and say, 'Right. Of course.'

Tom has one last look around the flat and claps his hands together. 'Sorted. If you need anything, I'll be in my office until five.'

'Thanks so much,' I say.

'Cheers.'

He leaves and closes the door behind him, and I head for the kitchen, where I find a large wicker basket wrapped in cellophane sitting on the counter. 'Oh, a *gift basket*,' I say out loud.

I quickly untie the silky ribbon at the top and peel back the cellophane. Beneath it, I find a pile of teas and snacks, along with a note:

Kelly,
Welcome! Here are a few essentials to get you started. The mobile has already been topped up. Please turn it on as soon as you arrive.
Best,
Natasha

I rummage through the basket and find a shiny black smartphone, which I power on, as per Natasha's (or, if I had to guess, Poppy's) instruction. Five minutes later, the phone rings, its jingle filling the kitchen as I study the various boxes of organic herbal teas.

'Hello?'

'Ah, brilliant, you've found the phone,' Poppy's voice trills in my ear. 'How was your flight?'

'Long,' I say. 'But otherwise fine. Thank you so much for the gi—' I clear my throat. 'The hamper. It's lovely.'

'Yes, well, we figured you wouldn't have anything in the house, so these are things at the very *minimum* we thought you would need.'

I scan the basket, which, among other things, contains a pot of wild boar pâté, a jar of organic Manuka honey, a package each of wild Scottish smoked salmon and venison salami, a tube of geranium and neroli hand lotion, and a lambswool hot-water-bottle cover. 'Yeah, it looks like you covered the basics.'

'I assume you've seen the ATM card Natasha has taken

out in your name.' I spot a Barclays Bank card sitting beside the salami. 'The PIN is attached. The cash from that account is meant for cookbook-related purchases only. Groceries, equipment, things like that. It is not for personal use.'

'Understood.'

'Good. Now, on to some business. Natasha wanted to have you round for supper tonight. Does seven o'clock suit?'

'I – oh. I didn't realize I'd be meeting her so soon.'

'She wants to get to work straight away. This book is very important to her.'

'I understand.' I rub my eyes. 'I'm just a little worn out. I didn't sleep much on the plane.'

'Supper won't take long. Natasha is very busy, as I'm sure you understand.'

'I do.'

'Good. We'll see you at seven, then. Oh, and if you decide to bring flowers – which of course you will – they must be white, and the stems must be trimmed to exactly six inches.'

'Okay…'

'And whatever you do, do *not* mention Matthew Rush. Do you understand? Under absolutely no circumstances.'

'I…Sure.'

'Good. We're in agreement. See you at seven.'

She hangs up abruptly, and as I stare dumbly at the phone, I wonder what the hell I've gotten myself into.

# Chapter 6

Hee-haw. Hee-haw. Hee-haw.

I startle awake to some sort of siren whizzing past my window, the flashing lights illuminating my darkened room like a disco. For a hazy moment, I think I'm back in Ypsilanti, where I spent nearly three weeks after Sam kicked me out of our apartment. But, as my eyes bring the room into focus, I realize, no, I'm not in Ypsi. I'm in London.

London.

Natasha.

Supper.

*Shit!*

I leap out of bed and grab my watch: six fifty-three. Oh, my God. How did this happen? The last thing I remember is sitting on my bed and writing a few notes in my project journal. That was at…what? Three o'clock? And now it's almost seven. I should already be walking to Natasha's house from the tube station. Crap!

I rush into the bathroom and grab my brush off the windowsill, trying to unfurl the gnarly knots in my long, unwashed blonde hair. No time to shower. No time for much of anything, really. Which, considering I'm about to meet one of the most gorgeous and famous women in the world, who happens to be my new employer, is freaking perfect.

The outfit I'd planned to wear still smells like the plane's luggage hold, so I reach for the medicine cabinet to grab a bottle of my perfume, and as I do, I catch a glimpse of my reflection.

Jiminy fucking Christmas. I have pen all over my face.

I grab a washcloth and begin scrubbing my skin, trying to remove the swirls of black ink from my cheeks and chin. What the effing eff? I must have fallen asleep on my journal. Jetlag: one. Kelly: nil.

By some miracle, the pen hasn't tattooed my face, although with all of the scrubbing, my chin is now red and raw and chapped. Whatever. Better to look as if I have a drooling problem than a beard.

I slap on some foundation and a coat of mascara before grabbing my jacket, purse and keys and rushing out the door. I glance at my watch: 7:05. Great. I'm already late, and I haven't even left the building.

When I get outside, I hurry across Weymouth Street and nearly die as a car almost hits me. I might have noticed the silver Mercedes if I hadn't been looking the wrong way, expecting the cars to be on the American side of the street.

'Sorry!' I shout, holding up my hands defensively. 'I'm American.'

The driver shakes his head and steps on the gas, ploughing onward.

My heart still racing, I flag a taxi on the other side of the road. I'd planned to take the tube – Poppy had told me I'd need to get an Oyster card for my travels around town – but, given that I'm already ten minutes late, I don't have time.

'Where to, love?' the driver asks, as I stumble into the taxi.

'Um…Belsize Park?' I rummage through my purse in search of the address Poppy gave me. 'Fifty-one to fifty-two Belsize Square. Across from St Peter's.'

'Lovely,' he says. 'Off we go.'

He steps on the gas and tears down the street, whisking me around parks, shops and cafés towards Natasha's house. As we speed through London, I stare out of the window and soak up the bustling city around me: bright red double-decker buses, shiny black taxis, block upon block of Georgian brick and knotted ivy. I can't believe that less than twenty-four hours ago I was standing in my dad's living room, trying to shoo Irene O'Malley out the door as she brought my father yet another casserole ('Well, a man has to *eat*,' she'd said, as she rolled back her shoulders, thrusting her ample bosom in my dad's direction).

Moving back into the house I grew up in was…well, let's just say it wasn't my favourite. My mom's death has made my dad even more irritable and loony than he was before, probably because he refuses to talk about it at all. Once the funeral was over and done with, he went back to his job with the Postal Service like nothing had happened.

He occasionally drifts away in thought, or pauses briefly when he finds one of her old crochet hooks or bobby pins, but if anyone brings up my mother by name, he snaps and says something like, 'Why does everyone have to *talk* all the time? Is there something wrong with silence?' So, being in the house with him for almost three weeks wasn't the most fun I've ever had.

That said, I didn't really have a choice. Sam gave me three days to pack up my things and leave the apartment, and since Poppy wasn't sure how long it would take to get me a work visa, rent me a flat and send me all of the paperwork (contract, non-disclosure agreement, and on and on), I couldn't just hang out in Chicago indefinitely without a place to live. And, as much as I dreaded living in close quarters with my father again, part of me was glad to leave Sam and Chicago behind. I felt – still feel – rotten about how I handled our break-up, and I worried that the longer I stayed in the apartment, the greater the chance I'd change my mind and beg Sam to take me back. Sam is comfortable. Sam is safe. But right now a voice in my head is telling me I don't need safe. I need risk. I need a change.

The taxi whizzes past a series of row houses made of rust-coloured brick, which eventually yields to rows of semi-detached white stucco mansions with big bay windows and column-clad front porticoes. The driver slows as he approaches a double-width white mansion with two driveway entrances, both of which are gated.

'Here we are, love. Ten pound twenty.'

I open my wallet, and when I look inside, I panic. I have only dollars. Thanks to my afternoon snooze, I never made it to the ATM.

'This is so embarrassing,' I say. 'I only have US currency. Do you accept dollars?'

''Fraid not,' he says. 'Pounds only.'

'What about credit cards?'

He shakes his head. 'I can drive round to a cash machine. There's one on Haverstock Hill.'

I look at my watch. It's already seven thirty. I don't have time to drive around for ten or twenty more minutes while we try to find an ATM. 'The thing is . . . I'm already late.'

The driver looks at me dumbly. What am I expecting him to say? *Oh, sure, well in that case, the ride's on me!*

Then it occurs to me: Poppy.

'Let me text my contact,' I say. 'She'll be able to help.'

I shoot Poppy a quick text, and seconds later, she is flying through the front gate, her phone clutched tightly in her hand. She is taller than I expected – probably five eight – with a slim build and straight chestnut hair that, tonight, is pulled into a slick high ponytail. Her silky cream top is tucked into a navy-and-green-striped pencil skirt that comes to her knees, and she sports a pair of low cream wedges.

'Come along,' she says, as she rushes to the taxi. 'You don't want to keep Natasha waiting more than you already have.'

I step out of the car as she hands the driver a neatly creased collection of bills and smooth my black pants and teal blouse. As the taxi pulls away, Poppy sidles up beside me and gasps. 'You haven't brought flowers!'

Fuck. The flowers. This jet lag is ruining my life. 'I'm so sorry. I've never had jet lag before, and I fell asleep by accident, and before I knew it—'

'Enough,' Poppy says. 'We'll just tell Natasha you're allergic.'

'To flowers?'

'Yes.'

'All flowers?'

She sighs. 'Oh, that won't work, will it? She has bloody flowers everywhere. Just say the flower shop near you was out of white flowers, and all they had were mums. She hates mums.'

'Okay...'

'Good.' She looks me up and down. 'What's happened to your chin?'

I reach up to touch it, the skin still sore from scrubbing away all of the pen marks. 'I fell asleep on a pen.'

A blank stare.

'I was writing notes in my project journal, and I must have—'

Poppy holds up her hand. 'That's enough, thank you. I don't need to hear any more.'

She leads me up the steps to the front door, which is painted dark grey. Unlike the other white houses on the block, this one doesn't have any protruding bay windows or rounded columns. Instead, the house has been remodelled with a contemporary flair, so that all of the windows lie flush with the façade, the window grids all painted the same deep grey as the front door. The front portico has a modern edge as well, with square columns and a thick rectangular overhang. Something about it screams California, even though we're in north London.

Poppy opens the front door and whisks me into the foyer, an airy, minimalist temple. White marble tiles cover the floor, gleaming like a single sheet of smooth ice, and the walls are painted the colour of snow, bare except for three abstract black-and-white paintings. Halfway down the hallway to the left, a curved staircase made of solid white marble sweeps to the upper floors, encircling a chandelier of dangling globe lights that hangs from the floor above. The living room is directly to my left, the blond hardwood floors stretching from end to end beneath a grey-and-black-striped rug and Mid-century Modern furniture. Like the entryway, the white walls are adorned with abstract expressionist paintings and prints, many resembling works I studied in college. I have seen no more than ten per cent of this house, and already it is the most amazing home I have ever entered.

'The kitchen is downstairs,' Poppy says, pointing to the stairway, which continues down to the ground floor. 'That's where you'll be doing most of your work.'

'Oh – I assumed I'd be testing the recipes in my kitchen.'

Poppy raises an eyebrow. 'Your kitchen?'

'The one in my flat.'

'No. You'll be testing the recipes here. At least, that's what Natasha told me.'

'What did I tell you?'

We both look towards the living room as Natasha glides our way, her long black hair tumbling in waves over her narrow shoulders. She wears a thin grey cashmere sweater, which dips over her left shoulder, revealing the black strap of a camisole underneath, and black leather leggings that stop at the ankle, right above her pointy black flats. Her features are even more striking in person: perfectly plump lips, chiselled cheekbones and hypnotic eyes as green and sparkling as emeralds. She is shorter than I'd expected, but also thinner, her head perched on her fragile frame like a lollipop on a stick.

Poppy composes herself. 'We were just talking about the recipe testing.'

'Ah.' Natasha smiles and extends her hand in my direction. 'You must be Kelly. So nice to meet you.'

I shake her hand, which feels smooth and delicate, like a Christmas ornament made of blown glass. 'Sorry I'm late. I…' Poppy shoots me a stern look '…was searching for flowers, but the florist by my flat only had mums.'

Natasha puckers her lips. 'Ick. Mums.'

'I know.' I look at Poppy, who gives me an approving nod.

'Anyway, so what were you ladies discussing about recipe testing?'

'Kelly thought she might be testing the recipes in her kitchen at Hampden House,' Poppy says.

'Oh, God, no. You're basically living in student housing. I can't expect you to cook out of that kitchen.'

The kitchen in my flat is nicer than the kitchen I grew up with and most of the kitchens I've called my own, as a student or otherwise. Frankly, if Hampden House is mostly student housing, it's the nicest student housing I've ever seen.

'You'll cook here, in my kitchen,' she says. 'But before we get into any of that, we should probably have something to eat.' She looks down at her watch. 'My husband said he'd be joining us, but he's running a little late. The dining room is up here, but I figured we'd eat in the kitchen tonight. Shall we?'

She gestures to the stairway, and Poppy and I follow her to the floor below, where we tread along a short hallway to the kitchen at the back of the house.

I cross the threshold and nearly gasp as I take in my surroundings. The entire back wall is one big window that looks onto a garden, which is landscaped with shrubs, hedges and a series of rectangular reflecting pools. The window actually extends upward to the first floor, with an overlook from the living room above. Like the rest of the house, the décor exhibits a contemporary flair, with glossy white cabinetry, dark grey marble counters, stainless-steel appliances, and white floor tiles that, when the light catches them in a certain way, appear to have the texture of alligator skin. A vast rectangular island sits in the middle of the room, beneath a light fixture consisting of shiny silver spheres of all different sizes, some as big as my head. Cooking in here on a regular basis? Yeah, I'll be just fine.

'Something smells delicious,' I say, as I breathe in a rich, herb-laced aroma. 'What's on the menu?'

'Stuffed Cornish game hens – or poussins as they call them here in the UK – steamed asparagus and truffled white bean purée.'

'Wow. That sounds … amazing.'

'You seem surprised.'

'Not at all. I just …'

My eyes trace her bony frame, and I think back to all the stories about her bizarre dieting habits – the enemas and liquid cleanses and her brief time as a vegan after she broke up with Matthew Rush. But then I remember Poppy's stern warning on the phone, and I decide to keep my mouth shut.

'I'm not surprised at all,' I say.

The oven timer starts beeping loudly from across the kitchen. 'Almost ready,' she says.

She motions for me to have a seat at the kitchen table, a long, rectangular slab made of brushed concrete. The table is set for four, with woven silver placemats, stark white plates, and sparkling crystal glasses.

'I hope you don't mind – we're going casual tonight,' she says, as she pulls the roasting pan out of the oven with Poppy's help.

I'm tempted to tell her that in my hometown, casual means paper plates and red plastic Solo cups. The Madigans don't really do crystal and silver.

As I take a seat at the table, a short, plump woman with cropped, reddish-brown hair emerges from a butler's pantry adjacent to the kitchen and assists Poppy in transferring the Cornish game hens to a rectangular white serving platter.

'Olga, this is Kelly. She'll be helping me with my cookbook.'

Olga looks up from spooning the pan sauce around the platter. 'Nice to meet you,' she says, with a thick Eastern European accent.

'Olga keeps this house from falling apart,' Natasha says. 'I literally couldn't function if it weren't for her and Poppy.'

Poppy flashes a self-satisfied smile. Olga's stony expression remains unchanged as she lifts the dishes of asparagus and white bean purée from a warming drawer and, with Poppy's help, brings everything to the table.

Natasha glances at her watch as Olga places a chicken on each of our plates. 'I guess we should start…'

60

Before I can say I don't mind waiting, I hear a door open and close in the hallway beyond the kitchen. 'Hello?'

'Finally,' Natasha mutters, under her breath. 'We're in the kitchen!' she calls, over her shoulder.

A tall man dressed in a slim-cut grey suit walks through the doorway and throws his leather briefcase to the side as he shimmies out of his suit jacket. 'Blimey,' he says, as he loosens his tie and pulls it over his head. 'That may have been the longest drive from Westminster in history – and that includes the era predating the car.' He lets out a sigh as he walks to the table, rolling his shirtsleeves up his long arms. 'And, to top it all, poor Sunil nearly hit some girl who leaped into the traffic on Great Portland Street. An American, of course.'

My cheeks flush. He was in the car that almost hit me? Perfect.

He approaches the table and rests his hands on the back of one of the chairs.

'This is Kelly,' Natasha says. 'The cookbook writer I was telling you about.'

'Oh, right, yes.' He starts to say something more but stops as he studies my face. I suddenly feel painfully self-conscious – not only because my chin is probably still red and hideous but also because he is so handsome I almost can't believe he is real. Like Natasha, he has dark hair and big green eyes, but his eyes are more of a bluish green, like the surface of the ocean. He has narrow shoulders, a slim waist and a perfectly chiselled jawline, and immediately I can see why he and Natasha are considered one of the most beautiful couples on Earth.

'Kelly, this is Hugh, my husband.'

'Nice to meet you,' I say, wondering if all women feel so lightheaded in his presence. I don't want to stare, but I can't tear my eyes from his face. I finally look away when our eyes catch again, hoping no one can see I'm sweating through my shirt.

'Likewise.' He rubs his hands together as he looks down at the table. 'Well, well – what does Olga have in store for us this evening?'

'*I* made this,' Natasha snaps back.

'Oh – right.' He clears his throat as he settles into his seat. 'It looks delicious.'

We tuck into our food, gobbling up forkfuls of meltingly tender chicken and smooth, earthy white bean purée. When I look up from my plate, I notice Natasha is taking a very long time to chew each bite and does so with an odd yet very specific rhythm.

'This is wonderful, Natasha,' I say.

She covers her mouth as she takes three more rhythmic bites and nods. 'Thank you. It's an old family recipe. My grandmother used to make it all the time when I was growing up.'

'And you've never made it for me?' Hugh says. 'I feel cheated.'

'I *did* make it for you. When we first started dating. Remember?'

He locks eyes with me and smiles guiltily. 'I do now ...'

Natasha lets out an exasperated sigh. 'Anyway, I definitely want to include the recipe in my book. That, and the white bean purée.'

I blot the corners of my mouth with my napkin. 'I thought your editor said this was going to be an everyday cookbook – recipes from your American and English kitchens.'

'Yeah, so?'

'It's just that Cornish hens and truffles…Well, to a lot of people, those aren't everyday ingredients.'

She purses her lips as she pokes at the asparagus on her plate. 'So we'll balance it out with more basic recipes. Like…sautéed spinach. And French fries.'

Hugh chuckles. 'French fries? When was the last time you ate French fries?'

She shoots him an icy stare. 'Not since I found out I was allergic to potatoes.'

'You're allergic to potatoes?' I ask.

'Just the white kind.'

'As opposed to…'

'Sweet potatoes,' she says. 'Those are fine.'

'Is that a common allergy? I've never heard of it before.'

Poppy kicks me beneath the table.

'More common than you'd think,' Natasha says, sawing off another asparagus tip. 'But plenty of people can still eat potatoes, which is why we should include a French-fry recipe in the book. And a hamburger recipe. Oh, and a recipe for my guacamole. I make the best guacamole.'

I tally the recipe list so far: Cornish game hens, truffled white bean purée, French fries, hamburgers and guacamole. This is the most eccentric cookbook I've ever worked on.

'Maybe we should sit down tomorrow and hash out a game plan of which recipes to include – from your child-hood, from your time in LA and your time here. Once we see everything written down, we'll have a better sense of what works with the narrative.'

Natasha stares at me. I sense she would like to furrow her brow, but her forehead is frozen and smooth as an ice rink. '*I*'m the narrative. Me.'

'Right. But we still need a thread that ties the whole book together, so that it's cohesive and not a bunch of random recipes thrown together. I think—'

'No offence?' Natasha cuts me off, her frosty tone belying the tight smile on her face. 'I'm not really interested in what you think. This is my cookbook, and I've hired you to do it the way I want. If I want a recipe for French fries, you'll help me develop a recipe for French fries. If I want a recipe for kale burgers, you'll help me develop a recipe for kale burgers. And if I want a recipe for sizzling hot ice cream, you'll help me develop a recipe for sizzling hot ice cream. Understood?'

My eyes dart around the table as I try to assess whether this moment is as awkward for everyone else as it is for me. Poppy is staring at her plate with laser-like focus as she cuts her asparagus into a million tiny pieces, and Hugh's eyes are locked on mine, with a gentle expression that says, *Just agree with her, if you know what's good for you.* So, yes. It would appear we're all in Awkwardville.

'Understood,' I say.

'Good. Because if we're going to work together for months on end, we'd better be on the same page.'

She pushes a few bits of stuffing around her plate, then stands up abruptly, dabs the corners of her mouth with a napkin, and excuses herself without looking me in the eye.

I think I've made a terrible mistake.

# Chapter 7

Natasha doesn't actually expect me to develop a recipe for sizzling hot ice cream, does she? There is no such thing. Even Ferran Adrià – the world-famous molecular gastronomist, who developed recipes for 'frozen chocolate air' and see-through ravioli – tried and failed to make ice cream hot. It cannot be done. Not for a three-star Michelin chef, and not for Natasha.

But whether she wants hot ice cream or not, one thing is clear: unless I want to pack my bags and board the next plane to Michigan, I will do what she says, no matter how outlandish or impossible. This shouldn't come as a surprise. That's the way it works whenever I ghostwrite a cookbook for a major personality, whether it's a renowned chef or a TV host. When I worked on the modern-art cake book, the pastry chef, Katie, often assigned me bizarre and random tasks, like refilling the bird-feeders in her yard and scheduling her hair appointments. But Natasha has an edge unlike my past employers – something I can't quite place – and I'm getting increasingly worried about what the future may hold.

Despite my misgivings, I set off for Natasha's home bright and early the next morning. I hop on the Northern Line at Warren Street and take my very first ride on the London tube, whizzing through the underground tunnels until I reach Belsize Park ten minutes later. The journey takes less time than I anticipated, so before I head to Natasha's house, I stop at a small grocery store called Pomona directly across from the tube station. Crates of fresh produce spill onto the sidewalk out front, containing everything from asparagus to rhubarb, and beside the front door, I notice about a dozen silver pails filled with fresh flowers, including a bunch of white roses.

I snatch up a bouquet and head inside to pay, where I find myself surrounded by freshly baked loaves of bread, dozens of English cheeses, fresh cream and butter, and more tins, jars and boxes of goodies than I can catalogue in my mind.

I pay for the flowers, along with a small pot of fresh yogurt coated with a layer of stewed plums. I tuck the yogurt into my bag and, flowers in hand, wind my way through the streets of Belsize Park to Natasha's house.

At just before nine, the streets are filled with people heading to work, along with moms and nannies walking hand-in-hand with their children on the way to school. In the chaos of last night's taxi débâcle, I hadn't appreciated how family-oriented this neighbourhood seems, but in the fresh light of morning, I notice how many strollers and skipping young children are on the sidewalks around me. I wonder if Natasha and Hugh are planning to have children. They certainly have enough room in that enormous house.

When I arrive at the front gate, bypassing a few shabbily dressed paparazzi loitering across the street, I press the bell and Olga buzzes me inside. I walk up the front steps, where she meets me with a typically bland and stony greeting.

'Natasha, she is downstairs with trainer,' she says, eyeing the roses. 'You wait in kitchen.'

I nod politely and make my way downstairs to the kitchen, which shows no signs of last night's dinner. The stovetop and counters glisten in the morning light, and the surface of the kitchen table is bare, with the exception of a few stone votives that run down its centre. I sit on one of the chairs, and as soon as I do, Natasha emerges from the hallway, her entire body dripping with sweat and her raven locks twisted into a bun on top of her head.

'Good morning,' she pants, making her way to the refrigerator, showing no sign of animosity from last night's dinner. She rubs her sweaty forehead with the back of her arm as she opens the door and takes out a bunch of kale, a few celery stalks, a peeled lemon and a knob of ginger. She dumps the produce on the counter and nods at the flowers. 'Are those for me?'

'Yes – I finally found a place that sells roses.'

'That's sweet. Thanks. Olga!' she shouts over her shoulder. Olga hurries into the kitchen. 'Could you put those in a vase? One of the tall ones. Thanks.'

She pulls out a large juicer from one of her cabinets, plugs it in and begins shoving the kale inside, leaf by leaf, creating a thunderous whirring sound that echoes through-out the kitchen as the juice empties into a tall glass.

'So I was thinking we could go over the recipe list today!' she shouts, above the roar of the juicer. She shoves in a stalk of celery. 'You know – get organized before we start testing everything.'

'Perfect,' I say.

Natasha cups her hand to her ear as she rams an entire lemon into the machine. 'Sorry?'

'Perfect!' I shout. 'That sounds perfect!'

She pushes the rest of the ingredients through the machine, shuts it off and, in a matter of seconds, downs the shockingly green contents of the glass.

'Aaah.' She sighs, smacking her lips. 'I am addicted to this juice. You have no idea. Obsessed.' She dumps the empty glass in the sink, and turns to Olga, who has re-entered the room with a tall crystal vase. 'Oh, not that one. Try the Christofle. And I'm finished with the juicer, so you can clean it now.'

Olga nods and leaves with the vase as Natasha turns to me. 'I'm going to hop in the shower, but why don't you start sketching out the recipes we discussed last night, and we can get going as soon as I come back down?'

'Sure,' I say. 'I brought the project journal I started, so we can use that as a springboard.'

'Great,' she says. 'And please – make yourself at home. I'll only be a few minutes.'

Ninety-three minutes later, I am still sitting at Natasha's kitchen table, alone.

In the time that has passed, Olga has cleaned the juicer,

arranged the flowers, mopped the floor, dusted the entire house and restocked the refrigerator with more kale, celery and ginger. I, on the other hand, have done nothing but read my recipe list twenty times and sketch the world's largest doodle of a cat with antlers.

Finally, after 103 minutes have passed, Natasha floats into the kitchen. She wears a drapy black sweater and black leggings, and her thick tresses are pulled into a taut low ponytail. Her smooth, fair skin practically glows, and I'm tempted to say she isn't wearing any makeup, except she must be wearing something because I can't imagine any-one's skin being so naturally luminous. Her plump lips are stained a fresh berry colour, as if she's just taken a bite of a ripe, juicy strawberry, and as she breezes past me and takes a seat at the table, the air fills with the fresh scent of white jasmine and sandalwood.

'Well,' she says, letting out a deep sigh as she slides into one of the chairs. 'That didn't take long.'

I study her face, trying to gauge her expression because, at 103 minutes, she can't possibly be serious. But there is not a trace of irony in it, which means the joke is on me.

'So,' she continues, 'what have you come up with?'

'Before we get to that, I was thinking we could talk a little more about the narrative.'

She rolls her eyes as she lets out another sigh. 'The nar-rative, the narrative – all you want to talk about is the narrative.'

'I just think it will help us figure out which recipes to include. Like, the main dish from last night. Why do you want to include that recipe?'

'Because my grandmother used to make it.'

'Okay. Tell me more about that. When would she make it? Where?'

'I don't know. I guess...' She pauses. 'She used to throw these amazing dinner parties. She was sort of known for them, even into her seventies. Sometimes she'd babysit my sister and me when my parents were out of town, and we'd get the leftovers the next day for lunch.'

I scribble in my notebook. 'What kind of leftovers?'

'You know, like leftover Cornish hens. Potato gratin. Cream of carrot soup. She used to make this chocolate mousse that was to die for.'

'Where did she live?'

'Elkins Park. A small suburb outside Philadelphia.'

'Is that where you grew up?'

She shifts in her seat. 'Sort of. Close by.'

'And was this your dad's mom? Or your mom's mom?'

'My mom's.'

'Were you close?'

She clears her throat. 'I'm sorry, I thought we were discussing a cookbook.'

'We are.'

'Then maybe we should discuss *cooking*, not my private life.'

'I'm sorry. I didn't...I just think readers and cooks would love a peek into your life. You're this megastar that people idolize, but if we pull back the curtain and show them a bit about you – that you cook, that your grandmother was a supreme hostess – I think people will love it.'

She twirls her oval diamond engagement ring around

70

her finger. 'That may be, but in my business, once you open the floodgates—'

'I'm not saying we open the floodgates. I'm saying we make you relatable.'

Natasha stares at me coolly. 'Don't interrupt me,' she says.

My cheeks flush. 'Sorry.'

'And, anyway, how are we going to get people to relate to me?'

'We'll make them feel as if they know you. Personalize some recipes from Natasha the movie star – green juice, truffled white bean purée – and recipes from before you were famous, like Cornish hens and chocolate mousse.'

She purses her lips and stares at me for a long while. 'I guess it isn't the worst idea I've ever heard.'

A weak endorsement if I ever heard one, but I'll take it.

We spend the next hour roughing out what recipes we'll include in the book, based on the outline her editor sent me: three sections, each devoted to a separate time in her life (childhood, LA, London), and each of those sections subdivided into courses. I'll have to double check with her editor to make sure we have the green light on the recipe list, but so far, things look good.

'Why don't you give me a copy of the Cornish hen recipe, along with another one or two dishes your grandmother made, and I can start working on those?' I say.

'I don't use recipes *per se*,' she says. 'It's all in my head.'

'Then just give me ballpark measurements.'

'Fine.' She flicks her diamond ring. 'But what about the French fries? And the guacamole? And all of the things we discussed last night.'

'Those recipes are all on the list. But maybe we start with the childhood recipes and then work our way up to the modern-day stuff.'

She doesn't look thrilled, but before she can argue, her cell phone rings on the table. She glances at the screen. 'I have to take this,' she says. 'But do whatever you need to do to get started, and fill me in on the rest later. Olga can help you get anything you need.'

'But what about the Cornish hen reci—'

'Jenny, hi – tell me you have good news,' Natasha says, as she picks up the phone and gets up from the table. She covers the receiver with her hand. 'Good luck. Oh – and before you leave today, if you could whip up a loaf of something sweet to have with tea, that would be great. Hugh has been asking.'

She resumes her conversation and heads out of the glass door into the back garden, leaving me alone to create recipes out of thin air and pull a loaf of quick bread out of my butt because, apparently, that is what I've been hired to do.

## Chapter 8

Here's the thing: I don't mind working for crazy people.
I've done that for years. Even before I landed my first job,
I was subject to my loony parents' whims. Dealing with
kooks – managing them, focusing them – is in my DNA.
I'm good at it. It's what I do.

But Natasha isn't crazy. Or, at least, not in the way I'm
talking about. Crazy was my mom telling me to wear a
bathing suit for underwear because she hadn't done the
laundry for a week and a half. Crazy was a famous food
personality asking me to make doughnuts six different
ways, then yelling at me for making doughnuts because
doughnuts are 'the Devil's victuals'. Crazy was a celebrated
pastry chef asking me to taste samples of cat food to make
sure they were suitable for her cat, Elizabeth Taylor. But
Natasha isn't crazy. She is selfish and oblivious and, combined, those traits could be even worse.

Since Natasha has left me with zero useful information about any of her grandmother's recipes, I decide to recreate the dish from last night's dinner based on memory. I'm good at what I do for several reasons but, first, because I have a pretty sensitive palate and can tell when a recipe needs an extra teaspoon of white wine vinegar or another dash of chilli. Sam and I used to play a game: he'd cook something, then blindfold me, and I would try to name all of the ingredients in the dish in as few bites as possible. He was always blown away by how quickly I could identify even the subtlest flavours – walnut oil, saffron, dried sage. What he found even more impressive was that I'd never tasted most of those ingredients until I was a teenager: my mom only made a handful of dishes, which together didn't use more than a dozen or so basic components.

I should probably add that, as a young girl, I didn't mind my mom's limited repertoire. By all accounts, until I was about eleven, I was a pretty fussy eater. I wouldn't touch anything spicy or sharp or 'tangy'. I much preferred my mom's tuna noodle casserole and ham salad to a dish of pasta bolognese. It wasn't that I feared foreign foods, just that my young palate was so sensitive I couldn't handle an onslaught of complex flavours. For me, eating a bowl of chilli was like walking into a crowded party and being able to hear every single conversation at full volume. The cacophony of spices and seasonings was too much. It wasn't until my taste buds matured and dulled with age that I could not only appreciate the many flavours of the world but also enjoy them.

As I sit at Natasha's kitchen table, I think through last night's meal. The chickens were filled with a fragrant stuffing that seemed to be laced with mushrooms, celery, and…was it sage? I think so. And the bread. It was rich and eggy, like a challah or brioche. The skin on each of the birds was crisp and salty, with pops of…garlic, I think. And paprika. The sweet kind, not the spicy one. But how did she get the skin so crispy? And did she brine the birds? Did her grandmother have a special trick for getting the meat so juicy? All of this would be a lot simpler if Natasha bothered to answer any of my questions, instead of talking to some stylist on her cell phone while she paces around her garden.

Rather than wait for her to make herself available, I decide to set off for the grocery store. I let myself out of the front door and, using the GPS on my phone, navigate the winding streets of Belsize Park to an ATM, where I withdraw a hundred pounds, using the card Natasha gave me. From there, I set out for Barrett's Butchers on England's Lane. The neighbourhood is a mix of colours and architectural styles – white stucco mansions, Victorian red-brick town houses, squat apartment buildings made of dull grey brick. Almost every block contains one house, if not two or three, whose face is saddled with metal scaffolding and bright blue tarpaulins. I can only imagine what Natasha's house looked like a year ago. From what Poppy had said, the contractors only recently finished what was a two-year renovation.

I pop into Barrett's, ducking beneath the bright red awning into the tiny shop, which is packed with fresh cuts of everything, from delicate lamb chops to meaty pork roasts covered with thick layers of fat. Mountains of sausages beckon from within the glass case, in more varieties than I could ever imagine – wild boar and apple, venison, chicken and sage, beef and garlic. A musty pong fills the store, giving the place an air of rustic authenticity.

I remember to order three 'poussins', then head back toward Pomona, the small food shop I visited that morning, remembering the fresh, crusty loaves of bread on their shelves. I grab a loaf of challah, its braided crust shiny and golden brown, along with some celery, an onion, some mushrooms and a few spices. Before I pay, I also throw a bunch of speckled bananas, a pot of Greek yogurt, some flour and sugar into my basket. The ingredients are slightly different here than they are back home – 'self-raising flour', 'caster sugar' – but I'm sure I can recreate the banana bread I developed for a famous morning-show host back in Chicago. It's one of my most popular recipes to date, and I'm sure it would taste great with a cup of tea.

When I get back to Natasha's house, Olga buzzes me through the front gate and grimaces as she eyes my shopping bags.

'Natasha say I do shopping for house.'

I shrug apologetically. 'I don't mind. Natasha gave me an ATM card. Sometimes it's actually easier to go myself.'

'Then you clean after, too, yes? Is *easier*.'

She purses her lips as I walk through the front door, where I run into Poppy, who is scanning emails on her phone.

'Oh. Hello.' She raises an eyebrow as her eyes land on my bags. 'You used the Barclays account, correct?'

'I did.'

'Good.'

I make for the stairway. 'Is Natasha around? I have a few questions about the recipe I'm working on today.'

'No, she's at Céline.'

'Céline?'

Poppy stares at me, apparently appalled. 'The *designer*?'

'Oh. Okay.' I'm embarrassed to admit I've never heard of this designer before. When I was a kid, we mostly shopped at Kmart and Sears, so 'designer' wasn't really a part of my vocabulary.

'She's getting fitted for a charity event she's attending later this month,' Poppy says. 'The dress her stylist originally selected was a total disaster, so we're hoping this one is acceptable. The incompetence Natasha has to put up with – you have no idea.'

I think back to my childhood. The time my mom forgot to pick me up in kindergarten and I had to walk home by myself, only to find her passed out on the couch in front of *General Hospital*. The time she sent me to school on Hallowe'en dressed in a trash bag because she'd forgotten to buy me a costume and said I should tell everyone I was 'white trash', which I did and then got sent to the principal's office. The time I found my twelve-year-old brother high and reeking of pot, while my parents watched *Judge Judy* in the family room. Incompetence? Yeah, I know a little about that.

But I don't share it with Poppy because she wouldn't be interested, and even if she were, she'd never understand. Instead, I simply say, 'Wow. I can only imagine.'

*

Here is what I can piece together of Natasha's day:

7–9 a.m.: Exercises with trainer
9–10.43 a.m.: Takes stunningly long time to shower, dress, do hair and makeup
10.43–11.43 a.m.: Discusses cookbook with me
11.43–12 p.m.: Complains to stylist on the phone
12–12.45 p.m.: Goes for fitting at Céline
1.00–4.00 p.m.: Spends three hours (!!!!!) getting a massage and facial

And that's all I have so far.
Meanwhile, here is what my day has looked like:

7–8 a.m.: Wake up, take cold shower, reply to emails from editors and agents about previous projects, make pot of tea that ends up burning my tongue
8.15–9 a.m.: Have weird interaction with Tom, the building manager, about my cold shower, head for the tube, make my way to Natasha's via Pomona
9–10.43 a.m.: Wait for Natasha, sketch out ideas for cookbook, draw doodle of cat with antlers
10.43–11.43 a.m.: Discuss cookbook with Natasha
11.43–1.00 p.m.: Shop for ingredients, draw up blueprint for Recipe Attempt No. 1, set out eggs for banana bread
1–3.00 p.m.: Navigate Natasha's kitchen, cut my finger with her chef's knife, bleed all over her marble counter (and onto her alligator-skin floor and onto my pants), wrap my finger with a paper towel and rubber band (which lasts only five minutes until I bleed through the towel and Olga gets me a bandage from upstairs),

78

set a tea-towel on fire as I attempt to light her La Cornue range, extinguish fire, finish preparing the stuffing, stuff the birds, lift massive roasting pan into oven, realize I have sweat through my shirt, consider making myself a gin and tonic, don't

And that's pretty much where I am at the moment.

Around four o'clock, the timer goes off, and I remove the Cornish game hens from the oven. Their skin crackles as I lay the pan on a trivet, the rich smell of mushrooms and sage filling the air. The scent is even more intoxicating than the one I remember from last night, but I know better than to think I've mastered a recipe at the first try. Even if it tastes perfect to me, I need to call upon my recipe-tester friends from home to see if they – and I – can repeat the recipe as I've written it. If not? Back to the drawing board.

I let the pan cool briefly, then transfer one of the birds to a plate and slice into the breast.

Heaven.

The meat is tender and juicy, perfumed with garlic and paprika and a hint of sage from the stuffing. It could use a bit more salt, so I'll have to try it again with that adjustment, and the stuffing could be a bit tighter. (An egg, maybe? Less butter?) But otherwise I've almost nailed it. I hope the rest of the recipe testing goes as smoothly. If it does, I'll finish the book faster than expected.

I tidy up the remaining mess around the kitchen, leaving the pan of chickens at the far end of the island for Natasha to try later. Then I grab the butter and flour and start on the banana bread, a recipe I've made so many times I know it by heart. I've made numerous variations over the years

79

– sometimes adding chocolate chips and crystallized ginger, at others drizzling a lime-coconut glaze over the top – but no matter what tweaks I make, licking the streaks of golden batter left in the bowl is pretty much mandatory.

Once I've poured the batter into the pan and stuck it in the oven, I finish cleaning up the kitchen, dusting the bits of flour off the counter and washing the bowls and spatulas. The caramel-laced scent of banana bread wafts across the kitchen, filling the room with its sweet perfume. If I had to draw up a list of the best baking smells in the world, banana bread would, without question, rank in the top five. Possibly the top two. I'm not sure why its smell is so intoxicating, but one whiff and I'm ready to attack that baking pan like a cheetah on a fresh kill.

While the banana bread bakes, I creep along the hallway to the stairway, hoping to hear some indication that Natasha has returned from her facial. The only sound I hear is Olga vacuuming the front hall. I linger for a few minutes, checking my phone and sending off a quick email to Meg, when I hear the clickety-clack of Natasha's heels coming down the marble staircase.

'How did the testing go today?' she asks, her formerly made-up face now bare and dewy, swathed in some sort of shiny serum. She wears a leopard-print bomber jacket over her black top and carries a purse the size of my torso over her shoulder.

'Pretty well, actually. I got really close on the Cornish hen recipe. They've been cooling in the kitchen – I'd love to hear what you think.'

Natasha brushes past me and marches to the kitchen but comes to an abrupt halt as soon as she walks through the doorway. She whirls around, her eyes wild. 'What is that *smell*?'

'What smell?' I sniff the air. 'You mean the banana bread?'

The timer starts beeping manically on the counter, so I rush across the room, grab two potholders, and pull the domed golden loaf from the oven, placing it on a trivet beside the stove.

Natasha's eyes widen as they land on the craggy, caramelized top of the bread. 'You made *banana bread*? Why would you do that?'

My cheeks flush. 'Because...you told me to?'

'When?'

'This morning. You asked me to make a loaf of something sweet to go with tea.'

She stares at me icily, her green eyes filled with contempt. I am so confused. 'I did *not* say to make banana bread,' she says.

I think back to this morning's events and replay them in my mind. Did I misinterpret something she said? No, I'm absolutely certain she asked me to bake a loaf of something sweet. Why else would I have bothered? She didn't say banana bread specifically but, seriously, who doesn't like banana bread?

'You asked me to bake something,' I say. 'Right before you went outside to take your call.'

'Are you calling me a liar?'

'No...I...Of course not.'

She narrows her eyes further. 'Good.' She purses her lips and waits for me to say something more, but when I don't, she looks away. 'Now get it out of my sight.'

She yanks open the refrigerator and pulls out a plastic bottle of ginger beet juice.

'Okay…But…do you want me to give it to Mr Ballantine? Or should I take it home?'

She takes a swig of juice and twists the cap back on the bottle. 'You can sell it on the street for all I care. Just take it *away*.'

She starts to stomp out of the kitchen, but I call after her. 'What about the Cornish hens?'

She pauses just shy of the doorway and whirls around. 'What about them?'

'Aren't you going to taste them?'

Natasha's eyes flit to the roasting pan sitting on the kitchen island. She shrugs. 'I'm sure they're fine.'

Then she walks out.

'What the eff?' I mutter to myself, staring at the banana bread.

'I heard that,' she calls from the stairway.

'Sorry!' I shout, my face burning up. Oh, God. I'm a dead woman.

'I bet you are,' Natasha says, her voice echoing down the hall. 'Just get back to work. And whatever else you do, get that *smell* out of my house.'

## Chapter 9

Okay. So Natasha is kind of crazy.

Who freaks out over a loaf of banana bread? It's not as if I'd fried ten pounds of oily fish or smeared her kitchen with blue cheese. What happens when I sauté garlic or hard-boil eggs? Should I expect a nervous breakdown? Will a potato gratin induce a psychotic episode?

With my first week in London already off to a rocky start, I spend the weekend getting to know my new neighbourhood, hoping to find the silver lining to my temporary expatriation. I grab an almond croissant and tea from the café across the street, stroll through Regent's Park, pop into a few shops on Great Portland Street, and explore the restaurants and stores along Marylebone High Street. On Sunday, I discover a bustling farmers' market in a big parking lot tucked behind the high street, where vendors sell everything from fresh milk and cheese to crusty loaves and thick cuts of beef and lamb.

That afternoon, after buying a dozen fresh eggs and a loaf of seven-grain levain, I sit in front of my laptop for a video chat with Meg. She'd begged me to call her as soon as I'd met Natasha for the first time, but I was jet-lagged and she was busy, so we decided to wait until the weekend. Knowing Meg, she's been sitting in front of her computer for at least thirty minutes, hoping I might log on early.

As expected, as soon as I power on my computer, Meg's name pops up, inviting me for a chat. When I accept her call, her cherubic face appears on my screen, her chin-length auburn hair full of kinks and waves, as if she's slept on it funny and hasn't bothered to fix it.

'Oh, my God, tell me *everything*,' she says, leaning dramatically into the screen, the freckles on her cheeks and nose blurring out of focus.

'You know I can't do that. I signed a non-disclosure agreement.'

'Puh-lease. Who am I going to tell? Other than my cat.'

'You work in news.'

'Public radio. I cover real news, not Hollywood news. And, anyway, I am your best friend – you know I'd never say a word.'

I hesitate, not because I don't trust Meg – I do, with every ounce of my being – but because once I start telling her things, I won't be able to stop. I've always trusted her with my deepest secrets, the ones I wouldn't tell anyone else. It's been that way as long as I can remember, ever since she brought me home to meet her family in third grade. They lived in a house like mine: a brick ranch with *faux*-clapboard and black shutters, three bedrooms and two baths, all crammed into about fifteen hundred square feet. But unlike mine, where knotty weeds poked through the cracked and crumbling driveway and shrubs grew wild and tangled over the front windows, Meg's house was neat and tidy. The lawn was mown, the bushes were pruned, and her driveway looked as if the asphalt had been poured that day.

We played for a few hours in her room, the walls of which were plastered with posters of Leonardo DiCaprio and Macaulay Culkin, and after a few hours, her mom knocked on her door.

'Kelly, sweetheart, what time did you say your mom was picking you up?'

I felt my cheeks flush as I realized it was already much later than whatever time I'd said. 'Oh…um…'

'I decided I wanted to walk Kelly home,' Meg said, jumping in. 'So we could play longer.'

Her mom looked at us sceptically. 'And your mom is okay with that?'

'Yeah, we called her,' Meg said. 'She said it was fine.'

None of that was true, but Meg had been to my house a few times, and though both of us were too young to explain my mom's weirdness, we both knew it wasn't normal for a grown woman to be in a bathrobe at four in the afternoon. Meg knew her mom would think so, too, and even though she couldn't pinpoint why my mom's behaviour wasn't quite right, she could sense it was something I didn't want everyone to know about. I didn't have to tell her. She just knew.

On the walk home, I thanked her for making up an excuse.

'It's okay,' she said. 'Friends don't tell each other's secret stuff.'

And she never has – not then, not ever.

'Come on, tell me!' Meg says, pressing her hands together and leaning even closer to the screen. 'What is Natasha like? Preposterously gorgeous?'

I relent. 'Yeah, she really is.'

'Of course she is. She's Natasha Spencer.' Meg wiggles in her chair. 'What else? Is she short? Tall? Thin? Funny?'

'She's shorter than I expected. And very, very thin.'

Meg shrugs. 'Of course.'

'She's also crazy.'

'Really? How crazy? Like, owning a diamond-encrusted spatula crazy? Or calling doughnuts "the Devil's victuals" crazy?'

I replay my interactions with Natasha in my mind. 'She straddles a pretty broad spectrum.'

A mischievous smirk spreads across her face. 'Excellent.'

'Not if you've been hired to work for her. She nearly had a panic attack yesterday when I took a loaf of banana bread out of her oven.'

'Wait – you were baking in her kitchen?'

'That's where I'm supposed to do all of the testing. Although I'm not really sure how that's going to work if she has a meltdown every time I bake something.'

'Well, banana bread is kind of at the extreme end of the spectrum. It's olfactory kryptonite. The smell is the enemy of diets everywhere.'

'True. Which begs the question, why did I bother making it in the first place?'

'Well, why did you?'

'Because she *asked* me to. Not banana bread specifically but "a loaf of something sweet".'

'And then she freaked out about it?'

'Yes.'

Meg snickers. 'Wow.'

'Right.'

'So what did you do with it, once it came out of the oven? Please don't tell me you threw it away. Your banana bread is like crack.'

'I didn't throw it away. She'd asked me to bake it for her husband to have with tea, so I left it for him in his office.'

'Amazing. Have you met him yet? The husband.'

'Yeah, I met him Thursday night, when they had me over for supper.'

'They had you over for *supper*?' Meg's eyes widen even further when I nod in reply. 'Oh, my God, stop it. *Stop it.* I can't take any more.' She tries to calm herself. 'So what is the husband like? Sexy as hell?'

I think back to Thursday night and recall Hugh's slim-cut suit, his chiselled features, and his sweet but puckish smile. 'He is definitely easy on the eyes.'

Meg sighs. 'Of course he is. And does he have a dreamy English accent?'

'He does.'

She clenches her fist and bangs on her desktop. 'You're killing me!'

'There's something off about their relationship, though. Like, when I went to drop the bread in his office upstairs, I passed a few rooms and…I think they might sleep in separate bedrooms.'

She lowers her voice. 'Really?'

'I'm not positive – and this is a hundred per cent confidential and stays between you and me – but…well, his office is attached to a bedroom that had a bunch of his suits and stuff lying on an unmade bed. And then when I peered into another room as I walked back to the stairs, I saw the housekeeper making another bed that had clearly been slept in.'

'Maybe he has a room just for his suits. Rich people have all sorts of crazy shit like that – an entire closet dedicated to their shoes, rooms meant only for "sitting", a glass-enclosed stovetop just for cooking fish.'

'No way – you're making that last one up.'

'Nope. True story. I covered it for our show – a local author here hates the smell of fish cooking, so he created a special fish stove that traps the smell. Hey, maybe you should get one of those for Natasha.'

'Ha-ha, very funny.'

'I'm serious.'

'Anyway, speaking of your show, how are things going?'

Meg's exuberant smile fades. 'Same old same. Too much news, too little funding. I feel like Sisyphus half the time.'

'Ugh. Sorry.'

'They haven't worn me down yet. I'm still fighting the good fight.'

I smile. 'Someone has to. If you ever need a piece about an Ypsi girl's adventures in England, let me know.'

'Don't say that if you don't mean it.'

'I highly doubt your managing editor would have any interest in a story like that.'

'You know, this whole "poor Kelly" act is getting old, my friend. You're on the other side of the ocean, skulking around Natasha Spencer's mansion. Tell me you *ever* thought that would happen.'

'You're right. Sorry.'

'It's fine – just don't be all boo-hoo-waah-waah. Okay?'

'Deal.' I glance down at my keyboard. 'By the way, you haven't heard from Sam at all, have you?'

'Me? No. Why would I?'

'You wouldn't. Sorry. I just wondered if he'd reached out to any of my friends because I haven't heard from him at all since I left Chicago.'

'You haven't heard from him because you broke up with him.'

'I know. But we were together six years. It's weird to go from sharing an apartment and a life to…nothing.'

'Imagine how he feels.'

'I was thinking of emailing him tonight, just to check in and see how he's doing.'

Meg sits upright in her seat. 'No. Nuh-uh. Don't you dare.'

I shrink back from the screen. 'Why not?'

'Because that isn't fair. You broke the guy's heart. If he wants to talk to you, he'll find a way of getting in touch with you. But, until then, you have to leave him alone.'

I slump down in my seat. 'You're right. I guess part of me feels guilty for how I handled things.'

'Sounds about right. I mean, I get why you did what you did, but it sort of came out of nowhere, especially considering he's kind of perfect. But you did it, and it's over, and emailing will only make things worse. Trust me.'

'You're sure?'

'Positive.'

'Okay. Thank you for being the voice of reason.'

'Any time.'

I glance at the clock. 'I should go. But, hey, could you do me a favour? If you drive through Ypsilanti in the next week or two, could you swing by my dad's place?'

'Sure.'

'Thanks. You don't have to get out of the car. Just drive by to make sure he hasn't burned the place down. Or, you know, added metal bars to the windows.'

She snickers. 'Will do.'

'All right. Time to figure out what the hell I'm doing at Natasha's tomorrow.'

'Living the dream?'

'Something like that...'

'Listen, any time you feel like complaining, remember this is a once-in-a-lifetime opportunity. Enjoy it. Savour it. At this moment in time, you are the envy of men and women everywhere.'

But as the words come out of her mouth, I have trouble believing they're true, because never in my twenty-eight years has my life been the envy of anyone.

## *Chapter 10*

Monday morning I embark on a second round of Cornish hen testing, this time using a bit more egg in the stuffing and a little more salt on and beneath the skin. Assuming I speak to Natasha today, I will also pick her brain about her grandmother's chocolate mousse and potato gratin – although, since Natasha is apparently allergic to potatoes, I don't expect her to have much to say on the latter.

When Olga buzzes open the front gate, I spot Poppy digging through one of the trash bins, the sleeves of her mint-coloured cardigan rolled up around her elbows.

'Poppy?'

She whirls around. 'Oh. Hello.'

She hurries me through the front gate so that no paparazzi can peer inside, then seals it shut behind me.

'Why are you digging through the trash?' I ask, my arms weighed down by grocery bags.

'Olga threw something away that she shouldn't have.'

'Was it important?'

'Oh, no – it was rubbish. But it should have been discarded separately. She's worried that if the paparazzi got hold of it…'

'The paparazzi dig through her trash?'

'They have done. You'd be amazed at the lengths they'll go to. You can never be too careful.'

She walks with me up the front steps and unlocks the front door.

'Do you need help?' I ask. 'I don't have to start cooking right away.'

'I'm fine looking for it on my own, thank you.'

'I'm sure you are. But it might go faster if there were two of us looking for it.'

She considers my offer. 'Fine. But put your shopping in the kitchen first. The last thing we need is you poisoning one of us.'

I hurry down to the kitchen, put the cold items in the refrigerator, then run back outside, where I find Poppy on all fours, searching through a trash bag she's ripped open.

'So what exactly are we looking for?' I bend down and begin sorting through the pile.

'One of her medicine packets. Olga saw the empty box on Natasha's dressing table and, like an idiot, threw it away, instead of shredding it.'

'Oh.' I sift through a few tissues. 'Is it for something …serious?'

'Don't think so. She's not ill, if that's what you mean. It's probably just her Adderall. She didn't say specifically.'

'Adderall? Isn't that for ADHD?'

'Technically. But it's also an appetite suppressant.' She casts a sideways glance. 'It's not like she takes it all the time. Just if she needs to lose a bit of weight quickly, like before an awards ceremony or something.'

She rummages through a few more crumpled bits of paper, then pulls a small, flattened box from the pile. 'Ah. Here we are.'

I catch a glimpse of the label: desogestrel/ethinyl estradiol. So birth control, not Adderall. It's actually the same birth-control medication I currently take – probably the only thing Natasha and I have or will ever have in common.

Seeing it triggers a thought. 'So...I have a question...' I say, figuring I may have found a way for Poppy and me to bond. 'Do Natasha and Mr Ballantine...well, do they sleep in separate bedrooms?'

Poppy stands and rolls her shoulders back. 'And what business is that of yours?'

'It isn't. But Friday I went upstairs to drop a loaf of banana bread in Mr Ballantine's office and—'

'Who said you could go upstairs?'

'Natasha.'

'When?'

'After she told me to get rid of the banana bread.'

This is only partially true. She never explicitly said I could go upstairs, but considering she said I could sell it on the street, I didn't think dropping it in Mr Ballantine's office would be a problem.

'No one is allowed upstairs but me and Olga,' Poppy says.

'Listen, I'm not trying to usurp your position.'

She looks as if she's been slapped. 'Good, because that would be impossible. I know everything that goes on under this roof.'

'Apparently not,' I say, before I can stop myself.

'What?'

'Sorry, I didn't mean—'

'For your information,' she says, her voice low and tense, 'I know all about Natasha and Hugh's arrangement. It's been like that for years.'

*Arrangement.* Ah.

Poppy dumps the bag back into the can and dusts her hands on her skirt. 'Now, I believe we both have work to do.'

She marches up the front steps, escorts me into the house and, with the crushed box held tightly in her hand, locks the door behind me.

To my dismay, Natasha has already left the house for the day when I finally settle into the kitchen, meaning we can't discuss any of the recipes I'd hoped to test today, including my second attempt at the Cornish hens. Olga informs me Natasha will be spending the entire morning with a perfumer about her new line of fragrances and does not want to be disturbed.

'She leave note,' Olga says, handing over a folded piece of paper.

It is written on thick cream paper, embossed with the initials NJS.

Kelly,

I was hoping you could recreate my grandmother's

chocolate mousse. I don't have a recipe, but I remember
it being smooth and chocolaty. I think she used liquor.
Thanks,
N


'That's it?' I say, more to myself than to Olga.

Olga shrugs. 'Natasha, she is very busy.'

'Did she say what time she'd be back?'

'Five o'clock. She say please for you to be here when she
return.'

I think back to Friday, when Natasha returned and
nearly self-destructed at the scent of banana bread. My one
saving grace is that chocolate mousse requires no cooking
and therefore doesn't give off a smell. The challenge, of
course, will be recreating a recipe I've never tasted, one
that, like any chocolate mousse ever made, is both
'chocolaty' and 'smooth'. At least she gave me a hint about
the alcohol – though whether the alcohol involved is rum
or Grand Marnier or crème de cacao, I haven't a clue.

I tuck the note into my pocket and rub my hands
together, ready to take on Natasha's latest challenge.

'So tell me,' I say, meeting Olga's stare, 'where does
Natasha keep her booze?'


By any measure, the day is a raging success. I tweak one of
my favourite recipes for chocolate mousse to match
Natasha's vague description, using both rum and crème de
cacao, along with a dash of coffee to heighten the chocolate
flavour. I'd originally developed the recipe with François
Bardon back in Chicago as the filling to his famous chocolate charlotte, a towering confection of velvety chocolate

mousse surrounded by fluffy ladyfingers, the whole thing capped with a billowy layer of whipped cream. But for this version I streamline the process and adjust the ratios of chocolate, cream and eggs so that it's more in line with what Natasha's grandmother might have made.

While the mousse chills in the refrigerator, I have another go at the Cornish hens, with the salt and egg adjustments I noted in my journal. I time it so that they will be done just minutes before Natasha returns at five o'clock. I doubt she will want to taste them, but I need them ready, just in case.

When they come out of the oven, their skin crackles and hisses, each one a rich golden brown. I leave the roasting pan on the counter to cool and watch as the clock ticks upwards.

Four forty-five . . .

Five o'clock . . .

Five fifteen . . .

Five thirty . . .

By five forty-five, the chickens are barely warm, and Natasha is nowhere to be found. I slip one of the birds onto a plate, grab a fork and knife, and dig in. As expected, the meat is nearly cold, but the flavour is perfect: rich and garlicky, with just a bit of kick from the paprika and enough salt to bring all of the seasonings alive. Now all I need to do is send the recipe to a few of my testers, then cross it off the list.

I dump my plate and silverware in the sink and wander into the hallway, where I find Poppy filling her bag with a few papers and heading upstairs.

'Have you heard from Natasha?' I ask.

'She's having drinks with Oliver Stone,' Poppy says, like it's nothing – like having drinks with Oliver Stone is as unremarkable as brushing one's teeth.

'Oh.' I bite my lip. 'Did she say how long she'd be?'

'No idea. I think they have quite a lot to discuss.'

'Then…do you think I can go? Olga said I should be here when Natasha returned at five, but since it's almost six…'

'If Natasha wants you to stay, then you must stay. She told me I could go, so I'm going.'

'So I'm just supposed to hang out until…whenever?'

She raises her eyebrows as she clutches her purse and heads up the stairway. 'It would appear so.'

I watch as Poppy disappears, and when I hear the door open and shut above me, I drag myself back to the kitchen. On the way, I catch a glimpse of the art on the walls. Four framed prints hang with about two feet between them, each one depicting a cartoonish explosion, like a frame of a comic strip. They remind me of Roy Lichtenstein's work, which I studied in college while writing my thesis. But when I take a closer look, I realize they aren't like Lichtenstein's work: they *are* Lichtenstein's work. I stare at the prints, my mouth hanging open, when I hear a door open and shut behind me.

'See something you like?'

I spin around and see Mr Ballantine standing in front of the door leading to the garage, his brown leather brief-case clutched in his hand. He wears a tailored navy suit and a stark white shirt, along with a silver pocket square and tie.

'Sorry,' I say. 'I wasn't…I hadn't noticed these before.'

'Are you a Lichtenstein fan?'

'I wrote my college thesis on his comic book art.'

'Ah. Brilliant.'

'I've never seen his work up close, though. Other than at a museum.'

'We're big fans. Well, Natasha is, anyway. I'm a bit of a Philistine when it comes to art, I'm afraid. I don't really understand how this is art if he just copied some cartoon artist's work and made it bigger.'

'That's actually what my thesis was about.'

'And what did you conclude?'

I smile. 'You'll have to read it some time to find out.'

He laughs. 'I see.' He nods at his briefcase. 'I'm sure it's loads more interesting than the stuff I'm supposed to be reading about.'

'I'd hold off on making that call until you've read it...'

He laughs again and places the briefcase on the ground next to the stairway. He sniffs the air. 'What's that I smell?'

My chest tightens. Here we go again. 'Just the Cornish hens...er, poussins I made earlier. But they've been out of the oven for a while. The smell won't last, I promise.'

He holds up his hands defensively. 'It's fine. I quite like the smell, actually.'

'Oh. Okay. It's just that on Friday Natasha got very upset about the way the house smelt.'

'Yes, well, that's Natasha,' he says, a slight edge to his voice. 'I wouldn't worry too much.'

'Okay. If you're sure...'

He shakes himself out of his jacket and throws it over the banister. 'Let's have a look at what you've made then, shall we?' He starts down the hallway towards the kitchen but stops in his tracks and whirls around. 'By the way, I've been meaning to leave you a note – that banana bread? The one you left in my office? Without question, the best I've ever had.'

My cheeks flush. 'Thank you.'

'No – thank *you*,' he says. He pats his belly. 'Let's see what else you've made to fatten me up.'

I follow him into the kitchen, and as I glance back at the prints hanging in the hallway, I try to ignore the flutters in my stomach.

## Chapter 11

'Bloody hell.' Hugh rests his spoon on the table and leans back in his chair. He wipes the corners of his mouth with a napkin. 'Now *that*'s what I call chocolate mousse.'

I run my spoon through a small bowl of silken mousse and take a long mouthful, letting the velvety chocolate coat my tongue. 'Not bad.'

'Not bad? It's bloody brilliant.' He leans forward and takes another spoonful. 'It's so...light. But rich. Which doesn't even make sense. If it weren't so bad for me, I'd trade it for cigarettes in a heartbeat.'

'I feel like chocolate is probably healthier than cigarettes.'

He smirks. '*Touché*.' He runs his spoon around his bowl. 'I'm trying to stop, actually. I'm down to one a day.'

'Natasha must be pleased.'

He raises an eyebrow. 'Are you joking? She's worse than I am.'

'Natasha? I thought she was always talking about…you know, clean eating and a healthy lifestyle.'

'Yes, well, talk is talk…' He glances into the bowl. 'But back to this mousse – what exactly is in it? Wait. Don't tell me. I probably don't want to know.'

'Let's just say it isn't health food.'

'I definitely taste booze of some sort. Rum?'

'And crème de cacao.'

'Where on earth did you find crème de cacao?'

'In your liquor cabinet.'

He rumples his brow. 'We own crème de cacao? Since when?'

I shrug. 'I'm probably not the best person to ask.'

He scoops out a heaping spoonful of mousse and shovels it into his mouth, but a not insignificant proportion lands on his upper lip, making it look as if he has a moustache. I hold back a laugh.

'What?' he says.

'You just…There's some mousse on your lip.'

'Oh dear.' He sticks out his tongue and tries to lick it off. 'Better?'

'No, here.' I grab my napkin and reach across the table, and as I do, I hear the clickety-clack of heels enter the room.

'I hope I'm not interrupting.'

I whip my head around to see Natasha standing in the doorway, dressed in high-waisted silky pants and a tight-fitting tank, both of which – like nearly everything I've seen of her wardrobe so far – are black. I immediately jump to my feet.

'Natasha – hi.' I throw my napkin on the table. 'We were just taste-testing the chocolate mousse you asked me to make.'

She eyes me coolly. 'I see.'

'It's brilliant,' Hugh says. 'You really must try it.'

'Here – I'll get some for you,' I say.

I scoop a small portion into a bowl and grab a spoon, feeling her husband's eyes on me. Natasha saunters towards the table and glances into the bowl.

'My grandmother's looked lighter in colour than this,' she says.

'Oh.' I hold out the bowl. 'Well…maybe try a spoonful and let me know what you think. If the taste is close, I can fiddle with the ratios or type of chocolate to make it lighter.'

She hesitates.

'Try it,' Hugh urges. 'It's better than the one I ordered that time in Paris, when you were shooting *Unhinged*.'

A beat passes. Then she takes the bowl from my hands, examining the contents warily. She picks up the spoon and measures out a small portion, enough to fit on only half the teaspoon. She stares at the spoon, as if she is confronting an old enemy. Finally, she lifts it to her lips and takes a little, leaving half of the half-portion behind. As soon as the chocolate hits her tongue, she closes her eyes and lets out a long sigh.

'See? What did I tell you?' He gives me a quick wink.

Natasha opens her eyes. 'My grandmother's was still lighter,' she says. 'And stiffer.'

'I can do lighter and stiffer. I'll tweak a few things and try again.'

'But why mess with perfection?' Hugh says, going for another big spoonful.

Natasha purses her lips. 'Because it's supposed to be my grandmother's recipe. And this isn't.'

Maybe it would be closer if you'd given me more to work with than 'chocolaty', 'silky' and 'used liquor', I think. 'It isn't a problem,' I say. 'I'm happy to rework the recipe.'

'Good,' she says. She hands the bowl back to me. 'Do that tomorrow. And see if you can do a version of her cream of carrot soup, without the cream. She used a lot of dill. That was always the best part.'

She whirls around and walks towards the hallway, the legs of her silky pants swooshing against each other as her hips swing back and forth. She pauses at the doorway and glances over her shoulder. 'Hugh, I need to brief you on my upcoming travel plans. Would you mind?'

He tosses his spoon into his empty bowl and wipes his mouth with his napkin. 'Right – coming.'

She turns and walks out of the door, and he starts to follow, but stops when he reaches me and rests a hand on my shoulder. 'Thank you for the mousse. It was lovely.'

Then he tucks his hand into his pocket, clears his throat and follows Natasha.

I should probably say up front that Hugh was right: that mousse was perfection. I could fiddle with the recipe all day and night to make it identical to Natasha's grand-mother's version, and it wouldn't be as good as the one I made tonight. But that's the funny thing about food. So much of our enjoyment of it stems from experience. Sure, there are foods almost universally agreed upon as good (chocolate) or bad (rotten eggs), but in between, the degree to which we love or hate a certain delicacy often has something to do with where we ate it and with whom. My mousse may, objectively, be the better dish, but that will never be the case for Natasha because it isn't how her grandmother made it. In the same way, I would kill for a bowl of my mom's spaghetti salad right now, but I'm pretty sure I'm the only one in the entire United Kingdom who would eat it.

Since ghostwriting cookbooks is all about pleasing the client, I spend the next two weeks doing as Natasha asks: refining the mousse recipe, developing a creamless cream of carrot soup, streamlining a recipe for baked apples, and concocting a gluten-free version of her grandmother's crumb cake. I manage to persuade Natasha to taste small amounts of all the recipes, except the mousse, and whatever is left after numerous rounds of testing I either leave in a special section of the refrigerator for Mr Ballantine or take home with me to my own tiny fridge, which, at this point, is bursting.

My refrigerator may be bursting but fortunately, even after all of the recipe testing, my waistline is not. I wish I could credit my steady weight to something other than genetics – a healthy devotion to exercise, say, or reasonable self-restraint – but a fast metabolism is one of the few genetic gifts my mother passed on to me. Given her diet, she should have weighed more than 200 pounds, but she never broke 120, even in her later years. It was one of the ways she could trick people into believing she was in decent health: sure, she might blow through an entire jar of sour cream and onion dip in one sitting, but she could still fit into the Lee jeans she bought in 1989, so everything was fine. Never mind that she could barely make it up a flight of steps without pausing to catch her breath.

But for me, the upshot is that I can basically eat whatever I want, within limits. In a job where I might have to eat chocolate mousse five times in a week, that's definitely an advantage. By my third week in London, my diet relies heavily on crispy sesame chicken, a dish Natasha says both her mother and grandmother used to make and was a staple at family gatherings. It's the first time she has mentioned her mother, but when I enquire further, she stiffens. 'She was a very good cook, just like her mother,' she says. When I try to push her and ask about her father, she says, 'Let's stick to the task at hand, shall we?'

So that's what I do. From what Natasha described, the sesame chicken is a variation on oven-fried chicken, with a crisp, garlicky coating speckled with sesame seeds. My first attempt is a total disaster involving burned sesame seeds, unappetizing flecks of fresh garlic, and more oil than all of Saudi Arabia. Whatever the chicken is supposed to taste like, I know this isn't even close.

I fine-tune the recipe all week, swapping out the fresh garlic for powdered and preheating the oiled pan in the oven for a good ten minutes before roasting. For what I hope is my final adjustment, I marinate the chicken pieces overnight in a dry rub, leaving them covered on a baking sheet in Natasha's refrigerator on Wednesday night.

When I show up at Natasha's place on Thursday

morning, Poppy is hurrying around the house, stuffing various odds and ends into a matching set of black Louis Vuitton suitcases congregated by the front door.

'Is someone going somewhere?'

She looks up from one of the bags. 'We're going to Paris for the week.'

'We?' My heart leaps. I've always wanted to go to Paris.

'Natasha and I. She's shooting an ad for her new fragrance and decided to stay the week.'

'Oh. Okay.' I watch as she stuffs a box of Vitamin C tablets into a carry-on. 'Does this mean I have the week off? Or should I work from my flat?'

She zips the carry-on shut. 'I believe Natasha still wants you to use her kitchen. Olga will be here. So will Mr Ballantine – though he will obviously be very busy with work.'

'So you'll be back when? Next Thursday?'

'Friday. That's the plan now, anyway. With Natasha… well, sometimes things change.'

'Do I overhear you two talking about me?'

Natasha glides into the hallway, dressed in a pair of black cashmere leggings and a grey blazer thrown over a dip-dyed grey-and-black tank top. She smiles, though a slight edge in her voice belies her relaxed expression.

Poppy immediately stands up straight and smooths the front of her coral wrap dress. 'No. I mean, yes. I mean…I was just telling Kelly about the Paris plans.'

'I'm jealous,' I say. 'I've never been.'

Natasha's green eyes widen. 'You've never been to Paris?'

'Until this job came along, I'd never left the United States.'

'You're kidding,' she says.

'Nope. I've had a passport for two years, just in case, but this is the first stamp on it.'

Natasha stares at me, wide-eyed, as if I've just told her I've never used a proper toilet. 'Well, now that Paris is right across the Channel, you have to make the trip before you head back to the States. Given how much you love food, it would be a crime not to.'

'I'd like to, if I can find the time,' I say.

Poppy clears her throat. 'Sorry to interrupt, but I'm going to keep packing. We still need a few more items in the hand luggage.'

'Sounds good,' Natasha says. 'Oh, but make sure you pack the active silver. Last time you forgot, and I swear that's why I got sick when we landed in Copenhagen.'

Poppy nods anxiously and rushes up the stairs, and Natasha turns back to me. 'Anyway, before we leave, I wanted to talk to you about how things will run while I'm away. Olga will meet you at the house at eight o'clock tomorrow to let you in. I know that's an hour earlier than normal, but she has a bunch of appointments and errands in the morning, so please, please, be on time. Olga has been a loyal and hardworking employee for years, and if you make her wait around…well, let's just say I won't be happy.'

'I'll be here at eight. Not a problem.'

'Great. And in terms of cooking, why don't you plan on finishing the sesame chicken and moving on to some of the recipes from my time in LA? Start with the poached salmon.'

'Remind me about that recipe?'

107

'When I first started working in LA, there was this restaurant that made the best cold poached salmon with a mustard-dill sauce. I'd murder for a plate of that right now. It was so good.'

'What was the name of the restaurant?'

'Bon Cuit. They closed about five years ago. So sad. They also made the best raw carrot salad, so take a stab at that, too. I can try them both when I return Friday.'

Before I can ask any more questions about my responsibilities in her absence, Poppy comes tearing down the stairs, visibly frazzled. 'There's a problem,' she says.

Natasha does not look happy. 'Oh?'

'I can't find either the magnesium tablets or the lavender eye mask.'

'Did you check the hall closet?'

'Yes. And they aren't there.'

Natasha checks her watch. 'Let me look. We'd better hurry. Sunil wants to leave at nine thirty sharp.'

She heads for the stairs, and Poppy follows.

'Have fun,' I call after them. 'I can't wait to hear all about it – especially the food.'

'We'll definitely report back,' Natasha says. Then she turns to face me, a tight smile on her face. 'Maybe we'll try that chocolate mousse Hugh ordered while I was shooting *Unhinged* – the one your version seems to have dethroned. I guess we'll see if he was right – or if he was just trying to make you feel good about yourself.'

Then she turns back and, with Poppy nipping at her heels, disappears upstairs.

# Chapter 12

*Bzzzz. Bzzzz.*

I roll over the next morning to the sound of my phone buzzing on my nightstand. I turned off the ringer, as I do every night, though that's more out of habit than necessity, seeing as no one has my number but Poppy, and we barely speak. But when I glance down at the screen, I see Poppy's name flashing up at me. Why would she be calling me? Isn't she in Paris?

'Hello?' I say, my voice still scratchy with sleep.

'Where are you?' Poppy barks into the phone.

'At home. Why?'

'Because Olga has been waiting for you for twenty bloody minutes, that's why.'

I glance over at the clock. It's eight twenty. Crap! 'I'm so sorry – I have no idea how this happened. I must have forgotten to set my alarm.'

'This is precisely the sort of thing Natasha didn't want to happen. She will be very unhappy when she hears.'

'Please don't tell her. Please? I'll leave right now – I'll just throw on clothes and grab a taxi. I won't even shower.'

'I don't need the details, thank you.'

'Okay. Just…don't tell Natasha. She'll kill me.'

Poppy hesitates. 'Fine. But I can't make any promises for Olga. I have no control over her.'

I jump out of bed. 'Thank you, Poppy. I swear this won't happen again.'

'Good,' she says, and hangs up.

I throw on clean underwear and clothes, and run a brush through my hair. I toss a random assortment of makeup into my purse, then burst out of the front door and hail the first taxi I see. Fifteen minutes later, after hitting a brief traffic jam on Chalk Farm Road, the cab deposits me in front of Natasha's house where I find Olga tapping her foot as she points to her watch. 'You late,' she says.

'I know – I'm so sorry. I forgot to set my alarm.'

'Natasha say eight o'clock.'

'I know,' I repeat. 'I made a mistake. It won't happen again. I promise.'

She lets out a grumpy *hmpf* and unlocks the front gate, leading me around the house to a side entrance I've never seen before. Her purse is slung over her shoulder, as if she plans to leave as soon as I get inside.

'I buy salmon and onion and extra carrots,' she says, as she opens the side door. 'For testing.'

'Perfect. Thank you. That will save me a lot of time.'

'No chicken today?'

'I think the version I made yesterday will do the trick.'

110

She nods without smiling. 'Was good. Very good. Mr Ballantine, he liked very much.'

'Really?'

'He finish whole plate.'

By the time I'd baked the chicken yesterday, Natasha and Poppy had already left for Paris, so I'd used Olga as my guinea pig and left a few pieces for Mr Ballantine. Olga never displays much emotion, but she wolfed hers, picking every last bit of meat off the bone. I'm glad to hear Mr Ballantine had a similar reaction.

Olga leads me through the door into a utility room, which connects directly to the kitchen through a closed door I'd never noticed before. I guess I'd always assumed it was a closet.

I make for the refrigerator, but when I don't hear Olga behind me, I glance over my shoulder. She is standing in the utility room, watching me.

'Could you...I mean, would you mind keeping all of this between you and me?'

She narrows her eyes. 'I no tell Natasha this time. But next time? Big trouble.'

'There won't be a next time – thank you.'

She stares at me, expressionless. 'You work now,' she says, then shuts the door and leaves.

Nine hours later, I stand in front of a thick piece of poached salmon, its surface carnation pink. I cooked the fish first thing this morning, slipping four fillets into a simmering bath of vegetables and white wine, then let it chill in the refrigerator all day, while I searched the Internet for descriptions of Bon Cuit's carrot salad. I made two different versions of the salad, neither of which was bad, but neither was very good either. The first was under-seasoned and bland, and the second tasted overwhelmingly of vinegar.

My fork glides through the salmon's supple flesh, meeting almost no resistance. I take a bite and close my eyes, trying to focus on all of the flavours: what works, what doesn't, what's too strong, what isn't strong enough. The silky texture is perfect, but the flavour could use a little…something. Maybe a leek in the broth? Or some shallots? I'll have to work on it next week. While Natasha is in Paris, surrounded by what are probably the most amazing pastries in the world. None of which she will eat.

I pack up the leftover salmon fillets and leave them in the refrigerator with a note:

Mr Ballantine –
    Please help yourself to the leftover salmon. I'm still working on the recipe, but this version is pretty good.
    Best,
    Kelly

I finish cleaning the kitchen and pack up my bag. As I zip it shut, Olga walks in.

'You ready?' She clutches her purse strap.

'Yep. There's some salmon in the refrigerator if you want to take some home with you.'

She looks as if she is about to decline, then stops herself. 'Is good?'

'Pretty good. Not perfect. I'm still working on it.'

She considers my offer, then waves her hand. 'Meh. I leave for Mr Ballantine.'

She escorts me out of the side door and locks it behind her. Then the two of us head for the tube station, where we take different trains on the Northern Line to our respective destinations.

As I emerge from Warren Street, I feel the split-splat of rain on the top of my head. It quickly escalates into a full-fledged downpour. This wouldn't be a problem if I had an umbrella or anything resembling appropriate footwear, but in my rush to leave this morning, I'd forgotten the umbrella, and thrown on a pair of flats that are quite possibly the least rainproof shoes ever designed.

I bolt into a small pharmacy on Tottenham Court Road, where I buy a cheap umbrella, but I'm already soaked. My cream T-shirt is dripping wet, and my jeans are thick and soggy with rain. As I leave the shop I catch a glimpse of myself in a mirror and flinch. My blonde hair clings to my neck and face in long, stringy hanks, and the mascara I applied during my cab ride this morning has stained my face with streaks of black. If I ran into someone on the street who looked like this, I would probably cross to the other side.

I wipe off the mascara as best as I can with the back of my hand, and then, with my new umbrella in hand, I rush outside and hurry along Warren Street towards my flat. I step in no fewer than six puddles, soaking and most likely ruining my shoes, and by the time I reach my building, my fingers have turned blue. Today definitely has not gone according to plan.

Just when I'm about to let out a sigh of relief that I'm back at my building, I reach into my purse for my keys and panic.

My keys. Where are they?

I rifle through my purse, digging past my wallet and notebook and various cosmetics I threw in this morning, but the keys are nowhere to be found. No. No, no, no. This can't be happening. How could I forget them? How?

Convinced I'm simply looking in the wrong place, I squat beneath the building's negligible overhang and dump everything in my purse onto the ground. No luck. I am officially locked out.

I stuff everything back into my purse, leap to my feet and press the buzzer for Tom, the building manager. No answer. I press again and again, but no one picks up. I glance down at my watch: 5:58. Tom works until five. Perfect.

As I get out my phone, a young woman comes out of the building, letting me in. I take cover in the warm lobby and head for my flat, though I'm not really sure what my plan is. I have no way of getting inside.

I jiggle the doorknob once I reach it, more out of hope than anything else, but as expected, I can't open the door. I let out a groan, and as I do, a middle-aged man comes down the stairs from the floor above and rushes past me.

'Excuse me,' I say. He slows his step and glances over his shoulder. 'I'm locked out of my flat. Do you know of anyone who can help? Someone who might have a key?'

He looks at his watch and frowns. 'Tom's left for the day, I'm afraid, and anything to do with keys has to go through him. Perhaps you could stay with a friend until the morning, when Tom gets in.'

A friend? Like…who? The only person I could maybe, possibly, call a friend is Poppy, and she is in Paris. Also, I'm pretty sure that if I referred to her as my friend in her presence, she would gasp in horror.

I brace myself for the awkward proposal about to cross my lips. 'I know this is going to sound crazy, since you don't know me, but...would you mind if I slept in your flat tonight? I don't really know many people in town and—'

'Sorry,' he says, his cheeks red. 'I'm...going out for the evening. You'd have better luck with an acquaintance, I'm sure. Good luck.'

He nods stiffly, then hurries through the lobby and out of the front door.

Great. Now what am I supposed to do? I don't know anyone in this whole damn city, other than those connected to the Ballantine-Spencer household. Natasha and Poppy are in Paris, Olga is...well, wherever the hell Olga lives, and Mr Ballantine is...

I catch myself mid-thought. Mr Ballantine. I can't call him. Can I? Maybe he could get hold of Tom or knows how to pick a lock. Or, at the very least, maybe he'll suggest something better than sleeping on a stranger's couch.

I grab my phone and run a search for his office number. He is a Member of Parliament, so his parliamentary address and phone number are easy to find. As soon as the number pops up, I dial it. The phone rings a few times, then a woman answers. 'Hugh Ballantine's office.'

'Could I please speak to Mr Ballantine?'

'I believe he's left for the day. Would you like to leave a message?'

I slump against the door to my flat. 'No, thank you. I need to speak to him tonight.'

'I'm sorry. Perhaps you could send him an email.'

'I guess that might work.'

'Best of luck.'

I'm about to hang up, when she yells into the receiver. 'Hello?'

I pull the phone back to my ear. 'Yes?'

'You're in luck. Mr Ballantine just popped back in to pick up some papers. Who shall I say is calling?'

'Kelly. Kelly Madigan. I work for his wife.'

She presses the phone to her chest, and I hear the muffled sound of her voice: 'A Kelly Madigan? She says she works for your wife.'

'Ah, right, yes. Put her through to my office.'

'Just a minute, please,' the woman says.

A few moments of silence pass, and then he picks up the phone. 'Hello?'

'Hi, Mr Ballantine, it's Kelly. The cookbook writer.'

'Yes, hi. To what do I owe the pleasure?'

I clear my throat. 'I…Well, the thing is, I've locked myself out of my flat, and the building manager's left for the day. I don't know what to do.'

'Oh dear,' he says.

'Do you by any chance have Tom's number?'

'Tom?'

'The building manager.'

'Afraid not.'

'Oh.' I grasp for an alternative. 'What about a lock-smith? I'm not supposed to, for security reasons, but I can't think of any other—'

'Why don't you just stay at our place for the night?'

My heart nearly stops. 'At your house?'

'Of course. We aren't exactly short of space.'

116

'I don't think Natasha would be happy with that,' I say. 'She's been pretty clear about maintaining…boundaries.'

'Then this can be our little secret. Really, I insist. It'll be a lot simpler than anything else.'

My heart is racing. 'Are you sure?'

'Absolutely.' He presses the phone to his chest and tells his secretary that he'll just be a moment. 'Where are you now?'

'In my lobby.'

'The flat Natasha rented you in Marylebone?'

'Yes.'

'Right. Okay. Sit tight, and I'll be there in fifteen or twenty minutes.'

'Oh, no, I can take the tube.'

'Don't be silly. Sunil is driving me home anyway. It's basically on the way.'

'Really? Because I don't mind taking the tube – honestly.'

'I'm sure you don't, but I'm offering to pick you up.'

'I know, but…' But what? I don't want to impose or overstep? A little too late for that, if I'm already planning on sleeping in their house. It's a free ride, after all, and he wouldn't offer if he minded…

'Okay,' I say. 'If you're sure it isn't any trouble.'

'None at all. See you soon.'

He hangs up, and I slip my phone back into my bag, wondering if what I feel deep in my chest is excitement or dread or, more likely, a combination of both.

# *Chapter 13*

Twenty minutes later, a silver Mercedes pulls up in front of my building, the same Mercedes that nearly hit me on my first day. I peer into the lobby mirror one last time, trying to make myself look like something other than a drowned rat, but my success is minimal. My hair is still damp, and though my clothes have started to dry, they are still soggy and uncomfortable. At least I no longer have mascara running down my face, although that also means I no longer have mascara on my eyelashes.

I hurry outside, and Sunil hops out of the front seat to open the car's door, holding a large black umbrella over his head. I slip into the back seat, where I find Mr Ballantine with a stack of papers on his lap.

'Hello,' he says. He eyes my sodden clothes. 'A bit damp, eh?'

'I forgot my umbrella this morning,' I say, by way of

explanation, though I quickly realize this will only make him think I'm more incompetent than he probably already does.

'Haven't you learned never to travel without an umbrella in England?'

'Apparently not.' I look down at my purse. 'Considering I also forgot my keys, I think it's safe to say I have a lot to learn about being a functional human being.'

Sunil pulls out from in front of my building and turns onto Great Portland Street, heading towards Belsize Park. I glance surreptitiously at Hugh, who sports yet another perfectly tailored suit, this one a deep grey with a maroon pocket square that matches his dark maroon tie.

'So do all Members of Parliament get their own chauffeurs?' I ask, trying to reboot the conversation.

'Uh, no,' he says, a lightness to his voice. 'Only those married to famous American actresses.'

'Oh. Right.' I fidget with the zipper on my purse. 'So...are there many of those?'

'Many of what? MPs married to famous American actresses?' I nod, realizing this is quite possibly the stupidest question I've ever asked. 'No,' he says. 'Last time I checked, I was the only one.'

I look out of the window and watch the drops of rain trickle down it as we drive through Regent's Park, willing myself into silence because, apparently, I am incapable of normal conversation tonight. We come to a stop at traffic lights, and men and women dressed in trench coats and wellies dash across the street, clutching umbrellas of various colours and patterns as they head to their Friday-night destinations. I wonder if it's raining in Paris...

'Let's hope so,' Hugh says. Our eyes meet. I said that aloud? Great. 'Serves them right for leaving us at home.'

I wonder – to myself, with my lips pressed together – whether leaving Hugh behind is part of the 'arrangement' Poppy mentioned. How often do they travel together? Certainly often enough to be photographed by the paparazzi now and then, but I'm not sure how regularly that is in the context of their relationship.

'Couldn't you have gone, too?' I ask, hoping the question isn't too forward. Given the idiocy I've displayed this evening, I don't think it is. Then again, I've only been in London three weeks, and even though it feels much longer, I'm still subject to personal boundaries.

'That wasn't an option,' he says. 'Especially not when this education bill has taken over my life.'

'What education bill?' My cheeks flush as Hugh raises his eyebrows in apparent shock. 'Sorry – I'm not up to date on British politics. I'm still trying to figure out the tube system.'

'The education secretary published a massive education bill last week, so as the shadow education secretary, I have to point out how terrible it is at least twenty times a day.'

'Sorry…the shadow secretary? What is that?'

'It's the equivalent role in the opposition party. So whatever party is in power, there's an entire cabinet of opposition members who scrutinize what the administration is doing and mimic their portfolio with policy prescriptions of their own.'

'Sort of like Model UN for grown-ups?'

'Something like that.' He smiles. 'You know, it's good having someone like you around to take me down a peg or two. I was one more *Newsnight* appearance away from thinking I was more famous than the prime minister. Thank you for giving me some perspective.'

'Happy to oblige.'

Sunil rushes through more lights and turns onto Chalk Farm Road, where dozens of shops sit side by side, their fronts festooned with three-dimensional ornaments, everything from giant Dr Martens to enormous black dragons. On one stretch, I count at least five tattoo and body-piercing shops.

'What's so terrible about this education bill?' I ask, as we drive beneath a bridge spray-painted with the words 'CAMDEN LOCK' in bold yellow letters.

'Well, for starters, it diverts money that could be used to bolster state primary schools to fund the Party's pet projects – the result of which will be huge classroom sizes, which disadvantage everyone, but especially poorer children without supplementary resources at home. The bill is a joke, really. Too bad the prime minister doesn't see it that way.'

'Do you think it will pass?'

He grins. 'It's my job to make sure it doesn't.'

Sunil veers onto Haverstock Hill, and as he does so, Hugh's cell phone rings. He glances down at the number. 'Dad – hi,' he says. 'Everything okay? Is it Mum? . . . Oh, good.' He sighs in relief. 'What's the problem?' He scratches his jaw as he listens intently. 'Have you spoken to your GP?' A pause. 'Well, perhaps you should call him first.' Another pause. 'I realize that must be very uncomfortable, but . . . No, I'm a doctor of *economics*. Not a medical doctor. Right, yes, but that doesn't mean . . .' He looks at me and rolls his eyes dramatically. 'Perhaps some prune juice would help. Or a pot of strong coffee.'

He continues walking his dad through various laxative strategies, until Sunil finally pulls onto Belsize Square and up to the gated driveway.

'Dad? Listen, I'm just getting home. Could we continue this another time? . . . Brilliant. Good luck with it all. I hope everything comes out okay.'

I snort as he hangs up. 'Sorry – I shouldn't . . .'

'Don't apologize,' Hugh says. 'My father is mad. My biggest champion and dearest inspiration, but completely and utterly off his trolley.'

'Sounds like my dad.'

'Does he regularly call you with bathroom emergencies?'

I quickly flip through my mental catalogue of bizarre father-daughter interactions. 'No. I guess I've been spared that horror.'

'Consider yourself lucky.'

He smiles and opens the car door, and I can't help but wonder whether he'd stand by those words if he spent a mere five minutes in the same room as my father.


'I hope this will do.'

Hugh escorts me into one of the bedrooms on the second floor, a lavishly appointed suite with two large windows and a wrought-iron four-poster bed. The room is a study in greys and whites – pale grey walls, stark white duvet, dark-grey-and-white Ikat headboard – with pops of peach from velveteen bolster pillows and fresh roses in tall mirrored vases. Every accessory and piece of furniture is artfully arranged, from the antique chest at the foot of the bed to the plush cushions on the two window-seats. I feel as if I'm a guest at a hotel that I could never, ever afford.

'This will definitely do,' I say.

I drop my purse on a gilded armchair in the corner of the room and crack my knuckles as I survey the rest of the room.

Hugh stands awkwardly in the doorway. 'Do you...Would you like some dry clothes? You must be miserable.'

I picture myself gliding down Natasha's turned staircase in one of her Dior dresses, just a little something I threw on while my clothes tumbled in the dryer. She'd be totally okay with that, right?

'I'm good,' I say. 'My clothes are almost dry.'

Hugh eyes me. 'They don't look it.'

'I'm fine. Really.'

'If you're sure...' He glances down at his watch. 'You wouldn't perhaps have left something delicious in the fridge?'

'As a matter of fact, there are a few pieces of poached salmon. And some mustard-dill sauce.'

'Brilliant. Care to join me?'

'I ate before I left for the day,' I say. 'But thanks for the offer.'

'That was nearly two hours ago. Surely you have room for a little something. Pudding, perhaps?'

'I'm okay. I don't think there's any in the house, anyway.'

'Given your ability to pull magical puddings out of thin air, I don't see that as a problem. And before you protest, let's just say *I*'d like some pudding, so you'd be doing me a huge favour. How does that sound?'

I hesitate, then relent. 'Okay. I guess I could throw together something. I think there's still some chocolate left from the mousse. Do you like chocolate chip cookies?'

'Does anyone *not*?'

Your wife, if I had to guess.

As if he's read my mind, he adds, 'They're my favourite. I'd love some.'

I follow him down two flights of stairs to the kitchen and start pulling the baking ingredients from the pantry while Hugh explores the contents of the refrigerator.

'What's this carrot business at the back?' he calls over his shoulder.

'Oh. That's a failed carrot salad. I don't recommend it.'

He chuckles. 'Then why don't you throw it away?'

I set the flour and brown sugar on the counter. 'Because I hate wasting food. For me, it's the hardest part of my job, throwing away failed recipes. I usually keep them around for a few days to see if I can salvage something from them, even if it's just a meal for myself. I thought maybe I could toss that salad with a bit of Greek yogurt and some toasted pumpkin seeds and have it for lunch on Monday.'

He looks at me sceptically. 'Yogurt and pumpkin seeds? I suppose that's why you do what you do, and I do what I do. I'd never think of eating yogurt with anything but muesli. And I'd never think of using pumpkin seeds...well, for anything, really.'

He pulls the platter of salmon from the refrigerator and lifts the note from the top.

124

'"Mr Ballantine"...You do know you can call me Hugh?'

'I just figured..."Mr Ballantine" seems more appropriate.'

'If you were addressing me on a Select Committee, yes. But in my house, please, call me Hugh.'

My cheeks flush. 'Okay. I will.'

I preheat the oven and start tipping the dry ingredients into a bowl, using the measuring cups I brought from America and left in Natasha's drawer. One of the biggest adjustments in relocating across the Pond has been familiarizing myself with the metric system. In the States, everything is measured in cups and pounds – three cups of flour, two pounds of chicken breasts – but here it's all grams and millilitres, and the ovens all register on the Celsius scale instead of Fahrenheit. I've made myself a cheater's conversion chart, and since Natasha wants her book published in many countries around the world, I've made notes using both measurements. But when it comes to a cookie recipe I know by heart, it's easier to use my American equipment.

I place a small saucepan on the La Cornue stove and melt half a cup of butter before mixing in two different kinds of sugar.

'Your kitchen is amazing,' I say. 'It's nicer than most of the professional kitchens I've worked in.'

'Natasha barely uses it,' he says, as he transfers a fillet of salmon to a plate. He looks up and catches my stare. 'Sorry – that wasn't very nice. She does use the kitchen. Just not with a frequency that necessitates such high-end equipment.'

'Lucky for me, then.'

125

He grins as he drizzles a bit of mustard-dill sauce over his salmon. 'You're right. It's lovely. I shouldn't complain. At times it just seems a bit…wasteful? But she's worked hard for her money, so I suppose she can spend it however she likes.'

I note the way he refers to it as *her money*. Do they have separate bank accounts, too? Do they have separate everything?

Hugh grabs a fork from the utensil drawer, rolls his sleeves up around his elbows, and digs into the salmon, standing as he shovels a forkful into his mouth. 'Mmm,' he says, grabbing for a napkin. He wipes the corners of his mouth. 'Lovely.'

I mix the wet and dry cookie ingredients together, then stir in the chopped-up bits of chocolate. 'The recipe still needs some work.'

He grabs my note off the counter. 'As you say here…'

'Next week I'll try adding some extra vegetables to the poaching stock. I might play with the temperature a bit, too.'

He takes another bite and rubs his chin. 'No. You know what this *really* needs?' He swallows and shakes a finger at me. 'Some pumpkin seeds. And possibly some Greek yogurt.'

I hold back a smile. 'Well played.'

'I thought so.'

Our eyes catch for a brief moment, but I tear mine away as I put the bowl of cookie dough in the freezer. Are we flirting? No. We can't be. He's married, and I'm…well, me. But I have to admit: this feels an awful lot like flirting. Which, obviously, is completely inappropriate.

I begin cleaning the counter, dusting off the specks of flour and scrubbing away the globs of melted butter and sugar.

'I'm sorry,' he says, as I toss the chocolate wrapper into the trash, 'but did you just put the bowl of cookie dough into the freezer?'

I wipe my hands on the kitchen towel. 'That's one of my tricks. You chill it for a bit before baking. That way the cookies don't spread out too much.'

'You are a fount of useful information,' he says.

'That depends on how you define useful.'

'Well, I suppose if Her Majesty demands a batch of chocolate-chip cookies that don't spread too much, you are the woman to call.'

'I guess I am.' I lay two cookie sheets on the counter. 'But if she needs any tips on how to set an alarm clock so that she doesn't oversleep and leave her keys and umbrella at home, she should probably ask someone else.'

He lets out a belly laugh as he swallows the last bite of salmon. 'Thankfully Her Majesty has people to worry about such trivial matters for her.' He rinses his plate in the sink and sticks it in the dishwasher. 'How long does the dough need to chill?'

'About thirty minutes.'

He groans and looks at the clock. He starts. 'Shit – I'm supposed to do an interview with Radio 4 in five minutes. I completely lost track of time.'

'Sorry. It's my fault. I shouldn't have kept you.'

He shakes his head and looks at me with kind eyes. 'Don't apologize. I lost track of time because I was enjoying myself.'

My heart thumps, and I look away, busying myself with finding a cookie scoop. 'You'd better do the interview. Someone needs to tell the masses why this education bill is a joke.'

I rifle through one of Natasha's drawers, and after several moments have passed without Hugh saying anything, I look up and find him staring at me.

'What?' I say, my cheeks red. The flirty feeling returns. *Go away!* I tell it. *Go away!*

He opens his mouth to say something but catches himself. He smiles. 'Nothing,' he says. 'You're right. I'd better go.'

He starts to walk out of the room but pauses when he gets to the doorway. 'Oh, but don't think I've forgotten about those cookies. When I've finished...' he points to his stomach '... I expect cookie nirvana.'

He winks and turns to leave. When he's vanished, I realize my hands are shaking.

# Chapter 14

This is ridiculous. Hugh is an MP. He is *married*. And not to just anyone – but to one of the sexiest, most beautiful women in the world. The only reason I should be nervous around him is because he is famous and important and could probably have me expelled from the country. I have no business shaking with excitement when he so much as smiles at me. But all of a sudden I feel like a giddy schoolgirl. It's pathetic.

While Hugh does the Radio 4 interview, I bake four sheets of cookies, transfer them to a cooling rack, and leave them in the kitchen with a note:

> Help yourself. Thanks again for bailing me out.

There. Not a whiff of flirtation. Straight and to the point. Appropriate.

I creep upstairs, and as I tiptoe down the hall, I overhear bits of Hugh's radio conversation as I pass his study.

'...but that isn't what it would do, is it? No, it would further penalize those without the means to find a smaller class size elsewhere...'

I slink into the guest room, lock the door behind me, and make my way to the en-suite bathroom, which gleams with white Carrara marble and shiny chrome fixtures. I gargle with a bit of mouthwash and splash some water on my face, but as I head back to the bedroom, I realize I have nothing to sleep in. My clothes are still damp, and as much as Natasha wouldn't like me sleeping in her guest bed, she'd be even less thrilled about me sleeping in it in damp clothes. And she'd really hate it if I slept in her bed naked. As, quite frankly, would I.

I rummage through the dresser drawers, but they're empty, so I sneak back into the hall, hoping I can find something in another room, even if it's just one of Olga's housecoats.

As I creep down the hallway, Hugh emerges from his study and stops me in my tracks. 'Can I help you?'

I whirl around, my cheeks balls of fire. 'My clothes...I just...' I grasp for a coherent explanation. 'I don't have anything to sleep in.'

Never mind that I told him an hour ago my clothes weren't a problem at all. He must think I'm insane.

'I'm sure I've got a T-shirt you can borrow,' he says. 'Wait there.'

He disappears into a room at the end of the hall and re-emerges clutching an oversized blue T-shirt with a logo for Cambridge University.

'This should do.' He tosses it in my direction and, in a rare display of co-ordination, I catch it. 'Won't you join me downstairs for a few cookies?'

My heart races but, though every ounce of me wants to say yes, I can't. 'Thanks, but no,' I say. 'I'm beat. I think I'll call it a night.'

'Oh. Okay. Well...goodnight, then.'

'Goodnight.'

I head back to the guest room, and when I grab the door handle, I look over my shoulder. Hugh is still standing at the end of the hall, and he doesn't move until I've shut the door behind me.

I need a friend. Obviously I need a friend. That's what all of this is about. If I had a friend, I could have called her instead of Hugh, and I wouldn't have put myself in a situation where I was sleeping in his T-shirt in his guest bedroom. But that's exactly where I am, and it's awkward and terrible, and I can't wait to get the hell out of here.

The next morning, I wake up at seven, slip back into my clothes, and tiptoe along the hallway and down the stairs, preparing to sneak out of the house before Hugh awakens. Tom won't be in his office until nine, but the coffee shops by my building will be open, and I can wait there until he arrives. It's better than staying here. At this point, anything is better than that.

When I reach the front door, I rest my hand on the knob and am about to unlock the deadbolt, when I hear footsteps behind me.

'Don't,' Hugh says. I spin around and find him standing at the base of the stairs, dressed in worn khakis and a rumpled blue button-down. He nods towards the knob. 'You'll set off the alarm.'

I loosen my grip. 'Oh. Right. Sorry.'

He glances at his watch. 'Sneaking out before breakfast?'

'I need to meet the building manager first thing. He's the only one with an extra key.'

'Let me at least make you a cup of coffee.'

I stare at him, my palms sweating. Well, maybe I could…It's just coffee. What's the harm in an innocent—

No. This is absurd. No, no, no.

'Sorry,' I say. 'I wish I could, but I can't. Not this morning.'

'Perhaps another time, then.'

He walks over to a keypad by the front door and deactivates the alarm system. I unlock the deadbolt and open the front door.

'Thank you so much for your help last night,' I say. 'I really, really appreciate it.'

'My pleasure. Truly.'

'If it weren't for you, I probably would have slept on my lobby floor.'

'Or found a dodgy bloke to pick your lock.'

'See? You saved me on multiple fronts.'

'Consider it my repayment for all the lovely food.'

'I'm not sure that's an even trade but…I'll take it. Anyway, thanks again. Have a nice weekend.'

'You too.'

I start down the front steps and make for the front gate.

'And thank you for the cookies,' he calls after me. 'They were amazing.'

I start to reply, but by the time I turn around, he has already gone back inside and shut the door, and I half wonder if he called after me at all, or if my imagination got the better of me.

As soon as Tom lets me back into my flat, I power on my laptop and scour every social media platform for someone – anyone – I might know in London. Considering my background, I know the odds aren't in my favour, but even if it's a friend of a friend of a friend of a friend…at least it's *someone*.

After several minutes of sleuthing, I come across a fellow U of M art-history major named Jess Walters, who graduated a year after I did and now works as a research associate at the Tate Modern. I vaguely remember Jess, even though we were in different years and were among some twenty-eight thousand undergraduates on campus. Whereas each graduating class produced more than four hundred economics majors and nearly the same number of psychology majors, there were usually only about seventy in art history, so we all sort of knew each other, even across years.

I fire off an email to Jess, trying not to seem as desperate for friendship as I feel. I don't remember much about her, other than that she had pin-straight, fiery red hair and lots of freckles, but she's worked at the Tate Modern for three years, so she seems to be doing pretty well for herself.

Once I've replied to an earlier email from Meg, I cobble together a breakfast out of leftovers and odds and ends from my refrigerator: poached egg on garlicky wilted greens, all piled on top of a toasted slice of three-day-old sourdough. As I poke the yolk with my fork, a thick yellow sluice trickles onto the plate, and I use another piece of toast to sop up the pool of gluey yolk as I rerun last night's events in my mind: the smile on Hugh's face, the smoothness of his voice, the softness of his Cambridge T-shirt.

No. Stop. *Stop*. There's no point in rehashing any of that. No point. It's over, and it will obviously never happen again, and the sooner I stop thinking about it, the better off I'll be.

I gobble down the last bit of breakfast and rinse my plate in the sink. When I get back to my computer, I see Jess has already replied.

Hi Kelly,
    Of course I remember you! I'm surprised you remember me. Anyway, very cool that you're in London for a while. I'd love to grab a drink some time. Actually, next week we're launching the new Lichtenstein exhibit and are having a cocktail thing on Tuesday evening. You're welcome to come. Any interest?
Jess

I write back immediately.

Yes! I'd love to come. I actually did my thesis on Lichtenstein. Just tell me where to be and when, and I'll be there.

I click 'send' and lean back in my chair, and when Jess writes again, moments later, with all of the details, I let out a huge sigh of relief because I've found someone to save me from myself.

134

# *Chapter 15*

I have a friend. *Finally*. An actual friend. Or, at least, someone around my age with whom I have a few things in common. This is what I need. After losing my mom, and then Sam, I've been...lonely. Two of the most important people in my life vanished in a matter of weeks, and then I moved to a country where I don't know a soul, and even though I think I made the right decision, the transition has been more difficult than I expected. But now I'll know someone in London besides Hugh, Natasha, Poppy and Olga, and I won't feel so isolated. Or I'll feel *less* isolated, which is a step in the right direction.

I work through the weekend and into Tuesday, perfecting the poached salmon and carrot salad and moving on to the mysterious 'kale burger' on Natasha's list of recipes from her LA period. She once described it as 'toothsome' and 'gluten-free' so my first attempt involves brown rice, kale and crushed lentils. It is not good.

As Tuesday evening approaches, I slip out of Natasha's house early, so that I can shower and change before heading to the Tate Modern to meet Jess. I have avoided Hugh all week and, conveniently, he is so consumed with this education bill that he hasn't been home anyway. Olga has given me a few strange looks, but I think that has more to do with her general demeanour and less to do with the fact that Hugh and I had a sleepover last weekend.

When I reach my building, I hurry through the lobby towards my apartment, but I slow my step as Tom calls to me from his office. 'Remembered your key this time, eh?'

I stop and smile politely, raising my keys and jingling them lightly. 'Yep. I won't make that mistake again.'

'Lucky it wasn't Saturday – then you'd really have been buggered.'

'Thank heaven for small mercies.'

'It's all relative, right, my dear?'

I offer another polite smile and head towards my flat, when Tom stops me.

'There's a letter for you, by the way. Left it on the table in the hall.'

'A letter? For me?'

'You are Kelly Madigan, yes?'

'I just...I didn't expect to get any mail. No one really has my address.'

'Well, somebody does. It's on the table.'

I hurry to the table, my heart thumping. It couldn't be from Hugh...right? No. He wouldn't dare. Would he? I sort through a stack of magazines and envelopes, my hands trembling ever so slightly. I shouldn't get myself all worked up. This is stupid. It's probably nothing.

But what if it isn't? I continue searching through the stack of mail and come across a white envelope addressed to me, with American stamps. I glance at the return address in the upper left corner.

Oh. It's from Dad.

I let out a sigh as I grab it, then let myself into my apartment. Why do I feel disappointed? I should be glad my dad is writing me. This letter is a sign he is still alive and working at the post office. That's a good thing. I should be happy. And I am. But I'm a little bummed, too.

I shake off my disappointment and tear open the letter, which is written in my dad's serial-killer script on plain white paper.

Kelly,

Greetings from the Mother Land. (That's America, in case you didn't realize.) How is England? Does everyone talk funny over there? And before you say, oh, there Dad goes again, let me just say I'm kidding. I know it's just talking, like how in China they don't call it Chinese food, they just call it food. In which case, I wonder if people make fun of *you* for talking funny? Ha!

Your friend Meg stopped by last week. I don't know why. She said she had a question about postage rates, but my guess is she was checking up on me. Any dummy knows you could go to the post office to ask about postage. She didn't need to make a special trip to see me.

Anyway, she said you're having a nice time in England, so that's good. Your mother always wanted to go, but we

137

never got around to it, so maybe throw a penny into the river for her or something. I always joked that she only wanted to go so she could meet a prince, but she said I was the only prince she needed, which is pretty funny considering. Anyhow, I know she'd be real happy about your trip, so enjoy it.

Okay, that's all I have to say for now. Drop a line and let me know how you're doing. I know you like to email but, hey, I'm a postman!
Love,
Dad

I stare at the letter for a few moments and then, as I lay it on the coffee table, my heart breaks a little because I notice the paragraph where he mentions my mom is smudged by tears.

Dennis Madigan and Cynthia Murphy met more than forty years ago at Ypsi High, back when the football team was called the 'Braves' before changing their name to the more politically correct 'Grizzlies'. My mom was captain of the cheerleaders, a marvel considering in her older years she viewed exercise as the devil's work. But she looked mighty cute in a short skirt and tight sweater and loved to dance so, by all accounts, she led the squad with verve and flair.

My dad, on the other hand, didn't play for the football team, meaning he and my mom didn't run in the same circles. My mom spent her days being wooed by the quarterbacks and linebackers, who'd strut down the hall in packs, like teenage gods. Meanwhile, my dad was off to the side reading the latest instalment of *The Amazing*

*Spider-Man*, self-conscious about his lanky gait and acne scars. He loved comic books – *The Fantastic Four*, *The Avengers*, *Superman* – and though he often couldn't be bothered to read the current history assignment, he was always up to date on the newest *Spider-Man*. He played trombone in the marching band, and at Friday-night games, he'd march up and down the field, stealing glances at my mom as she shook her pompoms in the air and rallied the crowd. He'd watch her blonde ponytail bob up and down, wishing she'd sit next to him when everyone went out for pizza at Mario's after the game. But he always got there a minute too late, after some Kevin or Johnny or Tom had already swooped in beside her.

Then one Friday night during their junior year, while everyone was piling into Mario's, my dad spotted my mom across the room, with a free seat beside her. She sat in a booth with two of her girlfriends, twirling the tip of her blonde ponytail around her finger as they all laughed together. My dad knew if he pushed through the crowd fast enough, he could snag the seat, so he elbowed his way through the mob, diving and ducking around people, until he made it to her table.

'This seat taken?' he asked.

'Might be,' she said, smiling coyly.

'How about if I buy each of you ladies a pizza and a pop?'

They looked at each other and giggled, and after a little more back and forth, they let my dad sit down.

She was completely out of his league, or so they both said, but my mom found him endearing. They were an unlikely pair – the blonde party girl and the taciturn nerd

139

– but my mom loved that he would read her his comic books and write her long letters, and my dad thought she was the cutest woman God ever created. They ended up dating for the rest of high school and for two years after, when they finally got married. Three miscarriages and thirty-three years of marriage wrung some of the romance out of their relationship, but they still seemed in love with each other until she died, or at least as far as I could tell.

I sometimes got the impression they were less in love with the Cynthia and Dennis of today and more in love with the Cynthia and Dennis of yore – the promise of young love, the mutual adoration, the unsullied simplicity of it all. In the end, neither of their lives turned out as they'd dreamed. My mom peaked in high school, never again achieving the same popularity or freedom she'd found in her teens. She discovered adult life wasn't so much fun, with all of its responsibilities and demands, and she tried to escape all of that by drinking a little too much and watching too much TV and generally not taking responsibility for anything. That was probably why she never followed up with her doctor – she was weary of life and figured she'd let nature take its course.

And though my dad did fine in school, he never went to college. Not many of his close friends did. They got jobs – with GM and Ford and Kmart. I suspect my dad would have loved college and often wonder what his life would have been like if he'd gone. Instead, he's worked for the Postal Service his whole life, feeling stuck and superior and, most of the time, bitter.

Bitter or not, for nearly forty years, it'd been Cynthia and Dennis, Cynthia and Dennis, two names that slid off the tongue together, like Sonny and Cher, Bill and Hill, Becks and Posh, Bogart and Bacall. But now it's just Dennis. Just Dennis, and nobody else.

Once I've put my dad's letter aside, I shower and change, throw on a fresh coat of makeup, grab my purse and head out of the door. As I pass Tom's office, I see he has left for the day, sparing me another jokey exchange about remembering my keys. I really hope that doesn't become an ongoing shtick.

I rush to the Great Portland Street tube, where I hop on a Circle Line train bound for Edgware Road, getting off at Blackfriars. I weave my way from the tube station across the Thames to the Tate. The brick exterior doesn't *look* very modern – the building served as a power station in the middle of the last century – but as soon as I walk inside, I'm swept away by the clean, minimalist lines, the plain taupe walls, the concrete floors, the steel beams running up the sides and along the ceiling.

I reach into my purse and pull out the instructions I scribbled down from the email Jess sent me: 'Tate Modern, Level 3 Concourse, Lichtenstein retrospective'.

I make my way towards the Level 3 Concourse, and as I step off the escalator I gasp. The entire space is lit in primary colours and actually *looks* like a Lichtenstein painting. Spotlights overhead dapple the floor with yellow Benday dots, like the ones in his comic book paintings, and the walls are uplit with fiery red bursts.

A woman in a black cocktail dress and wired headset stands with a clipboard in her hand near the entrance, and I approach her with awe in my eyes.

'Hi,' I say, still mesmerized by the décor. 'I'm here for the event?'

'Name?'

'Kelly Madigan.'

She flips through her list and furrows her brow. 'I'm sorry, your name doesn't seem to be—'

'She's with me.'

Jess emerges from behind the woman in black, her lustrous red hair drawn into a tight bun atop her head. She wears a bright green sleeveless dress and black-and-white polka-dot stockings, standing tall in her black platform heels. I suddenly feel very self-conscious about my conservative ensemble of black shift dress, black stockings and black ballet flats. Since I'd come to London to work, I hadn't packed much in the way of party clothes, but standing among the artsy hip set at the Tate Modern, I wish I'd bought something special for the occasion.

'Jess – hi!' I reach in for a quick hug. 'This is amazing. The lighting – I can't believe it.'

'Wait until you see the hors d'oeuvres. You'll die.'

She leads me towards a set of high cocktail tables, waving to guests on either side of the room as she glides through the narrow space.

'Thank you so much for inviting me,' I say, hurrying to keep up. 'I don't really know anyone in town, so I'm beyond grateful.'

Jess waggles her fingers at a woman in the corner and mouths a smiling *hiiii*. 'Yeah – why did you say you were here?'

'I'm working on a cookbook.'

She slows her step and air-kisses a man in an electric

blue suit. 'Let's talk later about the upcoming Judd exhibit,' she says, squeezing his hand and continuing towards the bar. She turns to me. 'Sorry – a cookbook? For whom?'

'Natasha Spencer.'

Jess comes to an abrupt halt. 'Natasha *Spencer*?'

I nod. The non-disclosure agreement doesn't say I can't tell people I'm working on her cookbook. I'm not supposed to give details about personal stuff – the kinds of things I told Meg when I swore her to secrecy. But I can talk about the book in broad terms and, per my contract, can even include it on my résumé. What I can't do is run to the tabloids and tell them Natasha and Hugh sleep in separate bedrooms.

'You know she's a huge supporter of the Tate, right?'

'I didn't,' I say. But, given the impressive work in her house, I probably could have guessed.

'Oh, yeah – huge. She gives like hundreds of thousands of dollars a year.'

'Wow.'

'Imagine having that kind of cash to burn.'

'I don't think I can.' I adjust my purse strap on my shoulder. 'So tell me more about—'

'Ruby!' Jess cuts me off as she waves at someone over my shoulder. 'Sorry,' she says, looking back at me. 'I have to talk to Ruby for a second. But make yourself comfortable. The food is free, and it's an open bar, so drink up! I'll only be a few minutes, and then I can introduce you to some of my friends.'

'Okay, sure.' I glance around the room. 'Where should I—'

But before I can finish my question, Jess is already on

143

her way to Ruby, and I stand in front of the bar, alone, fearing this night isn't going to be quite as much fun as I'd hoped.

Okay, so maybe Jess isn't going to be my new best friend after all.

It's not that she isn't nice or interesting or fun, but I haven't spoken two words to her since she ran off to speak to Ruby. She has waved to me a few times from across the room and mouthed, '*Sorry – work*,' several times while frowning apologetically, but that doesn't change the fact that, thirty minutes later, I'm still standing in front of the bar, alone. The only difference between now and thirty minutes ago is that I'm on my second glass of wine instead of my first. The crowd has also ballooned to a swarm of some three hundred people.

Rather than drink myself into a stupor, I decide to take a lap around the room and survey the art on display. I push through the smartly dressed masses, trying not to spill my Malbec on the various designer boots and heels. I know this is a work event for Jess, but part of me wishes I'd known in advance how much networking and schmoozing she'd have to do: I feel just as lonely here as I did three days ago – possibly more so, even though I'm in the midst of all these people.

I stop in front of Lichtenstein's *Drowning Girl*, which was always one of my favourites and a work I've never seen in person until now. I bought a poster of it in my sophomore year of college and hung it above my bed, and every time I walked into my room I'd smile on seeing it there. Everyone else I knew had the standard posters – *Starry Night*, 'My

Goodness My Guinness', *Animal House*, the Beatles – but my room was different. I didn't choose that poster because it looked cool or matched my comforter: I bought it because I liked *this* artist, *that* painting. I'd studied it and read about it and wanted a piece of it for myself, even if that piece was a ten-dollar poster. I loved – still love – the melodrama of it all, the woman drowning in a turbulent sea, the tears, the histrionic thought bubble – 'I don't care! I'd rather sink – than call Brad for help!'

'It's brilliant, isn't it?'

I look to my side and find a plump, middle-aged man with a dark, scruffy beard standing next to me, rubbing his chin.

'It is,' I say, offering a polite smile.

He removes his glasses and squints, inspecting the painting more closely. 'But I do think his appropriation of the tragic female is quite misunderstood.'

'Oh?'

'Indeed. One might say this woman is taking charge of her own life – choosing death rather than relying on a paternalistic figure to care for her. One might say it is, in fact, a *feminist* work.'

'I'm not sure I'd go that far…'

He puts his glasses back on and turns to face me. 'But why not, I ask? Why *not*?'

Oh, dear God. Leave it to me to find the lunatic in the crowd.

'Well, because…if you're asking me…'

'Kelly?'

I whirl around at the sound of my name. The air thickens.

'Hugh – Mr Ballantine.' His face is bright red – literally – thanks to the event lighting, and if I had to guess, I'd say mine is the same colour *au naturel*. 'It's…lovely to see you.'

'Likewise.'

The portly man beside me clears his throat and extends his hand in Hugh's direction. 'Fitz-Lloyd St John Kerr,' he says.

Oh, my God. Is that one name?

Hugh reaches out and shakes his hand. 'Ah, yes, of course. Good to meet you.'

'Indeed, the pleasure is all mine. I was just chatting to…I'm sorry, I didn't catch your name?'

'Kelly.'

'Right, right, right. I was just chatting to *Kelly* about how many of Lichtenstein's works could actually be described as feminist totems. Don't you agree?'

Hugh offers a jokey frown. 'I'm afraid you're asking the wrong MP. I still haven't figured out why, exactly, this is art.'

Fitz-Lloyd lets out a sharp gasp. 'You can't be serious, surely?'

'I'm afraid so. But I suppose that's why I'm in Parliament and not teaching history of art at Oxford.'

'Yes. Quite.' Fitz-Lloyd presses his glasses up the bridge of his nose and glances over Hugh's shoulder. 'Ah. I see Bryonie has arrived. If you'll excuse me…'

He leaves, and I shift my focus back to the painting, even though I can feel Hugh's eyes on me. He eventually looks at the work as well. 'A bit like you on Friday night, eh?'

146

'Assuming she's drowning because she forgot her keys and umbrella. And, anyway, I did call Brad for help.'

'Ah, so I'm Brad in this scenario?'

'You were more like the last resort.'

'I see.'

I take a sip of wine, trying not to act as awkward as I feel, which is very, very awkward. 'So…what are you doing here?'

'You mean other than saving you from boring nutters with six names?'

'Yes, other than that.'

'We're big patrons of the Tate – well, Natasha is, anyway – so we always get invited to events and exhibition launches. I don't often go, but since I saw this one was for Lichtenstein, I thought I'd call in.'

'I thought you didn't understand how his stuff qualifies as art.'

'I don't. But since you mentioned the other week that you'd done your thesis on him, well, I thought maybe I should learn more about him.'

'Ah, so it's my fault, then,' I say, trying to sound light-hearted even though what I'm really thinking is, *Oh, my God, you came because of me?*

'Yes, I think it's fair to lay the blame on you.' He smiles. 'Anyway, I might ask you the same question. How did you wangle an invite? This is a pretty exclusive crowd.'

'Oh, so cookbook ghostwriters don't qualify as exclusive?'

'No, sorry, I didn't mean—'

'I'm kidding. The only people who might use that word to describe me are a few Michiganders back home.'

'Who?'

'Michiganders. People from Michigan. That's where I'm from, originally.'

'Ah, I see. Where I'm from...I'm not really sure what we're called. Nottinghamians, I suppose? We don't really have a name.'

'You're from Nottingham?'

'Indeed.'

'So what you're saying is, you're Robin Hood.'

He laughs. 'Not quite.'

'I don't know...You're trying to help the poor, you're from Nottingham...Sounds pretty convincing to me.'

'Well, if you want to call me Robin Hood, who am I to argue?'

'Exactly.' I look at the floor, then back up at him. 'I think what you're doing about the education bill is great, by the way. You're very...'

'Stubborn?'

'I was going to say brave.'

He peers over his shoulder, then looks back at me, his eyes soft. 'Listen, I was wondering if you might like to—'

'There you are!'

Jess bursts between us and lets out a huge sigh. 'I am *so* sorry I abandoned you. Tonight's been insane. It's like everyone I've ever met in London is here. It's nuts.' She shakes her head. 'Anyway, I'd love to introduce you to some of my friends. They're all on the second-floor concourse.'

I glance up at Hugh, and as I do, Jess follows my gaze.

'Oh – unless you're...already busy?'

Hugh holds my stare for a beat. Then his shoulders

148

relax. 'I was actually just leaving,' he says. He reaches out and shakes my hand. 'Lovely running into you.'

He smiles and pushes his way through the crowd towards the exit.

'Sorry – I hope I wasn't interrupting anything,' Jess says, as she leads me to the escalator.

'It was nothing,' I say. 'Really.'

But as I look over my shoulder and watch Hugh's head disappear into the crowd, I know that isn't even close to the truth.

# Chapter 16

Were we flirting again? Because it sure felt that way. Granted, I'm out of practice and am hardly an authority on the subject. Before Sam came along, I was never particularly well versed in the art of seduction (example: my first interaction with Sam involved a conversation about a sandwich), and once we'd started dating, I didn't need to bother any more. But that conversation with Hugh...it felt different, somehow. Like we were both trying, like we both wanted to make the moment last. I called him *Robin Hood*, for crying out loud. Who does that? People who die alone, if I had to guess. And what would have happened if Jess hadn't interrupted us? Would we have spent all evening talking? Or would I have made another painfully moronic comment, this time about the Sheriff of Nottingham?

Once we arrive on the second floor, Jess introduces me

to some of her friends, who are around my age and at similar points in their careers. But as hard as I try to convince myself they will become my new best friends – that they must, that the only reason I'm flirting with an older, married man is because I don't know anyone else here – I find myself struggling to connect with any of them. When did making friends get so hard? In high school and college, I didn't even have to think about it. It just sort of happened. But ever since I left school and entered the real world, making friends has required a lot of effort, with mixed results. It's not that there's anything *wrong* with Jess or her friends. I just don't feel an instant connection. Not the way I do with Hugh – who obviously isn't a viable confidant.

I decide that if I can't fill my loneliness with friends, I'll fill it with work. And if any recipe can suck up a huge chunk of my time, it's Natasha's blasted kale burger. I'm stumped. I try lentils, I try rice, I try beans, in various combinations and proportions, but nothing quite works. Everything tastes so...*healthy*, and not in a good way. I've concocted many nutritious dishes over the years, and the key is to pack them with flavour and substance, but all of my burger attempts fall short.

Finally, after spending the entire week testing various incarnations, I get it right: crushed white beans, a handful of breadcrumbs, some smoked paprika and just enough egg to bind it all together with the chopped kale and other vegetables. It's smoky and toothsome without being heavy or gummy. I have no idea if it resembles what Natasha has in mind, but thankfully she returns from Paris today so I can have her taste it, along with the salmon and the carrot salad, which I've remade in anticipation of her return.

As I finish preparing the sauce for the salmon around three o'clock, I hear the front door open, followed by the click-clack of heels and the staccato of Poppy's voice as she marches into the kitchen, her phone pressed against her ear.

'No. Absolutely not. We said one o'clock. *One* . . . No, not Monday – tomorrow.' She lets out a heavy sigh. 'Fine. Yes. Tomorrow at one. Hot stones. Yes.'

She grunts as she hangs up.

'Welcome back,' I say. 'How was Paris?'

'Exhausting.'

'Eat anything good?'

'Anything? Try everything.'

'Where did you eat? What did you have?'

'Oh, you know, this and that. We ate at Joël Robuchon's place one night. That was lovely.'

'You ate at *Joël Robuchon*?'

'You've heard of it? I thought you'd never been to Paris.'

'I haven't. But I work with chefs for a living. Robuchon is a legend.'

'In that case, I should have asked for his autograph while he chatted up Natasha.'

'You *met* him?'

'Yes. He's charming.'

I'm trying not to geek out over this but, oh, my God! Back in Chicago, François would talk all the time about Robuchon as one of his idols. I can't believe Natasha met him.

'Anyway,' she says, 'now that we're back I need to do about five million things, and I'm already behind.'

'Is Natasha around? I have a few recipes I'd like her to taste.'

'Taste? Oh, no, no, no. We both overdid it in Paris. Too much wine and chocolate. She's juicing from now until Monday. We both are.'

I look down at the bowl of mustard-dill sauce. 'But I've prepared everything specially. Natasha said she'd do the tasting today, when she returned.'

Poppy shrugs. 'She changed her mind.'

'But all of the food – what am I supposed to do with it?'

'I don't know. I'm sure you'll think of something.'

'But can't she just—'

Poppy's phone rings in her hand, cutting me off. 'Her facialist. I have to take it.' Her eyes flit to the mustard-dill sauce. 'As for the food, just – whatever. Throw it out.'

She spins around, answers the phone and, as she schedules an emergency bird-poop facial for Natasha, waltzes out of my sight.

Throw it out? Throw it *out*? I poached a pound of salmon, meticulously julienned two pounds of carrots, pulled a recipe for freaking kale burgers out of my butt, and she wants me to throw it all away? No. I refuse. That isn't merely wasteful. It's also disrespectful and insulting.

Instead, I prepare a plate for Hugh, drizzling a bit of mustard sauce over a slice of salmon, which I place next to a mound of carrot salad and a seared kale burger. I wrap up the plate and leave yet another note:

Mr Ballantine

Sorry this is such a hodgepodge.

Kelly

He said to call him Hugh, but somehow that still doesn't feel appropriate, even though I've lived and worked here for a month. He is a Member of Parliament. He is *my boss's husband*. Never mind that he and Natasha sleep in separate bedrooms, or that he invited me to sleep in his house last Friday night, or that, against my better judgement, I am developing something of a crush on him. None of that changes anything. Or, at least, it shouldn't.

I take the rest of the leftovers home with me because I refuse to throw out perfectly good food it took me days to develop and prepare. That said, I've eaten salmon and kale burgers every day for the past week, so the idea of eating either for yet another meal makes me gag a little. Why couldn't we be stuck on the chocolate mousse recipe? Or even the sesame chicken? I'm not sure my gastrointestinal system can take another week of beans and kale.

When I get back to my flat, Jess Walters calls as I try to make room in my overstuffed refrigerator for more kale and salmon delights.

'Sorry again about Tuesday,' she says. 'I had no idea the night would be so crazy.'

'Don't worry about it – I had fun.'

'It was pretty cool, right? I'm glad you got to meet a few of my friends.'

'They seemed great,' I say, trying to sound more enthusiastic than I'd felt at the time.

'A bunch of us are meeting up at a bar in Soho tomorrow night – you should come.'

'I'd love to but…' But what? I have plans to sit home alone and eat kale-burger leftovers? Because, let's be honest, those are the only plans I have. I didn't feel an instant connection with any of her friends but that doesn't mean I can't hang out with them. And who knows? Maybe there'll be people I haven't met before. People who aren't Poppy or Olga. People who aren't Hugh.

'I'd love to,' I say, and I try really hard to mean it.

The next night I show up at the Blind Pig a little after nine, winding my way down Poland Street in Soho. It's one of those fake speakeasies, where the owners make the place feel hidden and a bit hard to find, even though everything about it is legal and publicized. The door is tucked away beneath a red 'Opticians' sign, the only indication I have arrived at the correct location being the doorknocker in the shape of a blindfolded boar.

I knock three times. A host lets me in and directs me up a narrow stairway, which is lit in various shades of red and purple. When I reach the top, I enter the cosy, dimly lit bar, which features an antique mirrored ceiling, a copper counter, plush leather banquettes and wood-panelled walls.

'Kelly!'

Jess waves to me from one of the banquettes, where she is surrounded by a group of about ten people, who sit on wooden chairs and tufted leather stools around a series of small, round tables. Everyone looks in my direction as she waves, making me the centre of attention, which I never enjoy.

As before, Jess looks hip and stylish, wearing a black-and-white checked skirt and silky black top, her fiery red hair pulled into a high bun. Given my wardrobe disaster on Tuesday, I bought a cheap, black peplum blouse this afternoon at Topshop, but the material is itchy, and the part around my hips kind of looks like a tutu.

'Have a seat,' she says, scooting over to make room for me on the banquette. 'Everyone, this is Kelly. We went to college together.'

Ten names fire at me like bullets, and I've already forgotten half of them by the time the last person – Harry – says his name. I recognize three of the people from the Lichtenstein exhibit, but the others, including Harry, are all new.

'So what are people drinking?' I ask. 'Any recommendations?'

'I have a Cuba Pudding Junior,' Jess says, handing me a drink list. 'But everything is great. You're a writer – you'll get a kick out of the menu.'

I scan the drink options: 'Rum DMC', 'Sidecar Named Desire', 'Dill Or No Dill'. When I reach one called 'Robin Hood, Quince of Thieves', I stiffen.

Robin Hood.

Nottingham.

Hugh.

'Fancy a serial killer?'

I look up to find Harry sitting beside me, having swapped places with Jess, who is now several seats away, chatting to a handsome man in a green polo shirt. Harry has reddish blond hair, which recedes a bit around his temples, and a long, lanky figure, with narrow shoulders and graceful hands.

'I…what?'

'A "Cereal Killer".' He points at the menu. 'It's supposed to be good.'

'Oh, right.' I read the ingredients: rum, white chocolate, Galliano, chocolate milk. 'Probably a little too sweet for me.'

'For me, too, if I'm being honest. I just want someone to order one because I love the name.'

'It's right up there with the "Cuba Pudding Junior" and the "Kindergarten Cup".' I glance at his hammered-copper mug. 'What are you drinking?'

'The "58 Poland". Leave it to me to pick the most boring name on the list.'

'That's the address, right? Or am I missing some sort of British pun?'

'No, it's the address. But I liked the ingredients. I'll try to order something more adventurous next time.'

I look back at the menu. 'Maybe I'll have the "Thermo Nuclear Daiquiri". How could I turn down a drink whose ingredients include "absinthe, glowing radiation and danger"?'

'Sounds like a recipe for a perfect Saturday night, if you ask me.'

He waves down the waitress, and I order my drink, and as she leaves, he rests his mug on the table. 'So you're American, then?'

'No. I put on this accent for fun.'

He blushes. 'Right, sorry, obviously.'

'I'm just giving you a hard time,' I say, though,

157

considering I have no friends here, I don't know why I think alienating a perfectly nice, attractive guy is a good idea.

'I should be used to it by now. I'm something of a specialist at pointing out the obvious.'

'Well, I'm something of a specialist at making situations as awkward as possible, so I guess we're even.'

He laughs. 'Where are you from in America?'

'Michigan. That's where Jess and I met – at the University of Michigan.'

'Ah, brilliant. That's in Ann Arbor, right?'

'Yeah, you know it?'

'Not from personal experience. But one of my mates from uni is doing a law degree there. He's in his first year.'

'Oh. So…you just graduated from college?'

'God, no – we graduated seven years ago. But he worked in the City for a while, met an American girl and they moved back to the States together. He decided to study law as part of his plan to stay there.'

'Ah, got it.'

'I've actually never been to America, if you can believe it.'

'Until now I'd never left. So, yeah, I can believe it.'

'I recently applied for a fellowship there, at Harvard. Not sure if I'll get it – or if I'd take it if I did. It's quite a long way.'

'What kind of fellowship?'

'At the Kennedy School. I work in public policy. International trade, mostly.' He grins. 'Don't worry, I won't bore you all night with talk of farm subsidies.'

I pretend to wipe my brow. 'Kidding – I'm sure your work is much more interesting than mine.'

'I somehow doubt that. What do you do?'

'I write cookbooks.'

'Like Nigella?'

'No. I mean, yes, but you won't see my name on the cover.'

'Oh. Then...where would I see it?'

'Buried somewhere in the acknowledgements, usually. I'm sort of the cook behind the cook. I test and write up the recipes for food personalities – chefs, TV hosts, actresses.'

'Ah, a bit like a ghostwriter.'

'Exactly like a ghostwriter. That's what I do.'

He picks up his drink and takes a sip. 'What brings you to London, then? Anyone I've heard of?'

'I'm helping Natasha Spencer with her cookbook.'

'Natasha Spencer? The actress?' He grimaces. 'She's always struck me as a bit of a nightmare, no?'

I choose my words carefully. 'She...is very good at what she does.'

He smiles. 'I thought so.'

The waitress arrives with my drink, and the entire group goes silent. The drink glows. The damn thing actually *glows* – not like, *Oh, there's a little sparkly twinkle from the ice and the glass*, but *Oh, wow, that chick is about to throw back a cup of neon green radioactive slush*. The daiquiri is piled high with crushed ice, and some sort of special cube sits inside, lighting up the entire glass, which is shaped like a chemical barrel. The glass is wrapped in bright yellow biohazard tape, with a biohazard flag attached to the straw, because apparently it isn't obvious enough that this is supposed to look like a container of nuclear waste. There might as well be a spotlight on me and a man bellowing through a microphone, 'HEY, EVERYONE! CHECK OUT THE LOSER IN THE TUTU!'

'Wow,' Harry says. 'They weren't kidding when they said "glowing radiation".'

'Apparently not.'

I pick up the glass, and Harry clinks his mug against it. 'Cheers,' he says. 'To living dangerously.'

Harry and I talk for the rest of the evening, and I learn about his years at University College London and his job at the Centre for Policy Research. He has pale blue eyes and an easy smile, but as much as I enjoy talking to him, my mind wanders every so often to Hugh: his chiselled jaw, his slim waist, his deep laugh. I hate myself for thinking about him, for wasting my mental energy on an implausible and immoral fantasy. But I can't help myself. Ever since the night I forgot my keys, his image keeps creeping into my brain, and no matter how hard I try to make it go away, it keeps finding its way back in. The 'Robin Hood' reference on the drink menu here certainly isn't helping.

At eleven o'clock, the group decides to move to another bar, and I take that as my opportunity to leave.

'Won't you come with us?' Harry asks, as we slide out of the banquette.

'I have to get up early tomorrow,' I lie. 'And I have to talk to my friend in Michigan in the afternoon.'

'Oh. I see.'

I follow the group down the stairway, and when we empty onto the bustling sidewalk, Harry sidles up next to me. 'I had a lovely time chatting to you tonight,' he says.

'Me too.'

That isn't a lie. I did like talking to him. He's smart and charming, with the sort of penetrating stare that indicates a genuine curiosity about the world. If it weren't for the fact that I'm exhausted, I would probably tag along. But the more tired I get, the more I think about Hugh, which means it's time for me to go to bed.

Harry reaches into his pocket and hands me a business card. 'If you fancy meeting up some time, here's my mobile number. I'd love to hear more about the cookbook.'

I stare at the card, holding it steadily between my fingertips. Why am I hesitating? Because he's attractive and single and age-appropriate? Because he and I had lots to talk about? Because he isn't Hugh?

'Maybe we can meet for a drink next week,' I say.

'That would be brilliant. I'm free any night but Friday. And Saturday, actually – I'm visiting family in Devon over the weekend.'

'Let's say Wednesday. I'll call you early in the week.'

His face brightens. 'Perfect. And I promise the evening won't involve "glowing radiation and danger" – unless you want it to.'

'I think I'm set on both those things for a while,' I say.

He smiles as if he understands, but what he doesn't realize is that when it comes to avoiding danger, I'm not talking about a drink.

# Chapter 17

On Sunday afternoon, I open my laptop for a video chat with Meg. I've been meaning to talk to her ever since I received the letter from my dad, but with the time change, only weekends work for both of us.

Meg's face appears on my screen after a few rings, her curls held back with a thick black headband.

'Top o' the morning to you, guv'nor,' she says, in an appalling fake English accent.

'No one actually talks like that here. In case you were wondering.'

'Cor blimey,' she says, her accent now sounding vaguely Indian.

'Seriously, stop. That accent is borderline offensive.'

'To whom?'

'The spoken word.'

She purses her lips. 'Don't tell me you've become one of

those Americans who spends a little time in England and suddenly thinks she's British. You're not one of them. You're one of us.'

I glance at the ceiling. 'Yes, thanks, I know.'

'I'm serious. The minute you start referring to lorries and loos, I'm sending someone to kidnap you and bring you home.'

'You should probably do that anyway.'

'Why?' She grins and rubs her hands together mischievously. 'Is Natasha still being crazy?'

'No crazier than before, really. I actually haven't seen her in about a week. She's been in Paris.'

Meg heaves an envious sigh and rests her chin on her hand. 'Of course she has.'

'I secretly hoped she'd take me but, alas...'

'Did you have the week off?'

'No, I still worked from her kitchen. Concocting a bunch of recipes she now won't try because she's "juicing" until Monday.'

'Well, I mean, obviously. She was just in Paris.' Meg says this as if she has intimate familiarity with juice cleanses and world travel, even though, like me before taking this job, she has never left the United States. 'So wait,' she says, 'you had her place all to yourself?'

'Sort of. Her housekeeper was there. And so was her husband.'

Meg wiggles her eyebrows up and down. 'Oooh, so you had Mr Hunky all to yourself?'

'No!' I take a deep breath and compose myself. 'He wasn't really around. He's been working on an education bill. It's been keeping him really busy.'

Meg holds up her hands defensively. 'Okay – sorry. Wow. Touched a nerve, apparently.'

'No, I'm sorry. I didn't mean to jump down your throat. Things have just been…weird, is all.'

'Weird how?'

'I shouldn't talk about it. I take that back – there isn't even anything to talk about.'

Meg narrows her eyes. 'Kelly Josephine Madigan. You are keeping something from me.'

I try to stop my cheeks flushing, but it's no use. My entire face is burning up. 'No, I'm not!'

She points at the screen. 'Yes, you are. How long have I known you?'

'Twenty years.'

'And how many secrets have you successfully kept from me over that period?'

I bow my head sheepishly. 'None.'

'Exactly. So out with it. What's going on?'

I look back at the computer screen. 'That's just it – nothing is going on. Nothing physical, anyway.'

'Nothing physical? That means it's something emotional. Are you…I mean, are you and her husband…?'

'No!' I say. 'I mean, there's been some mild flirting. And I guess technically I slept in his T-shirt last Friday night—'

'*WHAT?*' Meg stares at the screen, her eyes wild. 'WHAT DID YOU JUST SAY?'

She bangs on her desk so hard that, for a moment, I lose her picture, and the screen goes black.

'Hello? Meg?'

Her picture returns. I can't tell whether she's breathing or not.

'Ah, there you are,' I say. 'The screen went black for a second.'

'Did it? Well, good. Because that's exactly what just happened to my brain.' She presses her hand gently to her chest and takes a deep breath. 'So, take me through what you just said. Because I'm having trouble processing this. Why were you sleeping in Natasha Spencer's husband's T-shirt? And where were you while this was happening?'

I take her through the entire saga: oversleeping, forgetting my keys, calling Hugh, sleeping in the guest room. By the time I've finished the story, Meg's mouth is open so wide I can see her tonsils.

'Wait. Hold on. You're telling me you slept in Natasha's house while her husband was there and she was away?'

'That is the story I just recounted to you, yes.'

'What happened the next morning? Did you talk? Did you have breakfast together?' She leans closer to the screen. 'What did you do with the T-shirt?'

'I left it folded up on the bed. And, no, we didn't have breakfast. I tried to sneak out, but he caught me, so we talked for, like, three minutes before I left.'

'Have you seen him since?'

I blush again. The constant blushing is becoming a problem. It is one of the many disadvantages of having fair skin.

'You *have* seen him again!' Meg crows. 'Where? When?'

'At a Lichtenstein exhibit at the Tate.'

'You went *together*?'

'No, we ran into each other. I realized I have no friends here, so I connected with someone I knew at U of M who works at the Tate, and she invited me. Hugh just happened to be there. I had no idea I'd run into him.'

'A likely story!'

'Meg, stop.'

'Listen, I get it. The guy is a fox. I've seen pictures.'

'It isn't like that. There's nothing going on.'

'Yet.'

'Ever.'

'I wouldn't be so sure…'

'Okay, let me ask you the same question you asked me earlier: how long have you known me? Twenty years? And have I ever struck you as the kind of person who would sleep with a married man?'

She sighs. 'No, of course not. But that's a scenario in a vacuum. Life isn't a vacuum.'

'I know. Which is, no doubt, the reason I'm thinking about a married man at all. I just broke up with the guy I'd been dating for six years. I'm probably just lonely.'

'Probably? Definitely. But that doesn't mean the two of you don't have a legitimate connection.'

I think back to the night I spent at Natasha's house and the way Hugh made me feel – nervous, giddy, exposed. It was never that way with Sam. If anything, Sam made me feel the opposite: calm, steady, protected. Back then, that was what I wanted from a partner – what I needed. I knew I'd always be safe with Sam. What I didn't realize until a few months ago was that the more he protected me the more the world around me shrank. But with Hugh…it's different. Even though I've only known him a month, he has somehow made my world feel bigger and more complex, full of culture and excitement.

'Besides,' Meg continues, 'from what you've said, it

doesn't sound as if there's any romance between Hugh and Natasha. They're in separate bedrooms, right?'

'That's beside the point,' I say, shaking Hugh from my mind. 'Married is married. And, anyway, I met another guy last night who seems nice. He's around our age, single and interesting.'

'Well, well, well! Isn't it rough being Kelly Madigan? On the left, a famous, hunky politician. On the right, a dapper English gent. How *do* you find the time?'

I narrow my eyes, trying very hard not to rise to Meg's bait. '*Anyway*,' I say, changing the topic, 'tell me about my dad. He says you visited him. How's he doing?'

Meg grimaces and leans back in her chair. 'Not so great. I've been meaning to write you. He's…I think he's having a really tough time with your mom's death.'

'More than before?'

'Yes. Things have intensified.'

'How? What did he say?'

'It isn't anything he said. It's more like…' She trails off.

'It's more like what?'

She frowns. 'Well, he isn't showering, for starters.'

'How do you know that?'

'Because he stinks, Kelly. He stinks. Anyone within ten feet knows he isn't showering. You don't have to be Sherlock fucking Holmes.'

'Ew.'

'Correct.'

I run my fingers along my keyboard. 'I thought maybe he was doing better. He mentioned my mom in a letter he sent me. It's the first time he's mentioned her in a long time.'

167

She shrugs. 'I don't know. Maybe he started doing better after I visited. But when I was there...not good.'

'He's going to work, though, right?'

'I think so. I kind of feel bad for his colleagues. He really needs to get the shower situation under control.'

'I'll give him a call tonight to check up on him.'

'That's probably a good idea.' She pauses. 'Don't mention I brought up the shower thing, though.'

'You just told me he needs to get the shower situation under control.'

'He does.'

'And yet you don't want me to bring it up.'

'I don't want you to tell him I'm the one who told you. Just...weave it into the conversation naturally. Like, "I love my old-fashioned shower here. It's so great. Speaking of showers..." You know. Like that.'

'I'll see what I can do.' I glance at the clock on my computer. 'Shoot – sorry to cut this short, but I have to finish prepping three recipes for Natasha to taste tomorrow since she wouldn't eat anything on Friday.'

'Cry me a river...'

'Hey – you have no idea. You'd last five minutes in this job. Trust me.'

'Not if I had Mr Foxy Ballantine nearby.'

'Meg – enough. Stop.'

'Fine, fine. I won't mention him again. But if anything else happens, I want to be the first to know.'

'Nothing else is going to happen,' I say, but as I sign off, I'm not sure if I'm telling her that because I truly believe it or because I know I should.

# Chapter 18

The conversation with my dad never happens. I call, but when I do, Irene O'Malley answers the phone and tells me he's picking up a new hose at the hardware store. 'I'm happy to give him a message,' she says.

'I'm sure you are,' I mumble, under my breath.

'Sorry?'

'Nothing.' I clear my throat. 'Just tell him Kelly called and that I'll try him later in the week.'

'Will do. Oh!' She lets out a yelp as something crashes in the background. 'Jeez, Kelly, your mom sure stacked her pots high.'

'Why are you sorting through my mom's pots?'

'Your father needs a good home-cooked meal in his own kitchen is why.'

My jaw tightens. Man, my mom called this one. 'How kind,' I say.

'It's how I'm built,' she says. 'I'm a giver. I can't look at a handsome, lonely man like your father and not help out. No, ma'am. Not me.'

I'm about to jump in and tell her she could help him most of all by getting him to scrub himself with a little soap and hot water, but then I think back to my mom's note. She would, without question, rather my father stank up the entire state of Michigan with his stench than have Irene O'Malley insinuate herself into a potential sponge bath. The shower conversation will have to wait.

'Thank you for your generosity,' I say. 'I know it would have meant a lot to my mother.'

'Yes,' she says, her voice tart. 'Well.'

'Anyway, please tell my dad I called.'

'You got it.' Another pot crashes in the background. 'Gosh, darn it! This shelving system makes no sense at all.'

'Maybe you can reorganize it next time you stop by,' I say. 'You'll need to make room anyway for all that Tupperware of my mom's you still need to return.'

Irene goes silent.

'Bye now.' I smile to myself, and before she can say anything else, I hang up.

On Monday morning I show up at Natasha's house carrying two bags of food: poached salmon, carrot salad, and the early makings of a kale burger. Poppy sent me a text last night saying Natasha would be ready for the tasting at noon, after which we can discuss the next recipes on the list – but only briefly because Natasha has an appointment with her acupuncturist at one o'clock.

Olga lets me in at the front door and follows me as I

170

hurry down the stairs to the kitchen. I begin unloading my containers into the refrigerator, while she stands at the edge of the counter, watching me.

'Mr Ballantine, he say thank you for the…"hodge podge".'

I freeze. 'He did?'

'Yes. He say the salmon is best yet. And the carrot salad…no needed Greek yogurt after all.'

I try to contain my smile. 'Good. I'm glad he enjoyed it.'

She eyes me as I continue putting food into the fridge. 'Miss Natasha, she is very happy you feed Mr Ballantine so well.'

'It's no trouble at all,' I say, my face hot. 'If someone didn't eat the leftovers, I'd end up throwing them out.'

'The cookies – those leftovers, too?'

My chest tightens. The chocolate-chip cookies. The ones I made the night I slept over.

'Oh, those…' I don't know what to say. Do I make up some elaborate story? No, I can't do that. I'll just get myself into more trouble. 'No, they weren't leftovers. Mr Ballantine asked me to make some, so I did.'

'When?'

'Sorry?'

'When he ask?'

Why is she suddenly so curious? I can't tell her the truth. At the same time, I can't pretend he asked me while I was here at work. She knows that isn't true.

'You know? I can't remember,' I say, reaching into the bag for the container of carrot salad. 'The past few weeks have been a blur. For all I know, I imagined he asked for the cookies.'

Okay, so that's kind of a lie, but not really. The past few weeks have been a blur, especially that Friday night.

'Ah.' She runs her eyes across my face. 'Mr Ballantine, he is happiest I've seen in very long time.'

'Oh?'

'Yes,' she says.

I close the refrigerator door, about to concoct some sort of explanation for his happiness, when Olga cuts me off. 'Is good,' she says. Then she shrugs. 'To me, is good.'

I'm about to ask what she means by that when we hear footsteps overhead.

'No more talk,' Olga says.

She grabs a duster from inside one of the kitchen cupboards, and as she makes her way to the hallway, I could swear she offers me a slight smile before disappearing through the door.


Later that morning, I put the finishing touches to the carrot salad and assemble the kale burgers, which I will sear to order once Natasha comes down. At five minutes to noon, I plate up the salmon, drizzling the mustard-dill sauce over the top in a zigzag pattern, and scoop out a portion of carrot salad into two small bowls, making sure I get sufficient amounts of both grated carrot and chickpeas.

Ten minutes later Natasha storms into the kitchen, with Poppy close behind, a notebook and pen clasped in her hand.

'So where is this salmon I've been hearing about?' Natasha says, flicking her long, glossy hair over her shoulder. She is, once again, dressed in blacks and greys, this time dark grey harem pants and a silky black tank.

I grab the plate of salmon and push it towards her on the marble island. 'I think I finally got it right. The coriander seeds really make the flavour pop.'

'Let's hope so,' she says, 'considering Hugh has mentioned it twice since I got back.'

'He has?' I say, before I can stop myself. Then I quickly add, 'Your opinion is the one that matters, so I hope you like it.'

I hand both her and Poppy a fork, and Natasha slices off a small piece of salmon and swirls it around in the sauce.

'Mmm,' she says, covering her mouth as she chews in her odd, rhythmic pattern and swallows. She nods at Poppy. 'Try it – it's good.'

Poppy pokes at the fish and takes a small bite. 'Lovely,' she says.

Natasha holds the fork upside down in her mouth, tapping the tines against her teeth. 'But I wonder...could we maybe add some rosemary?'

'No,' I say, probably a bit too quickly.

Natasha raises an eyebrow. 'No?'

'What I mean is, rosemary is a very strong flavour. Probably too strong for a preparation like this. Especially given the dill in the sauce. The flavours don't really go together.'

'Hmm, you're probably right...' She lays her fork on the counter. 'But why don't you take a crack at it, just to see?'

I clench my fists beneath the counter. 'Okay...I can do that. But the more times I retest things, the more trouble we run into with your deadline.'

'Not if you work quickly.'

173

'Even if I work quickly, we still have a long way to go. I can retest this recipe if you aren't happy with it, but we'll probably have to borrow that time from another recipe.'

'She...isn't wrong,' Poppy says timidly. 'Your editor wrote today asking how things are progressing. You have time, but not loads of it.'

Natasha raps her fingers against the counter. 'Fine. We can keep this version for now. But if there's time at the end, I'd like to try it with rosemary. Just to see.'

'Okay,' I say. 'Deal.'

*Even though I already know rosemary won't work.*

I bring out small bowls of the carrot salad for both her and Poppy, and while they sample small portions, I finish off the kale burgers.

'I'm sorry, what are those?' Natasha asks, nodding at the burgers I've transferred to a plate.

'Kale burgers.'

'Why aren't they green?'

'I needed to add a few other ingredients to make everything stick together.' And not taste like a tree branch.

'The kale burgers I used to eat in LA were much greener than that.'

I push the platter towards her. 'Maybe you could try a bite and let me know what you think of the flavour, and we can work backwards from there.'

She wipes the corners of her mouth with a napkin. 'Or we could start with wanting them to be greener, and you could work forwards from there.'

I try not to lose my cool. *It's her book, not your book, it's her book, not your book.*

'Okay,' I say. 'Sure.'

Not that it took me a week to develop the recipe or anything. Not that refusing to taste so much as a single forkful is rude and disrespectful and utterly infuriating.

She takes another bite of the carrot salad and twists her lips to the side. 'This is good,' she says. 'But now that I'm tasting it…I'm reminded of a raw zucchini salad I once had while on location in Italy. Could we make this with zucchini instead?'

'Sure. But I'd have to change a few things, since zucchini can be really watery. Do you want the same dressing, just with zucchini?'

She rubs her fingers along her lower lip. 'No, actually…The salad I'm thinking of was zippier. It had lemon juice in it, I think. And Parmesan shavings. And toasted nuts.'

'Pine nuts?'

'Almonds, I think. Or was it pistachios?' She shakes her head. 'I don't know – I'm sure you can figure it out.'

I take a calming breath. 'So, just to clarify: we're swapping out the carrot salad for an Italian zucchini salad.'

'Yes, I think so. I think that's for the best.' She dabs at the corners of her mouth as Poppy scribbles furiously in her notebook. 'Oh, and don't bother leaving any of the zucchini salad for Hugh. He *detests* zucchini.'

'Ah, so no zucchini bread, then.'

She narrows her eyes. 'What?'

'Zucchini bread. For Hugh – Mr Ballantine. I guess that's out.'

'Why on earth would you bake zucchini bread for my husband?'

'I wouldn't. I just meant, since you asked me to bake banana bread that one time...' I trail off, as I remember the finer points of the banana-bread incident.

'I never asked you to bake banana bread,' she says.

'Right. Sorry. My mistake.'

She glances at Poppy. 'Where do we *find* these people?'

Poppy does not respond. A wise choice, as far as I can tell.

Natasha studies her manicured fingers, then looks back up at me. 'Are we done?'

'I...guess so,' I say. 'That's all I have for you to taste today.'

'Then we're done.' She motions for Poppy to follow her out of the room but pauses before leaving. 'Why don't you plan on having the zucchini salad and kale burger ready for me to taste on Friday? And if you can start working on a version of my grandmother's scrambled eggs, that would be great. I know we already finished that section, but I'd like to add this recipe. Her eggs were fluffy and creamy without being wet and gross.'

Not wet and gross. Got it.

She struts out of the kitchen, with Poppy following close behind, and when she gets to the door, she rests her hand on the frame.

'Oh, and I've been meaning to mention – from now on, when you arrive, could you please use the servants' entrance?'

'The what?'

'The servants' entrance. The one on the side of the house.'

'Oh,' I say, trying not to sound as taken aback as I feel. 'Okay. If that's what you'd prefer.'

'It is. I know I can be low-key about a lot of things, but I'm not okay with my staff coming in and out of the front door.'

*Her staff.* Is that what I am? I guess so. In that case, I wonder how she'd feel about her staff sleeping in her guest bedroom...

'Then I'll use the servants' entrance. Not a problem.'

'I'm sorry,' she says. 'I should have mentioned it sooner.'

She turns and walks out of the room, and all I can think is how she just apologized for entirely the wrong thing.

# Chapter 19

.

Natasha is my boss. I know this. She is the one who hired me, and she is the one paying me – although I have not yet received any money since I arrived in England. Her business manager, Larry, cut me a cheque as soon as I signed the contract (a small amount to 'get me started'), but he was supposed to arrange for the rest of the money to be deposited directly into my US bank account in instalments. I emailed his assistant last week when nothing had appeared, and apparently they'd lost some of my paperwork, so I needed to resend all of my banking details. They are allegedly processing my information, but it's taking an awfully long time, and no one seems all that concerned. I suppose that's what happens when you're rich and famous. You never worry about money, so you don't understand why anyone else would.

But somehow, even though Natasha is my boss, I'm still

a little offended that she considers me a servant. I'm pouring my soul into this book so that she can achieve her dream of writing a cookbook. Without me, this book would be nothing more than an idea. If she is the architect, then I am the engineer, contractor and handywoman, taking her pie-in-the-sky blueprints and turning them into something functional, sturdy and real. I don't expect her to treat me as an equal, or even as a friend, but I don't think a little respect is too much to ask.

Nevertheless, I do as she asks and start using the servants' entrance the next morning when I arrive. I follow the small pathway around the side of the house to the door I used with Olga the morning I overslept and forgot my keys. Olga opens the door seconds after I press the small round buzzer.

'I buy more kale,' she says, as she lets me in. 'And zucchini.'

I've decided to let Olga do most of the shopping from now on. The control freak in me would rather do it myself, but my inner pragmatist knows having Olga do it will save me time, and given my increasing antipathy toward Natasha, the faster I can finish this project, the better.

I set my bag on the counter, open the refrigerator and stare into its chilled interior. The mere thought of tackling the kale-burger recipe makes me want to set this kitchen on fire. The burger I developed was good – really good. It had texture and substance, rich with garlic and onion and perfumed with smoky *pimentón*. Okay, so it wasn't green. But it had green flecks. I did use kale. Just not enough of it, I guess.

Instead of delving back into my recipe nemesis, I decide

to start on the zucchini salad. I remember once making a recipe for sautéed zucchini based on one from the Red Cat in New York City. The recipe calls for cooking a mess of julienned zucchini for barely a minute – just enough to warm it through, while tossing it with toasted almonds and olive oil. The dish gets a few quick shavings of Parmesan at the end, and *voilà*: zucchini perfection.

Natasha specified a zucchini salad, not a zucchini sauté, and she said the dressing was 'zippy' and involved lemon juice, but I can use the Red Cat recipe as a springboard to develop the sort of salad she has in mind.

I grab two zucchini from the fridge and, using one of Natasha's bespoke Kramer knives, meticulously slice each one into even matchsticks. I dump the matchsticks into a colander and sprinkle them with salt, leaving them to shed some of their water while I brainstorm what type of lemon vinaigrette to make. For as long as I've been cooking, I've never loved a big, lemony slap in the face. For me, a little lemon goes a very long way. But this isn't supposed to be my recipe. It's supposed to be Natasha's, and Natasha wants it to be zippy and lemony, which means I'll have to create a dish I might not otherwise make or enjoy.

That's one of the toughest parts of my job: the palate meld that accompanies the mind meld. I have to create a dish Natasha would like and write up the recipe the way Natasha would present it, taking myself out of the equation, even though I'm the one responsible for all of it. I'm like the man behind the curtain in *The Wizard of Oz*, except that guy had it easier because the wizard wasn't real.

Since the dish is based on a salad she had in Italy, I decide to use one of my standby vinaigrettes, which uses lemon, olive oil, mustard, a little garlic, and – the secret ingredient – an anchovy. The anchovy gets mashed up with the garlic and some salt, so you barely even know it's there, but it adds extra oomph to the dressing and gives it an Italian flair (not that I've ever actually been to Italy).

I find a jar of anchovies in Natasha's pantry, and as I mash one with a garlic clove and a fat pinch of salt, Poppy drifts into the kitchen, tapping on her phone. She approaches the counter, still glued to her device, and when she gets within three feet of me, she sniffs the air.

'What, in God's name, is that smell?'

'What smell?' I take a whiff. 'You mean the anchovy?'

Poppy makes a gagging sound. 'Oh, my God. Of all the unbearable smells!' She claps a hand over her nose and mouth.

'It's one anchovy. That's it.' I squirt some lemon juice into the bowl. 'There – you can barely smell it now.'

She slowly removes her hand but quickly slaps it back over her nose. 'Nope – still there.'

'Sorry. It's part of the recipe.'

'Well, thankfully this conversation will be brief. Natasha wanted me to tell you she plans to go to Paris next week and wanted to know if you'd like to come, since you've never been.'

My heart leaps. 'Really?'

'Apparently.'

'When would we leave?'

'Monday morning, first thing. It'll be a quick trip this time – only three days. Just enough time for a fitting at Dior and a facial.'

'Would you be coming as well?'

181

'Obviously.'

'So would we share a room, then?'

Her eyes widen, as if I'd just proposed waxing her bikini line. 'Certainly not.' She suddenly seems very worried. 'At least, I don't think so. I'll have to ask Natasha.'

'I promise I'm not as scary as I look.'

Given Poppy's expression, I must look terrifying.

She blinks, her hand still covering her nose. 'You're in, then?'

'Definitely.'

'Good. I'll let Natasha know.'

She whirls around, scurrying away from the vinaigrette as quickly as possible, and as I whisk the olive oil into the bowl, I can barely contain my smile.

# Chapter 20

Paris! I can't believe it. I've dreamed about going to Paris ever since I was a little girl. I first caught a glimpse of the city on *Dallas*, when Bobby and April went on their disastrous honeymoon. I was only five at the time, and the show was on past my bedtime, but I snuck downstairs and watched through the spindles on the banister while my mom sat in front of the TV with her tumbler of blackberry brandy (which, at the time, I thought was juice for grown-ups). I couldn't really follow the plot, but I thought the city looked like something out of a fairy tale, and I've wanted to visit ever since.

And now I have my chance! I'll be accompanying Natasha, which puts a dampener on things, but I'll probably get the royal treatment as part of her entourage. Considering how posh the guest room in her house is, I can't imagine her staying anywhere that isn't fabulous.

Maybe I'll even meet Joël Robuchon, or Pierre Hermé. I can't wait.

The only downside to this sudden news is that I now need to cancel my date with Harry. If I'm going to Paris for three days, I'll lose half a week of testing and, given how behind we are, I need to use every available hour before we leave to stay on schedule.

When I call him on my way home, he doesn't even try to mask his disappointment. 'I suppose next week is out then, too, if you'll be in Paris,' he says.

'Sorry. Maybe we could do something next Saturday instead?'

'Yeah, okay. That sounds good. There's a great pizza place in Brixton – assuming you like pizza.'

'Love it.'

'Great,' he says, his tone brighter. 'Shall we say eight o'clock? The queue can get rather long, but it's worth the wait.'

'Works for me. Sorry again about having to cancel – this trip came out of nowhere.'

'Not a problem. Have fun in Paris. Eat a few croissants for me.'

I spend the rest of the week working at a frantic pace, perfecting the zucchini salad and refining the dreaded kale burger so that it is almost entirely green. When I'm not testing recipes, I spend nearly every waking minute researching which restaurants, *boulangeries* and *pâtisseries* I will cram into my three-day trip: Poilâne, Le Relais de l'Entrecôte, Ladurée, Gérard Mulot, Pierre Hermé, L'As du Fallafel, Le Bistrot Paul Bert, Le Comptoir. Considering I will be there for just three days, I'm not exactly sure how

I will fit everything in, but I'll find a way. Who knows when I'll have another opportunity to go to Paris? I have to make every second count.

As soon as I arrive on Friday morning, I start preparing the zucchini salad and kale burger for our noon tasting. I think I've finally nailed both recipes, developing versions that not only taste good but that Natasha will like. The zucchini salad is zippy, but not overly lemony, and the flavour is rounded out with the touch of anchovy and garlic in the dressing, the toasted almonds and nutty Parmesan. I also managed to preserve the flavour of my original kale burger while making it greener, and I've improved the texture. The only dish I don't have lined up for the tasting is her grandmother's scrambled eggs, but I've started working on them and will have something for her soon. And, anyway, Parisians are the masters of all things *oeuf*, so I can do research while I'm there.

By eleven fifty-five, all of the dishes are ready. By twelve fifteen, I start looking at my watch. By twelve forty-five, the toasted almonds in the zucchini salad are getting soggy. By one o'clock, the uncooked kale burgers look a little sad. And by one thirty, I am officially pissed off.

At two o'clock, Natasha bursts into the kitchen, dressed in leopard-print Spandex pants and a sports bra. As usual, Poppy trails behind.

'Hey,' Natasha says, dabbing at her forehead with a small towel. She lets out a big sigh. 'We made it.'

I glance at the clock. 'I thought we said noon.'

'Yeah, but my trainer wanted me to check out the new Pilates equipment in her studio, and noon was the only time she could meet me.'

'Oh. I wish I'd known. I'd have worked on a few other recipes this morning before prepping the tasting.'

'I'm sure you survived. Anyway, where's the food? I just got my period and could eat the whole house.'

I pull the dishes from the refrigerator. 'Do you want to start with the kale burger or the zucchini salad?'

Natasha wipes her neck. 'Why don't I try a bite of the zucchini while you cook up the burgers?'

'Perfect.'

I scoop some of the salad onto two plates, and as she and Poppy dig in, I heat a frying pan.

'Is this the dressing with the...?' Poppy trails off.

'The what?' Natasha asks.

I look over my shoulder. 'Oh. I think she's referring to the anchovy. I used one in the dressing.'

Poppy spits her salad back on the plate, and Natasha rolls her eyes. 'You're such a prole,' Natasha says. 'I love anchovies.'

Out of the corner of my eye I notice Poppy's cheeks are bright red.

'It's something to do with the smell,' Poppy says. 'I just...I can't.'

Natasha takes another forkful of the zucchini salad. 'More for me, then.'

I finish cooking the kale burgers and transfer them to a large platter. 'One for each, or one to share?'

'One each – I'm starving,' Natasha says.

I place the burgers on two separate plates and push them across the counter. They cut into them and take small bites.

'Now this I like,' Poppy says.

Natasha scrunches up her nose. 'Do you?'

Poppy's cheeks flush again. 'I do. Don't you?'

'I mean…it's *nice*. It's tasty. But I wonder…is it clean enough?'

'Clean how?' I ask.

'I don't know. Like, all that smokiness? What is that?'

'Smoked paprika,' I say.

'And what about these chunky bits? What's that?'

'Mashed white beans.'

'See? That's what I mean. All those beans, it seems a bit heavy, doesn't it?'

'We need something to bind all of the kale together,' I say. 'We can't only use kale.'

'Why not?'

'Because the burgers wouldn't stick together.'

'What about an egg?'

'I used one of those, too.'

'Oh.' She taps her fork against the plate. 'Well, could you maybe try it with chickpeas instead of white beans?'

Oh, dear God, this recipe is going to kill me.

'Sure,' I say. 'Whatever you want.'

'And maybe cut back on the smokiness.'

'No!' Poppy jumps in. 'Sorry – I just…I don't know much about food, but I think the smokiness is lovely. It makes the burger feel meaty without the meat.'

My eyes flit between Poppy and Natasha. *Please agree with Poppy, please agree with Poppy.*

Natasha throws up her hands. 'Fine. Keep the *pimentón*. But try to make the taste…cleaner. And lighter.'

'Okay.' I look down at the plates of zucchini salad. 'What about the zucchini?'

She gives a drawn-out sigh. 'Oh, I don't know. I mean,

I love it. But hearing Poppy talk…maybe she has a point. A lot of people don't like anchovies.'

'But you do.'

'But I don't want a bunch of people skipping a recipe in my book because it has anchovies in it.'

'Okay. Maybe I could try the dressing without the anchovy. Or tweak it in another direction.'

She shifts her jaw from side to side. 'You know what? Why don't we ditch the zucchini salad and go back to the carrot salad.'

'The one I made for you on Monday?'

'No…I mean, yes, that *kind* of carrot salad, but could we get rid of the chickpeas? And maybe add sunflower seeds. Or almonds. I don't know – something crunchy.'

I try very hard not to combust.

'Okay, but like I said before, with your deadline…The more we retest, the trickier things become. At some point we're going to have to start cutting recipes.'

'What? No. No way are we cutting any recipes.'

'I don't *want* to cut any recipes. It's just with all of this retesting, and the Paris trip next week—'

'Well, you'll just stay here and work,' she says.

I freeze. 'What?'

'If we're running into deadline problems, then you shouldn't come with us to Paris.'

'No, no – I'm not saying we're running into problems yet. I'm saying we could run into problems down the line.'

'And that's the last thing I want to happen. I'd much rather you stay here and get us on track.'

My heart sinks. 'But I'm sure I could make it work. It's only three days. And it could be good for research…'

188

I realize I'm backtracking on everything I just said, but I've been thinking of nothing except this trip all week. I have to go.

'Nope,' she says. 'I've made up my mind. You're staying here. I'm sure you'll have plenty of other opportunities. It's not like I needed you to come with me, anyway.' She looks at Poppy's notebook. 'Are we done?'

I nod, unable to speak through the lump in my throat.

'Great. Good luck with those recipes. I'll see you next Wednesday afternoon when we're back.'

She throws her exercise towel over her shoulder and turns to leave. 'Oh,' she says, turning back around, 'and see if you can come up with a fun topping for those burgers. Like, maybe a plum ketchup or a honey mustard. You'll certainly have the time.'

I hate her. Oh, my God, I hate her.

What kind of person dangles a trip to Paris in front of someone, then yanks it away? It isn't my fault we're running into deadline issues. She's the one who keeps changing her mind: 'Carrot salad! No, zucchini salad! No, carrot salad!' If she would just stick to the plan, we'd be fine. But she's capricious and thoughtless, and now I'm stuck dealing with the consequences. In London.

Not only am I in London – I'm in London *alone*. Harry is visiting family in Devon, and Jess is on some weekend trip in the Lake District, and they are the only two people I know well enough to call. Part of me is tempted to move up my date with Harry to earlier in the week since I'll be around, but instead I decide to use the time I would have been in Paris to get ahead of schedule. If I'm not going, I

189

need to make this time count. The sooner I get out of here, the better.

So on I go, using my weekend to mash, blitz and sear my way to veggie-burger perfection. This time I use chickpeas and a bit of lemon juice to brighten and lighten the flavour. Once I've completed that recipe, I move on to a new carrot salad and a recipe for the fluffiest, creamiest scrambled eggs I've ever tasted. If Natasha doesn't like these eggs, it's official: her taste buds are up her asshole.

On Monday, I decide to tackle three new recipes: a topping for the kale burger, a spicy Brussels-sprout hash, and a rendition of seafood paella, inspired by a dish Natasha once ate while on location in Spain. Neither plum ketchup nor honey mustard really goes with the kale burgers, but I develop a garlicky aïoli that is perfect: creamy and peppy, with just the right amount of kick from the garlic. It's the ideal foil for the burger, which means Natasha will probably hate it.

By the time I finish that evening, it's well past six o'clock, and Olga has already left for the day, having shown me how to lock the servants' entrance behind me. As I scrub down the counter, my feet throb while a dull ache wraps itself around my lower back and down my legs. Putting in extra hours will help me finish this project sooner, but it may also kill me. I haven't been on my feet for so long since my first job washing dishes at Abe's Coney Island, and that was when I was a fit, energetic fourteen-year-old. I may only be twenty-eight, but I'm rapidly losing the ability to stand on my feet for ten hours at a time.

The mere thought of walking a half-mile to the Belsize Park tube station makes me want to cry, so I plop down on one of Natasha's kitchen chairs and kick my feet up on the seat of another. I close my eyes and allow myself a quick catnap, drifting off to the rhythmic sound of the dishwasher as it whooshes through its cleaning cycle. Visions of croissants and steak *frites* float through my mind as I picture Natasha and Poppy prancing down the Champs-Élysées, cackling loudly as they mention my name and how sad I must be sitting in London alone. I bet that was part of the plan all along. I bet it's some big joke between the two of them.

As I envision Natasha tripping over a crack in the pavement and falling face-first into a tower of éclairs, I'm awoken by a voice in the kitchen.

'Hello?'

My eyes bolt open, and I leap up from my seat. 'Hugh – Mr Ballantine. Hi.'

'I've told you, call me Hugh.' His brow furrows. 'What are you doing here? Shouldn't you be in Paris?'

I wipe beneath my eyes, certain I have gobs of mascara and gunk stuck there. 'I had to stay back and work on some recipes.'

'What? That's rubbish. Why?'

'We're starting to run into some deadline issues. Natasha – we didn't think I could spare the time.'

'Oh dear. How far behind are you?'

'Hard to say. We could be fine, if we stick to the plan, but she keeps—' I catch myself. 'The plan is a little…in flux.'

'Ah. Right. With Natasha, that tends to happen.'

He drops his briefcase by the door and shimmies out of his suit jacket, a navy one with a slight sheen. He loosens his pink tie as he makes his way to the refrigerator.

191

'So what have you left for me tonight, then? Something delicious, or something gone very wrong?'

'I'd never leave you a stinker.'

He laughs. 'Yes, well, thank God for that. Though admittedly even the recipes you consider disappointments have been lovely.'

'Thanks.' A familiar warm feeling washes over me.

He opens the refrigerator and pulls out the dish of paella and the plate of kale burgers.

'More bloody kale burgers?' he says, his eyes wide.

'Yes. Sorry. Natasha wanted me to tweak the recipe. Again.'

'Good grief. What version is this? The fifth?'

'Of the ones you've tried? The third.'

'And of the ones I haven't?'

'I've lost track. The eighth, maybe?'

'All this for a burger made of *kale*?'

I shrug. 'It's what she wants.'

He scratches his temple as he lowers his voice to a mumble: 'And we all know what that means…'

'They're not that bad, are they?'

'No – sorry. They're not bad at all. The last version was quite nice, actually.' He grins. 'For a kale burger.'

'Well, for both your sake and mine, I hope she likes this version. Because if I have to eat one more kale burger, *I* might start turning green.' I crack my knuckles and eye the door. 'Anyway, I should take off. But let me know what you think of the paella. And the kale burger, if you dare.'

I grab my bag off one of the kitchen chairs and head for the utility room.

'Have a nice evening,' I say.

I lay my hand on the door handle, when Hugh interjects: 'Where are you going?'

I turn around, my hand still resting on the handle. 'Home?'

'No, I mean why are you going into the utility room?'

'Because that's where the servants' entrance is.'

'Why are you using the servants' entrance?'

'Because Natasha asked me to.'

'When?'

'Last week.'

He rolls his eyes. 'Such bollocks.'

'It's fine. Really.'

'No, it's not fine. It's ridiculous. We don't live in Downton bloody Abbey. There's no reason you can't come in and out through the front door.'

'Well, technically, I am her employee.'

'Nevertheless. It's silly.'

I shift uncomfortably from side to side, not knowing what to say. He runs his fingers through his hair. 'Sorry,' he says. 'I shouldn't...It's just that Natasha and I come from different places on this sort of thing. She grew up the daughter of a wealthy lawyer, and I grew up the son of a factory worker who put together bikes for a living. The entire notion of having staff is foreign to me.'

'You have a driver, don't you?'

'Natasha's contribution to the household, not mine. That isn't to say I don't appreciate the convenience of having these people around, but the idea that they have to use separate entrances and kowtow to us makes me uncomfortable.'

Part of me wonders why he doesn't say something to

Natasha if it makes him so uncomfortable, but somehow asking seems a bit too forward, even though I've spent a night in his house, wearing his shirt.

'Sorry – it's none of my business. I shouldn't have said anything.'

'No, no – I'm the one who opened the door in the first place. Here I am, an advocate for the poor, and meanwhile I'm running a household where I make people feel like worthless underlings.'

'You don't make me feel like a worthless underling.'

'No? Well...good. Because that certainly isn't how I think of you.'

*How do you think of me?* I want to ask. But I can't. Because that's wrong. So instead I simply say, 'I'm glad.'

We stand silent for a few awkward moments until Hugh glances down at the bowl of paella. 'Are you sure you don't want to join me for supper? Because there's no way I can finish all of this myself.'

I grip my purse strap tightly. 'I really should go. I need to call my dad.'

'In Michigan?'

'Yeah, how did you...'

'At the Tate. You mentioned being a Michigander.'

'Oh, right. I forgot. That night is kind of a blur.'

'Funny. I remember it quite clearly.' He pauses. 'I think of it often, actually.'

My fingers start tingling, and I want to tell him, *Me too – I think about it all the time*. But, ever the realist, I hug my purse tighter, smile, and say, 'Have a nice night. I hope you enjoy the paella.'

# *Chapter 21*

I do have to call my dad. That wasn't a lie. But, oh, how a part of me wanted to stay and share a bowl of paella with Hugh. It's all I can think about the entire journey back to my apartment. Why couldn't I have accepted his invitation? No, scratch that. I know why. Anyone with a brain knows why. But part of me still wishes I'd said yes. Every time we talk, all I can think is, *I want to know everything about you.*

But never mind. No point thinking about something that will never happen. It will only make me feel sadder and more alone.

Instead of losing myself in the world of fantasy, I dive face first into the fiery pit of reality by trying my dad for the third time in eight days. I called him yesterday but, like the Sunday before, he wasn't home, and I ended up speaking to Irene O'Malley for a second time. Apparently this time she was ironing his uniform – 'Because, dear, *somebody* has to take care of the poor man.'

Since it's Monday afternoon back in Michigan, my dad will still be at work, so I call the post office directly, saving myself another awkward interaction with Irene. Aside from the fact that I have run out of things to discuss with her that do not involve my father, her ongoing presence in his house violates my mom's number-one dying wish. I don't believe in ghosts, but if ever there was a woman who would rise from the grave merely to prevent some other woman making off with her widower, it's my mother.

My dad picks up on the fourth ring, his cantankerous voice blasting through the receiver with his typically impassioned yet confrontational greeting, everything shouted like an accusation: 'Ypsilanti Post Office! Can I help you?'

'Dad, hi. It's Kelly.'

'Kelly? Hang on a sec.' He puts me on hold, and two minutes later he picks up again. 'Hi. Sorry. Had to wait on a customer.'

'Not a problem.' Not that I'm calling from England or anything…

'So how's it going? I got your letter. Sounds pretty fancy over there.'

'It's definitely a different lifestyle, that's for sure. Not so much for me as for my employer. But still.'

'Have you met the Queen yet?'

'No, I haven't met the Queen. Nor will I, if I had to guess.'

He snorts. 'I'm just joshing. How old is she now, anyway? She must be getting up there.'

'Old enough to be your mother,' I say.

196

'So not that old, then.'

As usual, I can't tell if he's joking. 'I guess it depends on your reference point. So how are things with you? I...understand Irene has been spending a fair amount of time at the house.'

'Yeah, but don't worry, she's in your old room.'

I start. 'I'm sorry – what?'

'She's staying in your old room. Not mine.'

'Wait. Hold on. What do you mean she's "staying" in my old room?'

'It means what it means: she's sleeping in your old room.'

'She's *living* with you?'

'No.' He pauses. 'It's just temporary.'

'It's just *temporary*? Why is it anything? Why is she there?'

'To help around the house. Y'know – doing the stuff your mom used to do.'

I sit on my couch with my mouth open, unable to process what my dad just said. Aside from the fact that my mom probably never did half the things Irene is currently doing, she always saw Irene as her arch-rival, the woman who'd hijacked my mom's Queen Bee status in adulthood. When she was a student, my mom always showed up to school with her hair perfectly feathered and her bright pink lipstick artfully applied. But as she got older, her style remained the same – the same haircut, the same colours of lipstick and eye shadow, as if her teenage look had been fossilized – but its application suffered. Most of the time, she'd pick me up from school in a sweat-suit, but sometimes she'd be dressed in a bathrobe with rollers still in her hair.

Irene, meanwhile, always showed up in full makeup and freshly pressed pants, her hair teased and sprayed into puffy stasis. My mom was thinner and probably naturally more beautiful, but Irene's doughy face glowed with a bright, unblemished complexion, helped along by a thick coat of foundation ('She must apply that gunk with a trowel,' my mom always said). My mom's skin, meanwhile, always looked reddish, even more so when she'd had a few drinks, and her makeup application was always a little slapdash, with a glob of mascara here and a smudge of eyeliner there, assuming she'd had the energy to use either.

The competition between the two of them wasn't overt. They'd be perfectly cordial when they ran into each other at the supermarket or neighbourhood gatherings. But they also couldn't get through a conversation without making some sort of veiled criticism, and Irene was always worse than my mom ('Cynthia – my goodness, I almost didn't recognize you without your curlers!'; 'Now, tell me – is making the macaroni real gummy part of the recipe?'; 'My gosh, I haven't seen pants like those since 1975!'). The fact that she is sleeping in my old bedroom would make my mother's head explode.

'Does helping around the house really necessitate her sleeping under the same roof as you?' I ask. 'Can't she sleep at her own place and swing by during the day?'

'That's kind of an imposition, don't you think?'

'Dad, she's the one who's supposed to be helping you. Out of the kindness of her heart, allegedly.'

'I don't care for your tone.'

'Sorry – you'll excuse me if I'm not overjoyed that Mom's former arch nemesis is now residing in her abode.'

'Well, look at you and your ten-dollar words.'

I pause. 'Which words are we referring to?'

'"Nemesis". "Residing". "Abode". I think those English folks are wearing off on you.'

'Dad, I assure you I used those words long before I moved to England. Along with millions of other Americans, none of them particularly fancy.'

'I'll take your word for it.' Then he quickly adds, 'I know what they mean, by the way. Those words.'

'I never doubted you did.'

'Well...good,' he says.

'Why do you always play down your intelligence? Mom always said you were a bookworm in school.'

'That was high school. A long time ago.'

'So? You don't need to play the dummy. You're way smarter than most people I encounter on a daily basis.'

'Bah,' he growls.

'I'm serious. I've always thought you'd have made a great lawyer.'

He snorts. 'Not a chance.'

'Why not? You certainly like to argue...'

'Because lawyers are assholes,' he says.

'QED...'

'What?'

'Nothing. Never mind. So how long is Irene planning to camp out in my old bedroom?'

'How the heck should I know?'

'Because it's your house, and there is a random person sleeping under your roof. I figured perhaps you might know when she planned to leave.'

'She hasn't said.'

199

'Well, maybe you could gently suggest she return to her own house.'

'Why? She's helping me.' There is a brief silence. 'I've been lonely, Kelly. I miss your mom.'

'I know. Me too.' A lump forms in my throat. I've managed to distract myself with work since I arrived in London, like a bandage over a cut, hoping if I can't see it and don't think about it, it'll go away. But it's still there, and talking to my dad is reopening the wound.

My relationship with my mom was unconventional and strained at times, but even when we hadn't talked in a while, I liked knowing she was there, that if I wanted to, I could call her or send her a card. When I moved to Chicago and started working on the cake book, I remember calling her one evening after a particularly gruelling day at the bakehouse. My boss, Katie, had given me instructions to start working on an Andy Warhol-inspired Napoleon. The idea was completely insane – layers of coloured puff pastry, in shades ranging from brown (chocolate) to pink (strawberry), and filled with multicoloured pastry cream, to represent Warhol's pop palette. I tried to tell her pink puff pastry was beyond my skill set, and certainly beyond that of the average home cook, and anyway, puff pastry wasn't cake, the subject of the book. But she wouldn't listen and gave me her standard puff-pastry recipe, and off I went to recreate the worst idea I'd ever heard.

I'd made puff pastry a few times before, but I wasn't an expert, so even when I thought the amount of butter seemed obscene, I told myself Katie knew better than I. Besides, this was chocolate puff pastry, an entirely different beast. As it turned out, I should have trusted my gut. Katie had

200

forgotten to scale down the butter with the flour and salt, so the dough was a mess, and when I tried to bake it, the butter melted out of it onto the floor of the oven and caught fire, like the world's biggest oil lamp. Katie screamed at me, made me clean up the mess, then scrapped the recipe for a multicoloured pound cake, even though the whole thing had been her fault.

I called my mom that night in tears. I didn't expect her to do anything – she was in Michigan, and she'd never been a problem-solver anyway – but I just needed her to listen. Sam was always trying to fix my problems, but I didn't need a fixer. I needed a mom. She listened to my story and, outraged, hooted, 'But it wasn't even your fault!' Then she sighed. 'Pour yourself a Scotch, sweetie. You deserve it.'

It was exactly what I needed to hear. But now she's gone, and I can't ever call her like that again, even if I wanted to.

'I guess I'm having trouble ignoring how Mom would feel about all of this,' I say, wondering if my dad has considered this too. 'You know she wasn't Irene's biggest fan.'

'Yeah. But don't worry. I'm not planning to marry the woman or anything. She's just helping out with housework and stuff. Some ironing, some cleaning, a few nursing duties.'

'Nursing duties?'

'You know, like picking up my cholesterol meds and making sure I take my vitamins. Oh, and last week she drew me a bubble bath.'

'A *bubble bath*?'

'Yeah. Apparently it had been too long since I'd given the old pits a good scrubberoo.' He chuckles. 'Irene got in there good and cleaned me out.'

'Oh,' I say. 'Okay.'

I need to get that woman out of his house.

The only good news to come out of that conversation with my dad was that he has started bathing again. Which, given that his stench had grown foul enough for Meg to express concern, is a very positive development. Other than that, I fear I am mere days away from an unpleasant encounter with my mother's ghost.

If I have any hope of finishing this project ahead of schedule, the only ghost I should be thinking about is my ghost writing for Natasha, so the next day I show up at her house, armed for a second go at the Brussels-sprout hash and paella. The Brussels sprouts I made yesterday were a bit *too* spicy and still need an extra something to make the flavour pop – maybe a little honey or bit of garlic, if not both. I also want to improve the seafood paella and add a little more smokiness to the finished product.

I work at a dizzying pace, slicing, searing and sautéing as fast as I can so that I can leave early, call Stevie and come up with a plan to evict Irene O'Malley. I emailed my brother last night, asking how he was doing and telling him I wanted to talk but, in classic Stevie fashion, he did not reply. If he knew about Irene, he'd probably be even less thrilled with the current state of affairs than I am, but saying so would require typing out an email, which he can't be bothered to do, unless the reply is something simple like 'OK' or 'No'. The only way I can brainstorm eviction strategies with him is to ambush him with an unexpected call.

The Brussels sprouts come out perfectly – a little sweet, a little spicy, with a slight tang from some apple cider vinegar – and the paella is nearly there, though I'll need to try one more tweak tomorrow. I box up the leftovers, stick them in the refrigerator, and wipe down the counter. Once I've grabbed my bag and taken my share of the leftovers, I head out with Olga and make my way towards Belsize Park tube station. Olga stops halfway up the road, beneath a bus stop. 'I take bus today,' she says. 'See you tomorrow.'

I say goodbye and continue to the tube station, cutting through the neighbourhood onto Glenloch Road, passing all of the ruddy-brick row houses with bright white trim. Small hedges line the sidewalks, some painstakingly trimmed with sharp edges and others wild and bushy and overgrown. I love the way all of the front doors are a little different – some fiery red, some cobalt blue, others stained wood with Tiffany glass. As I reach the point where the road merges with another, I hear someone call my name.

'Kelly?'

I look around, trying to locate the source of the voice, then see Hugh walking towards me, crossing from the other side of the street.

'I thought it was you,' he says, smiling as he approaches, his briefcase clasped in one hand and a brown-paper bag in the other, a baguette poking out of the top. 'On your way home?'

'Yep. Olga's at the bus stop on Belsize Park, so if you need anything, you might be able to catch her.'

'I'll be fine. But thanks.'

I peer over his shoulder. 'Where are you coming from,

203

anyway? I thought Sunil drove you to work.'

'He does, most of the time, but today he has a family matter to deal with, so I got on the tube.'

'Slumming it like the rest of us, huh?'

He laughs. 'I often take the tube. I'm not the prima donna you seem to think I am.'

'I don't think you're a prima donna. Honest.'

'Just a bit of a prat.'

'I don't think you're one of those either. Although I'm not really sure what that word means.'

'Perhaps I shouldn't be the one to inform you,' he says.

'Perhaps not.' A beat passes. 'Anyway, I should go – I have to get home so I can call my brother.'

'You're very in touch with your family, aren't you?'

'A bit. Not as much as I should be.'

'You seem pretty in touch to me. Last night it was your father, tonight it's your brother. I expect tomorrow it will be your mother.'

'My mom is dead.'

'Oh.' He flushes. 'Oh dear. I'm sorry.'

'It's okay. There's no reason you would have known.'

'Yes, but still. It wasn't very politic.'

'Can a politician be impolitic?'

He grins. 'Is there a politician who isn't?'

'*Touché*. But, really, don't sweat it. It's been more than two months now.'

'That recent? Now I really feel terrible.'

'Don't – seriously.'

'Well, I do.' He glances down at his paper bag. 'I popped into Pomona on the way home and picked up a few nibbles

204

– a baguette, some cheese, wine. Why don't you come back to the house and have a quick bite to eat? It's the least I can do to make it up to you.'

'You don't have to make up anything. I'm fine.'

'Then let me do it to make myself feel better. Because, regardless of what you say, I feel rotten.'

I look at the clock on my phone.

'Ah,' he says, 'you have a call with your brother. Right. Sorry.'

'We didn't officially set one up,' I say, ruining my one easy excuse for declining his invitation. 'It was going to be more of an ambush.'

'That sounds sinister.'

I slip the phone back into my bag. 'It's a long story. My family is crazy.'

'Whose isn't? May I remind you about my father's call a few weeks ago?'

I laugh. 'Like I could forget.'

He tightens his grip around the paper bag. 'So will you join me? I promise I won't keep you – just a glass of wine, a few bits of cheese.'

I fix my eyes on his, and though a voice in my head tells me to say no, to run, to get as far away from him as I can, I can barely hear it above the sound of my heart beating wildly.

'Okay,' I finally say, my eyes still fixed on his. 'Why not?'

My stomach flutters as the words come out of my mouth because I know, fully and clearly, the answer to that question.

# *Chapter 22*

'If you can't go to Paris, then Paris will come to you.'

Hugh unwraps a large hunk of Brie and places it on a plate next to a slice of Bûcheron.

'*Merci*,' I say, resting my bag on the counter.

He grabs two wine glasses and ushers me to the table, then puts the cheese next to the baguette and a bottle of red. He pulls out a corkscrew and opens the wine, which he pours generously.

'*Bon appétit*,' he says, handing me a glass. He clinks his against mine and takes a sip. 'Please, sit. Enjoy.'

I slide into one of the chairs and reach for the baguette. 'Do you have a knife?'

He swallows his wine and waves me off. 'Let's just do like the French do and tear into it. We're going to finish it anyway.'

'A whole baguette?'

'Easily. I realize you've probably been feasting on *la bonne cuisine* all day, but I've eaten nothing but a jacket potato, and I'm famished.'

I tear off a piece of bread and hand the baguette to him as he settles into his seat. 'Nice wine, by the way. What is it?'

He picks up the bottle and scrunches up his face as he examines the label, holding it progressively further away. 'A shiraz, I believe.'

'Eyesight going already?'

'Yes. Apparently forty is the age when everything goes downhill – eyesight gets worse, joints start aching, bits fall off.'

'Bits fall off? Which bits?'

'Nothing important. Just hair, really.'

'Okay. Good. You had me worried. I thought like maybe you've started losing toes or something.'

He laughs. 'No, nothing like that. At least, not yet. Perhaps that's what happens when you're fifty – I still have a decade to work it out.'

I spread a bit of buttery Brie on my bread. 'When did you turn forty?'

'April. Though in my mind I'm still thirty-five.' He pauses. 'I'm being charitable. In my mind I'm probably still fifteen.'

'You and every other man I've ever met.'

He winces as he stuffs a piece of bread into his mouth. 'Oooh, she went there…'

'Actually, I take that back. My ex-boyfriend was the opposite. He was probably thinking like a forty-year-old when he was fifteen.'

'Sounds like a fun chap.'

'He was fun in his own way. He was a good guy.'

He takes another sip of wine. 'So what happened to the two of you, then? If you don't mind my asking.'

'I got the job offer from Natasha and moved here.'

'And?'

'And…that was it.'

'But it's not as if you're staying here for ever.' He holds up his hands defensively. 'Not that I'd mind if you did, of course.'

'It wasn't just the move. I think I outgrew the relationship.'

It's the first time I've said those words out loud, but as soon as I do, they sound both right and strange – right because that's exactly how I feel, but strange because it makes our relationship sound like a pair of shoes that doesn't fit any more. It's also the first time I've admitted to myself that there is no going back to Sam, not only because I fell out of love with him but also because I'm no longer the person he fell in love with. 'Sorry – that must sound odd,' I say.

'Not at all. I know exactly what you mean. Believe me.'

I finish my wine, and Hugh refills my glass as I reach for some of the goat cheese. 'What about you and Natasha? How did you meet?'

'A long story for another time,' he says.

I want to ask about their marriage – about the separate bedrooms and the fact that they never seem to spend any time together – but it's none of my business, and his tone tells me it isn't up for discussion anyway. I change the topic.

'Yesterday you mentioned your dad built bikes for a living?'

He licks a blob of cheese from his thumb. 'I suppose technically he didn't build them. He worked for Sturmey-Archer, a manufacturing company. They primarily made bicycle gear hubs.'

'Made?'

'The firm was sold to some Taiwanese outfit in 2000. He bounced around a few other jobs after that, then retired four years ago.'

'And has since taken to calling you with his constipation woes.'

'Indeed.'

'What was it like growing up? I'm guessing you didn't live like this.' I gesture around his kitchen.

'Definitely not. We were never exactly poor, but money was always tight. Our entire house was smaller than the ground floor here.'

'Mine, too. By a lot.'

'What did your parents do?'

'My dad works for the Postal Service.'

'Really? My uncle worked for the Royal Mail for years. He retired a few years ago.'

'My dad is a long way from retirement, if I had to guess.'

'Money?'

'That, and I have no idea what he'd do with himself if he didn't have to go to work every day.'

'I'll tell you what he'd do. He'd call you asking about prune juice and strong coffee.'

I laugh. 'Exactly.'

'And your mum? Did she work?'

I finish my second glass of wine, my head a bit woozy. 'Kind of. She had mainly part-time gigs – cashier at one of the local grocery stores, sales clerk at Kmart, that kind of thing. She had trouble holding down anything more permanent. She wasn't the most reliable person.'

'No?'

I consider my response, wondering how much I can or should tell him about my mom, but the wine has loosened my inhibitions, so I decide there's no harm in telling him the truth.

'She drank too much,' I say. 'Not like an alcoholic or anything, although…I don't know. Maybe she was. We never really talked about that kind of thing. It's not like she was hitting the sauce at ten in the morning. That much I know. And she never drove us to school drunk or picked us up drunk. Frankly, if she'd been drinking, she just wouldn't show up. But by four or five o'clock, she always had her glass of blackberry brandy nearby – either that or a Rum Runner.' I meet Hugh's eyes. 'Sorry – too much information. You probably think my family is nuts.'

'Like I said before, whose isn't?'

'Yeah, but mine is sort of on a different level.'

'Not really. Not from mine, anyway. My dad, as you know, is lovable but mad, and my mum…' He trails off. 'Well, she sounds a bit like yours.'

'She drinks blackberry brandy at four in the afternoon?'

He forces a smile. 'She tends to prefer sloe gin. Or she used to. But yes.'

'Oh, I'm sorry. I didn't realize…'

210

'No need to apologize. She's been on and off the wagon for years. Currently she's on it, but who knows how long that will last?'

'Did you...I mean, was it an issue when you were growing up?'

'A bit. But, like you say, we never really talked about that sort of thing – I mean, God, on top of everything else we're British. The "stiff upper lip" isn't fiction. Anyway, she was never an embarrassment, always managed to keep it together, but I lived my entire adolescence fearing she was just one drink away from crossing the line. And I've spent my adult life worrying about her constantly – whether she'll slip up, whether she'll be okay if, God forbid, something happens to my dad. I can never rest easy. I feel like I'm always on guard.'

'I wish I'd been more like that. Maybe if I had, my mom would still be around.'

'Don't blame yourself. It isn't your fault. At some point people need to take responsibility for their own actions. At least, that's what my therapist told me.'

'You're in therapy?' I say, before I can stop myself.

'Was. Briefly. When my mum's drinking got really bad, and I developed a bit of insomnia over it. I'm very good at solving problems – it's part of the reason I became a politician – and it bothered me that I couldn't solve hers, the woman who'd raised me and whom I loved dearly. I think I also blamed myself a bit. Was I too naughty as a child? Was my brother? Should I have done more? It's taken time for me to grasp that it's no one's fault.'

'Did she ever work?'

'Nope. Spent all her time raising me and my brother

211

– hence the guilt on my part. Even if she'd wanted to, my dad felt pretty strongly about providing for the family.'

'My dad was like that, too, although for all his talk, he never tried all that hard to make something of himself. It's almost as if he'd rather complain about his situation than do something about it.'

'Maybe he didn't want to disappoint all of you by trying and failing. Maybe he didn't want to disappoint himself.' He swirls his wine. 'Sometimes success requires a leap of faith, and not everyone has the courage to take it.'

'You obviously did. How did you end up here?'

'In Belsize Park?'

'Not just that. Shadow education minister. A rising star in your party. Potential future prime minister.'

'I worked hard at school. Got a cricket scholarship to Cambridge. Worked even harder. Got a PhD. And…well, here we are.'

'But how could you see all of that from your small house in Nottingham when you were a little boy?'

He shrugs. 'Dunno. I was always a bit of a dreamer, I suppose.'

'But even those dreams…I mean, I went to a great college, but it was twenty minutes from my hometown. The American equivalents of Cambridge – Harvard, Yale – weren't even on my radar.'

'Surely you'd heard of them.'

'Of course. But applying to those schools would have been like saying, "I want to go to the moon" or "I want to become a famous actress". Those things happen, just not to people like me.'

'Why not?'

212

'Because I am who I am. I'm from where I'm from.'

'So? That doesn't mean anything. You can be whatever you want to be. There's no reason you can't become the next Nigella.'

The wine rushes to my head. 'There are plenty of reasons.'

'Like?'

'Like…I don't look like Nigella, for starters. And I don't have her connections. Her parents were famous and wealthy. My parents didn't even go to college.'

'So? Neither of my parents went to college either. That didn't stop me.'

'Yeah, but you're…you. I'm a nobody.'

'What are you talking about? You aren't a nobody. You're well-spoken and clever, you can make some of the best home-cooked food I've eaten in my life, you're confident and funny, you're bloody beautiful—'

He stops, his cheeks blossoming with pink. The word rings in my ears as my heart pounds. *Beautiful*. He thinks I'm beautiful?

'Sorry – I hope I haven't made you uncomfortable,' he says.

I wave him off, trying to disguise the fact that my hand is trembling. 'You haven't at all.'

I reach across the table and rip off another piece of baguette, but as I pull, my hand snaps back and knocks my wineglass onto the floor. It shatters into dozens of tiny shards, sending burgundy-coloured wine sailing across the white tiles.

'Oh – I'm so sorry.'

I leap up from my seat and rush to the sink, feeling a bit

off-kilter from all of the wine. I grab a roll of paper towels and bring it back to the table. Crouching beside a chair, I sop up the spilled wine, brushing the bits of glass into another paper towel.

'Be careful,' he says, squatting next to me. 'You'll cut yourself. Here, let me.'

'I'm fine. Really. I just need to – shit!' Sure enough, I've pierced my index finger on a small piece of glass next to one of the chairs. Blood gushes onto the floor. 'I'm such an idiot.' I jump up and head for the sink again, running my finger under the cold water. Hugh chases after me, the roll of paper towels in his hand.

'Here – use this.' He wraps a clean paper towel around my finger and presses hard as he lifts my hand over my head. 'Hold it like this for a few minutes until it starts to clot, and then I'll get you a plaster.'

'A what?'

'A plaster.' I stare at him blankly. 'A bandage. Whatever you Americans call it.'

'Oh. Right. Thank you.' Hugh continues to hold my hand above my head, his hip nearly touching mine. 'I'm so sorry,' I say. 'Natasha's going to kill me.'

'If she kills anyone, she'll kill me. I'll tell her I broke it.'

'Why would you do that?'

'Because getting rid of me is a lot more complicated than getting rid of you.' He goes quiet and searches my face. 'We aren't in love, you know. Me and Natasha.'

'It isn't really my business…'

'Perhaps not, but I thought you should know. It's more like…a business arrangement. We help each other professionally, but it's not…There's no romance.'

'You're still married.'

'Technically. But she's had a lover for a while now, and we barely see each other. Even when we do, it's all very buttoned up. We never really...talk about things.' He tightens his grip on my hand. 'Not like this. Not like I can with you.'

My heart races, his words echoing in my head. I want to kiss him. God, I want to kiss him. He gets me – who I am, where I'm from, what I want in life. And he sees something in me, something I've never seen in myself, that makes me feel capable, worthy – invincible. Sam shrank my world to make it manageable and safe, but Hugh has blown it wide open, releasing me into a sea of adventure and possibility. I like the person I am when I'm with him, the way I act, the way I feel. It's as if he's unlocked a part of me I didn't know existed, and now that I've caught a glimpse of the woman I could be, I don't want to let her go.

'You shouldn't say things like that,' I say.

'You're right,' he says. 'I shouldn't.'

He holds my stare, and then he slowly moves closer, until his hips are touching mine, pressing me against the kitchen counter. He leans towards me, his breath hot on my face, and I slowly lean towards him, my skin tingling. He rubs his thumb gently along my lower lip, and then he kisses me, softly at first, then with more intensity. My heart is beating so hard and fast I'm afraid it will burst. He pulls me close and starts kissing my neck, his skin smelling of cedar and pine, his touch electric.

'Tell me if you want to stop,' he whispers in my ear.

He kisses my neck again, and I pull him closer. 'I don't want to stop,' I say.

I grab at his shirt and run my hands up and down his back, and he presses against me harder, rubbing his knee along the inside of my leg. My entire body shakes, out of fear or desire or a combination of both, but he holds me close, his body warm and solid. Every touch and kiss feels like the first – not with Hugh, but with anyone – as if everything that came before this was, on some level, pretend.

He reaches down and pulls my T-shirt over my head, exposing my pale skin to the glow of the kitchen light. He runs his hands over my stomach and hips, and I shiver as I unbutton his shirt, feeling feverish, dizzy. His chest is smooth and muscular, his skin warm and pale. He pulls away for a moment and smiles, and my legs go weak, trembling as I look up at him – those eyes, those lips. I fumble with his belt buckle, tugging at it manically, like a woman possessed, wanting him so intensely my bones ache. My breath quickens, the air thick and strange, as if something in the room has suddenly changed, as if we have crossed some sort of threshold.

He unbuttons my jeans, hoists me onto the counter, and wraps my legs around his waist. I run my fingers through his hair, my heart beating faster and faster, my head dizzy with wine and longing, and then, as I pull him into me, I let my mind go blank.

# Chapter 23

What have I done? What have I *done*?

This is terrible. Oh, my God, this is terrible. I mean, it wasn't terrible at the *time*. It was magical and emotional and was, quite literally, the best sex that has ever happened – if not in the history of the act, then at least in my personal history. But now that it's over, I'm left with the glaring reality that I just slept with a married man. Not just any man. An MP. An MP who, for the sake of publicity or not, is married to Natasha fucking Spencer.

Oh, God. I think I'm going to be sick.

I rush over to the kitchen sink and vomit, while Hugh is in the bathroom down the hall. I flick on the water, washing the wine-soaked hunks of regurgitated baguette down the drain.

'Everything okay in there?' he shouts from the end of the hall.

'Fine,' I call back, even though that isn't even close to the truth.

I blot the corners of my mouth with a paper towel, a thin stream of blood still trickling from my index finger. Hugh walks back into the kitchen, his white shirt half buttoned and stained with blood.

'Jesus, it looks like you murdered someone.'

He glances down at his shirt. 'Indeed it does.'

'I'm really sorry. I shouldn't have— I should have gotten a Band-aid. A plaster.'

'It's fine. There wasn't exactly a lot of … planning going on.'

'But your shirt is ruined.'

'Probably.'

We stare at each other for a few uncomfortable moments, and my queasiness returns.

'Listen,' he says, and as soon as he does, I know what will follow. *This was a mistake. This can't happen again. I'm sorry. You should go.* So instead, I hold up my hand.

'I know,' I say. 'It's okay. I'm leaving.'

'That isn't what I meant – you don't have to leave.'

'I think we both know that isn't true.'

He stares at me for a long while. 'Could I at least call you a taxi?'

'I can take the tube. It isn't a problem.'

He looks at the clock. 'Nonsense. I'd worry the whole time. I'll call a taxi right now. And then I'll get you a plaster.'

He walks out of the kitchen, and I finish cleaning the floor, sweeping up the glass with one of Olga's brooms and wiping up the rest of the spilled wine with a paper towel.

Aside from a bit of grout that now bears a pinkish hue, there is no trace of my clumsiness.

Hugh comes back, waving a bandage over his head. 'Taxi called. Plaster ready.'

He approaches and unwraps the bandage, crumpling the paper into a ball. I stick out my finger, and he gently applies it. When he's finished he looks down at me, my finger still held in his hand.

'Could you please call when you get home? To let me know you got back safely.'

'Sure. If you want.'

'I do. Thank you.' He holds my finger tight.

The doorbell rings, and we turn towards the hall. 'Sounds like the taxi's here,' I say.

He gradually lets go of my finger, and I grab my bag off the counter and follow him upstairs. He unlocks the front door, but as I reach out for the knob, he presses his hand on top of mine.

'I…had a lovely time tonight,' he says.

My chest tightens. This is awkward. Why is this so awkward? 'Me too,' I finally say.

'You promise you'll call when you get home?'

He stares at me earnestly, and my heart races. He rubs his thumb along my hand, and I say, 'I promise,' even though I know that's a lie.

Promising to call him wasn't a wilful lie. I would have called him if I'd had his cell-phone number, but I knew I didn't, and I wasn't about to ask for it. For privacy reasons, I don't even have the house line. The only person's number I have in connection with this house is Poppy's, and somehow I didn't think calling her in Paris to say, 'I made it home safely after sleeping with your boss's husband – just thought I'd let you know!' was wise.

Instead, when I get home, I head straight for my bedroom, dump my bag next to my bed and hop in the shower, as if cleaning myself will erase what happened tonight. Unfortunately, the plumbing in my building is about two hundred years old so the water alternates between too hot and too cold, providing little comfort and no absolution.

What little sleep I get that night is besieged by dreams of Hugh and me, our legs intertwined, our lips pressed together. I can't decide whether these are dreams or night-mares. Didn't I want that to happen? Haven't I wanted it ever since I met him?

My great fear is that when I arrive the next morning, his will be the first face I see, and we'll fall into a clumsy, stilted interaction that I won't know how to resolve. But my worries are for naught because when I arrive at the house Hugh has already left for work, so Olga and I are the only two people there.

'Miss Natasha, she return today,' Olga says.

'Do you know what time?'

She shrugs dispassionately. Apparently she neither knows nor cares.

Given that last time Natasha returned from Paris, she drank nothing but juice for three days, I decide not to prep the Brussels sprouts, since doing so will inevitably result in throwing them away. Instead, I get going on what I hope will be my final test run of the paella, followed by a first attempt at sweet potato fries, a compromise Natasha and

I came to, since she wanted fries in the book but doesn't eat white potatoes and therefore wouldn't be able to try them.

As I trim and soak the sweet potatoes, the house phone rings, and I hear Olga's footsteps race down the hallway above me as she goes to answer it. The ringing stops, and a few moments later, I hear her thumping down the stairs to the kitchen.

'A call for you,' she says.

'For me? Who is it?'

'Mr Ballantine. He have question.'

My pulse quickens. 'Oh. Okay.' I wipe my hands on my apron. 'Is it okay if I take the call down here?'

'Please.'

I pick up the phone and press it to my ear, my eyes locked on Olga, who stands frozen in the doorway. 'Hello?'

'Hi – Kelly. It's me. Are you okay?'

'Fine,' I say, flashing a friendly smile for Olga's sake.

'Thank God. I was worried. You never called.'

'I don't have the number,' I say, trying to make my dialogue as vague as possible. To Olga, that could mean anything. It doesn't mean *Sorry for not calling you last night.* It doesn't mean *Sorry for sleeping with you.*

'Right – of course. I didn't even think of that. I suppose I assumed you had the house number, but I forgot Natasha doesn't give it out. Shall I give you my mobile?'

'What for?'

'I don't know, in case…' He fumbles over his words. 'No, I suppose you're right. It's probably not a good idea. You should have the house number, though. I don't care what Natasha says. Have you got a pen and paper?'

'Let me ask Olga,' I say. I move the receiver away from my mouth. 'Olga, do you have Natasha's number in Paris?'

'I think...maybe. I go check,' she says, heading for the stairs.

'Ah, sorry,' Hugh says. 'I didn't realize she was standing right there.'

I redirect my voice back into the phone. 'Listen, I appreciate your concern, but I'm fine. Made it home in one piece and back to work in one piece, and everything is great.'

'Good. Lovely. I'm...glad to hear it.'

Olga re-enters the kitchen with a scrap of paper. 'I have number.'

She goes to hand it to me, but I stop her. 'Why don't you give it to Mr Ballantine?' She shrugs in acquiescence. 'Lovely speaking with you, Mr Ballantine,' I say. 'I'm glad I was able to help.'

I hand the phone to Olga, and as she takes it, I head back to my station at the counter, pretending not to notice that she is eyeing me warily the entire time.

Natasha returns at four o'clock that afternoon, just as I am up to my elbows in sweet potato fries – not figuratively, but quite literally, as I scoop the soaking slices of sweet potato out of an elbow-deep bowl of water.

'*Bonjour!*' she says, as she waltzes up to the kitchen island, across from where I'm standing.

*Yes, by all means, speak French and remind me that you went to Paris without me.*

'How was your trip?'

'*Magnifique*. The weather was amazing. And the food.' She sighs. 'Pierre really outdid himself this time.'

222

'Pierre?'

'Gagnaire.'

My jaw drops. 'You know Pierre Gagnaire?'

'Oh, sure. I've been going to his places for years – Paris, Tokyo, Dubai, Hong Kong. I love his approach to food: new flavours, classic techniques. He's such a genius.'

She's right: he is. The man has three Michelin stars. He's one of the greatest chefs in the world. But more astounding than the fact that Natasha has met him – *knows* him – is her ability to speak with such knowledge about his cooking. And not just his cooking, my cooking, too. As annoying as her fussiness may be, she does have an extremely well-cultivated palate. I suppose if I regularly ate at Pierre Gagnaire and Joël Robuchon, I would, too. But if she derives such pleasure from fine food, then why did she have a meltdown at the mere whiff of a loaf of banana bread? It makes no sense. *She* makes no sense.

'So,' Natasha continues, 'what do you have for me to taste today?'

I freeze, my hands clasped around a bunch of raw sweet potatoes. 'Oh – last time…I thought…' I clear my throat. 'I thought you'd be doing another cleanse.'

'A cleanse? Why would I be doing a cleanse?' She looks down at her waist, then back up at me. 'Do I look fat?'

'No – my God. You're, like, the thinnest person I've ever met. No, it's just that last time you were in Paris you didn't want to do a tasting for a few days. I figured it would be the same this time around.'

'Did I say that?'

'No…I just assumed.'

'Well, you know what my eighth-grade English teacher

told me about assuming?' She stares at me coolly. 'It makes an "ass" out of "u" and "me".'

How does this woman manage to get through a day without someone punching her in the face?

'I'm sorry,' I say. 'Next time I'll be sure to ask.' I nod towards the sweet potatoes. 'I'm about to do a first test run of the sweet potato fries, so if you want, you can stick around to try them. Oh, and the paella should be ready in an hour or so, if you're interested.'

She scrunches up her lips and looks at the clock. 'No on the sweet potato fries. Yes on the paella. I'll be down in an hour for a taste.'

'Perfect.'

She taps her hands on the counter. 'Oh – and before I go, I almost forgot: Hugh and I want to throw a dinner party for some friends on Saturday, and we were hoping you could cook. I'm thinking...tapas.'

'This Saturday?' As in three days from now?

'Yeah. That isn't a problem, right?'

'Nope. It's fine.' Aside from the fact that I now have three days to pull a tapas menu out of my butt. I was also supposed to meet up with Harry for pizza that night, and now, thanks to Natasha's capriciousness, I will have to cancel. Again.

'Excellent. I think there will be twelve of us. I'll double check with Hugh – I haven't spoken with him since before I left. You haven't run into him, have you?'

'Me?'

'Yeah. I know he's been swamped with work, but I just wondered if you'd seen him or if he's been living at the office.'

224

I swallow hard, trying to keep my voice from quavering. 'I ran into him the other day for a second as I was leaving. He seemed fine.' I suddenly remember this morning's call. 'Oh, and he called this morning asking for the number at your hotel. Not sure what that was about, but Olga gave him the number.'

She looks confused. 'Why would he need to call me in Paris this morning, if I was returning this afternoon?'

'I—'

—have no idea how to answer that question. Why *would* he need her number, especially if, as he said, their marriage is one of convenience and they never talk? What seemed like a plausible lie now seems preposterous.

'I'm not sure,' I say. 'He didn't call?'

'No. And, anyway, he knows where I was staying. I sent him an email weeks ago.'

'Oh. Weird.'

She looks annoyed, and I'm certain she is about to call my bluff, but instead she clenches her fist and lets out a grunt.

'God, he's such a flake. This is why – *this is why* I send him a monthly calendar. He never remembers *anything*. Jesus.' She points her finger at me. 'I'm telling you, Kelly, when you find the right man some day, you'd better pray he isn't like Hugh. Because if he is, it'll drive you up the freaking wall.'

I laugh nervously as I reach for the bottle of olive oil and try to stop myself saying out loud the words that have been running through my head – that I've met the right man, and he isn't like your husband. He is your husband.

# *Chapter 24*

What am I saying? Hugh isn't the right man. He is the wrong man. He is, in fact, the very definition of 'the wrong man'. He is married, he is a politician, and he is twelve years older than me. Wrong, wrong, wrong.

But if that's the case, then why can't I stop thinking about him?

I suppose Harry has been on my mind as well, but only in the sense of *Crap, I need to call Harry and cancel our date* or *Ugh, I still haven't called Harry, I really need to get on that*. It really isn't the same thing.

On Thursday evening, I manage to get Harry on the phone, bracing myself for the inevitable disappointment in his voice.

'This dinner came out of nowhere,' I say. 'But she's my boss, so I kind of have to do it.'

'I understand,' he says, though, as expected, he doesn't

sound thrilled. 'Shall we try for a third attempt? Or is this your polite way of telling me you're not interested?'

'No – that isn't it at all. I promise. I'd still love to meet up.'

This is sort of true. I genuinely liked him when we met a few weeks back, and I feel like a huge jerk for constantly cancelling on him. But ever since the incident on Tuesday night, Hugh has been pumping through my veins like a virus, an infection I can't seem to shake. Sometimes, in the middle of sautéing Brussels sprouts or chopping an onion, I'll flash back to his thumb grazing my inner thigh or his lips lingering on my neck, and my hands will start shaking, my skin so hot I need to open the refrigerator to cool down. But no matter how phoney his marriage is, Hugh still isn't available, and Harry is, which means I should at least give him a shot.

'What about next weekend?' Harry suggests. 'I'm free Saturday night.'

'Me too. You pick the place, and I'll be there.'

'Unless you cancel again,' he says.

'I won't cancel – I swear.'

'Famous last words…'

'I guess swearing is a little risky. For all I know, my boss will ask me to build a replica of Buckingham Palace out of *macarons*.'

'Is that even possible?'

'I have no idea. Which probably means she'll ask me to do it.'

'Well, if she does, I could always keep you company while you assemble the balcony. Or, you know, make a *macaron* stick figure of Prince Charles.'

'I'll hold you to that.'

'I hope so.'

My shoulders relax. 'I'll call you next week, okay? We can discuss the details – whether they entail French cookies or not.'

'Sounds brilliant. I look forward to it. In the meantime, let's hope you don't come down with some terrible virus.'

'Let's hope not,' I say, wondering if he knows I already have.

The next day, I start drawing up a menu for Natasha's tapas party. Apparently the number is now up to fourteen, which wouldn't be a problem if she had requested something like a roast or a pasta dish, but for tapas, I now have to make a million little things, and I have one day to figure out what they will be. Everyone always assumes hors d'oeuvres or tapas parties are easier because you don't have to roast a massive slab of beef or braise a huge pot of pork, but really, making lots of little dishes involves infinitely more work, even more so when there are more than a dozen guests.

I decide to make a massive *tortilla española*, since that's something I can prepare in advance and serve warm or at room temperature. I add a Manchego and apple salad to the list, along with a watermelon and tomato salad, and shrimp and squid *a la plancha*. For fourteen people, I will need a few more vegetable dishes – maybe some roasted red peppers stuffed with goat cheese and a green bean salad with apricots and *jamón serrano* – along with a few more hot meaty dishes, like ham *croquetas* and grilled hanger steak. Once I come up with a list on Friday afternoon, I send it off to Natasha, who signs off with a perfunctory 'Fine.'

Later that evening, I return to my messy flat. Laundry from two days ago still hangs on the drying rack, a disorganized stack of magazines covers the coffee table, and my bed is unmade. This would never be the case if I still lived with Sam. He never went to bed without making sure the counters were wiped down, the laundry was put away, and the day's papers were dumped in the recycling bin. Good old reliable Sam. I miss him. I don't miss us – who I was when I was with him, who we'd become as a couple – but I miss having him as a friend, the person I could always count on. I could use someone like that in my life right now. Meg said I shouldn't email him, but it's been more than two months now. Maybe…

No. Meg is right. It isn't fair. I should talk to my brother instead. Actually, I should probably clean my apartment, but I've been meaning to call Stevie since Tuesday night, when everything with Hugh derailed my plans and, apparently, my life. Stevie picks up on the third ring, much to my surprise, given that speaking on the phone is his second least favourite way of communicating after email. Frankly, the only way he really likes to communicate is in person, through mumbles and grunts, preferably while sitting in front of the TV.

'Stevie – hey, it's Kelly.' There is a long pause. 'Your sister?' I add, trying to be helpful.

'Yeah, hey, how's it going?' He doesn't sound at all surprised to hear from me, as if I live down the street and am calling for our regular afternoon chat.

'It's going fine. A little hectic. A little crazy working for a movie star.'

'Oh, right, you're working for ... what's her face ...'

'Natasha Spencer.'

'Riiiiight.' He lets out a slow and sloppy laugh. 'Man, she's hot.'

'Stevie, are you high?'

'What? No.' He clears his throat. 'Barely a joint. It's cool.'

'What time is it?' I glance at my clock. 'It's one thirty in Ypsilanti right now. What are you doing smoking a joint at one thirty in the afternoon?'

'It's Friday.' He titters. 'Friiiday.'

'Stevie ...'

'I told you – stop calling me Stevie. It's Steve.'

'Okay, Steve. Maybe you shouldn't be smoking joints at one thirty in the afternoon, Steve. Maybe you should be studying, Steve.'

'Studying for what?'

'What do you mean "for what"? For school.'

'Oh. Right. Nah, I'm taking some time off.'

'Time off? You mean you dropped out?'

'For now.'

'Why?'

'It wasn't working out. And I wanted to have the summer off.'

'Stevie – sorry, Steve. You're twenty-freaking-five. Why are you trying to draw this out as long as possible? Just get the degree and be done with it.'

'And then what?'

'Oh, I don't know – get a job?'

'But I already have a job.'

'Cleaning the deep-fryer at Abe's Coney Island.'

'I'm beyond that now, thank you very much. I run the entire deep-fry station.'

'That isn't the kind of job I'm talking about. I basically had that job when I was fourteen.'

'Well, excuse me for not being as brilliant and successful as you.'

'That's not what I'm saying. You're better than a job at the Coney Island. You're too smart for that.'

'I take it you haven't seen my college transcript…'

'I'm not talking about grades. I'm talking about smarts.' I click my tongue. 'You're just like Dad.'

'What did you just say?' His voice is suddenly sharp.

'I said you're just like Dad – never wanting to apply yourself, always settling for "honest" work, when really you're too afraid to do anything remotely challenging because you don't want to fail at it.'

'That isn't true.'

'It is, and you know it.'

He huffs. 'So is this why you called? To check up on me? To harass me?'

I take a long, deep breath, thinking back to my mom's letter, where she asked me to keep an eye on Stevie. That wasn't my initial reason for calling, but now that I've called, I'm glad I did. Somebody needs to look out for this kid, and it sure as hell isn't going to be my father.

'No,' I say. 'I called because I wanted to talk to you about Irene O'Malley.'

He snickers. 'What about her?'

'Did you know she's living with Dad?'

'What do you mean "living"?'

'Sleeping under the same roof. Cohabiting. Shacking up.'

He goes silent. 'Wait. Hang on. Dad's banging Irene O'Malley?'

'I don't know that they're "banging",' I say, trying to dismiss that foul image from my mind. 'But she's sleeping in my old room. And every time I call the house, she's there. Has she not been there when you've visited?'

'I haven't really visited.'

I start. 'Why not?'

'Because Dad's been so weird ever since Mom died. Seeing him like that…it just makes me sad. I don't need that.'

'Maybe he'd be less sad if you were around.'

'Because we were always so close…'

Dad and Stevie's relationship was a little like mine and Mom's in so far as it was complicated and layered and somewhat fraught. Stevie was more like my mom – a partier, a social butterfly – where I was more like my dad, minus the cynicism and *ennui*. If Stevie had been the kind of kid who wanted to read *X-Men* or *The Avengers*, my dad would gladly have taken him under his wing. But Stevie just wanted to hang with his friends and smoke pot, and my dad had no idea what to do with him. I think Stevie always mistook my dad's incompetence for a lack of interest, so instead of extending an olive branch, he withdrew from him further.

'Would you rather have Mom's nemesis sinking her claws into our father?' I ask.

'No. Irene is kind of the worst.'

'Exactly. So you and I need to find a way to get her out of that house. Any ideas?'

232

'Other than hiring another chick to stand in her place?'

'Yes, please, other than that.'

He hums into the phone. 'I don't know. I'll think on it.'

'Great. I'll do the same. We can catch up some time next week and trade ideas back and forth.'

'Cool,' he says. 'And I promise I won't be high next time.'

'Thank you.' I pull at a thread on the hem of my shirt. 'I mean what I said, by the way. About you being smart.'

'Yeah, yeah, yeah…'

'I'm serious. Don't settle because you think it'll prevent you from being disappointed in life. Trust me – disappointment finds all of us, one way or another. Better to have—'

'—loved and lost than never to have loved at all.'

Not exactly what I was going for, but okay. 'Something like that,' I say.

'I got it. Message received.' He yawns. 'Anyway, have fun in jolly old England. Oh, and do you think you could snag Natasha's autograph for me?'

'Probably.'

'Sweet. Tell her a shot from *The Devil's Kiss* used to be my screen saver. I used to jerk off to it all the time.'

'Stevie!'

'Steve.'

'Whatever! Ick! Gross!'

He lets out a lazy laugh. 'I'm your little brother. Grossing you out is my job.'

I groan and concede that, whatever failures Steve has experienced in his life, annoying me has been, and will always be, one of his great achievements.

Thirty minutes before Natasha's guests arrive on Saturday

night, she enters the kitchen, her sleeveless silk duster jacket fluttering behind her. It is a rich cream, and beneath it she wears a plunging sleeveless black top and black cigarette pants. She tosses her long, dark waves over her shoulder as she marches towards me in her black stilettos.

'Where are you planning to put the stuffed dates?' she asks.

I freeze halfway through transferring the early makings of a ham croquette to a plate. 'What stuffed dates?'

'The ones stuffed with almonds and blue cheese and wrapped in bacon.'

This was not one of the recipes we agreed to.

'There are no stuffed dates. They weren't on the menu.'

'Are you on drugs? Of course they were. I've literally never had tapas where there weren't stuffed dates on the menu.'

I wipe my hands on my apron and pull out a copy of the menu I sent her yesterday afternoon.

Spanish olives
Boquerones
Apple and Manchego salad with toasted walnuts
Tomato and watermelon salad
Green bean salad with apricots and jamón serrano
Tortilla espagñola
Croquetas de jamón
Squid and shrimp a la plancha
Grilled hanger steak with salsa verde
Raw sheep's milk cheese with quince paste, chocolate-fig jam, and fruit-and-nut toasts

She grabs the paper from my hand. 'What is this?'

'The menu you approved yesterday.'

She looks at the list, then up at me, her expression just shy of ferocious. 'Are you challenging me?'

'No, I'm just—'

'You're just what?'

*Calling you insane.*

'I guess I misunderstood,' I finally say.

'Perfect. Perfect!' She lets out a dramatic cry as she looks at the clock. 'What the eff am I supposed to do now? Everyone will be here in twenty minutes.'

'I'm sure no one will mind if there aren't stuffed dates on the table.'

'You're joking, right? Have you even *eaten* tapas before?'

'I have, actually.'

'Where? In bumble-fuck USA?'

'In Chicago.' *At some of the best tapas restaurants in the country.*

'Well, I don't know how they do it in Chi-CAH-go, but in New York and London and freaking SPAIN, they have stuffed dates.'

I'm tempted to tell her I'm sure they do, but that this is a home-cooked dinner party, not an exhaustive gastronomical tour of a country's cuisine. But given the fierce look in her eyes, I decide there is no point.

'Okay…Well…I'm sure there's something we can do to fix this,' I say, though to be honest, unless the solution involves teleporting or time travel, I'm not sure what that is.

'There'd better be,' she says. 'I want this dinner to be perfect.'

I hold my breath and race through my mental recipe catalogue. There are no dates in this house – that much I know – because Natasha used the last of them in her kale smoothie yesterday afternoon. But I do have some dried apricots left over from the green bean salad. I could do something with those.

'What if instead of stuffed dates wrapped in bacon, we served dried apricots topped with herbed goat cheese and a crisped shard of serrano ham?'

'Would they be warm?'

'No. But at this point, it's the best riff I can come up with.'

She bites her lip, and after a few moments of consideration, she shrugs in exasperation. 'Fine. Whatever. Just do it.'

She turns to leave, and as she does so she grunts, 'God, this party is a disaster before it's even started.'

She tosses her hair over her shoulder and hurries out of the room. As the hem of her duster jacket billows behind her, I can't decide whether it makes her look like a dragon or a queen.

# *Chapter 25*

The apricot canapés are phenomenal – so good, in fact, they should have been part of the menu all along. I lay them on Natasha's cocktail table next to the warm olives and *boquerones*, and as her guests arrive and begin grazing on a few light bites before I bring out the rest of the tapas, I can hear the *ooohs* and *aaaahs* echoing from the overhang above.

Under Natasha's strict instructions, I should allow the guests to mingle and graze in the living room for an hour, at which point the dinner party will progress into the dining room, where Olga will bring up the rest of the dishes and, along with another hired hand, fill wine glasses, clear plates and otherwise attend to their needs. I need to time everything down to the minute, so that there aren't awkward gaps between dishes or a rush of too many at once. I also need to make sure nothing sits on the kitchen counter for too long before Olga takes it upstairs.

I pull the apple and Manchego salad from the refrigerator and divide it among three serving bowls, which I will give Olga to take upstairs and lay along Natasha's walnut dining table. The table itself is a spectacular work of craftsmanship: a twelve-foot slab of raw-edged claro walnut, as if a lumberjack had sliced a massive tree from top to bottom, then placed it upon a polished bronze base. The base has been crafted to look like branches, crawling outward from the centre across the floor, and Olga set the table with similarly chic but rustic tableware and linens. I won't spend any time upstairs during the party, but I managed to sneak a quick peek while Olga set up, and the table setting – the entire room, actually, with its Lucite chairs, petrified wood stools and what appeared to be a painting by Robert Motherwell – took my breath away.

I divide the tomato and green bean salads in the same way I did the apple one, so that the first wave of tapas will feature a variety of cool dishes scattered along the table. The *tortilla espagñola* will follow, then Olga and her helper will clear the plates, set new ones, and prepare for the wave of hot foods. That's when the timing could get a little hairy. I'll need to fry the *croquetas*, then immediately get going on the seafood and steak.

The volume of the crowd dissipates as the guests upstairs move from the living room into the dining room, and soon there is a hush in the kitchen, nothing but the sound of bowls and serving spoons clanking against the marble counter. Olga and her assistant whisk the salads upstairs, and I swirl my two tortillas with aïoli, before slicing them into thick wedges. I set them out for Olga to take up when the crowd is ready, and while I wait for her to return, I adjust the heat beneath a pot of oil, not wanting it to boil over and start a grease fire before dinner is even halfway through.

The tortillas go up, a few empty salad bowls come down, and when Olga gives me the high sign, I fry the *croquetas*, dropping the breaded balls of smoky ham and creamy béchamel into the hot oil. The oil foams and sizzles as I plop in each ball, and the kitchen fills with the smell of deep-fried bacon. Using a skimmer, I scoop out the crispy croquettes, each one a deep golden brown, and lay them on paper towels to drain while I fry the next batch. Once I've cooked them all, I quickly transfer them to platters, which Olga takes upstairs.

As I root through the refrigerator for the marinating shrimp and squid, I hear Olga re-enter the kitchen. 'Hey, before you add any more dishes to the dishwasher, could you do me a favour and grab another roll of paper towels from the pantry?'

'I'm … afraid I don't know where Olga keeps them.'

I whirl around and find Hugh standing on the other side of the island. My pulse quickens. He looks, as always, absurdly handsome, dressed tonight in a crisp white button-down, which he has tucked into dark grey trousers. He carries a glass of white wine in one hand, the other tucked into his pocket. This is the first time I've seen him since The Incident on Tuesday night.

'Oh,' I say, trying to catch my breath. 'I thought you were Olga.'

'Sorry to disappoint you.'

'I'm not disappointed. Just…' *Flustered, nervous, guilt-ridden.* 'Surprised,' I say.

'Happily, I hope.'

'I…' I don't know how to respond to that. Happy to see him? Happy doesn't begin to describe it.

'I'm sorry – I'm really busy,' I finally say. 'I still have a few courses to go, and if I don't stay on schedule, everything will fall apart.'

'Sorry – of course. I just wanted to tell you everything has been brilliant so far. Everyone is making a huge fuss.'

'Well, that's good to hear.'

'You have many fans,' he says. 'Though I am probably one of the biggest.'

I tear my eyes away and turn back to the refrigerator, loading up my arms with the marinating seafood. 'Listen, I really need to start cooking this seafood or I'll be—'

'I can't stop thinking about you,' he says.

I freeze. Only when I begin to feel dizzy do I realize I've been holding my breath.

I turn slowly, letting the refrigerator door close behind me as I set the shrimp and squid on the counter. 'Don't say that.' My voice is a trembling whisper.

'But it's true. I can't.'

'Don't say that,' I repeat.

'Why not?'

'You know why.'

'Yes, but…Can you honestly tell me you don't feel the same way?'

'So what if I do? You're married.'

240

'I told you – our marriage, it isn't real. We aren't in love.'

'That doesn't matter. As far as the outside world is concerned, you're happily married.'

He stares at the floor. Then he looks up at me, his eyes intense. 'But if that were to change…'

'If what were to change?'

'Where the hell is Hugh?' Natasha's voice echoes down the hall, cutting off Hugh before he can answer. She pokes her head through the kitchen door. 'There you are. What are you doing down here? Everyone's asking where you went.'

'I was just complimenting Kelly on the lovely meal.'

'Yeah, well, it isn't over yet, so maybe you shouldn't get ahead of yourself,' she says. 'And, anyway, you're making me look bad.'

'Not as bad as I would have done had I stayed and listened to bloody Imogen prattle on about the lack of suitable holiday homes in Avignon.'

Natasha rolls her eyes. 'Please. Like it's half as bad as listening to some of your friends talk politics. Or fucking cricket.'

'Yes, please do remind me of your thoughts on cricket. I'd quite forgotten.'

She shoots him an icy look, then glances at me. 'Could we not do this in front of the help?'

'She isn't "the help",' Hugh says. 'She has a name.'

'It's okay…' I say, wanting both of them to leave immediately. Aside from this situation being awkward beyond belief, I really have to start cooking the seafood, and it seems kind of inappropriate to do so in the middle of their argument.

'Whatever,' Natasha says. 'Just come back upstairs. *Kelly* needs to finish cooking the meal.'

She grabs his arm and pulls him away, and as the two of them walk through the doorway, I pretend I don't see him glance back over his shoulder.

The party is a massive hit. Except for a slight hiccup in timing between serving the *croquetas* and squid, everything runs smoothly, each dish hitting all the right notes. The squid come out tender and garlicky, with a slight char from the iron griddle, and the grilled steak is the perfect medium-rare, its flavour set off by the piquant *salsa verde*. When Olga finally returns after bringing up the cheese course, she dumps the rest of the dirty plates in the sink and says, 'Miss Natasha, she is happy.'

'Really?' Because she didn't seem all that happy the last time I saw her.

'Yes. Everyone love the food.' She pats my shoulder as she helps me wipe down the counter. 'Is good.'

Olga and her helper – a surly forty-something brunette whose name I never catch – help me unload the first wave of dishes from the dishwasher, then we quickly reload with more dirty dishes from the sink before the two of them return upstairs. After a few more trips up and down, they help me finish cleaning the kitchen, and by midnight, nearly everything is back in its right place.

Around twelve thirty, Natasha wanders down to the kitchen. I heard the door open and shut a few times, so I know some guests have left, but I still hear the muffled echo of chitter-chatter coming from the floor above, so I know at least a few guests are still here.

'Nice job,' she says, gliding up to the counter. She stops when she reaches the edge and presses her hands against the surface.

'Thanks. I'm glad everything turned out the way you wanted.'

'Well, let's not kid ourselves. It wasn't really the way I *wanted*. I *wanted* stuffed dates. But everyone seemed to like those apricots, so I guess it isn't the end of the world.'

'Maybe we could add the apricots to your book,' I say. 'Assuming you liked them.'

'Maybe. I'll think about it.' She raps her fingernails against the counter. 'Oh, and I'm sorry about earlier,' she says. 'With Hugh.'

I try not to look as nervous as I feel. 'You don't need to apologize.'

'You're right. I don't. He's the one who acted like an ass. But I feel like I need to apologize on his behalf.'

'Really, there's nothing to be sorry about.'

'Whatever. It's over.' She sighs. 'Anyway, given his behaviour tonight, I cannot *believe* I'm even asking you this, but I was wondering…Next weekend we're hosting a dinner party in Nottingham for a bunch of people in his constituency – the local treasurer, some other random officers – and I could use your help.'

'Okay. Sure. Sort of like tonight?'

'No. Not at all, actually. These people, they're much more…Well, Hugh would say "down to earth" but I'd say "unsophisticated". You should see some of the haircuts – unreal. But there's a general election next year, so he needs to rub elbows with all of the local people and make a good impression.' She rolls her eyes. 'Politics.'

'I could draw up a simple menu – a roast, something very traditional and English.'

'That would be perfect,' she says. 'Oh, but here's the hitch: it needs to seem as if I cooked it.'

'Oh.' I hesitate. 'Okay…'

'I know. It's ridiculous. But Hugh doesn't want to seem like the guy who married a movie star and lost touch with the common folk. Never mind that he *did* marry a movie star, but whatever. It's what I signed up for when we got married.'

I try not to dwell too much on her reference to their marriage, even though I have a vast array of questions.

'I could make a bunch of dishes that you could bring up with you and just reheat in the oven,' I say.

'How would we transport them?'

'I could put the food in some hotel pans. And for last-minute things, like Yorkshire puddings or whatever, I could send a list of instructions.'

'No. That won't work.'

'Why not?'

'I don't eat the way those people eat. I've never made Yorkshire puddings or bread sauce or whatever the hell they cook for their Sunday lunches. The last thing Hugh needs is for me to ruin dinner for the major players in his constituency. No, I think it would be better if you came with me – sort of played the woman behind the curtain.'

'But would Hugh – sorry, Mr Ballantine – be okay with that?'

'It was his idea, actually. Given how successful tonight's dinner was, he was all, "Oooh, we should bring Kelly along next weekend."'

My head feels light. 'He said that?'

'Believe me, I'm as surprised as you are. We can talk through the details next week, but count on coming up with Sunil next Saturday. Hugh and I will come separately on Friday.'

Shit. Saturday. I'm supposed to see Harry on Saturday. I can't cancel on him a third time. He'll never speak to me again. Maybe we could meet for a nightcap after the dinner in Nottingham. It isn't ideal, but it's better than bailing.

'What time will I be able to leave after the dinner?'

'Sunil will take you back with me on Sunday.'

I hesitate. 'On Sunday?'

'It'll be too late to drive back to London by the time everything wraps up. And just because I'm playing house-wife doesn't mean I plan to clean all of those dishes myself.'

Or, if I had to guess, at all.

I'm about to ask if I can slip out early, but she cuts me off by slapping the counter.

'Good. It's settled, then.' She makes like she's about to leave the room, then stops herself. 'You know what? Let's not include those apricots in the cookbook after all. They weren't *that* good.'

Her hips shake from side to side as she glides out of the room, and I have to muster every ounce of self-control not to call after her, *I bet your husband disagrees.*

# Chapter 26

Fact: those apricot canapés were delicious.

Part of me wonders if the reason she doesn't think they were 'that good' is because everyone else did, including Hugh. It often seems the more Hugh likes something I've made, the less she does. Some days I wonder how they manage to fake a marriage at all. She seems to regard him with such disdain. Why bother?

The next day, before I draw up a menu for Nottingham, I call Harry. My stomach churns as the phone rings, my mind running through various iterations of the same apology: 'I'm sorry. I'm the worst.' Aside from the fact that cancelling yet again makes me feel like a horrible person, the incident with Hugh has dampened my interest in Harry. I wish I wanted him as much as I do Hugh, but lately Hugh is occupying precious real estate in my heart and mind, and I'm having trouble making room for anyone else.

The phone rings and rings, and finally it goes to voicemail.

'Hi, you've reached Harry Swift. Please leave a message and I'll get back to you soon. Cheers.'

'Harry – hi, it's Kelly. You're going to kill me.'

I leave a message explaining Natasha's unexpected catering request, apologizing profusely for breaking my promise. At this point, he probably thinks I'm making up all of these excuses when, really, if I didn't want to see him, I'd just come out and say so. But he doesn't know that, so I try to sound as sincere as possible without over-egging my apology.

'Anyway,' I say, 'I'd still like to meet up some time, so give me a call when you get this, and we can set a date.'

I know there's a very high probability I'll never hear from him again, but I hope I do, at least to know I haven't hurt his feelings.

Once I've left a message, I move on to next weekend's menu. I'm not very familiar with traditional English cuisine, so I scan the Internet for ideas I can present to Natasha tomorrow. I really should present them to Hugh, since he is English and Natasha is not, but that would involve a one-on-one encounter, and I don't want to think about where that could lead. Or, rather, I think about it often, and it fills me alternately with lust and fear. And, anyway, if Natasha is going to cook these dishes with me and pretend they're her handiwork, she should have some say in what we make.

As I compare a few different recipes for rhubarb crumble, Meg's name appears on my computer screen as she calls for a video chat. We haven't spoken in two weeks – not since Natasha offered and revoked the trip to Paris, and not since The Incident with Hugh. If I'm being honest with myself, I've been avoiding her because I don't want to tell her about The Incident, and I know I won't be able to lie if we speak. But I miss her – I miss having a friend – so I answer her call.

'Oh, my God, *finally*,' she says, throwing her head back dramatically. 'It's been two weeks. I'm dying.'

'There isn't much to report.'

'Lies. I've been stalking Natasha online. I saw somewhere that she was spotted in Paris – looking fabulous, of course.'

'Yeah, she went again. She was supposed to take me, actually, but she left me behind.'

'Why?'

'Because she keeps changing her mind about what recipes she wants in the book, and I need to keep us on track to meet our deadline.'

'That sucks.'

'A lot. Especially since I've always wanted to go to Paris.'

'You'll get there some day. In the meantime, how is Mr Hottypants?'

'I'm sorry, I don't know anyone who goes by that name.'

'Last we talked, you knew *two* people who might go by that name. Let's start with the famous older one. How is he? Still setting your lady parts ablaze?'

'Meg, stop.'

'No, I will not stop. I spent last week reporting on white-nose syndrome in Michigan bats, and then I went on a date with an accountant who smelt like onions. I need some juicy gossip. Come on – help a sister out.'

'Why did he smell like onions?'

She rolls her eyes. 'I don't know. He still lives with his mother. It was a mistake.'

'Are we talking raw onions or caramelized?'

'Does it matter?'

'Kind of. If the answer is caramelized onions, maybe his mom was cooking something, and the smell kind of…stuck.'

'That doesn't change the fact that he is thirty-one and still living with his mother. The man is an accountant. He has means.'

'Maybe he isn't very successful…'

'Oh, good, that's what I need: an unsuccessful accountant who still lives with his mother and smells like onions. Someone call Father Francis and set a date at the church.'

'Sorry. Didn't mean to pour salt on the wound.'

She waves me off. 'It's fine – as long as you give me a full and unabridged update.'

'Unabridged? Okay, well, after we talked two weeks ago, I did a load of laundry, which I hung on my drying rack because I don't have a dryer. Then I tidied up the apartment and—'

'Okay, okay – abridged. Abridged. For the sake of all things holy, abridged. Just give me the high points. Did you see Foxy Ballantine?'

I swat a fly off my table. 'I did.'

Meg rubs her hands together. 'That's what I'm talking about. Details, please – where, when, yada yada.'

'Well, I saw him a few times while Natasha was in Paris—'

'You saw him? How? Where?'

'In the house, mostly.'

'Mostly? What does that mean? Were you alone? Tell me you were alone.'

'Yes, we were alone.'

'Where?' She lowers her voice. 'Was it in the bedroom?'

'No – Jeez. What kind of person do you think I am?' My cheeks flush. 'It wasn't like that at all. I just…ran into him.'

'With your vagina?'

'MEG!'

'Sorry. But I know you, Kelly Madigan. You're equivocating.'

'I'm not!'

Meg raises an eyebrow and says nothing.

'Okay, fine. I saw him as I was leaving on Monday night. Then on Tuesday, I ran into him on the way to the tube, and he invited me back to the house for some wine and cheese.'

'Oh, my God. You had a date. You had a date with Natasha Spencer's husband.'

'It wasn't a date! It was wine and bread and cheese.'

'And sex?' Meg asks, smirking. When I don't answer, her smile fades. 'No. Shut up. No. Oh, my God. No. Shut up. Holy Jesus. I can't breathe.'

'No – it wasn't…I mean…Meg, calm down.'

She gasps for air. 'Oh, my God. Oh, my God. This is…Oh, my God.' She fans herself with her hand. 'I can't. I just…Oh, my God.'

'Stop – you're going to pass out if you carry on like that.'

She closes her eyes and takes a deep breath, letting the air out in a slow, steady stream. 'Okay. I'm calm. Now. Walk me through this. What happened?'

250

'Well, things sort of…progressed…'

Meg starts to get riled up again but presses her hand against her chest. 'Okay. And how, exactly, did they progress? Be specific.'

I contemplate glazing over the details, but before I can even attempt to do so, the entire story comes pouring out, every aspect of it, from the moment I ran into him on Glenloch Road to the encounter in the kitchen last night. On some level it feels good to lay everything out in the open, like a confession. That was one of my favourite parts of church, growing up, when I still actually went to church. I remember going to confession in second grade and pouring out everything, even things I hadn't done ('…and I ate too much chocolate…and then I coveted my neighbour's wife…and also his goods…'). It just felt so good to unload, to share my sins and then expunge them with a few Hail Marys. If only adult life were that simple.

When I've finished telling Meg everything, including the planned dinner next weekend in Nottingham, she sits in silence, staring back at me through the screen. She nods slowly, her lips pressed together. Given her earlier behaviour, I expected her to respond with fits of squealing, but now that the fantasy she hinted at has become real, her excitement has cooled.

'Right,' she finally says. 'Well.'

I rest my head in my hands. 'It's awful. I know it's awful. And the worst part is I still have to be around him. If I could avoid him, I could pretend like none of this ever happened.'

'And what good would that do? It did happen.'

'But I wish it hadn't.'

251

'Really? Deep in your heart, do you really wish none of it had happened?'

'Of course I do.'

'No, you wish it had happened under different circumstances,' she says. 'I know you. I can see the look in your eyes, even through a computer screen. You like this guy. You *really* like this guy. You just wish he weren't married.'

'But he is married, so it doesn't matter what I wish, does it?'

'It isn't a real marriage, though. You've said so yourself.'

'So? The rest of the world doesn't know that.'

'Didn't he say something last night about how that might change? Maybe he and Natasha are considering divorce.'

I replay the interaction in my mind, as I've done countless times since last night. Could he really have meant divorce? And if he did, would he honestly ever consider me in Natasha's place? Of course he wouldn't. In what world would I, a blonde slip of a thing from Michigan, be a rival for Hollywood royalty? No world I can think of.

'So what if they are? That doesn't make what we did right.'

'But it kind of makes it less wrong.'

'And how is that?'

'I don't know…Like, if you two end up together some day—'

'End up together? Meg, I've known the guy for like six and a half weeks. A little soon to be talking marriage.'

'I didn't mean marriage.'

252

'Then what did you mean?'

She leans back in her chair. 'I don't know. You're right. You haven't been there all that long. And you're lonely. I get it. But hearing you talk, seeing your face…Kel, you were never like this with Sam.'

'Like what?'

'Smitten. Enchanted. Besotted. Pick your adjective. Like, you're telling me sleeping with him was a mistake and you regret it and blah-blah-blah, but the way you look, the tone in your voice – you obviously have feelings for him.'

I look at the keyboard. 'And what if I do?'

'Then maybe you should figure out how serious those feelings are. Like, is this some crazy rebound crush after Sam? Or is this something more serious and real? Because if it's the latter, you should probably find out if he feels the same way, if only to prevent yourself getting hurt.'

'I guess…'

'I'm just trying to look out for you. I don't want you to waste your time. It's like your mom always used to say: "You get one life, so you'd better make the most of it."'

'I think her exact words were, "You get one life, so don't waste it drinking bad whiskey."'

'Whatever. Same idea.'

We stare at each other through the screen, then burst into laughter, cackling like wild hens until tears roll down our cheeks. If there's anyone who knows my mother as well as I do, it's Meg, and though we may both be misquoting her terribly, we know exactly how she would feel about this entire situation: she would love it. She'd love the sense of adventure, the messiness of it all, and would support my missteps wholeheartedly, prodding me on like the devil on my shoulder. 'Have fun while you're still young!' she'd say. 'Be the dancing queen!' It's why she loved that ABBA song so much. She never left the Midwest and didn't do much with her life, but if she closed her eyes and turned up the music, she could pretend she was the girl in the song, living life to the fullest and enjoying the ride. That's what she wanted for me. She wanted me to live a life filled with passion – with adventure.

Tears of laughter stream down my face, and I wonder if it's a coincidence that, for the first time in my life, I'm embracing my mother's sense of irresponsibility and running with it full steam ahead and that, in spite or because of this, my heart has never been fuller.

## Chapter 27

The following week, in addition to testing a new round of recipes for the cookbook, I firm up a menu with Natasha for the dinner in Nottingham. We decide on a simple meal of roast beef with horseradish and mustard sauce, sautéed green beans with caramelized shallots, and rosemary-and-garlic roasted potatoes, to be followed by an offering of Cheddar and Stilton, and a warm rhubarb crumble. To me, the menu strikes the perfect balance of sophisticated and homey, but Natasha is already having a mild panic attack about the main course because she's (allegedly) allergic to potatoes and, apparently, hasn't eaten red meat since 1995.

'We can make something else,' I suggest on Thursday, as she picks manically at the hem of her shirt. 'Rice instead of potatoes. And roast chicken for beef. Or maybe duck?'

'Do you have any idea how many ducks and chickens

we'd need to roast for ten people? Eleven, if we're including you, which I guess we are. No, it has to be beef.'

'We could do pork,' I say. 'I know that's red meat, too, but it's less red, I guess.'

'That's the dumbest thing I've ever heard. No, we'll stick with the beef and potatoes. It's what these people eat, and the whole point of this dinner is to cement their relationship with Hugh. I'll just...figure it out as we go.' She rests her hands on her hips. 'Some days I think this marriage is going to kill me.'

*Then why don't you end it?* I want to ask, which makes me think of Hugh's comments last weekend, which, of course, makes me think of Hugh. Every time I'm convinced I've put up an emotional barrier between him and me, someone says something to knock it down. Ironically, that person is usually Natasha.

The next thirty-six hours fly by in a blur, and before I know it, I'm standing in front of my building on Saturday morning, waiting for Sunil to pick me up. Natasha and Olga left yesterday morning, and Hugh left in the afternoon so that they could get the house in order. I sent many of the ingredients up with Olga ahead of time: the cheese, the produce, the beef. By the time I arrive, she will have unpacked everything into the refrigerator and cupboards, and I can dive right into preparation for this evening.

Sunil arrives in his silver Mercedes and pops the trunk, lifting my small suitcase and battery of kitchen equipment inside. I slip into the back seat, my tote beside me and a brown shopping bag on the floor. The bag contains a vat of horseradish and mustard sauce, which I made last night, and a tin of homemade oatcakes, which I plan to serve with the cheese. I'll do most of the recipe prep at the house in Nottingham, but to save myself time, I decided to make a few accessory dishes in advance.

Once Sunil has packed up the car, he hops into the front seat and zips out from his parking space, heading north onto the M1 towards Nottingham. I doze off in the back seat, resting my head on the window frame, and the next thing I know, Sunil is pulling into a gravel driveway, nearly two and a half hours later.

'Are we here?' I ask.

'Yes, ma'am.'

I look out of the window as he continues along the crushed gravel path towards a two-storey Victorian house made of orange brick and covered with thick patches of ivy. The front bay windows are framed with bright white sashes, and a brick chimney rises high above the rooftop. The house isn't vast, but it certainly isn't the 'quaint little cottage' I'd imagined when Natasha said Hugh had bought an old vicarage for next to nothing and turned it into his local residence. The house is easily three times the size of the one I grew up in and is surrounded by a smorgasbord of shrubs – rhododendrons, hawthorns, viburnum, holly – all interspersed with wild flowers, ferns and green mosses.

Sunil parks the car in a large area that looks a little like a parking lot and opens my door. I grab my things and make my way across the crushed gravel to the entrance. Olga opens it and greets me with the sort of unreadable salutation that has become her signature.

'Miss Natasha, she is resting,' she says.

'Is Poppy here?'

Olga's brow furrows. 'No. Poppy is home. In London.'

Given the purpose of tonight's dinner, it makes sense for Poppy not to come, but I have never known Natasha to travel without her. She must not know what to do with herself.

'Maybe you could show me around the kitchen,' I suggest. 'So I know where everything is when Natasha wakes up.'

Olga leads me into the house, the inside of which is covered with rich wood panelling and parquet flooring. A baronial staircase rises to the floor above, and Olga leads me through the reception hall, past the drawing and dining rooms, to the kitchen at the back. The floor is made of square terracotta tiles, which run up to the oak cabinetry and jet-black Aga. Silver and copper pots and pans hang from the ceiling, along with a few terrine and cake pans that appear never to have been used. The entire room feels very self-consciously 'English Countryside'.

'Ah, you made it,' Hugh says, as he walks into the kitchen. He wears beige chinos and a baby-blue-and-white striped Cambridge rugby shirt.

'The house – it's lovely,' I say.

'You sound surprised.'

'Natasha made it sound a little more…rustic, I guess.'

'As she would.' He looks around the kitchen. 'I suppose it was a bit more rustic when I first saw it. It was a run-down vicarage in need of repair. I bought it for a song and made it my little project. Natasha has helped with a lot of the decorating – though I made her promise to stick to the English spirit of the place.'

'Ah, so no Lichtenstein paintings.'

He laughs. 'No Lichtenstein, I'm afraid. Unless there was

an English Lichtenstein who happened to be chums with Constable or Turner.'

'I'll go out on a limb and say there wasn't.'

'There you have it, then.' He smiles softly, then stops as he catches Olga's stare. 'Anyway, sorry for interrupting. I know you have lots to do to prepare for tonight. You're okay with the plan?'

'Fine,' I say.

'Good. I promise these people aren't as tiresome as Natasha says. Some do, indeed, have frightening haircuts, but they're lovely people. Once you and Natasha have got dinner on the table, you can relax and have a good time.'

'I look forward to it,' I say, even though I cannot imagine a scenario in which Hugh, Natasha and I sitting together around a dinner table could possibly be fun.

Five hours before the guests are supposed to arrive, Natasha joins me in the kitchen, dressed in black leggings and an oversize grey sweatshirt. Her hair is tied in a messy bun atop her head, and even though she doesn't appear to be wearing any makeup, she is more beautiful than almost anyone I've ever met.

'Sorry,' she says, covering her mouth as she yawns. 'I needed that nap. Last night really took it out of me.'

'Oh?' I ask, trying to sound casual, even though what I'm thinking is, *Why? Why did last night take it out of you? Were you and Hugh having sex? I thought you didn't do that.*

'Hugh had a few old friends over for drinks. I haven't drunk that much Scotch in years. And now I remember why.' She rubs her forehead.

'Well, the good news is that we're in really great shape for tonight. I already made the horseradish and mustard sauce and the oatcakes. I've trimmed the beans and prepped the shallots. I was actually just about to start on the rhubarb crumble, if you wanted to help.'

She glances up at the clock. 'You're making it now?'

'I figured we could reheat it just before we serve it. And then you could bring it to the table.'

'I was hoping to squeeze in a workout before getting ready…'

'No worries. I can do it myself. I just thought I'd extend the invitation.'

She considers the offer. 'You know what? Fuck it. I'll cut the workout down to one hour instead of two. Where's the knife? I'll trim the rhubarb.'

I hand her the chef's knife and the ruby stalks of rhubarb, which I picked up from the market yesterday morning. Natasha grabs a wooden cutting board and begins chopping the rhubarb into inch-long chunks, and as she does, I'm impressed by the finesse and dexterity of her knife skills.

'Where'd you learn to hold a knife like that?' I ask.

She scoops up the rhubarb and dumps it into a large bowl. 'I don't even remember at this point. My mom, maybe? And then people like François and Pierre sort of refined my technique along the way.'

'You haven't mentioned much about your mom,' I say. 'Does she still live in Philadelphia?'

Natasha hesitates. 'She's dead.'

'Oh,' I say. 'I'm sorry.'

'It is what it is.'

'When did she…?'

'About six years ago. Cancer.' She smooths the front of her sweatshirt. 'I don't really want to talk about it.'

'Of course – I just…My mom is dead, too. She died a few months ago. Right before you hired me, actually.'

Natasha fixes her eyes on mine. 'I'm sorry. I had no idea.'

'There's no reason you would. It's not something I tend to bring up.'

'Yeah,' she says, her voice almost sympathetic. She runs her fingers along the cutting board. 'Were you…close?'

'Not exactly. I mean, we weren't *not* close, but we were very different people. My mom, she was a little…quirky.'

'Quirky? Like how?'

'Like…when I was in third grade, she started singing "Dancing Queen" in front of all of my friends at my birthday party because she'd had a little too much to drink, and then tripped, fell and knocked over the birthday cake. Though I'm not sure if that was worse than my fifth-grade birthday party, when I had to bake my own cake because she forgot…'

'Oh,' Natasha says. 'I see.' Clearly this is beyond her notion of what 'quirky' might entail.

'I take it your mom didn't do those sorts of things,' I say, trying to defuse the awkwardness.

'No.' She clears her throat. 'She was a class act, all the way around. My best friend, actually.'

'And she liked to cook?'

'Loved it. So did her mom.'

'The one who made the Cornish hens?'

'That's the one.' She plays with the hem of her sweatshirt. 'My mom had a few specialties, too. She used to make

261

this banana bread that...' She takes a deep breath. 'I can't even think about it without getting choked up.'

I think back to the banana bread I baked for Hugh, and the shit fit she threw when she caught a whiff of it baking in the oven. Maybe that was why she freaked out – not because she fears gluten or sugar but because the smell reminds her of her dead mother.

'Losing her must have been very hard for you.'

She nods. 'It was.'

Her voice is soft, and I realize this is the most real I've ever seen Natasha: sad, honest, with unwashed hair and no makeup. Until now I have, on some level, regarded her as if she weren't a real human being. She was a diva. A prima donna. A bitch. But standing with her in the kitchen, talking about our dead mothers, I'm grasping, as if for the first time, that there is a person inside that polished shell, an actual person, with emotions and fears and regrets. Maybe she isn't so horrible after all.

'Anyway,' she says, after a long silence, 'I told you I didn't want to talk about this. So let's not.'

'Okay. Sorry.'

'What's next? What do I add to the rhubarb?'

'A cup and a half of sugar, some cornflour, and a vanilla bean.'

I grab the bag of sugar and deposit it next to her on the counter. She picks it up as if it's toxic. 'A cup and a half of *sugar*? God, I can't believe how these people eat. It's a wonder they don't all have diabetes.'

'Everyone deserves dessert once in a while,' I say. 'I'm sure they don't eat like this every night.'

'I wouldn't be so sure.' She measures the sugar into the

bowl and sighs. 'Some days I'm really not sure how much longer I can play the politician's wife.'

My breath shortens. *Then don't*, I think. *Leave*.

She stirs the sugar into the rhubarb and catches my stare as she reaches for the cornflour. 'What?'

I hold my breath for a beat, trying to keep my thoughts from pouring out in a messy gush. 'Nothing,' I finally say, and reach for the flour.

## Chapter 28

Natasha and I have turned a corner. Maybe. At the very least, we've bonded. I still don't fully understand the bizarre arrangement behind her marriage, but we now have something in common – not a favourite designer or matching timepiece, but a deep, emotional connection. We've both lost a mother, an event understood only by others who have experienced the same sort of loss. We can relate to each other now. Our relationship has reached a new level.

Or, at least, that's what I think until she struts into the kitchen an hour before the guests arrive.

'What the hell are you wearing?' she says, a scowl on her face.

I glance down at my outfit, a black sleeveless blouse that I've tucked into a pair of black cigarette pants. 'Clothes?'

'Whatever. I guess it's fine.'

I'm not sure why it wouldn't be. I always wear all black when I cook for a party I'll also attend because black hides any potential stains. And, anyway, black seems to be Natasha's favourite colour. She's even wearing black pants tonight – a pair of pressed sateen culottes – though instead of pairing them with a black or grey shirt, she wears a crisp white blouse, the sleeves rolled up to her elbows. Between the two of us, her outfit seems like more of the problem. That white shirt is begging for a grease stain or spatter of beef *jus*.

'I'm sorry – this is the only outfit I brought, aside from the clothes I'll wear home tomorrow.'

'I said it's fine. I just wish you'd cleared it with me before you packed.'

I still don't understand why my outfit is even remotely problematic, but I decide to let it drop. 'I was just about to put the beef in, if you want to help.'

'I'd rather not mess up my shirt…' she says.

I repeat: and my outfit is the problem?

'That's fine,' I say. 'I can do it.'

I finish tying the beef and slather it in salt and pepper, place it on a bed of rosemary and stick the roasting pan in the oven. Natasha eyes the pan warily.

'You do realize people won't be here for almost an hour,' she says.

'The beef takes a long time to cook – I'm roasting it low and slow. It won't be ready to eat for another two hours.'

'Fine.' She smooths her shirt sleeves. 'I still can't believe I'm serving red meat.'

'It'll be great. I promise.' I smile, trying to revive the

bond we formed earlier. 'If you don't want to eat it, I'm sure you can hide it under the potatoes, since you can't eat those anyway.'

Her expression indicates this is the most unwelcome advice she has ever received. 'Do you honestly think I need your advice on how to handle a dinner plate?'

'No, I was just trying... I just thought...'

'You thought what? That I needed diet help from a twenty-something cookbook writer?'

'It wasn't diet help. I was just trying to be... friendly, I guess.'

'Friendly?' Natasha sneers. 'I hate to break it to you, but we're not friends. You work for me. Remember?'

'Right, but I figured that after you told me about your mom, and I told you about my mom...'

'What? That because both our moms are dead we'd somehow become BFF?'

'No. I thought...' What did I think? That she'd finally treat me with respect? 'I don't know,' I say. 'I guess I thought we'd reached an understanding.'

'Sorry to disappoint you.'

And for a lot of reasons I don't even fully understand, all I can think is, *Me too*.

From the moment the guests arrive, the house bustles with activity. Natasha and Hugh greet them and introduce me as 'the woman helping with Natasha's cookbook', though I do notice that Hugh uses 'woman' and Natasha tends to favour 'girl'. They make it sound as if Natasha has been slaving away, page after page, and I am merely the assistant helping with odds and ends, even though the opposite is true. But tonight that doesn't matter. Tonight, I am whatever Natasha needs me to be.

I help Natasha shuttle light hors d'oeuvres back and forth from the kitchen, while Hugh works the room, chatting with various members of his constituency. Natasha wasn't entirely wrong about the haircuts. One sixty-something woman sports a spiky brown coif, which she appears to have highlighted with tiger stripes of red and platinum blonde, and there is a man wearing what is surely the most unnatural toupee on planet Earth. But considering I grew up in the eighties and nineties in a small Midwestern town, all of these styles are well within my comfort zone, and frankly, I feel much more at home here than I did among Natasha's 'fabulous' friends in London.

While the beef rests on the counter, covered with a tent of aluminium foil, Natasha dons a grey-and-white striped apron from one of the cupboards.

'All right,' she says, rubbing her hands together. 'Where are the potatoes?'

'Still in the oven.' I point to the large white bowl at the far end of the counter. 'I was about to dump them in there, if you want to take them out.'

I half expect her to balk, but ever since the guests arrived, she has been all business – serving hors d'oeuvres, taking drink orders, shaking hands. When we get back into the kitchen, I'm the one doing most of the work, but she puts on a good face in public. I suppose that's part of her job – she *is* an actress, after all. I'm starting to understand how she makes her marriage look so convincing.

'I'll take them out, but maybe you can scoop them into the bowl,' she says. 'I don't want to get too messy.'

She grabs a pair of potholders and pulls the pan from the oven. I scrape the crispy, rosemary-scented potatoes into the bowl and sneak a taste of one for quality control. They've come out perfectly: golden brown and crusty on the outside, soft and creamy on the inside, with enough salt, garlic and rosemary to make the flavour pop.

'They're going to love these,' I say.

'They'd better. Although who knows with this crowd? Did you see that one woman's top? Nineteen eighty-three called. It wants its shirt back.'

I'm not exactly sure which top she is referring to, though my guess is it's the blue bow-tie-neck blouse with small white polka dots, which looks as if it could have come out of Margaret Thatcher's closet. My mom had one of those when I was growing up – a hunter green one by Liz Claiborne that she called her 'fancy shirt'. She often wore it at Christmas, tucked into a tan A-line skirt, and perhaps for that reason, I actually smiled when the woman walked through the door. It's strange the things that remind me of my mother and where they appear. I never would have expected to find comfort in a fifty-five-year-old woman from Nottingham, but seeing her made me feel unexpectedly at home.

Natasha and I cart out the bowls of potatoes and green beans to the dining-room table, and once everyone takes their seats, including me, Natasha appears in the doorway, the platter of roasted beef resting on her arms.

'Dinner is served,' she announces.

She parades into the room and lays the beef in front of Hugh, the apron still tied around her neck and waist.

'I figured I'd leave you with the honour of carving,' she says.

'Ah. Right.' Hugh claps his hands together. 'Where's the knife?'

I reach for a large carving knife on the table and hand it to him. We lock eyes for a brief moment. 'Thank you,' he says.

I tear my eyes away. 'You're welcome.'

Hugh carves the beef to the *ooohs* and *aaahs* of the crowd, and everyone passes along their plates, before digging into the beans and potatoes. Then Hugh raises his glass.

'A toast – to all of you, for everything you do to keep this town the lovely, vibrant place it is. Cheers.'

Everyone clinks glasses, then dives into the meal. My knife glides through the slice of beef without resistance, like cutting through a softened stick of butter.

'Natasha, you really have outdone yourself,' says the woman in the Thatcheresque top. 'This beef is absolutely *gorgeous*.'

Natasha doesn't respond at first, as if she hasn't heard, but then she snaps to attention and smiles. 'Thank you. I'm so glad you like it.'

'It really is brilliant,' Hugh says. His eyes shift to me. 'You'll have to make sure you include this one in the book.'

'Yes! Tell us more about the cookbook,' says the man with the horrendous toupee. 'When can we buy our copy?'

Natasha cuts her beef into minuscule pieces. 'Probably about a year from now, maybe sooner. It depends on how quickly I finish testing the recipes.'

'And now – Kelly, was it? Kelly, what exactly is your role?'

I open my mouth to speak, but Natasha cuts me off. 'She brings a method to my cooking madness,' she says.

'And what, exactly, does that entail?' he asks.

I try to jump in, but once again Natasha speaks before I can utter a word. 'Oh, you know...Following me around in the kitchen, writing down what I do, trying to take my improvisational style and turn it into something people can do at home.'

'Do you know each other from America?'

'Oh, God, no.' She clears her throat, then flashes a smile, bringing herself back into character. 'Sorry – no, I got her name through an American chef I know. She worked on his book.'

'And how does one get into that line of work?' he wonders, finally asking a question Natasha can't answer for me.

'It's kind of a long story,' I say, 'but I got interested in cooking when I was a teenager, and I always loved writing, so when I had a chance to help with a cookbook after college, all the pieces sort of fell into place.'

'Did you go to a catering college?' the woman with the tiger-striped hair asks.

'No, sadly not. All of my training has been on the job. I've worked in kitchens ever since I was a kid, though – washing dishes, working the sandwich line – so I have a decent amount of experience.'

'Ah, yes, washing up,' the man with the toupee says. 'That was my first job, too, many, many years ago. I worked at the local pub and made a tenner a week.'

'Did you, Nigel?' Hugh says. 'I never knew that.'

'Hard work, isn't it, dear?' Nigel says.

'Let's just say I was glad when I got promoted to the deep-fryer – although that was significantly messier.'

He laughs. 'I once worked at a chip shop. Smelt like the place for days, even after showering.'

'Right? No matter how much I showered, I always smelt like someone had fried *me*.'

'Was your job also at a chip shop, then?'

'No, it was at a place called Abe's Coney Island.'

'Coney Island in New York? I think my son-in-law went there once.'

'No, this is a chain of restaurants called "Coney Islands". They're basically big American diners that serve everything you can imagine.'

'Natasha, have you been to one of these Coney Islands?'

She looks up, as if she hasn't been listening. 'Sorry?'

'A Coney Island – have you eaten at one?'

She pushes the meat around her plate. 'No...I don't think so...'

'It's very much a Michigan thing,' I say, trying to save her. 'Especially in and around Detroit.'

'Are you from Detroit?' a spectacled gentleman asks. 'I've read some terrible stories in the paper about what's happening there.'

'I'm from a small town about forty minutes west,' I say. 'But yes, what's happening in Detroit is heartbreaking. The entire city has basically collapsed. There are a lot of reasons why, but what's saddest, to me at least, is that I can't imagine the city bouncing back in my lifetime. It was badly managed for so long.' I look up at Hugh as I cut into my beef. 'Now, perhaps if they had *Mr Ballantine* to lead the way, they would be on stronger footing…'

The table erupts in laughter, with the exception of Natasha, who looks startled, as if the laughter has jolted her out of a daydream.

'It's quite scary, though,' says Nigel. 'If it could happen to a city like Detroit, it could happen anywhere. It wasn't long ago that entire cities in this country were decimated after the coal mine closures in the eighties. That's why we need sensible policies, locally and nationally.'

'Indeed,' Hugh says, 'and that's why I feel so very strongly that this education bill will put our city – and all English cities, for that matter – at a serious disadvantage in the future.'

The woman with tiger-striped hair blots the corners of her mouth. 'But is it wise to challenge the prime minister on his signature piece of legislation? Surely, as a party, we're setting ourselves up for failure.'

'In actual fact, I believe challenging him on it is the only way for us to succeed,' Hugh says.

He goes on to explain his strategy for blocking the prime minister's bill and for leading his party to victory in next year's election. As he speaks, the entire table is quiet, every pair of eyes fixed on Hugh as he speaks with enthusiasm and passion about his visions for the future – both for his constituency in Nottingham and for the entire United Kingdom. The more he speaks, the faster my heart beats. Aside from being charming and absurdly handsome, he is the kind of person who could change the world – who wants to, who seems to have been designed for that very task. How could I not fall for someone like that? How could I possibly look away?

When he has spoken for a good five minutes without interruption, he stops himself abruptly and smiles. 'And now I'll stop talking because I fear I'm boring my wife and Kelly to tears.'

'No, no!' I blurt out, before I can stop myself. I cover my mouth when I catch Natasha's unfriendly expression, confirming that I have, indeed, spoken out of turn.

Hugh laughs, defusing the tension. 'No, no?'

'I'm sorry – I didn't mean…All I meant was, I wasn't bored to tears. I don't know anything about British politics, but what you were saying…it was inspiring.'

Nigel guffaws. 'A British politician inspiring an American? I say, Ballantine, perhaps you really are the young hope for the party.'

There is a collective chuckle around the table, and Hugh smiles. 'Dearest Nigel, thank you for calling me young.' He raises his glass. 'That, my friend, is something I can drink to.'

Everyone clinks glasses, and then the hum of conversation returns as the guests break off in smaller groups around the table. Hugh catches my stare for the briefest of moments, and as our eyes meet, I pray Natasha can't see my blush or, even worse, that I am, against my better judgement, falling in love with her husband.

# Chapter 29

In love? How can I be falling in love? With Sam, it took three months of exclusive dating before we exchanged I-love-yous, and even then it was another month before I really felt as if I meant it. I've known Hugh for barely two months. But in that brief time I've felt something click between us, like two jigsaw pieces snapping into place. I'd always assumed love was complicated and layered – like my relationship with my parents or Sam – but maybe I was wrong. Maybe love is as simple as an arrow through the heart.

Once Natasha has served the rhubarb crumble and there isn't a speck left in the dish, or on anyone's plate, she and I clear the table with the help of a few of the guests.

'Ms Spencer, that crumble was divine,' says the woman in the Thatcheresque top. 'It's lovely to meet someone as beautiful and talented as you who can actually *cook*.'

'Thank you,' Natasha says, accepting a compliment about my cooking without hesitation.

'I can't wait to buy a copy of your book when it comes out.'

'You'll only have to wait about a year, assuming we don't run into any more unnecessary *delays*.' She lets the word linger, as if any of the delays so far have been my fault. She reaches for the dessert plates the woman is carrying. 'Here, I'll take those.' She passes them to me. 'I think Hugh, Nigel and Malcolm were going to talk shop over some Scotch. You should join them.'

'Oh, no, I'm afraid I must go. But thank you very much for having me.' She grabs Natasha's hand and squeezes it. 'I am truly such a fan of your work.'

'Thank you,' Natasha says.

'And lovely to meet you, Kelly. I hope you enjoy your time in England.'

Natasha escorts her to the front door, and soon the others follow, until the only people left are Hugh, the toupeed Nigel and the spectacled Malcolm, who chat in the drawing room while they sip their Scotch.

'I'm really sorry about earlier,' I say, when Natasha comes back into the kitchen.

'When?'

'At the table. When Hugh – Mr Ballantine – was talking politics. I didn't mean to speak out of turn.'

She waves me off. 'Oh, that. Don't even worry about it. At least one of us was paying attention. My mind was elsewhere.'

'Well…good,' I say. Then I quickly add, 'That I didn't speak out of turn. Not that your mind was elsewhere.'

She stares at me for a beat. 'You're weird, you know that?'

'Yes, actually, I do.'

She rinses her hands in the sink. 'Anyway, my agent called right before we sat down to dinner, and I need to leave for Paris *again* tonight for this lame promotional thing, so I basically spent dinner going through my mental checklist. Poppy usually takes care of packing everything but since she isn't here…'

I glance at the clock. 'You're flying to Paris tonight? It's almost ten. And Heathrow is more than two hours away.'

'Oh, I'm flying privately,' she says. 'The company behind my perfume needs me there for a Sunday breakfast event, so they're flying me from the Nottingham airport. Sunil will drive me there in a few minutes.'

'But…where am I supposed to go? I thought I was driving back with you and Sunil tomorrow?'

'Sunil will take you home tomorrow morning.'

'Oh…So…I'm staying here tonight? Alone?'

'Not alone. Hugh will be here. And Olga and Sunil are in the guesthouse.'

'Oh, okay. That's good. At least there will be other people around.'

'Don't worry – this place may be old, but I promise it isn't haunted. There's no reason to be scared.'

'Right,' I say, trying to sound relieved, 'of course not,' even though I am scared, and not of the house.

Within minutes, Natasha has dashed upstairs, grabbed her bags, and rushed out the door to meet Sunil, who was already waiting with the car running. Olga joins me in the kitchen to finish scrubbing the pots and pans and load the dishwasher.

'The dinner, it was good?' she asks.

'It was *great*,' Hugh says, appearing in the doorway, a nearly empty glass of Scotch in his hand. 'Kelly and Natasha really outdid themselves.' He smiles. 'Mostly Kelly, I'm guessing.'

'Natasha helped make the crumble. And she trimmed some of the green beans and peeled a few potatoes. She has excellent knife skills.'

'I'll have to compliment her when I see her. I hear she's off to Paris again?'

I nod. 'I didn't realize there was an airport in Nottingham.'

'It's very small – mainly for private planes. Not that I've had the chance to fly on one myself.'

'That makes two of us.'

He smiles again, then shifts his gaze to Olga. 'Olga, you've done quite enough this evening. Please, allow me to take over.'

He rests his glass on the counter and takes the tea towel from her hands.

'Please,' she says, resisting, 'is my pleasure to help.'

'Nonsense. You do plenty to help at home. You deserve a break. You, too, Kelly. Go and put your feet up. Relax.'

'I still have to pack up the leftover cheese and oatcakes,' I say.

'I'm quite confident I can do that myself. I'm not as incompetent as I look.'

'Okay…If you're sure.'

'Absolutely.'

I wipe my hands on a tea towel, then follow Olga out

of the kitchen and down the hallway. She and Sunil are staying in the small guesthouse next door, but since it has only two bedrooms, I am in a small room in the main house, down the hall from Hugh and Natasha's separate bedrooms. I close the door behind Olga, then head up to my room, which is tucked in the far corner of the house on the second floor, just above the kitchen. I kick off my shoes and plop down on the bed, a narrow twin covered with a blue-and-white patchwork quilt. I lean my head against the white metal headboard and take a deep breath as I close my eyes, letting the sounds of Hugh rattling around in the kitchen wash over me. I try not to think about him, try not to picture his face or wonder what he's doing down there, but I can't help myself. Hearing him speak tonight ignited something inside me, and the more I try to extinguish it, the hotter it burns.

The kitchen suddenly goes quiet, and a few moments later there is a knock on my door.

'Kelly? Are you awake?'

I bolt upright and swing my legs over the bed. 'Yes – come in.'

He opens the door and pokes his head through the crack. 'Sorry – I saw the light was on.'

'That's okay. What's up?'

'I just wanted to thank you again for tonight. Despite what you say, I know it was mostly your doing, and I really appreciate it.'

'My pleasure.'

'And I also wanted to thank you for...well, being so lovely at dinner. I haven't seen Nigel that engaged in quite a while. And Malcolm was very interested in what you had to say about Detroit and your background. It all went down very well.'

I pretend to tip an imaginary hat. 'Happy to be of service.'

He rests his hand on the doorway. 'Listen, I was wondering…would you care for a glass of Scotch? There's only a bit left, and it seems a shame to leave it…'

I wrinkle my nose. 'I'm not a big fan of Scotch. Not really my thing.'

'I could rustle up some port as well. Or perhaps some cream sherry?'

'No, really, I…' I clear my throat. 'I'm fine.'

'It's no trouble. Honestly.' He raises his eyebrows earnestly. 'I'd love the company.'

'I'm sure, but…' I trail off, as I glance down at my feet.

'But what?'

I look up. 'You know what.'

A brief bout of silence passes. 'Yes. I suppose I do,' he says. He rubs his hand up and down the doorframe. 'I'm sorry. Sleep well.'

He turns to go, but before I can stop myself, I call after him. 'Wait!'

He turns back. 'Yes?'

I get up from the bed and walk to the doorway, my heart racing. What am I doing? Have I no sense at all? 'One drink,' I say. 'But then I'm going to bed.'

'Okay. Right. Great.'

I meet his eyes. 'But you should understand, what happened before, between us, in your kitchen, it can't happen again.'

'I know.'

'It just…it can't.'

'I know,' he says again. 'It won't.'

We stare at each other for a long while in silence, and the next thing I know, we are pressed up against each other, kissing wildly and hungrily, as if we're animals, clawing at each other, trying to tear each other apart. I grab at his shirt and untuck it, and he pulls mine over my head in one swift motion, so quick I don't realize he's done it until I feel his hands on my skin. We head clumsily to the bed, tripping over my shoes and overnight bag as articles of clothing fly off one by one: my bra, his belt, my pants, his shoes. A voice in my head tells me to *stop*, to *think about the consequences*, but as Hugh runs his hand along my inner thigh, the voice becomes softer and softer, until all I can hear is the creaking of the bed and the sound of his breath in my ear.

## Chapter 30

It happens again. And again. And again. Four times, in fact. After the first time, the guilt lessens, and the resistance falls away. It's not that I think what we're doing is right. But once we'd slept together twice, once this was no longer a 'one-time mistake', the damage had already been done. Is three times really worse than two? Is four worse than three? Is there something more wrong than wrong?

The next morning I open my eyes just before sunrise, my legs knotted with Hugh's as we lie together in the narrow twin bed. The mechanics of this arrangement are much more romantic in theory than in practice, especially considering I haven't shared a twin bed with anyone since college, and even then it was never comfortable.

'Good morning,' he says, smiling as he wipes the sleep from his eyes. I am suddenly very aware that this is the first time he has seen Morning Kelly, who is probably five thousand times less attractive than Morning Natasha.

'Good morning,' I say, arching my shoulders as I attempt to crack my back. 'What time is it?'

'Not quite five.'

'Jeez, the sun rises early here.'

'That's because it's summer. You should see what it's like around Christmas. The sun doesn't come up until after eight, and it sets around three thirty. The joys of a northern latitude.'

'And I thought Michigan had it bad...'

'So tell me more about growing up in...Where did you say it was? Gypsy something?'

'Not gypsy – Ypsi. Short for Ypsilanti.'

'Right. What's it like there?'

'It's a small working-class town. A lot of college kids, thanks to Eastern.'

'Eastern?'

'Eastern Michigan University.'

'Ah. Different from the University of Michigan?'

'Yeah. U of M is next door, in Ann Arbor. That's where I went to college.'

'Yes, I know.'

'You do?'

His cheeks redden. 'After you mentioned your thesis on Lichtenstein, I Googled you to see if I could find a copy.'

'That's kind of creepy.'

'Is it?' He takes a moment to reflect. 'Yes, I suppose, saying it out loud, I do sound like a bit of a stalker. Honestly, I'm not. You just piqued my interest when you mentioned you'd written about the very question I'd always asked about his work.'

I smile. 'It's fine. A little stalking never hurt anyone.'

'I'm fairly certain that isn't true, but I'll take it.' He props himself on his elbow. 'So tell me more about growing up in Ypsilanti.'

'My childhood is not that interesting. Trust me.'

'It involves you, so it's interesting to me.'

'Why?'

'What do you mean, "why"?'

'Why would you be interested in my life story?'

'Well, in case you hadn't noticed, I fancy you quite a bit.'

'Do you?'

He sighs. 'No, I slept with you because I find you repulsive.'

I kick him lightly beneath the covers. 'You don't have to fancy someone to sleep with her. Men sleep with women they don't fancy all the time.'

'I don't.'

'A likely story…'

'It's the truth. You are the first person I've slept with in an embarrassingly long time.'

'Embarrassingly long as in?'

'Years. Several.'

'What about Natasha?'

He flushes. 'We don't sleep together.'

'Any more? Or ever?'

He considers his words carefully. 'Any more. We did when we first met, but things were different then.'

'Different how?'

He sits up and leans against the headboard. 'We were

dating. There was romance. I did, indeed, fancy her – or, at least, the idea of her.'

'And then?'

'And then…At some point the spark died.'

'So you decided, "Hey, you know what? Let's get married."'

'A bit glib when you put it that way. But yes.'

'You realize that makes no sense at all, right?'

'It's easier to understand when you know the full story.'

'Which is?'

He breathes in slowly. 'We dated seriously for about six months, but between her shooting schedule and my spending eighty hours a week at work, we didn't actually see much of each other. We considered calling it off, or I did, but Natasha convinced me we were useful to each other. I make her look sophisticated and worldly, and she raises my profile by being who she is. And, realistically, with our busy schedules, we didn't have time to date anyone else seriously either. So we agreed to stay together to help each other. Marriage was just a more serious extension of that plan.'

'But that's so…'

'Calculating? Abhorrent?'

'Well…yeah.'

'It is. Thinking about it now, I can't believe I agreed to the whole arrangement. But, at the time, Natasha convinced me it was a good idea. She's very persuasive. It's easy to get caught up in the Natasha whirlwind when she's enthusiastic about something. And in terms of my career, she hasn't been wrong. She's definitely been an asset.'

'Yeah, but is that enough to sustain a marriage?'

'No. At least, for me it isn't. When we negotiated the agreement, I wasn't in a place where I was even thinking about children or family or any of that. I was completely focused on my career. But now...' he rubs a palm across his forehead '... now I want a true partner – not a business partner. I want to be with someone I love. I want to start a family.'

'So what are you going to do?' I think back to my conversation with Meg. 'Have you ever...would you ever consider getting divorced?'

He looks at me, and for a moment I think I've gone a step too far. I'm about to clarify that I wasn't asking whether he'd leave her for *me*, only if he'd ever leave her in general, when he nods.

'Yes. I've been thinking about it. Quite a lot over the past year, actually. I used to worry that being divorced would damage my chances of becoming prime minister, but now I'm not even sure I care. And in today's environment, I'm not sure the public would either.'

'You want to become prime minister?'

'Some day. Maybe.'

'In that case, maybe Natasha really could be an asset. She'll be your Carla Bruni.'

'Oh, so now I'm Nicolas Sarkozy?'

'If the shoe fits...'

'Sarkozy is about five foot five. His shoe definitely would not fit.'

'All I'm saying is, maybe being with someone like Natasha could help you get what you want.'

'Being prime minister isn't all I want.' He motions to the space between us. 'I want this. I want someone I can talk to, someone who understands where I came from and what makes me tick. I want to be with a person I can't stop thinking about, who sets me on fire every time she walks into the room.'

'Uh, Natasha is one of the most beautiful people on the planet. If she can't set you on fire, I think you might have a problem.'

'Natasha is beautiful. No question. But I want more than that. I need more than that. I could never talk to her the way I talk to you. She doesn't even know about my mum. Can you believe that? Six years, and I've never told her how worried I am about my own mother.'

'Why not?'

'Because, with Natasha, I never feel like I'm talking to a real person. It's all artifice. The hair extensions, the Botox – even her name is made up. She was born Natasha Horowitz, but she thought that was too "ethnic" so she changed it. It's not that I think she's incapable of understanding about my mum. It's that I don't think she cares enough to bother.' He reaches out and touches my hand. 'The way I feel with you, the way we can talk, it was never like that with her. It's never been like this with anyone.'

My heart races as he leans in and kisses my forehead. 'But enough talk about my dysfunctional marriage,' he says. 'We have a few hours until Olga starts banging around downstairs, and I would like to cook you a proper English breakfast.'

'You, cooking for me?'

'Indeed.' He hops out of bed and throws on his shirt from last night. 'Meet me downstairs in half an hour. You're in for a treat.'

He leans in for one more kiss, and as he turns his back and disappears through the door, I wonder if he finally told me everything I wanted to hear or if I just imagined it.

'Breakfast is served.'

Hugh lays a plate filled with beans, sausages, eggs, mushrooms and tomatoes in front of me, as the pop of the toaster signals the toast is ready. 'White or granary?' he asks.

'Granary. Thanks.'

He grabs the hot toast with two fingers and tosses it onto my plate, then assembles his own, standing at the kitchen counter with his back to me. He has clearly showered and changed since I last saw him, now dressed in khakis and a white polo shirt that has 'Cambridge University Cricket' printed on the back.

'Did you play cricket throughout college?' I ask, as I scoop up a forkful of beans.

He looks over his shoulder and smiles. 'I did. And then for Nottingham for a few years.'

'It's like baseball, right? Except the games last for, like, a week or something.'

He laughs as he licks a bean from his thumb. 'It's quite different from baseball, actually. To my mind, the rules are much simpler.'

He brings his plate to the table and starts explaining cricket to me. None of what he says makes any sense at all. He might as well be speaking Farsi. After he has been talking about *wickets* and *creases* and *overs* for what feels like ten minutes, I hold up my hand. 'I'm going to stop you right there,' I say, 'because I didn't catch any of that.'

'Shall I start again?'

'Please don't. Unless you want my ears to start bleeding.'

He winces. 'You do realize you're talking about one of my favourite sports?'

'Don't say things like that. It makes me question your taste.'

He kicks me jokingly under the table. 'You sound like Natasha.'

My eyes widen, and I kick him back. 'You did *not* just say that.'

'I think I did.'

'Fine. Please – tell me more.'

He laughs as he bites into a piece of toast. 'No, I understand. If you didn't grow up with it, it isn't the easiest sport to take up. But cricket has been a part of my life since … God, as long as I can remember. My dad took me to Trent Bridge when I was maybe six to watch a Test match, and it became a bond between the two of us. We'd go every year. Still do.'

'Did he play cricket, too?'

'With his mates at school, but not seriously. Not like I did.'

'Ah, so you were a *seriously* boring cricketer.'

He grins as he cuts into one of his sausages. 'It paid for most of my education, so I can't complain. I was on the verge of playing for England, actually, but I hurt my knee and had to give up.'

'How did you get into politics, then?'

'My dad's influence again. He took me to a political rally when I was about twelve, and it sparked an interest in politics that stuck with me. It seemed like the most direct way of making a difference.'

'You certainly have a knack for it. Last night at dinner, you were amazing. I can see you leading the country some day.' I poke at a mushroom with my fork.

He smiles softly as he rubs his foot up and down the inside of my leg, but he stops abruptly when we hear the snap and click of the front door opening. Hugh leaps up from his seat as Olga makes her way down the hallway and into the kitchen.

'Olga! You're up bright and early this morning.'

Her eyes wander over his shoulder and land on me. I haven't showered, but thankfully I threw on a pair of jeans and the T-shirt I planned to wear for the drive home.

Hugh catches the direction of her stare and gestures at the stove. 'Fancy a bit of breakfast? Kelly and I are both, apparently, early risers, though it doesn't help that those bloody curtains don't block out any light. But I have plenty of ingredients left. Please, join us.'

She keeps her eyes trained on me. 'No, thank you. I not hungry.'

'Oh, come on,' he says, nudging her playfully in the side. 'Don't make Kelly suffer through one of my boring stories on her own. I'm sure she'd love the company.'

I nod encouragingly, but she shakes her head. 'I clean sheets.'

It suddenly occurs to me that, although my sheets have clearly been slept in, Hugh's bed probably hasn't even been unmade, but before I can start panicking, he jumps in.

'If you insist. But at least allow me to get them for you. You shouldn't have to trundle up those creaky stairs.' He turns to me. 'Kelly, would you mind if I gathered the sheets from your room? I promise not to snoop.'

'Sure,' I say. 'That's fine. I already packed most of my things anyway.'

'Lovely. Back in a tick.'

He dashes down the hall and, as I follow him with my eyes, I feel Olga's stare bearing down on me, wringing the delusion out of me drop by drop, until all that's left is guilt.

# Chapter 31

By the time Olga and I get back to London, it's already after noon, meaning I have less than two hours to make it to the Marylebone Farmers' Market before it closes. Sunil drops me at my door before heading back to the Spencer-Ballantine residence with Olga, who will prepare the house for Natasha's return late this evening. Hugh stayed in Nottingham, where he will deal with some business before heading back to London tomorrow night.

I let myself into my flat and dump my bags next to my couch, then make my way into the kitchen, where I scan my recipe list for the coming week:

- Shrimp tacos
- Asparagus frittata
- Asian poached chicken breasts

- Paleo seed bread
- Motherfucking kale burger

I choose not to address the emotions brought on by the last item because doing so will only amplify them into a seething, uncontrollable rage, so instead I grab the list, my wallet and my shopping bags and head for the farmers' market. Olga will buy most of my ingredients for the week, but I like to shop for myself at the weekend, in the hope of stumbling across a bit of inspiration, especially on a warm and sunny day like today.

The market bustles with activity, the parking lot crammed with colourful tables selling everything from bunches of golden beets and fresh spinach to plump gooseberries and glistening cherries. I take a deep breath and close my eyes, drinking in the summer air as I replay the weekend's events in my mind. A mere eight hours ago I was lying in bed with Hugh, yet somehow it feels as if it happened weeks ago, if it happened at all. That's always the way it is with Hugh. In the moment, everything feels hyperreal, every word and touch laced with electricity. And then suddenly – poof! – I'm back to the daily grind, wondering if I imagined it.

I take another deep breath, picturing Hugh's gentle hands running up and down my thigh, when I feel a tap on my shoulder. 'Kelly?'

I open my eyes and find myself standing face to face with Jess Walters, her fiery red hair tied in a messy bun on top of her head and her pale freckled arms sticking out of a flowing purple sundress. I haven't seen her since we met at the Blind Pig.

'Jess – hi.' I shake myself out of my daydream. 'Sorry, I was somewhere else.'

'Obviously. How are you? I've been meaning to email you about getting together, but my job has been nuts lately.'

'Mine, too.'

'You're still working on Natasha Spencer's cookbook?'

'Slowly but surely.'

'Very cool.' Her eyes wander over my shoulder, and she waves to someone behind me. 'Listen, I have to run, but I've been meaning to ask, what's up with you and Harry?'

'What do you mean?'

'I thought you were supposed to meet up for a date.'

'We were, but I've been running into deadline issues with the cookbook, so I've had to cancel.'

'Several times, from what I hear.'

I flush. 'It's been a busy few weeks.'

'Well, whatever the case, Harry thinks you aren't interested.'

'Really? I haven't been bailing on purpose – honestly. We've just had really bad luck.'

'I'm only the messenger. Maybe you could try calling him again. Unless you really aren't interested.'

'I am. I mean, I think I am.' I flash back to the smile on Hugh's face after he kissed me goodbye this morning.

'Are you seeing someone else?'

'No. Not really…'

She holds up her hands. 'Say no more. I get it. I'll let Harry know you're spoken for.'

'No, I'm not—'

'Gemma!' Jess shouts, and waves to someone over my

shoulder. 'Sorry,' she says to me, 'I have to run. But let's grab a drink soon, okay? There's a fun wine bar near Trafalgar Square I think you'd like. I'll send you the details.'

She gives me a quick hug and scampers off. Another escape plan slips through my fingers.

I buy a loaf of multigrain, some strawberries and a dozen eggs before heading back to my flat. When I get there, I start catching up with the chores I neglected all weekend due to my stay in Nottingham, and in between loads of laundry, I notice an email in my inbox from my brother.

Subject: hey
i have an idea how to get Irene out of the house call me when u get this I don't have ur number.

I ignore the fact that the email contains neither punctuation nor capital letters and focus instead on the fact that (a) Stevie has emailed me, (b) he has done so before noon his time, and (c) he has come up with an idea to evict Irene. Either a ghost has possessed my brother, or miraculous things are happening in my absence.

I grab my phone and dial his number. When he picks up, I have to pull the phone away from my ear as the *thump-thump* of Eminem blasts through the receiver.

'Stevie – Jesus! Turn it down, will you?'

The music fades. 'Sorry,' he says. 'Didn't realize you could hear that.'

'You didn't realize I could hear that? I'm pretty sure people in Belgium heard that. You're going to blow out your eardrums. How can you concentrate when the music is that loud?'

'I'm not trying to concentrate.'

Of course he isn't. 'Right. Anyway. I got your email. What's the plan? How do we get Irene out of there?'

'Hang on a sec.' I hear him get up and shut a door. 'Okay,' he says. 'I'm back. So, here's what I'm thinking. The other day I was watching TV, and *Home Alone* came on, and I was, like, Whoa, I haven't seen that in a while. So I watched it.'

'Okay…'

'And remember the part where Kevin is watching that black-and-white gangster movie? The one where the guy's, like, "Keep the change, ya filthy animal"?'

'Uh-huh…'

'So he uses that later when he orders takeout pizza. He just, like, plays the movie, and the pizza-delivery guy thinks he's some gangster, and it's hilarious.' He laughs to himself.

'Right. But what does that have to do with Irene O'Malley?'

'Well, I was thinking – I have a few recordings of Mom from, like, home videos and stuff. I could string together a few audio recordings, then call Irene in the middle of the night or something and make her think Mom is calling her from beyond the grave, being, like, "Stay away from my husband." And Irene will freak the fuck out and leave.'

A long silence ensues, as Stevie awaits my reply. I'm not exactly sure what to say. Aside from the fact that he is basing his plan around a 1990 John Hughes film that

295

centred on the plight of an eight-year-old boy, the entire scenario seems like an overly elaborate solution to a relatively simple problem, like calling in the fire department to blow out a birthday candle.

'It's...creative, I'll give you that,' I say.

He huffs. 'You hate it.'

'No, no – I just...It seems like a lot of work on your part. All the dubbing and editing. And what if Dad were to answer the phone and not Irene?'

He hesitates. 'I hadn't thought of that.'

'It might really freak him out. He hasn't exactly taken Mom's death easily.'

'True.' He sighs. 'It's the best I could come up with, okay? Sorry it's a dumb plan. I don't know why you expected anything better.'

'It isn't dumb,' I say.

'Yes, it is, and you know it. Everything I do is dumb. I'm Stevie the Dummy. Everyone knows that.'

'I thought you were Steve now, not Stevie.'

'Whatever. Same difference.'

'You're not dumb,' I say.

'Oh, yeah? Were *you* still trying to get your college degree at twenty-five?'

'There's a difference between being unmotivated and dumb.'

'I'm motivated.'

'To do what?'

'I don't know. Live. Eat. Meet chicks.'

I close my eyes. 'That's not the kind of motivation I'm talking about.'

'I know. I'm working on it.'

'Listen, I'm not ruling out your *Home Alone* idea, but maybe we should come up with a few others first, and then we can decide which is the best way to go.'

'Other ideas like what?'

'I don't know. Let's keep thinking and talk next weekend. Okay?'

'I guess. But I'm not making any promises. This might be the best I can come up with.'

'And if it is, well, maybe that's what you do. But I think we should explore all our options before you start creating a poltergeist.'

'Yeah, okay. I guess that makes sense.'

'Maybe if you visited Dad, you'd get some ideas...Have you been since we last spoke?'

'No.'

'Stevie. Come on. What did we talk about?'

He groans. 'All right, all right – I'll stop by later this afternoon. I don't have to be at work until five.' He snickers. 'Maybe I can stick a fake mouse in her bed or something. That'll creep her out.'

'I'm pretty sure Mom never threw out Oreo's toys when he died. There's a toy mouse somewhere in that house.'

'Wait – so you're cool with me actually doing that?'

'Let's just say if a toy mouse ended up in Irene's bed, I would have no problem with that.'

'Sweet. Consider it done.'

We share a mischievous laugh, and once we've said goodbye and ended the call, I lean back in my chair and realize that the two developments currently dominating my time involve having an affair with a married British politician and devising childish pranks to pull on my dead mother's nemesis. And, to whatever extent my mom would enthusiastically endorse the latter and possibly support the former, I can't help but think this somehow represents a disintegration of my moral compass, and I'm not sure what, if anything, I can do to restore it.

## Chapter 32

When I show up at Natasha's house the next morning, I run into Poppy, who arrives at the gate at the same time as me, dressed in a sleeveless azure sundress.

'Poppy! Long time no see.'

She offers a polite but stiff smile, then nods at one of Natasha's security guards as she punches the access code into the front gate, which opens into the driveway. 'It has, indeed, been a while.'

'Admit it, Poppy, you missed me.' I wait for her to agree. 'Well, I've missed you,' I say, when she doesn't respond. I'm not sure which I find more shocking: that I say this, or that I also mean it.

'Have you?' She eyes me warily, her words more like a statement than a question.

'I have. How have you been?'

'Busy beyond belief. Between all of these trips to Paris

and the early publicity for the cookbook, everything has been complete madness.'

She heads for the front door, and I follow her hesitantly, knowing I should probably use the servants' entrance but figuring if Poppy is using the front door maybe I can too, at least for today. I still don't fully understand Natasha's underling hierarchy.

'Did you go with her to Paris Saturday night?'

'No. As you know, she left me in London, so it was impossible for me to get to Nottingham airport in time, and it was too late to book me on commercial.'

Her voice is tart. She clearly does not appreciate having been left out of the weekend's events.

'At least you had a weekend off, right?'

She hurries up the front steps. 'I suppose.'

I follow her into the house and make my way to the stairway leading to the lower floor. 'I assume Natasha is back, then?'

'She is. But she's with her trainer now, and then she has an appointment with her acupuncturist, after which her publicist must brief her on her upcoming interview with British *Vogue*. Speaking of which…' She pulls her phone from her purse and begins scrolling through her inbox. 'The journalist writing the piece wanted a sneak peek of the cookbook manuscript. Natasha, of course, will have the final say over what recipes he sees, but could you pull together what you have so far and give it to her to read?'

'Oh. Sure. Although, as you know, we're a little… behind.'

'Yes, I know. I've been emailing her editor.' She continues scrolling through her email.

'Okay. As long as Natasha is cool with sending the journalist something very rough.'

'Natasha will have the final word on that. But assuming the recipes you send are well tested, I don't see a problem.'

'Great.' I grab hold of the banister. 'By the way, is Olga downstairs?'

She looks up from her phone. 'I have no idea. I arrived with you.'

'Right. Sorry. I guess I'm used to you knowing the ins and outs of everything that goes on in this house.'

'Well, I do. Normally. All of the major things, anyway.'

She looks back down at her phone and begins typing rapidly, and I have to bite my tongue to stop myself saying, *Except the most major thing of all.*


'I not find poblano peppers,' Olga says, as soon as I walk into the kitchen.

I drop my bag on one of the kitchen chairs and head for the sink to wash my hands. 'That's okay. I can work on something else this morning. I sometimes forget certain ingredients are easier to find in America.'

She heads for the door. 'Everything else is in refrigerator and cupboard.'

'Thank you,' I call after her. She nods without turning. I notice she hasn't made eye contact with me since we returned from Nottingham.

Once she's out of sight, I scan the pantry and refrigerator and decide to start on the asparagus frittata, since that's something fairly quick and easy I can make and cross off my list. I also didn't eat much breakfast this morning, so I'd kill for some eggs.

To make the dish a little more interesting, I decide to roast the asparagus, giving it a nice char in the oven while I whisk together the eggs and slice and wash the leeks. As I measure the oil into a frying pan, I glance over my shoulder and see Natasha walk into the kitchen, dressed in black Spandex workout clothes and dripping sweat.

'Natasha – hi. I didn't think I'd see you this morning.'

'You won't. Pretend I'm not here.'

'Oh. Okay. Sorry. I won't say another word.'

'You've already said eight too many.'

I turn around, my jaw clenched, and toss the leeks into the pan of hot oil, pushing them around with a wooden spoon. Natasha scoots behind me and gets out her juicer, along with a bunch of vegetables from the fridge, including the knob of ginger I planned to use later when testing a recipe for Asian poached chicken.

Given her frosty directive, I am hesitant to say anything, but as she dumps the produce on the counter, I decide I need to speak up. 'The ginger … I actually need that today.'

'Sorry?'

'For the chicken. I need ginger for the poaching liquid.'

She stares at me coolly, then flicks on the juicer, its noisy drone filling the room. 'Then tell Olga she needs to buy more.'

She pushes the entire knob through the juicer, followed by a beet, an apple and a carrot. She gulps down the glass of burgundy juice, her eyes fixed on mine, as if she is daring me to say something, daring me to cross her. But what would I say? And what would be the point? She knows what she did was rude, and she doesn't care.

She finishes the last of the juice and pushes the dirty glass in my direction. 'Make sure you put this in the dishwasher.'

Then she leaves, and I wonder what it says about Hugh that he could fake a marriage to this woman for five minutes, much less five years.

Later, as I sink my fork into the fluffy frittata, which is studded with leeks, roasted asparagus and fluffy blobs of ricotta, Poppy storms into the kitchen as she taps on her phone.

'An update,' she says, without looking up or saying hello.

'On?'

'The *Vogue* article. The writer wants to cook a few of the dishes with Natasha, here, in her kitchen.'

'When?'

'Her publicist is trying to set a date. The writer would like to come some time in July. Obviously the article will come out much later, close to the launch.'

'Tomorrow is July first...'

'Yes, I am aware. I think they're aiming for later in the month. I'll co-ordinate with Natasha, but the two of you will need to decide what dishes they'll cook together, and you'll need to run through them with Natasha.'

'Does she want my help on the actual day?'

She looks up from her phone. 'She hasn't said. But I doubt she'll want you here during the interview. Before, yes, but not while he's here. It looks bad if she needs someone holding her hand the whole time.'

'What about you?'

'Well, of course I'll be here. She'd be lost without me.'

303

Given that Natasha survived both Nottingham and Paris without Poppy, I don't think that's entirely true, but I'm learning that Poppy's entire self-image and self-worth are defined by her importance to Natasha.

'Just let me know what Natasha needs,' I say. 'I'm happy to help.'

'Good,' she says. 'Oh, and I chatted to Mr Ballantine earlier today. He wanted me to relay a message.'

Her words cut through the air, which still smells of caramelized leeks. 'Oh?'

'Yes, something about one of your kitchen utensils. He said, "Tell Kelly she left one of her implements behind."'

'Did I?'

Instinctively I reach up for my earlobe to make sure I haven't lost an earring, even though I know I put on the pair I'm wearing this morning and, as far as I know, am not missing one.

'Apparently,' she says.

'But I don't remember leaving anything behind.'

'I suppose that's why you forgot it.'

'I guess…'

'Anyway, he said he has it and will bring it with him when he returns to London.'

'And when will that be?'

'Later this evening.'

I run my fingers along the edge of the counter. 'Did he want me to meet him?'

Her brow furrows. 'Why would he want you to meet him?'

'I don't know. So that he could give it to me in person.'

'And why would he want to do that?'

Because this message might be some sort of code? Because he might want to see me again? Because I really want to see him?

'I don't know,' I repeat.

'I imagine he'll leave it for you on the counter. He's very busy. And, anyway, it's not as if returning the likes of a spatula requires a formal meeting.'

'A spatula?'

She sighs. 'Whatever it was. He didn't say.' She glances down at her phone. 'Ah. It looks as if Natasha has appointments for the rest of the day. She won't be able to sit down with you to discuss the book until tomorrow at eleven.'

'That should be fine.'

'As I'm sure you're learning, with Natasha "should" is not an option. We'll see you then.'

She turns and flounces out of the room, and I'm left wondering what I could have left with Hugh in Nottingham, other than my heart.

## Chapter 33

I stay as late as I can that day, stretching out the recipe testing as long as possible in the hope I might run into Hugh. But when Olga meets me in the kitchen at nearly six and asks if I'm ready to walk to the tube with her, I can't think up a decent excuse that won't make her more suspicious of me than she already is. So, grudgingly, I pack up my bag and walk with her toward the station, my mind awash with questions about Hugh's cryptic message.

Desperate for answers, I decide I'll show up a half-hour early the next day so that I can run into Hugh before he leaves for the day. But when I arrive that morning, I find he has already gone to work and, perplexingly, has left neither an 'implement' nor a message on the kitchen counter. The only thing waiting for me is a knob of ginger, supplied by Olga, with the message 'For Miss Kelly'.

I spend the morning refining the frittata recipe, which I

plan to offer to Natasha when we meet at eleven to discuss her book and the *Vogue* interview. As usual, she is late, and when she finally arrives, she is on the phone.

'Fine. Send the Lanvin and the Versace. But just so you know, that Prada dress was a fucking joke.' She hangs up and plops down in a chair across from me. 'Yeah, because I want to look like a fucking ballerina on acid.'

'Sorry?'

She looks up, as if she is noticing for the first time that I'm sitting across from her. 'Nothing. Stylist issues.'

'Ah.'

'Anyway, I hear Poppy briefed you on the *Vogue* interview.'

'She said you're looking at some time later this month?'

'She and my publicist are dealing with the details, but yes. I think we're looking at some time around July the fifteenth.'

'So…two weeks from now.'

'Like I said, I'm not the one working out the details.'

'Assuming it ends up being the fifteenth, we have two weeks to practise a few recipes together so that you're comfortable cooking on your own.'

She shrinks back defensively. 'I *am* comfortable cooking on my own.'

'Of course you are. All I meant was, I've been the one developing and testing a lot of these recipes, so I should probably get you up to speed on what I've been doing.'

She tosses her hair over her shoulder. 'Well, yes. That would be helpful.'

'Here's what I've written up so far.'

I push a stack of paper across the table and take her

through all of the recipes I have developed over the past two months. She has, of course, tasted all of these dishes, but the last few weeks have been such a whirlwind that it's helpful to have everything spelled out in an organized list, even for me.

Once we have gone through the manuscript-in-progress, I look down again at the list of completed recipes.

'So in terms of dishes you'll cook with the *Vogue* writer, I was thinking your Cornish hens should be at the top of the list.'

She groans. 'I feel like I make those all the time.'

Considering the last time she made them for Hugh was five years ago, I don't see how that could possibly be the case, but whatever.

'That's the reason you should make them,' I say. 'You're comfortable with the recipe. You could probably make it blindfolded. That's good. You don't want this guy writing some sort of hit piece about how you don't know what you're doing, right?'

'No. Definitely not.'

'Exactly. So why don't you make that recipe, and then maybe your grandmother's chocolate mousse? Or maybe the sweet potato fries. Those came out really well.'

She twirls her wedding ring around her finger. 'What about the kale burgers?'

'No,' I say, probably more quickly than I should.

'No?'

'The recipe isn't ready.'

'You have two weeks.'

'I'm not sure that's enough time.'

'Why not?'

Oh, I don't know, maybe because I've been testing kale burgers for more than a month and still haven't made one you like?

'It's a tricky recipe to get right,' I say. 'And, anyway, I realize this is your publicist's domain, but do you really want to cook a recipe that makes you seem like a health nut?'

'Excuse me?'

'I'm not calling you a health nut. I'm saying a recipe like kale burgers might make you *seem* a certain way, and I'm not sure that's the image you're trying to convey.'

She taps her fingers against the counter. 'I see what you're saying. Fine. Let's do the sweet potato fries. Those were good.'

'Perfect. I'll let Poppy know. And if these recipes and headnotes look okay to you, I'll touch base with your editor and pass them along for the journalist to see.'

'Great. Do it.' She gets up from her seat as if she's about to leave.

'Wait – before you go, when do you want to go over the recipes together? I know you know how to make the Cornish hens, but maybe we could do a test run, along with the sweet potato fries.'

'Co-ordinate with Poppy. But I leave Thursday for LA, and I won't be back until Tuesday, so it'll have to be next week.'

'Oh. Wow. So that gives us less than a week to practise.'

She waves me off. 'Plenty of time.'

'Okay. If you're sure.'

'Of course I'm sure.' She heads for the refrigerator,

where she grabs a pitcher of water filled with lemon slices. 'On a totally different topic,' she says, pouring herself a glass, 'I talked to Hugh last night.'

'Oh?'

She walks over to one of the kitchen drawers and pulls out a set of measuring spoons. 'Are these yours?'

I squint from across the room as I look at them more closely. They are one of the sets of measuring spoons I brought from the States.

'Oh, yes,' I say. 'They are.'

'Hugh found them in the Nottingham dishwasher and assumed they weren't ours.' She saunters over to the table as she sips her water and dumps them in front of me. 'Good catch, huh?'

'Thank you,' I say.

'Don't thank me. Thank Hugh.'

'You'll have to do it for me.'

I scoop up the spoons, and as I tuck them into my bag, I try to act something other than disappointed, even though that's exactly how I feel.

In the two days before Natasha leaves for LA, I manage to finalize the recipes for the asparagus frittata and Asian poached chicken, and I come very close to nailing the Paleo seed bread, which makes Natasha very happy. I will never be someone who gives up wheat or grains (give me gluten or give me death), but I'm surprised at how delicious the nut-and-seed-based bread is and how much of that is down to Natasha's guidance. Unlike most of the recipes, she had a lot of specific instructions with this one ('Almonds and hazelnuts, coconut oil, and a mix of seeds – try sunflower, pumpkin and sesame. Maybe some flax. A little honey as well, but no more than a tablespoon'). I wish she were that prescriptive with her stupid kale burger. When she tries, she can actually be helpful, but most of the time, she doesn't bother.

When I arrive on Thursday morning, Natasha has already left for the airport, but I find a note from her on the counter:

> Kelly –
> Please try to have the seed bread ready for me when I get back. Also, the shrimp tacos and the kale burger (I really don't see why you're having so much trouble with that one). Oh, and if you could prepare a few things for Hugh to have for dinner while I'm gone, that would be great. Try to keep it light. He's looking a little soft.
> N

Looking at the note, the significance of her absence finally sinks in. It's not that I didn't grasp before what her trip meant – that she'd be gone for more than five days, that I'd have Hugh to myself – but I was so busy testing recipes and trying to polish the manuscript that I didn't have much time to dwell on it. I also think part of me didn't want to wallow in the disappointment of his not-so-cryptic message and the cold reality that I might be more emotionally invested in our liaison than he is.

I spend the day finalizing the seed bread and also making a variation with dried sour cherries, which add a lovely sweet-and-sour tang and yield a loaf that would be equally delicious topped with cheese or slathered in fresh jam. Since both loaves will keep for up to a week in the refrigerator, I leave half of each in Natasha's fridge and decide I'll take the rest home with me. In my head, I'm already concocting uses for both: a smoked trout spread for the plain version, and a whipped vanilla-bean ricotta for the one with cherries.

Rather than take another stab at the kale burger, which I know Hugh won't want to eat for dinner, I decide to whip up another frittata, using up the leftover odds and ends in the refrigerator. Even though I've made my fair share of frittatas recently, it's a dish I can make with an endless number of ingredients and, most importantly, can be served hot or at room temperature. And though part of me fantasizes about making something elaborate, like a creamy lobster risotto, and having a steaming bowl of it on the table when he returns, while I sit in a chair wearing nothing but an apron, I know I can't do that. That would be a step too far, an overt act of seduction as opposed to the relative happenstance of what has taken place so far. I'm not sure what basis I have for these arbitrary moral boundaries, but having them in place gives me at least the illusion of virtue.

I leave the frittata on the counter with a note for Hugh ('For dinner – enjoy. Thanks for returning the measuring spoons'), then head out with Olga, who locks the door behind her.

'I come late tomorrow,' she says, as we make our way up Glenloch Road.

'How late?'

She nods. 'Ten. Eleven, maybe. I have doctor's appointment.'

'Okay. What time should I meet you, then?'

'Mmm, noon? Mr Ballantine, he will be at work.'

'Noon works. Oh, but were you able to find any jalapeño or poblano peppers?'

'No. But I keep trying. Tomorrow, maybe.'

We go our separate ways, and the next morning I take advantage of the late start time to catch a few extra hours of sleep and grab a relaxing breakfast across the street at Villandry. But when I arrive at Natasha's house at noon and ring the bell beside the gate, Olga isn't there to greet me. Hugh is.

'Hello,' he says, as he meets me in the driveway.

'Hi.' I peer at my watch. 'Shouldn't you be at the office?'

'Nope. I took off early because I'm heading back to my constituency this afternoon. And, anyway, it's a slow Friday. There isn't much going on.'

'Where's Olga?'

'Running a bit behind. Apparently she's on a quest for some specific ingredient you've asked her to buy.'

'Oh. Probably the peppers.'

'Peppers?'

'Jalapeños and poblanos. You can find them almost anywhere in the States, but we've had a lot of trouble finding them here.'

'Have you tried Borough Market?'

'No. I've actually never been there.'

His eyes widen. 'You're joking. Surely you, of all people, must know about Borough Market.'

'I've heard of it. I've just never been there.'

'You must. Really, you'll adore it. It's open today. In fact...' he glances down at his watch '... I haven't had any lunch yet. Why don't we go together?'

313

'Right now?'

'Right now. I wasn't planning to leave for a few hours anyway.'

'But what will Olga think? She already seems suspicious of the two of us.'

'Because of the sheets?'

'Not just the sheets. She's made comments.'

'I wouldn't worry about it. Olga may report to Natasha, but she's always had a soft spot for me. She's sort of like a great-aunt. If I told her I was giving you a tour of the market, my guess is she wouldn't give it a second thought.'

'But what if we run into someone? Or someone recognizes you?'

'People rarely recognize me unless I'm with Natasha. Much as I'd like people to be as passionate about politics as they are about celebrity culture, they aren't. To most people, I'm the lanky git on Natasha's arm.'

'If you're sure...'

'I am. And even if someone does recognize me, it's not as if we'll be snogging in the middle of the market. There's nothing wrong with me showing you a bit of British food culture.'

'I guess that's true.'

'Of course it is. Come on – let's write Olga a note telling her we've stepped out and get on our way.'

I follow him into the house and realize I'm not the only one inventing ethical boundaries to suit my needs, and I wonder how many times we can rewrite the rules before they cease to exist.

## Chapter 34

Borough Market is like nothing I've ever seen. I've been to farmers' markets before – in Ann Arbor growing up, in Chicago, here in London, my local market in Marylebone – but Borough Market is like all of the others combined, times a thousand.

As soon as we emerge from the tube and walk through the limestone archway on Borough High Street, we are bombarded by purveyors of everything from fresh vegetables and buttery pastries to goat's milk ice cream and soft, eggy strands of pasta. Hugh lets me wander up and down the aisles, and I stop to watch one vendor stir a three-foot-wide paella pan, offering up piping hot bowls of tender prawns and rice to a throng of hungry customers. The market is vast, occupying three distinct spaces – the Green Market, Three Crown Square and Jubilee Place – and as I zigzag through the maze of stalls, I'm glad Hugh is there to keep me from getting lost.

'This place – I feel like I'm in a fairytale.'

'I thought you'd like it.'

'Like it? I *love* it. I may never leave.'

'Ah, so my plan to get you to stay in London is working…'

I catch his stare but look away, afraid someone might see us, as if anyone around us even cares. 'You have a plan?'

'Not really. I was kidding. Sort of.'

'Ah.' I try not to sound disappointed but, like the measuring spoons, I keep looking for signs that I'm more than just an easy shag – that he cares about me, too.

'I've been thinking about you a lot,' he says, as if on cue. 'Not that I didn't think about you before, but since Nottingham…I don't know. It's been different. More real.'

I scan a table of Turkish pastries. I want to ask how much he thinks about me, if it's even half as much as I think about him. But I can't – partly because I can't get up the courage and partly because I'm not ready to hear the answer.

'I thought you were trying to send me some sort of message with those measuring spoons the other day,' I say.

'I was. Well, sort of.'

'What was it? Because I'm pretty sure I missed it.'

'Just that you'd left something behind. But I also wanted to let you know that I was coming back, and that I'd been thinking about you.'

'Oh.' I try a sample of baklava from a tray resting on top of the table. 'Then why did you give the spoons to Natasha?'

'I didn't. I gave them to Poppy.'

'Natasha said you gave them to her. She said you found them in the dishwasher and figured they were mine.'

'No, that's what I told Poppy.' He rumples his brow. 'Did she not give you the note?'

My stomach curdles. 'What note?'

'The note I left with the spoons.'

I suddenly feel sick. 'There was no note. Natasha reached into the kitchen drawer, pulled them out and gave them to me. That was it.'

He goes pale, then takes a deep breath. 'Oh dear.'

'Why? What was in the note?'

The colour returns to his face, and he waves me off. 'It was nothing, really. Nothing Natasha would care about, anyway. It said something like, "I expect you'll need these. Thank you again for making everything so lovely."'

'And you don't think that might rankle with her?'

'Not really.'

'Come on – after everything that happened with Matthew Rush? He cheated on her with her trainer.'

'That was different.'

'How?'

'Because she was madly in love with him. She's never felt like that about me. Even in the early days, it was strictly lust. And now she has Jacques. Why do you think she's always jetting off to Paris?'

'I thought that was for her new perfume.'

'Which Jacques helped her launch. Convenient, isn't it?'

'If she wouldn't care, then why didn't she give me the note?'

He shrugs. 'Probably because she didn't want you to feel too pleased with yourself. I wouldn't worry. Honestly.'

But as we make our way towards a towering stack of cookies, I'm not sure if he actually means that, or if he's just saying whatever he can to keep me from panicking.

We share a bowl of silky, fragrant paella for lunch, and then we split a pillowy doughnut from one of the bakery stands for dessert. As much as I enjoy the food, I can't help but feel a little nauseous. What if Natasha knows? What happens then?

I find some poblano peppers at a stall that specializes in chillies and Mexican ingredients. In addition to the poblanos, I load up on corn tortillas, dried ancho chillies, chipotles, and a few chilli powders, but when I open my wallet to pay, I only have a five-pound note. Before I can reach for my personal credit card, Hugh stretches over me and hands the vendor a stack of bills.

'I'll do it,' he says. 'Cash is easier.'

'Thanks,' I say, as we stroll down the thoroughfare. 'I should have stopped at the ATM.'

'I hear Natasha set you up with a Barclays account?'

'Just for cookbook-related expenses. But it's been useful. At least one of my bank accounts is flush.'

'What do you mean?'

'I haven't really been...paid since I got here.'

Hugh stops in his tracks. 'What?'

'Nothing. Never mind.'

'Are you saying Larry hasn't paid you yet?'

'There've been some issues with setting up the direct deposit.'

'That's ridiculous,' he says. 'You've been here two months.'

'I know. But I'm the only one who seems at all concerned. Larry's assistant treats me like a massive headache – as if I'm the cause of these problems and not the recipient.'

'Typical.'

'Maybe you could say something to Natasha…'

'That won't help. Larry deals with all of her financials, and when it comes to money she's totally clueless. She'll pay two thousand pounds for a doorstop, then wonder why people have trouble relating to her.'

'She paid two thousand pounds for a doorstop?'

He gives me a sideways glance. 'Yes. Apparently it was handmade.'

'Out of gold?'

'Concrete. She also paid to have it engraved with her initials.'

'No. Stop.'

'I know. It's absurd. Apparently she couldn't use a rubber door wedge like the rest of us. Or, Heaven forbid, a large stone.'

'Wow.' I glance up at him as we walk to the market exit. 'Does she use cashmere toilet paper?'

'Ha! Not yet. Though whenever she goes to LA, she comes back with a new fetish. Last time it was some "biological terrain analysis" nonsense.'

'Biological what?'

'You don't want to know. Trust me.'

As we wind our way past a stand selling sheep's milk cheese, I spot a man with a camera around his neck at the end of the aisle. I can't say for sure, but he reminds me of one of the men I've seen outside Natasha's house. He lifts the camera and adjusts the focus, pointing the lens at Hugh and me.

I tug delicately on Hugh's sleeve. 'I think that man just took a photo of us.'

He looks over his shoulder. 'Who?'

'Him.'

I point down the aisle, but a throng of tourists blocks our view, and by the time they're out of the way, the man has gone.

'He was right there,' I say. 'Right in front of the olive oil stand.'

'Probably just a tourist taking photos of the market.'

'But he looked like one of the paparazzi I've seen in front of your house.'

'Really?' He cranes his neck to see if he can catch a glimpse. Then he shrugs. 'I didn't see anyone. You must have imagined it.'

I search the crowd one last time. 'I guess so,' I say, even though I'm positive I didn't.

A little more than thirty minutes later, we emerge from Belsize Park tube station and head back to the house.

'What time are you leaving for Nottingham?'

'Around three or four.' He looks at his watch. 'You're welcome to come with me, if you like.'

My heart leaps, but I quickly decline the invitation. 'I don't think that's such a good idea.'

'Maybe not.' I feel his eyes on me. 'But it would be fun.'

'Fun or not, how would you explain my presence to

320

your Nottingham friends? Not to mention Sunil and Olga.'

'There's a summer festival going on this weekend. I could be showing you a slice of English culture.'

'Will they be burning effigies?'

'No. Why?'

'I'm kidding. Today is our Independence Day. I figured you don't exactly have the same perspective on the holiday over here.'

'Ah, right – the Fourth of July. Then you really must come with me. You can gloat as you tuck into your clotted-cream fudge.'

I come to an abrupt halt. 'Clotted-cream fudge?'

'And clotted-cream ice cream, if memory serves.'

'A weekend with you I could turn down. But a weekend with clotted cream, now that's intriguing.'

'So I've been outranked by fudge now?'

'Oh, you've always been outranked by fudge. Everyone is outranked by fudge. And clotted-cream fudge…Well, I can only imagine.'

He chuckles as he opens the front gate. 'So what do you say? Will you join me?'

I play out the scenario in my head. 'I want to. Like, a lot. But I just don't think it's a smart move.'

'You don't have to come for the whole weekend. You could take the train up tomorrow and leave whenever you like.' His hand grazes mine. 'It's up to you, but I'd love it if you came.'

The words rattle around my head. *I'd love it if you came.* That isn't the same as wanting me to come, though, is it? He didn't say, *I want you to come to Nottingham* or *I need you to come to Nottingham.* On the other hand, he didn't say, *It would be nice if you came* or, as a guy once said to me in college before I met Sam, *I'll be in my room around eleven, so if you want to come by maybe text me and I might be there.* Compared to the last, Hugh's invitation is basically a marriage proposal.

As I parse every word of Hugh's offer, he moves closer, as if he's about to kiss me, when the front door rattles. He pulls away, and seconds later it opens with a snap.

'Ah, Olga – hello,' Hugh says. He clears his throat. 'Kelly and I are just getting back from a little tour of Borough Market.'

Olga's eyes flit between the two of us. 'Yes. I see her note.'

'It's unreal – I can't believe I hadn't been.' I grip my shopping bags tight to keep my hands from shaking. 'I even managed to find some hot peppers.'

She glances at my bags. 'I have little luck, too. On Edgware Road. Come. I show you.'

We follow her into the house, but as Olga heads downstairs, Hugh grabs my arm and pulls me back.

'So will you come?' he whispers.

'I don't know. Maybe. I'll think about it.'

He looks over my shoulder to make sure Olga is no longer in view, and then he leans down and kisses me, rubbing his thumb along my cheek. 'I'll leave it up to you, but for what it's worth, I really, really want you to join me.'

He gives me another quick kiss, then disappears into the living room, and I tread carefully down the stairs, dizzy as a drunk.

# Chapter 35

I shouldn't go. Definitely, definitely not.

I should stay in London and work on the tacos and the kale burger. I should do laundry and call my father and do all sorts of other chores, alone, in my apartment.

But I don't want to do any of those things. I want to take the train up to Nottingham and spend Saturday afternoon with Hugh. I want to eat clotted-cream fudge and see where he grew up and lie with him in his bed as he tells me more about his years at Cambridge. I want to hear more about his hopes and dreams, about his vision for Britain and for the world, about all of the things that make him tick. And I want to kiss him, and for him to kiss me back, and to pretend Natasha doesn't exist.

Which is why, even though I know I shouldn't, I show up at St Pancras station on Saturday morning and board a train for Nottingham.

Hugh left the address in a drawer in the downstairs bathroom, along with his mobile number and sixty pounds to cover the journey there and back. If it weren't for the fact that we recently discussed my cash problem and Larry's incompetence, I'd feel icky taking his money – like some sort of kept woman. But I do have a cash problem, and Larry is incompetent, so I accept the free ticket, even though I still have doubts about going at all.

The train arrives in Nottingham just before noon, and I take a taxi from the station to Hugh's house, soaking up the bustle of the city as we make our way out of the centre of town. About twenty minutes later, the taxi pulls onto Hugh's crushed-gravel driveway, where I find a white Volkswagen parked at the end.

I pay the driver and sidle up to the front door, suddenly nervous I've made a huge mistake. But as soon as Hugh opens the door and I see his face, I'm glad I came, mistake or not.

'You made it,' he says. 'How was the journey?'

'Fine.'

'Great.' He waves me inside. 'Come in, relax for a bit. Can I get you something to drink?'

'Some water, thanks.' I clasp the strap to my bag as I follow him down the hallway.

He leads me into the kitchen and pours me a glass. He starts to pass it to me across the counter but stops. 'Before I give this to you, have you ever had elderflower cordial?'

'You mean like a cocktail with St Germain?'

'No, no – this is a non-alcoholic drink made with elderflowers.'

'Then no, definitely not.'

'Would you like to try it? I think you'd like it. It's a very English thing to drink in the summer. That, and Pimm's. But it's a bit early for Pimm's.'

'It's afternoon…'

He holds up his hands defensively. 'If you'd like Pimm's, I'm happy to make it.'

'No, elderflower cordial sounds great. I'd love to try it.'

He grabs a bottle of sparkling water from the refrigerator, along with a bottle of elderflower syrup, and mixes them together in two highball glasses, one of which he hands to me. 'Cheers,' he says, clinking his glass against mine.

I take a sip, and the fizzy drink tickles my tongue with its delicate floral flavour. 'Yum,' I say, going for another sip. 'Very refreshing.'

'I thought you might like it.'

I glance down the hallway. 'Is Olga here?'

'No, she stayed in London. I told her I can manage on my own for the weekend.'

'And Sunil?'

'In London as well.'

'Then how did you get here?'

'I drove. Believe it or not, I do know how.'

'So…it's just the two of us?'

'Indeed.' He sets his glass on the counter and makes his way over to where I'm standing, wrapping his arms around my waist. 'Just the two of us.'

He leans in and kisses me, but instead of relaxing into his arms, I stiffen. He pulls away. 'What is it?'

'Nothing. I'm just…nervous, I guess.'

'Why? We're the only ones here.'

'I know…'

'Is it something I've done?'

'No, no – of course not.'

He looks down at his outfit, then sniffs his shirt. 'Do I smell or something?'

I laugh, stand on my toes and kiss him. 'No, you do not smell.'

'Then why are you nervous?'

'Well, first of all, I've thought about having you all to myself for a long time, and now that I do…'

'…you're worried you'll discover I'm not that interesting after all.'

'The opposite, actually – that you'll discover *I'm* not that interesting.'

He kisses my forehead. 'Rest assured, if anyone will fail to meet expectations, it will be me. It's sort of my speciality.'

'Yeah, shadow minister at forty, possibly future prime minister, I'd say you're really slacking.'

He squeezes me. 'Always ready with a witty retort.'

I breathe in his skin, which smells like the sea. 'But that isn't the only reason I'm nervous,' I say, before I can stop myself.

He pulls away again. 'Oh dear. I do smell, don't I?'

'No – I mean, you smell, but you smell great. You smell…' I take a deep breath '. . . perfect.'

'Well, thank you. But then why are you nervous?'

Because we're here alone? Because Natasha doesn't know? Because I'm falling in love with you, and I have no idea if you feel the same way about me?

'Because we're crossing a line,' I say.

'I…think we already have.'

'But this weekend, I came out here. By myself. I took the train. You *paid* for it. Before, everything we did was circumstantial – one thing led to another, there was drinking involved. But now…Now we're actively breaking the rules. We're trying.'

'I understand.' He hesitates, and then he adds, 'And I agree.'

Part of me hoped he'd counter my argument, that he'd somehow convince both of us this weekend was no different than any of the other times. But it is different, and we both know it.

'Maybe I should go back to London,' I say.

'No – please.' He grabs my hands. 'Stay.'

'Why?'

'What do you mean, "why"? Because you're beautiful and brilliant, and I can't stop thinking about you. Because I love being with you. Because you're a total breath of fresh air.'

'But what about Natasha? She's your wife. And my boss.'

'She won't be your boss for ever, or my wife.'

'What do you mean?'

He sighs. 'I've been planning to talk to Natasha when she returns next week. I can't keep doing this. She may be able to keep up a sham marriage while sleeping with someone else on the side, but I can't. I'm sick of this. I'm sick of pretending.'

'Listen, I don't want to be responsible for a messy divorce…'

'You aren't responsible. I mean, yes, meeting you has certainly been a catalyst, but only in the sense that you've motivated me to do what I should have done a long time ago.'

'But shouldn't we press pause until you've actually separated? Or at least until you've spoken to Natasha?'

'I don't want to wait. I'm crazy about you, Kelly. Being with you, I suddenly feel like me again – the way I felt when I played cricket, the way I felt the first time I heard live music. I don't want that to stop, not even for a few days.' He clasps my hands tightly in his. 'Please stay. I want you to stay.'

I drink up his words and fall into him, my body melting against his chest.

'Okay,' I say, 'I'll stay,' as if I've made a choice, even though I'd already made up my mind before I even stepped on the train.

## Chapter 36

The inevitable occurs: on the kitchen floor, a location steamier in theory than in practice, given the cold and uneven nature of the terracotta tiles. With Sam, I always fantasized about having sex in some unconventional place – in the woods or a public bathroom or on a beach somewhere – but he was always too uptight and traditional for that kind of thing, so we never did. 'There's a reason beds were invented,' he'd always say, or 'You do realize sand is an abrasive, right?' But with Hugh, for better or worse, there is no discussion or deliberation. It's all hot, steamy passion, which – given the circumstances – has its downsides.

As I lie on Hugh's chest, breathless, as he rubs his thumb up and down my arm, his phone rings on the counter. He sits up and reaches for it, then groans. 'My father,' he says. He presses ignore. 'I'll call him back later.'

'Is he still having trouble pooping?'

'No, he's moved on to an ingrown toenail. Which, again, I have no qualifications to treat.'

'He still lives around here?'

'He does. I had dinner with him and my mum last night. I'll pop round again tomorrow, although if he tries to show me his toe, I might leave.'

'How is your mom doing?'

He tosses the phone onto the counter and sits next to me, leaning against the cupboards. 'Good. The best I've seen her in a while, actually. She's got serious about her gardening. I think that's helped. It's a good distraction. What about your dad?'

'I haven't talked to him in a while. If I had to guess, he's probably been taken prisoner by my mom's nemesis.'

Hugh laughs. 'What?'

'Long story. Growing up, there was this woman who kind of turned into my mom's rival, and now she's sleeping in my old bedroom while she "helps" my dad with odds and ends around the house.'

'And your mother wouldn't like this, I gather.'

'She'd *hate* it. She left me this list of dying wishes, and right at the top was "Keep Irene O'Malley away from your father."'

He rubs his chin. 'I know a few people from school who are in MI6 now. I'm sure I could arrange something.'

'Thanks. I'll let you know. For now, my brother is coming up with a plan. Assuming he can get his lazy ass off the couch for long enough...'

'Is your brother older or younger?'

'Younger. In every way.'

He rolls his eyes. 'Sounds like my brother.'

'Has yours finished college?'

'He's thirty-seven, so, yes, thank Christ. It certainly took him long enough, though. He sort of faffed about for a decade, trying his hand at a bunch of businesses that never amounted to anything. But a few years ago he met Cleona, and she finally seems to have set him straight.'

'I wish my brother would meet a Cleona.'

'She's great. You might even meet her today – she'll probably be at the fair. Speaking of which...' he looks at the clock '. . . we have forty-five minutes before it starts, but I wanted to show you something first, if you don't mind.'

'Does it involve clotted cream?'

He smiles. 'No. But it's still good – I promise.'

I follow Hugh out of the front door and towards the white Volkswagen in his driveway. He opens the passenger door for me, and within seconds we are zooming back toward the centre of town. He drives along a few fast roads, then crosses a bridge over the River Trent, zipping past a strip of shops until we approach a tall Victorian building made of red brick. A sign hangs just above the ground-floor windows: 'Trent Bridge Inn.'

I eye him warily. 'Are you taking me to a cricket match?'

'Not a match, no. But I wanted to show you the grounds.'

He pulls around a curve in the road, taking us past the inn, and drives beside a white metal fence until he reaches a short driveway. He turns in and stops when he reaches a locked gate. A security guard approaches the car, and Hugh rolls down his window.

'Hello, Charlie,' Hugh says.

'Ah, Mr Ballantine. Here to see Mr Hutchley?'

'Not today, I'm afraid. Just wanted to have a look around.'

The guard hunches over and peers through Hugh's window, laying his eyes on me. 'I see.'

'This is Kelly,' Hugh says. 'She's helping my wife with her cookbook.' He says this as if it were the most natural thing in the world to have me in the car with him, as if any normal man would hang out with his wife's ghostwriter.

'Ah, lovely,' the guard says. 'It's a bit quiet today. You'll have to come back when there's a match on. The England–India Test starts next week. Perhaps Mr and Mrs Ballantine can bring you back then.'

'Perhaps,' I say, trying to seem as natural as Hugh.

'Anyway, enjoy,' he says, as he opens the gate. 'It's a lovely day.'

Hugh puts the car into gear and waves as he pulls into a small parking lot behind a sign for the William Clarke Stand. We make our way around the outside of the grounds toward the pavilion, and once we're inside, Hugh leads me down a hallway that empties outside, where a cluster of seats looks onto an enormous field. The manicured lawn is striped with alternating bands of dark and light green grass, with a few rectangular sandy patches in the middle, and is surrounded by bright white bleachers and a large scoreboard.

'Wow – the playing field is huge,' I say. 'It looks bigger than a baseball field.'

'I think it is. More like an oval than a diamond, though.'

'How many people can come here at once?'

'About seventeen thousand.'

'Really? Wrigley Field can seat, like, forty thousand.'

'The seats don't go very high here. Not nearly as high as a baseball stadium.'

I scan the seats around us, then look back at Hugh. 'Where would you sit with your dad? Here?'

'God, no, we sat far away from the pavilion – usually over there.' He points to the stands across the field. Then he waves at another set of stands with a modernistic over-hang that looks a little like an aeroplane's wing. 'Occasionally for a treat we'd sit over there, but of course it looked much different then. Not nearly as nice.'

I walk closer to the green and breathe in the summer air. 'Would you come for the England–India Test matches?'

He snickers. 'I wish. No, we mostly went to crap matches that were really cheap – the Nottingham reserve team versus the Sussex reserves or something like that. But I didn't care. I still loved it.'

'So what does one eat at a cricket match?'

'The English equivalent to what you'd eat at a baseball game – fish and chips, burgers, pasties, ice cream.' His lips curl to the side. 'You really do have food on the brain con-stantly, don't you?'

'Pretty much.'

'Whose influence is that? Your mum's?'

I snort. 'Hardly.'

'Was her cooking dreadful?'

'Not dreadful. Just…limited. It mostly involved pro-cessed food. Her most famous dish was a spaghetti salad.'

'What's wrong with spaghetti salad? Sounds okay to me.'

'It was. But it wasn't exactly gourmet.'

'What's in it?'

'Let's see...Spaghetti. Ham. Cheese. Miracle Whip.'

'Miracle what?'

'Whip. It's sort of like mayonnaise but not.'

'Sounds a bit like salad cream.'

'The dish also has something in it called "Accent", which is basically straight-up MSG.' I give Hugh a sideways glance to see if he looks appalled. To my surprise, he doesn't. 'Like I said, it isn't gourmet, but it's one of my top comfort foods, probably because it reminds me of my mom.'

'I have a few things like that,' Hugh says. 'My grand-mother used to make the most brilliant bubble and squeak. There's no science to it – it's just leftover mash and veg – but hers always tasted better than everyone else's. Never mind that it was one of the few edible things she could cook. Any time I eat it I think of her.'

'It's funny how food can do that, isn't it? Remind you so strongly of a person? Ironically, I think it must happen more often with people who don't cook much. I cook so many different things all the time that I can't imagine any one dish reminding my kids of me some day.'

'Then all food will remind them of you. Which will be even better.' He scratches his jaw. 'So you want children, then?'

'I do. At least one.'

'One? Oh, no. I want at least three.'

'Three? I don't know...That sounds like a lot of work.'

'Nonsense. It'll be wonderful.'

'If you say so. I'd rather see what one is like and make up my mind then.' I jokingly glance down at my watch.

'You'd better get a move on, sir. You aren't getting any younger.'

He hip-checks me. 'Thanks for reminding me.'

'I'm just saying.'

He gently brushes his fingers against mine. 'You'll make a lovely mother one day.'

'I guess if our moms could do it, anyone can.'

'I mean it. You're thoughtful and kind and self-assured. You have patience and empathy. You're the whole package, really.'

'You're not so bad yourself.'

He smiles and rubs his hands together. 'Right. Shall we head to the fair, then?'

'Sure. Lead the way.'

He turns around and goes back into the pavilion, and as I follow him, I glance over my shoulder and take one more look at the cricket pitch before walking through the exit.

The fair is almost exactly like the ones I've been to in America – rides, games, face painting, music, food – with a few exceptions. For one, there are fewer fried things. The festivals I went to as a kid relied heavily on fried Oreos and corn dogs, both of which my mom ate with relish. I remember going to the Ypsilanti Heritage Festival one summer with her and Stevie when I was seven, and she introduced me to my first Elephant Ear.

'They fry elephants' EARS?' Stevie said in horror.

'No, no – it's just fried dough,' my mom said. 'But it's big and flat and kind of looks like an elephant ear, so that's what they call it.'

335

She ordered three – overkill, given that each was the size of a dinner plate – but we demolished them, scarfing down the pillowy, cinnamon-sugar-topped dough with relish.

'Pretty good, huh?' she said, winking. Then she bought us each a corndog and a Pepsi ('pop', as she called it), followed by funnel cake for Stevie. I knew Stevie had already eaten too much – he was only four – but he kept whining for a funnel cake, and she wanted to play bingo, so she bought it for him anyway. He wolfed it down, then proceeded to barf all over himself, but Mom was one number away from having BINGO and didn't want to leave. So I took Stevie to the bathroom and cleaned him up, and when I got back, she was waiting for us, her hands on her hips.

'All I needed was seventeen. That's all! But damn Irene O'Malley got twenty-six and BINGO!' She groaned. 'Anyway. Everyone ready to go?'

We piled into the back of the Buick station wagon and headed home, Stevie's soiled shirt stinking up the car the whole ride.

The memory of that afternoon floats away as a gentle breeze blows across the Nottingham fairground, the sun beating down on my bare shoulders. I breathe in the fresh summer air as I pass a table covered with all sorts of cakes – Victoria sponge, Madeira, Battenburg, lemon drizzle. Again my mind drifts to my childhood, this time to the Michigan State Fair, which my family would visit at the end of every summer. It had all sorts of contests – pie eating, hog calling, watermelon-seed spitting (Stevie's favourite) – but the cake competition was my favourite challenge of all. Every year I'd eye the confections longingly: the fluffy coconut cakes, the fudgy chocolate towers filled with gooey caramel or silky buttercream, the cinnamon-laced bundts topped with buttery streusel. The competition was divided into adult and youth categories, and when I turned twelve, I decided to enter a recipe for chocolate cupcakes with peanut butter buttercream and peanut brittle.

My mom was a little befuddled by my participation (her idea of baking involved brownie mix and canned icing, preferably in a blinding shade of neon), but she rode along with me, my dad and Stevie as we carted two dozen cupcakes to the fairgrounds in Novi. The competition was steep – pumpkin cupcakes with cream-cheese frosting, German chocolate cupcakes, zucchini cupcakes with lemon buttercream – but my entry outshone them all, and I ended up taking home the blue ribbon, along with a gift certificate to King Arthur Flour.

'Cash would be a little handier, wouldn't it?' my mom said, as I stroked the silky tails of the blue ribbon. Then she bent down and kissed the top of my head. 'Proud of you,' she said, her breath bearing its signature ketonic sweetness. 'You're my superstar. You know that, right?'

Hugh's gentle laugh shakes me out of my daydream, my mom's face evaporating into the air. I spot him across the fairground, chatting with a bunch of locals. He looks so relaxed, so self-assured, his smile taking up his whole face as he shakes their hands. I'm learning that Hugh is comfortable around everyone, or even if he isn't, he certainly makes everyone feel comfortable around him. There is an easiness to his smile, something that takes the edge off, like a glass of good wine. Part of me wonders if I'm just another sucker for his charm, another sycophant who wants a piece of the Hugh Ballantine pie. But when he catches my stare and gives me a subtle wink, I tell myself, *No, I'm different*, because even if I'm not, I have to believe I am. Otherwise, what am I doing?

While Hugh glad-hands with his constituents, I continue strolling around the fair, on a quest for clotted-cream fudge. I find some at a small stand next to the Ferris wheel and, with the little cash I have left, I buy three flavours: traditional, peanut butter, and chocolate. The traditional, I discover, is not traditional American fudge, which would be chocolate, perhaps studded with toasted walnuts. Instead, this version is blond in colour, with a milky, burned-sugar flavour, like a square of caramel, only less sticky and with a soft, velvety texture. It's almost too sweet, but only almost, and part of me wonders how much I could reasonably eat without making myself sick.

Once I've wolfed down the clotted-cream fudge and sampled my fair share of cakes and clotted-cream ice cream, I wander back to the area beside the bouncy castle, where I last saw Hugh chatting to some locals. Despite his assurance that my presence isn't unwelcome or inappropriate, I've kept my distance, but now that we've been here for an hour and a half, I'm running out of distractions that don't involve eating clotted cream. I'm also pretty sure I'm sunburned because my cheeks sting and the back of my neck is suspiciously itchy.

Hugh waves to me as I approach, continuing his conversation with a woman whose back is to me. Her long, strawberry-blonde hair spills down her back, and she wears a gauzy jade sundress that comes to her ankles. I slow my step when I realize I might be interrupting their conversation, but Hugh waves again, nodding for me to join them.

As I get close, the woman spins around, tempering her smile as she gives me a quick once-over.

'Having fun?' Hugh asks, when I finally join them.

'I am,' I say cautiously. 'I think I've eaten pretty much everything here.'

'I'm not sure where you put it,' the woman says, scanning me up and down.

I smile politely, trying to figure out who she is, when Hugh speaks up, as if he has read my mind. 'Forgive me – Kelly, this is Cleona.'

'Oh, Cleona – of course.' My shoulders relax. 'So nice to meet you.'

She slowly shakes my hand. 'And who are you?'

Hugh jumps in. 'This is Kelly, Natasha's ghostwriter.'

'Oh! Right.' Her smile warms. 'Sorry, I hadn't realized Natasha mentioned me.'

I am about to say it was actually Hugh who mentioned her, but before I can speak, Hugh interrupts. 'Cleona and Natasha are friendly,' he says.

'Ah.' Perfect.

'We don't talk every day or anything,' Cleona says, as if she's embarrassed to be friendly with Hugh's wife.

'Maybe not, but she likes you better than anyone else in my family – including me.'

They laugh, and I wonder how much Cleona knows about the terms of their marriage.

'Anyway,' Hugh continues, 'Natasha is in LA for a friend's movie première and some meetings, so Kelly was at a loose end for the weekend – especially since, in her country, it was Independence Day yesterday.'

'Oh, right, of course,' Cleona says. 'So you decided to get pissed with your oppressors?'

'That was the idea, anyway,' Hugh says. 'I told her about the festival, so she took the train up today to get a slice of English culture.'

Cleona offers a mock-frown. 'Oh dear. I hope you haven't been thoroughly traumatized.'

'Not yet. All of the clotted cream is definitely working in your favour.'

Hugh's eyes light up. 'Brilliant – you tried the fudge.'

'And the ice cream. On top of a few cakes. And a pie or two.'

Cleona's eyes widen, and she cranes her neck as she peers behind me. 'Are you carrying an extra stomach somewhere, or do you have a hole in your leg?' Hugh elbows her in the side. 'Well, I mean, honestly. Where does she put it? If I ate that much I'd be mammoth.'

'You would not be mammoth,' Hugh says. 'Henry, on the other hand...'

'Oh, please. Henry has the Ballantine metabolism. Thin as a rail, no matter what.'

'That's not what Natasha says.'

'About Henry?'

'About me,' Hugh says. 'Apparently I'm getting "soft".'

'Perhaps she's talking about your politics. You let the education secretary walk all over you last week. You didn't pin him down on anything. What happened?'

'I was a bit distracted.'

'By what? His hideous tie?'

He laughs. 'Well, yes, there was that...'

'The man is an idiot,' Cleona says. 'We'd all be a lot better off if you were running the department. Don't you think, Kelly?'

I smile politely. 'Yes,' I say. 'I do.'

'See? Even an American thinks you'd be better.'

'Natasha is American,' he says.

'I suppose so. But she's a woman of the world, really. Born in America, living in London, jetting off to Paris and Tokyo, appearing in films around the globe. She sort of belongs to everyone, doesn't she?'

'Or no one,' Hugh says.

Cleona clicks her tongue, then glances at her phone, which trills in her purse with a text message. 'Oh dear. Must go. Apparently Freddie's in tears because they've run out of green balloons. Disaster.'

'Let me know if there's anything I can do to help,' Hugh says.

'Pay for his therapy one day. That'll do.' She leans in and kisses him on the cheek. 'Drop in later. We're having a barbecue – just us and another couple with a two-year-old. Your parents were coming, but apparently your father's having problems with his toe.'

'Oh, God. He's told you about that too?'

'In more detail than I'd care to know. Anyway, come if you can. We'd love to see you.'

'I'll try,' he says. 'I have a bit of other business.'

'I understand. The life of a politician and all that.' She waves in my direction. 'Lovely meeting you, Kelly. I can tell Natasha's in good hands.'

Her phone rings, and she waves goodbye as she picks

up and moves away. When she's out of sight, I fill my lungs with the sweet summer air, thankful I can breathe again.

Hugh does not go to the barbecue at Cleona and Henry's. Instead, after a long day at the fair, he takes me back to his house and cooks me dinner, a simple meal of grilled steak, baked potatoes and red wine.

Over dinner, we talk more about his childhood in Nottingham and my childhood in Ypsilanti, and I tell him about the Elephant Ears and bingo and my award-winning cupcakes. He tells me about his first crush, a girl in primary school named Samantha Humphrey, who wore her blonde hair in braided pigtails that he'd pull to get her attention. We talk about losing our virginity: for him, in a field house by his school's cricket pitch when he was fifteen, with a girl named Lucy Pitts; for me, in Pete Giovanni's twin bed the summer before senior year of high school. We talk about other past relationships – which ones were mistakes, which ones we were too young and foolish to appreciate.

When we've cleaned our plates, I help him clear the table, and as I dump the dirty dishes in the sink, he presses against me from behind, wrapping his arms around my waist. Whatever hesitation I felt before has vanished, and I lean into him, wanting this moment to last for ever, for him to keep holding me and never let go. Everything about this feels like a fantasy, as if it couldn't possibly be real, but as we peel off each other's clothes and stumble upstairs, a trail of shirts and pants in our wake, I decide I don't care if it's real or not. I just don't want it to end.

*

As we lie in his bed, the sweat drying on our skin, Hugh rolls over and grabs a pack of cigarettes and a lighter. He pulls out a cigarette and sticks it into his mouth, but I yank it out before he can light it.

'I thought you were trying to quit.'

'*Trying* being the operative word.'

'Not very hard, apparently.'

'Oh, come on. Just one. There's nothing like a cigarette after a good shag.'

'You're such a cliché.'

'But an endearing one, no?' He goes for another cigarette.

I grab that one, too, along with the entire pack. 'I don't care how endearing you are. Smoking is gross.'

He groans. 'You're no fun.'

'I don't know…You seemed to be having fun a few minutes ago…'

He flicks me in the side.

I dump the smoking paraphernalia on the floor and roll back over to face him. 'You never told me you had a nephew.'

He smiles. 'Freddie. He's three.'

'And apparently obsessed with green balloons.'

'Ha, yes. He does fixate on things. But he's a laugh. I adore him.'

'Do you see him much?'

'Not as often as I'd like. But enough. He calls me Uncle Hughie.'

'Sorry I kept you from seeing him tonight. You should have gone.'

He runs his thumb along my arm. 'I'll see them another

time. Tonight I wanted to be with you. And, hopefully, in the not too distant future, they'll all meet you. I know Freddie would love you. Henry, too.'

'I don't know. I'm no Natasha.'

He kisses my shoulder. 'Exactly.'

He pulls me close, and I nuzzle into him, and then I close my eyes and pretend that when I wake up tomorrow, I won't have to pack my bag and return to London and go back to being a nobody.

## Chapter 37

When I get back to my flat the next morning, I grab my laptop and sink into my couch, scanning through my emails, which, uncharacteristically, I haven't checked since Friday night. There's one from Meg, begging and pleading with me to talk to her later this afternoon, and, buried in the mass emails from the *New York Times* and Serious Eats, another email from my brother from yesterday morning.

Subject: mouse
i found some real dead mice so i think i'll use those instead of oreo's toys, like in the bed or maybe under irenes pillow. what do u think?

I write back immediately.

Subject: Re: mouse

Stevie. No. NO, NO, NO. That is MY old bed, in case you forgot, and when I get back from England I will probably be sleeping in it again. I do not want real dead mice in my bed. I repeat: NO DEAD MICE IN MY BED.

I'm tempted to call him immediately to underscore my opposition to this plan, but I realize it's not quite noon here, which means it is barely seven a.m. in Ypsilanti. There's no way he's awake. He probably went to bed an hour ago.

Instead, I bide my time by cleaning my apartment, doing laundry and running through the recipes I will test next week, along with the lessons I'll give Natasha so that she's prepared for the *Vogue* interview. When I open my laptop three hours later to see if Stevie has replied, I discover he hasn't. Meg, however, is apparently up and ready to talk because, within thirty seconds of me being online, her name pops up on my screen for a video chat.

'Are you stalking me or something?' I say, as I accept her call.

'What choice do I have? We haven't talked in two weeks. You haven't replied to any of my emails. I was getting ready to send out a search party.'

It's true that I haven't written or talked to Meg in a while, mostly because I'm not sure what to tell her. The events of the past couple of weeks will, quite possibly, give her a heart attack, and saying everything out loud makes these developments seem even more surreal and ill-advised than they do in my head.

'I've been busy. We're hurtling toward our deadline, and

346

I have to prepare Natasha for a *Vogue* interview, and she's never around.'

'Where is she now?'

'LA. And last weekend, she was off on another quick jaunt to Paris.'

'I assume Foxy Ballantine didn't join her.'

'No. She didn't need him. And, anyway, he has work to do.'

'In your pants?'

'Meg!'

'Let's dispense with the pleasantries, shall we, and get down to business? What's going on with you and Foxy B?'

I tread carefully. 'We've…spent more time together.'

'Time? Where? When?'

I tell her about the dinner in Nottingham and my second visit this weekend.

'So, wait, are you guys like an item now?' she asks.

'An item? Who says that?'

'I do.'

'Apparently…'

She glares at me through the screen. 'You still haven't answered my question.'

'I don't know. I guess we are.'

'But he's still married, right?'

'Technically, but apparently he's planning to talk to Natasha this week about separating.'

Meg raises her eyebrows. 'He's leaving her for you?'

'No. I mean, he isn't leaving her *for* me. I'm more like the catalyst, I guess.'

Meg goes quiet for a few seconds. She doesn't seem nearly as excited as I expected.

'What?' I say.

'This all just seems really...fast.'

'Faster than it seemed before?'

'No, but before it was all crazy and circumstantial. Now that he's actually planning to leave her...I don't know. Shit's getting real.'

'True. But he's miserable. Their marriage is a sham. And we're crazy about each other.'

'Of course you are. You just lost your mom and long-time boyfriend, and he's getting laid for probably the first time in years. You're in the sex-crazed honeymoon period.'

'Yeah, but...there's more to it than that.'

'Even if there is, you've only been banging each other for a matter of weeks. What happens once they separate? What happens when there's no more sneaking around? Are you going to be part of a media circus? And what are you going to do, professionally speaking? I doubt Natasha will keep you as her ghostwriter if you're screwing her husband. Or ex-husband. Or ex-husband-to-be.'

'They're not in love.'

'So? Movie stars are obsessed with their public image. Do you really think she'll want it to get out that her husband slept with her ghostwriter? After what happened with Matthew Rush?'

'But that was different. She was head over heels for him. Natasha and Hugh – it's all business. She's even seeing some guy on the side – Jacques something-or-other.'

'Your average Joe doesn't know that. If I had to guess, the last thing Natasha wants is for people to think she got dumped again. She'd probably do whatever she could to prevent that happening – including ruining your career. She knows a lot of people.'

'A lot? Try *everyone*.'

'Exactly. And my guess is she could destroy you if she wanted to.'

My breath shortens. Why hadn't I thought of that before? Natasha could end my career. Easily. All it would take is a few phone calls to the right people, and she could single-handedly flush my reputation down the drain. Even if she is a narcissistic bitch, she's the kind of narcissistic bitch any moderately successful chef would want on his or her side. One offhanded comment in an interview that 'Restaurant X' is her favourite place to grab a bite, and suddenly that chef's restaurant and profile have skyrocketed overnight. She makes them more famous by association. They need her. They don't need me.

'You're right,' I say, my heart racing. 'Oh, my God, you're right.'

'Of course I'm right.'

I massage my temples, suddenly feeling very, very stressed. 'What should I do? Should I tell Hugh not to leave her?'

'I am totally unqualified to answer that question. I'm just trying to get you to think of this outside the lovesick bubble you're in. I'm not saying you have to choose between love and your career but . . . well, yeah, you might have to choose between love and your career. Or at least consider the impact your decisions might have on both.'

I weigh the options: giving up the man I can't stop think- ing about, or throwing away a career I love. I don't like either. Why can't I have both? Why does it have to be one or the other? 'Maybe I could talk to Natasha myself.'

Meg cackles. 'Yeah, because she sounds like such an understanding person.'

'I just...I love my job, you know?'

'I do. And you're good at it. I wasn't kidding when I said I'd be interested in a column about your food adventures in England. You write so well, and your recipes always come out perfectly. I guess you have to decide how important all that is to you.'

I stare at the screen, wishing a decision would leap forth and illuminate a path forward, but all I see is Meg's cherubic face and glossy curls. Figuring all of this out will take time, and I don't have much.

Meg takes a sip of water as various scenarios play out in my mind. 'Anyway,' she says, 'on a different note, I ran into your brother yesterday. He asked if I had any dead mice he could borrow.'

She raises an eyebrow, and as she does, I realize that if I had to choose a moment when I suddenly didn't recognize my life any more, this conversation, in all of its soul-crushing absurdity, would probably be it.

The more I reflect on my conversation with Meg, the more nauseous I feel. Natasha really does know everyone. *Everyone.* Artists and chefs, politicians and princes, directors and Fortune 500 CEOs. She has drinks with Oliver Stone and dinner with Joël Robuchon and managed to eat at El Bulli twice before it closed. Throughout this affair with Hugh, I have worried about what our dalliance could mean for him and his career, but apparently I haven't spent enough time worrying about what it could mean for mine. Natasha could not only trash my reputation with other chefs, she could also make sure no one hires me again.

That being the case, my goals for this week are as follows:

- Get on Natasha's good side: have at least four recipes for her to taste on Tuesday, compliment her skin, ask if she's lost weight
- Talk to Hugh: arrange time for one-on-one conversation; figure out if I want him to talk to Natasha about divorce or not; figure out what, exactly, we are doing
- Implement plan discussed with Hugh
- Prevent Stevie from infesting house with live or dead rodents

My ability to achieve those goals becomes increasingly tricky the further down the list I go, particularly when it comes to controlling my brother and his potentially calamitous schemes. By Tuesday morning, I still haven't heard from him, and I think there's about an 80 per cent chance my childhood bed is currently filled with dead vermin.

Churning out four new recipes, however, is something I can do. While I wait for Natasha to return from LA, I perfect the recipe for shrimp tacos with the ingredients I procured from Borough Market. After that, I develop a recipe for a brown rice salad with roasted cauliflower and sweet potatoes. I also muster the fortitude to give the kale burger another try, even though a very large part of me thinks we should throw in the towel and forgo including the recipe at all.

When Natasha finally returns on Tuesday afternoon, she blows into the kitchen looking tanned and firm, like a mannequin brought to life by an evil sorceress.

'God, I miss LA already,' she says, as she sweeps past me on her way to the refrigerator. She doesn't speak to me so much as to the room, as if she were addressing an audience.

'Good trip?'

She pokes her head out from behind the refrigerator door and stares at me, as if she's noticing me for the first time. 'Perfect, actually. The weather was amazing. Unlike this place.'

'The weather was actually really nice while you were gone. Warm and sunny most of the time.'

She closes the fridge door. 'Whoop-dee-doo. Five days of nice weather. In LA it's nice *every* day.'

*Then maybe you should move back there.*

'Your skin looks great,' I say, remembering my earlier plan. 'You look like you got some sun.'

She glances down at her arms. 'This? Oh, this is fake. A friend recommended a new bronzing guru, so I gave him a try. I never tan. After everything that happened with my mom, the last thing I need is skin cancer.'

'Trust me, I understand. I burn if you wave a flashlight at me. I'm not a tanner.'

'I can see why. You're really pasty.' She studies my face. 'Although your cheeks look a little pink. Must have been all that London "sun" while I was away.'

I think back to the carnival in Nottingham and the sting in my cheeks as the sun beat down all afternoon. 'Like I said, I burn really easily,' I say.

'You should be careful. You're a perfect candidate for skin cancer.'

I take a deep breath, noting that the first time Natasha has called me 'perfect' in any context is one in which I contract a life-threatening disease. 'I wear sunscreen,' I say. 'At least, most of the time.'

'Most isn't enough. Seriously, you should wear it every day. What is your morning skin regime?'

'I don't really have a regime *per se*. I just blot my face dry after my shower and put on some moisturizer with SPF.'

She stares at me blankly. 'That's it?'

'That's it.'

'No antioxidant serum? No face oil? No eye cream?'

'Nope.'

'And what SPF?'

'I don't know. Fifteen, I think. Maybe eight.'

She shakes her head. 'I can't believe this. Okay, first of all, you should be using at *least* SPF thirty. But you should also definitely be using a serum and an eye cream. You're what? Thirty-three?'

'Twenty-eight.'

'See? Your regime is ageing you already. I'll have my facialist recommend some products for you. Talk to Poppy. She'll liaise.'

'Okay, thanks.' I appreciate her sudden interest in helping me with…well, anything, but now I'm wondering if I really do look five years older and, if so, why no one told me until now.

She takes a sip of purple juice. 'Anyway, where do we stand with the recipes?'

'We're in great shape. I've done the shrimp tacos, Paleo

bread, rice salad and another kale burger. There is some leftover Paleo bread in the fridge, along with some of the rice salad, which I made this morning.'

She reopens the refrigerator and pulls out one of the half loaves of Paleo bread wrapped in foil.

'That's the one with sour cherries,' I say.

'Sour cherries? That wasn't on my list of ingredients.'

'I know, but I decided to make a variation. We don't have to include it in the book if you don't want. I just thought it might be a fun addition.'

She unwraps the foil, slices off a thin sliver, and takes a bite. 'Fine. It's good. Let's include it.' She wraps the loaf, returns it to the refrigerator and pulls out the bowl of rice salad. 'What's this?'

'The brown rice salad. With roasted cauliflower and sweet potatoes.' She looks at me dumbly. 'Based on one of your last meals in LA before you moved?'

'Oh, right.' She glances down at the bowl. 'What's the green stuff?'

'Arugula.'

'The salad in LA didn't use arugula.'

'I know, but after testing it a few different ways, I really think it adds something. Try it. I think you'll like it.'

She grabs a fork and digs a small portion out of the bowl. She takes a bite, chewing with the strange rhythm I've come to expect, and once she has swallowed she scrunches her lips to the side.

'It's good,' she says. 'But it still needs something.'

'Like?'

'I don't know. Something sweet. Or a spice. Maybe a sweet spice.'

'You mean like cinnamon?'

Her eyes widen, and she bangs her hand on the counter. 'Yes. Cinnamon. Exactly.'

'Easily done. I'll work on that tomorrow morning, and we can arrange a tasting for tomorrow afternoon. I'll remake the tacos and kale burgers, too. Or we can do those on Thursday. Your call.'

'Oh, no. We can't do a tasting Thursday. I'm doing the *Vogue* interview that day.'

I start. 'What?'

'The *Vogue* interview.' She waves her fork in the air. 'The one we've discussed a billion times?'

'You said that wasn't happening until the fifteenth.'

'No, I said it would happen mid-month.'

'Thursday is the tenth.'

She sighs, clearly exasperated. 'So it's five days early. *Whatever*. It's not like you're the one doing the interview.'

'I know, but we were supposed to cook together, to get you ready.'

'So? We'll cook together tomorrow.'

'Yeah, but that's only one day.'

She sets her fork on the counter. 'You're saying I need more than a day? To make a dish I've been making for years?'

'And sweet potato fries…'

'They're sweet potato fries. How hard can they be? It's not like I'm trying to make a fucking *croquembouche*. One day is plenty of time.'

'Okay, if you're sure…'

'I am.' She grabs her juice off the counter. 'Oh, and I'd

like to have some of those kale burgers ready in the refrigerator for me to throw on the indoor grill.'

Oh, dear God, the freaking kale burgers again.

'I really think you're better off sticking with the Cornish hens and sweet potato fries,' I say. 'Two recipes is plenty.'

She smiles coolly. 'Good thing I don't really care what you think, then, isn't it?'

She takes another sip of her drink, screws on the cap, and leaves the kitchen without another word.

## Chapter 38

As usual, the next morning Natasha shows up late, strolling into the kitchen forty minutes after our agreed meeting time of ten a.m. She wears a pair of distressed jeans and a grey V-neck T-shirt, her hair tied into a low ponytail.

She approaches the opposite side of the kitchen island. 'Where do we start?'

No apology for keeping me waiting, no explanation for her tardiness. In other words: the usual.

'First, we peel the sweet potatoes,' I say. I push two red-skinned sweet potatoes across the counter.

She reaches tentatively for them. 'Okay. But tomorrow have them peeled before he arrives. It'll make everything go a lot quicker.'

'Sure.'

'And the stuffing for the Cornish hens – have the bread cubed and ready to go, too.'

'No problem.'

'I can take care of the rest,' she says. 'Aside from the kale burgers.'

'Right. Those.'

'You'll have a version I can taste after we do the sweet potato fries, right?'

'Yep.' And you'll probably hate it.

'Good,' she says. 'Now, where's the vegetable peeler?'

I hand it to her, and she begins skinning the sweet potatoes while I preheat the oven and grab the cornflour, salt and pepper. When she finishes, I instruct her to cut the potatoes into batons, which she does with finesse.

While she slices the potatoes, I pour some cornflour into a large plastic bag along with some salt and pepper.

'Once you finish cutting up the sweet potatoes, we'll soak them in water for a bit, and then we'll toss them with this cornflour, which will help them develop a nice crust in the oven,' I say.

'Why not plain flour?'

'I tried them that way, but they turned out kind of gummy. The cornflour is finer. And it happens to be gluten-free, which I know is something you care about.'

I fill a large bowl with water, and she dumps the raw fries into the bowl, then rinses her hands in the sink, wiping them on a fresh tea towel.

'Now what?'

'We wait while the oven preheats. With regular potatoes, you soak longer because it removes some of the starch, but sweet potatoes are less starchy, so it isn't such a big deal. If you want, we can have them soaking when he arrives tomorrow so that you can skip this step.'

'Yeah. Do that.' She tosses the tea towel onto the counter and watches as I assemble the ingredients for the spicy aïoli. 'So…I hear you kept Hugh company while I was away.'

Her comment lands in the silence between us with a thud.

I freeze. 'I…What do you mean?'

'Exactly what I said: that you kept him company while I was in LA.'

A wave of nausea crashes over me, and I stare at her stupidly as I try to figure out what she knows and how I should respond. Does she know about Borough Market? Or that I spent the night in Nottingham? Or both? And if the answer is both, what else does she know?

'I ran into him a few times, I guess.'

'And Cleona,' she says.

Cleona. That means she knows I was in Nottingham. But who told her? If it was Hugh, that means he may already have talked to her about separating. If it was Cleona, well, that's different. But even if it was Cleona, that doesn't mean Natasha knows I spent the night.

'Oh, right, I ran into them at the fair in Nottingham,' I say. The lie rolls off my tongue, but my mouth feels as if it's stuffed with cotton balls. I've never been a liar, and now that I'm becoming one, I hate it. I wish I could tell her the truth. I wish this charade were over.

'What were you doing there?'

'I ran into Mr Ballantine on Friday, and he mentioned there was a carnival in Nottingham on Saturday that I might enjoy.'

She runs her fingers along the edge of the counter.

'That seems like a long way to go for some lame little fair.'

I try to keep my cool. 'I guess, but it was Fourth of July weekend, and I felt a little homesick. I thought a carnival might lift my spirits.'

She keeps her eyes fixed on mine. 'I still think it's a little random. I'm sure there would have been plenty in London to keep you busy.'

'You're probably right,' I say, still unsure what she knows or where she's going with this, still hating that I'm lying to her face. 'It wasn't much fun. The clotted-cream fudge was good, but otherwise...nothing special.'

'Blech,' she says, sticking out her tongue. 'Clotted-cream fudge – that stuff makes my teeth ache.'

'Yeah, it's pretty sweet.'

'Pretty sweet? *Sickeningly* sweet. It literally makes me nauseous.' She shivers. 'Anyway, Cleona said you seemed very...friendly.'

I stiffen. So she spoke to Cleona. That isn't necessarily a bad thing, but it isn't good either. I wonder what else Cleona said. I wonder if Hugh knows.

'She was sweet,' I say.

'Sweet?' Natasha cackles. 'I wouldn't say that. She's great, but she definitely has an edge. That's what I like about her.'

'I only met her for a few minutes. It's hard to tell in such a short time.'

'I guess.' She raps her fingers against the counter. 'She seemed to think I'd mentioned her to you before. I don't remember bringing her up.'

'Really? I could have sworn you said something about Hugh's sister-in-law...'

She shakes her head. 'No, I don't think so. Definitely not, actually.'

'Huh. Maybe I got her confused with someone else.'

'Considering that we don't talk about much other than this cookbook, I find that a little hard to believe.'

My heart thumps in my chest. What the hell is this? If she suspects something more sinister is going on, why doesn't she just say so? Does she want me to come out and say, *I'm sleeping with your husband*? Because I'm one more pointed question away from doing just that. But I try to keep it together because I haven't talked to Hugh. It isn't fair for me to pull the yarn that unravels his life without speaking to him first.

'Well, anyway,' I say, trying to change the topic, 'if nothing else, it was a nice day out.'

'And evening?'

My cheeks flush. God, I hate this. 'No, just day.'

'Because Cleona says Hugh never made it to their barbecue, which is really unlike him.'

I shrug. 'I don't know. I only ran into him at the fair. I'm not sure what he was up to the rest of the day.'

She stares at me coolly. 'It just all seems very odd.'

I shrug again and offer an innocent smile, and then I look at the clock on the wall. 'The sweet potatoes should be ready. Shall we?'

I reach for the bowl of soaking potatoes and pull them from the water, feeling Natasha's stare bore into me as I pretend none of what she said bothers me at all, that everything is fine, fine, fine.

Everything is definitely not fine. No matter what Natasha

actually knows or thinks she knows or doesn't know yet, she obviously suspects something strange is going on, and she is correct. No matter how insufferable she is, no matter how platonic and business-like their relationship is, she doesn't deserve to find out about our affair through Hugh's sister-in-law. She should hear it from Hugh.

I try to find a time to talk to him that evening, lingering as late as possible as I finish testing a few more recipes, but at nearly six thirty, Poppy swoops into the kitchen with her hands on her hips and her tote bag slung over her shoulder. 'Are you coming?'

I toss a dirty paper towel into the trashcan. 'In a few minutes. I have a little more cleaning up to do.'

'I'd appreciate it if you could hurry. I have plans.'

'You don't have to wait for me,' I say, unsure why she's even implying she would. She never waits for me.

'Yes, unfortunately, I do. Olga left early because she isn't feeling well, and Natasha just left for a cocktail reception at the Savoy.'

'I can let myself out. It's fine. I know how to lock the door behind me.'

'I'm sure you do, but Natasha isn't comfortable with that.'

'Okay. Well, maybe I could wait until Mr Ballantine gets home and then leave.'

'No, that won't work at all.'

'Why not?'

'Well, aside from the fact that he's appearing on *Newsnight* tonight and won't be home until very late, she specifically asked me to see you out.'

362

'She did?'

'Yes. Specifically.'

'Oh.' I try to buy myself time. 'I thought by this point Natasha would trust me to lock up.'

'Natasha doesn't trust anyone,' Poppy says.

My face grows hot. 'She must trust you.'

'That's because I'm the only person she *can* trust. She needs me.'

'She doesn't trust Olga?'

'A bit. She isn't too keen on trusting staff in general. The poor woman has been burned one too many times. You do know about the Matthew Rush saga, don't you?'

'He had an affair with Natasha's trainer, right?'

'And the housekeeper.'

'I thought the housekeeper was the one who sold the story to the tabloids.'

'Yes, and why do you think that was? Matthew had ended things with her, and she was jealous.'

'Oh. Wow. I didn't know.'

'Well, now you do. She used to have a big entourage – bloody sycophants, the lot of them – but after the débâcle with Matthew, she keeps a close circle. The fewer people she lets into the inner sanctum, the fewer people there are to let her down.'

'That seems like a really sad way to live – never trusting anyone.'

Poppy shrugs. 'It comes with the territory. And, anyway, sad or not, it's a far better way to live than having people constantly betray you, isn't it?'

'I guess.'

'Luckily, she's been in this business long enough to sniff

out the liars and the cheats. Those people get what they deserve.'

I flush. 'Like...how?'

'She has her ways.'

'Ways? What ways?'

'I wouldn't be a very good assistant if I told you, would I?'

'I guess not.'

She purses her lips. 'Anyway, as I said, I have plans for this evening, so could you *please* hurry up?'

'Two seconds – I just need to finish wiping down the counter.'

I grab a fresh rag and begin polishing the surfaces, trying not to dwell on the fact that Natasha did hire a person who betrayed her and, worse, she married one, too.

# Chapter 39

Natasha is going to destroy me. Meg persuaded me that was a possibility, but if what Poppy says is true, my demise is both imminent and certain. Is there anything I can do to forestall catastrophe? Or am I gagged and bound to the tracks, while Natasha barrels towards me like a freight train?

The only person who might be able to save me is Hugh, but thanks to his *Newsnight* appearance, I can't talk to him until after the *Vogue* interview. I don't want to wait that long, but I also don't want to risk calling or texting or emailing him. Doing any of those things would leave a paper trail for Natasha or the paparazzi to pursue, and that's the last thing I need.

So I do the only things I can do: I focus on work, and I wait. The *Vogue* interview is set for eleven a.m., so I arrive at Natasha's house two hours earlier than normal to prep all of the food. I peel and slice the sweet potatoes and dump them in a large bowl of cold water, then grab the tray of cubed challah I left to dry out the night before and place it next to the other ingredients for the stuffing: the diced onion and celery, the sliced mushrooms, the powdered sage, salt and pepper. I throw together the kale burgers and stick them into the refrigerator to chill and firm up before Natasha cooks them. She finally approved a version yesterday, though to be honest, at this point, I can't tell how or why she likes this recipe better than the others. I added puréed sautéed mushrooms into the mix, so maybe she likes the meaty kick they add. I honestly have no idea.

Natasha arrives in the kitchen a little after ten, looking typically chic in a pair of silky black harem pants, a flowing white tank, and a long silver pendant that hangs from her graceful neck.

'You look nice,' I say. 'I love that necklace.'

She touches the pendant absently. 'Thanks...So how are we doing? Is everything ready?'

'Nearly. I just have to set out a few more ingredients, like the cornflour and the olive oil.' I glance quickly at her white tank top. 'I assume you have an apron?'

'Why?'

'You're wearing a white shirt.'

'Are you suggesting I change?'

'No, no – you look great. I'd hate for you to ruin your shirt, though.'

'Since when do you care what happens to my clothing?'

'I don't.'

'Oh, so you don't care if I destroy a brand-new Alexander McQueen tank?'

'I mean...I guess that's your decision.'

'Oh, so now I've *decided* to ruin my own clothes?'

Dear God, what did this woman eat for breakfast this morning? Nothing, if I had to guess.

'I...' I shrug helplessly. 'I don't know. Forget I said anything.'

She flicks her hair over her shoulder. 'Whatever. Could you at least walk me through where everything is?'

'Sure.'

I gesture at the bowl of soaking sweet potatoes, then show her where I've left the ingredients for the stuffing. I take her through the steps of the sweet potato fries one last time, even though we made them yesterday, because I figure it always helps to have a recipe fresh in your mind. She seemed comfortable with the whole process yesterday, but the last thing I want is for her to freak out in the middle of the interview and blame me later for not preparing her.

'And here are the raw Cornish hens and uncooked kale burgers,' I say, opening the refrigerator door.

She peers over my shoulder. 'Those look disgusting.'

'The hens?'

'The burgers. What the hell did you do to them?'

'The same thing I did yesterday...' *When you told me they were good.*

'No. Those look completely different.'

'I don't think so. I used the same recipe – the same proportions of everything.'

'Are you calling me crazy, then?'

'No. Of course not.'

'Because only a *crazy* person would claim two identical things were totally different.'

'I don't think you're crazy,' I say, even though *Oh, my God, yes, I do*.

'Then what am I?'

Dozens of words whizz through my head: crazy, insecure, self-centred, gorgeous, rude, bitchy, thin, inconsiderate, fit, forgetful, fashionable, paranoid, rich. And then it occurs to me: nervous. She's nervous about this interview. She's worried she'll make a mistake or that he'll write something unflattering about her, and she's taking it out on me. But I know better than to suggest she has a case of nerves. That won't end well for anyone.

'I don't know,' I say. 'Maybe I did do something slightly different,' even though I know that isn't true.

'Well, they look totally disgusting, so there's no way I'm making them.'

'I promise they'll taste delicious,' I say. 'Just like yesterday.'

'How could they taste "just like yesterday" if you did something slightly different?'

Because they are *exactly the same*.

'They will,' I say. 'Trust me.'

'Famous last words.'

'We don't have to make them. As I said before, I think the Cornish hens and fries are plenty.'

'I know *you* thought that, but *I* wanted to make kale burgers, and now you've ruined everything. Did you at least bring pages from the manuscript for him to read?'

'I did.' I head for the kitchen table, where I grab a bound

stack of papers. 'I made sure your editor signed off on these pages before printing them out.'

Normally, when a project is running on schedule, I don't send off a manuscript until I've completed the entire thing. But since we're running behind, I've decided to submit the book to the editor in parts. If I'd known earlier about the potential for a *Vogue* interview, I probably would have approached the testing and writing more strategically. Then again, knowing what I know now about Natasha and Hugh and everything else, I would have done a lot of things differently. Maybe I never would have accepted this job to begin with.

Natasha flips through the manuscript, then nods curtly. 'Fine. I'll give it to him when he arrives.'

This is also a little unconventional – letting a journalist see a book when it's still in early manuscript form. The thing isn't even copyedited. But apparently Natasha's publicist thinks giving a high-profile publication a sneak peek will build interest, especially since we will be much closer to publication by the time the profile comes out. The cookbook editor told me she's fine giving *Vogue* a preview of the manuscript, as long as whatever the writer prints doesn't 'cannibalize' the book, but considering we haven't even started on the recipes from Natasha's time in London, there isn't much to cannibalize.

I take one more look around the kitchen. 'So if that's it, I guess I'll head out until you've finished the interview.'

'What? No, you have to stay here.'

'But Poppy said you wouldn't want me here. That it would make you look bad to have me cooking with you.'

'Well, obviously, I don't want you *cooking* with me.'

'Then what would I be doing?' Sitting with my thumb up my ass?

'You'll be here with Poppy as one of my assistants. These writers always figure I have a legion of assistants, so he won't care.'

'But if I'm not cooking, why do you need me here?'

'I don't *need* you. Believe me, in no way do I need you.'

'Okay.' Good to know I'm completely unnecessary.

'But I do think it would be very useful for you to sit in on this interview,' she says. 'You will learn some very... interesting information.'

'Oh?' Something about her tone sets me on edge.

She simpers, her green eyes twinkling in the light from the globular pendants. 'I don't want to spoil it,' she says. 'But I think you'll find the interview enlightening, to say the least.'

Her lips curl ever-so-slightly upwards, and as she hands the manuscript back to me, I can't help but think things are about to go very, very wrong.

*

The *Vogue* writer is named Thomas, and he arrives at eleven on the dot, dressed in jeans, a white T-shirt and a black blazer. He has a bit of a potbelly, which pokes out from above his black leather belt, and his curly ginger hair is pulled into a low ponytail.

'Lovely to finally meet you in person,' he says, as he shakes Natasha's hand. According to Poppy, they spoke on the phone last week before she left for LA. 'I happened to be passing through Paris over the weekend and picked up some of that tea you recommended – divine.'

Natasha smiles, obviously tickled he took her advice. 'I'm so glad you like it.'

'Adore it. In fact, as a little thank you…' He reaches into his worn leather briefcase and pulls out a small tin. 'They mentioned this is a new herbal tea they just started selling over the weekend. I thought you might enjoy it.'

'My goodness – thank you,' she says, taking it from his hand. 'That was so thoughtful of you.'

I notice how gracious Natasha is being now that Thomas is in the room, almost as if she has transformed into a different person – the Natasha I imagined working with rather than the Natasha I actually got.

'My pleasure,' Thomas says. He looks around the room. 'What a fantastic kitchen. Absolutely stunning.'

'Thank you. We put a lot of thought into getting it right.'

'I'll make sure the photographer gets plenty of shots of the space to accompany the piece.'

I crane my neck, looking for a photographer, but don't see anyone.

'The photos happen later,' Poppy whispers in my ear, assuming – rightly – that I'm a total newbie when it comes to celebrity magazine profiles.

'I actually have something for you,' Natasha says. She grabs the bound manuscript off the kitchen counter. 'An early look at the text.'

'Ah, brilliant. I can't wait to dig in.'

'It obviously still needs polishing, but at least you'll get an idea.' She glances at the clock. 'Anyway, I'm on a bit of a tight schedule, so we should probably get started…'

'Right. Of course. Where should we begin?'

'With my grandmother's poussin recipe. Come on. I'll show you.'

She leads him to the area along the counter where I laid all of the ingredients for the chickens and throws on a crisp navy-and-white striped apron.

'I hope you don't mind,' she says, as she ties the apron strings behind her back. 'I told my assistants, Poppy and Kelly, they could hang around for the interview.'

'No problem at all,' he says, smiling in our direction. Poppy and I are still standing by the kitchen table, our hands clasped in front of us.

'Good,' Natasha says. 'Now, let's start with the stuffing.'

Thomas places a small recorder on the counter, and Poppy and I take a seat at the table while the two of them start cooking. As Poppy taps away on her phone, I try not to jump in with a suggestion or correction as Natasha sautés the onions and celery or seasons the mushrooms. It's not that she's doing anything wrong, but she isn't executing the recipe the way I wrote it in the manuscript – the very manuscript she just gave Thomas to read and cook through on his own. If he tries to replicate this recipe, it will definitely taste different – possibly better, given how much testing I did, but different nonetheless.

As they slice and sauté and stuff, they chat about Natasha's mother, her grandmother, her favourite restaurants growing up in Philadelphia. Thomas occasionally pulls a small notebook from his pocket and scribbles in it, especially when Natasha says something touching about her mom or a particular childhood memory. Having spent a decent amount of time around Natasha by this point, I'm impressed by her ability to seem so open and forthcoming, when I know she's holding a lot back. She gives just enough information to make herself seem real and rounded, but not quite enough to seem flawed. It's masterful.

Once the chickens are in the oven, they move on to the sweet potato fries, which Natasha prepares exactly as we did yesterday, a huge relief on my part. I worried she'd decide I'd used too much oil or not enough cornflour and go rogue at some point during the cooking process but, unlike the Cornish game hens, which she's made many times, she only did the fries with me, so she seems more comfortable sticking to the playbook.

Thomas opens the door to the second oven, and Natasha slides the tray of sweet potato fries inside. After she's rinsed her hands and wiped them dry, she offers Thomas a glass of Chablis, which he gladly accepts. She grabs a glass, pausing momentarily as she notices there is one red wine glass missing from the shelf above. My breath shortens as I recall the night – *the* night – when everything changed, right here in this kitchen. Did Hugh ever explain about the broken glass? Did he tell her he did it? Or did he forget?

She shakes herself out of her trance and places the glass on the counter, filling it with a crisp white wine that spar-kles as it splashes into the glass. I notice she does not pour herself any, which seems a little odd, but then again, I've never seen Natasha drink very much. Even at the dinner in Nottingham, she only had a single glass of wine, though maybe that's because she was still hung over from the Scotch the night before. That, or she decided she didn't need the extra calories.

She carries Thomas's wine and a glass of water for herself to the other end of the kitchen table, where she and Thomas sit and carry on with the interview while they wait for the chickens and fries to come out of the oven.

'So,' he says, 'we've talked a bit about your family's influence on your interest in food and cooking, but what about your husband?'

'Oh, Hugh adores food. I have yet to find a dish he doesn't like.' She pauses. 'I take that back. A friend made us kale burgers a few weeks back, and he thought they were disgusting.'

Thomas wrinkles his nose. 'Kale burgers?'

'They're not as bad as they sound, at least when you make them right. But this friend, let's just say she didn't. She's actually made a few doozies, but of course Hugh is too polite to say anything.'

My cheeks flush as I clench my jaw. Hugh loves my food. He's *told* me he loves my food. He even said the kale burgers were good, although he normally doesn't like that kind of thing – never mind that it was Natasha's idea I make them in the first place.

'Do you two ever cook together?'

'Oh, God, no. Hugh loves to eat, but cooking…Let's just say it's a good thing he leaves that to me.'

*Not true!* I want to say. He made me a delicious English breakfast the morning after the Nottingham dinner, and after the fair, he cooked steaks and potatoes. He may not be Joël Robuchon, but he knows how to cook.

'It must be difficult to find time to eat together,' Thomas says, 'given that you both have such high-powered careers.'

'It's definitely a challenge.'

'How often are you able to?'

'Not as often as either of us would like.' She tosses her hair over her shoulder and sits up straighter. 'But we make time whenever we can. We are both very committed to our marriage.'

Her voice hardens in the last sentence, as if she is putting particularly emphasis on this point. Is she doing that for Thomas? Or for me?

'That's lovely to hear,' Thomas says. 'Most people with your kind of jobs would be like ships passing in the night.'

'It can feel that way sometimes, but we make an extra effort to reconnect. A marriage requires work and attention, and we both feel really strongly that we want to put in that time.'

'There's talk of your husband becoming prime minister some day.'

She shrugs coyly. 'Talk is talk.'

'But how would you feel about that?'

'I'd be supportive, of course. I think he'd make a great leader. He really does love this country. Having lived here a while, I can understand why. People here are so…likeable. And sophisticated. Just the other week, we hosted a dinner for some of Hugh's constituents in Nottingham, and all I could think was, These people care about all the right things.'

I take a calming breath, trying not to erupt in the midst of this sham of an interview. Natasha is so full of shit it's a wonder her sparkling green eyes haven't turned brown. Likeable? Sophisticated? Since when does she think that? And what's all this about being committed to their marriage? What a load of crap.

'Has that not been your experience in America?' Thomas asks.

'Americans are just…different.'

'Different how?'

'I don't know. Less worldly, I guess. And just generally… different.'

Thomas nods and jots something in his notebook. 'Two countries divided by a common language,' he says, with a smirk.

She sips her water. 'Anyway, all of this is speculative. Right now, Hugh is content with his post as an MP for Nottingham and as shadow education secretary. Anything to do with Downing Street would be way, way in the future.'

'Speaking of the future,' he looks up from his notebook, 'do you two have any plans for children at some point down the line?'

Given what Hugh has told me about their relationship, I expect Natasha to shift in her seat, blush and dismiss his question with a perfunctory *Of course…some day*. Instead, she takes another sip of water, places the glass on the table and smiles gently.

'Actually, I hadn't intended to bring this up yet, since it's very early, but…' She rests her hand gently on her stomach. 'Hugh and I are expecting.'

Poppy's head whips up from her phone, and for a moment, I stop breathing. Did she just say…No. No, that can't be right.

Thomas raises his eyebrows. 'I – I'm sorry…Are you…You're pregnant?'

She beams. 'I am.'

'How far along?'

'Still early in the first trimester, which is why we haven't told anyone.'

My gut churns. That can't be right, can it? The room starts spinning. If she's pregnant, then that means...No. No, she can't be. That's impossible. Unless it's Jacques's?

'When do you plan to make an announcement?'

'Initially we wanted to wait, but...well, I guess the cat's out of the bag.'

'So I can report this?'

She shrugs. 'Sure, why not? My publicist will probably flip, but the news will come out eventually, so it might as well be now.'

'As you know, this profile won't come out for many months, but if you don't mind me filing a quick newsflash sooner about the pregnancy...'

'Sure,' she says. 'Go for it.'

Thomas starts to say something, but the timer for the sweet potatoes starts blaring and interrupts him.

'Ah, sounds like the fries are ready,' Natasha says.

'Brilliant.' He clears his throat. 'Would you mind if I...popped outside for a moment to call my editor? I'd like to brief her on all of this.'

'Sure,' Natasha says.

She lets him out of the door to the back garden, and as she makes her way to the oven, she glances over her shoulder, and for a fleeting instant, so brief I could have imagined it, I swear she fixes her eyes on mine and smiles.

## *Chapter 40*

No. This can't be happening. She can't be pregnant. She *can't*. Aside from the fact that she and Hugh allegedly never have sex, she is on birth control. Or, at least, she was in early May, when I helped Poppy sort through her trash. I realize birth-control pills aren't 100 per cent effective, but they work most of the time. And didn't she just have her period a few weeks ago?

I need to talk to Hugh. That's what I need to do. I need to talk to him and figure out what is going on. Has he been lying to me? Or is Natasha lying to all of us? What if she's pregnant with her lover's baby? What if she isn't pregnant at all?

My head is still spinning when Thomas comes back inside, feverish with excitement over this latest turn of events. 'I've spoken to my editor,' he says. 'She wants to run something within the hour, but she wanted me to double-check with you first. Are you sure you're okay with doing it this way? It's…quite unconventional.'

'It's fine,' she says.

'Okay. If you're sure.'

I know what he's thinking: *Are you sure your publicist will be okay with this? Are you sure your HUSBAND will be okay with this?* Because even I know the answer to those questions is a resounding *NO*. This is Natasha going rogue, for reasons only she knows, and part of me senses she cares less about the immediate impact on her own reputation and more about the impact on others. But whether that reputation is mine or Hugh's or someone else's, I'm not sure.

'What, then, is the quote you and your husband would like to give about this happy news?'

She bites her lip as she shovels the sweet potato fries into a napkin-lined basket. 'How about, "We're thrilled that our dream of becoming parents has finally come true, and we cannot wait to meet the new addition to our family."'

'Lovely.' Thomas smiles as he writes furiously in his notebook. 'If you'll give me one more quick second to send this along to my editor, I'll be back to join you for what looks like a delicious lunch.'

She looks up at the clock. 'I'm a little tight on time…'

'Not to worry. I won't be more than a moment.'

He steps outside again, and once he has closed the door behind him, Poppy clears her throat. 'Shall I contact Nicole?' she asks, referring to Natasha's publicist, who is based in LA.

'Yeah, that's probably a good idea,' Natasha says, as she brings the fries to the table.

'And Mr Ballantine?'

'What about him?'

'Shall I contact him as well?'

'To tell him I'm pregnant?'

'No, to tell him *Vogue* will be reporting the news within the hour.'

'Oh. Right.' She pauses. 'No, why don't you stick to Nicole? You'll have your hands full with her.'

'I can call Mr Ballantine,' I blurt out, before I can stop myself.

They lock eyes with each other, then look at me. Poppy frowns. 'Why would *you* call him?'

'Just to, you know, cover the bases. Since you'll be busy dealing with Nicole.'

'You don't think I can handle my own husband?'

'Of course! It's just…you're having lunch with Thomas, and you still have to finish the interview. I thought I'd save you time.'

My real motive, of course, is to speak with Hugh before the news comes out so that I can figure out what the hell is going on and what this means for me – for *us*.

'Thanks, but I have this under control,' she says. 'And, anyway, Hugh will be impossible to get a hold of today. He's in Nottingham again, in meetings all day.'

My stomach sinks. 'He is?' I try not to show my disappointment. 'When will he be back?'

'Why do you care?'

'I don't. I was just curious.'

She takes the chickens from the oven. 'I have no idea when he'll return. I'm going up tomorrow to meet him, and we're spending the weekend together, and I'm not really sure when either of us is coming back.'

'Oh.' My hand starts shaking beneath the table, and the air in the room feels thicker with each passing second. She doesn't know when they'll be coming back? What does that even mean? Surely Hugh has to return to London at some point because that's where Parliament is. On the other hand, from what Hugh told me, nothing really happens in July or August. Does that mean Hugh could be in Nottingham for the rest of the summer? Would he really do that without even saying goodbye to me?

I take a deep breath, trying to keep my composure. 'We still have a lot of recipes to test for the book,' I say.

'So?'

'So it would be great to have you around for tastings and advice. Do you think you'll be back within the next week or so?'

She places her potholders on the counter. 'Probably. And if not, I'll make sure Poppy has all the information you need.'

'Okay.'

I can't ask the follow-up questions I really want to ask: *Will Hugh come back with you? And, if not, when does he plan to return?* But that's all I really care about, and something about Natasha's demeanour tells me she is hell-bent on my not knowing the answer.

Thomas reappears as Natasha places the platter of Cornish game hens on the table, a big smile on his face. 'All settled,' he says. 'The story should appear online within the hour.'

Natasha gently presses her hand against her stomach as she slides into one of the kitchen chairs. 'I should probably prepare for an onslaught.'

'If anyone can handle it, my guess is you can,' Thomas says.

'Yeah, this isn't my first time at the rodeo…' The anxious edge in her voice belies the smile on her face.

Thomas pulls out a chair across from Natasha and claps his hands together. 'Right. So shall we dig in? This all looks marvellous.'

'Please – help yourself.'

She passes both platters to Thomas, while Poppy and I sit, gawking at the two of them from the other end of the table. When he has filled his plate, he passes them back to her, and she helps herself to one of the birds, along with a small portion of fries.

'Better take more than that,' Thomas says, with a wink. 'You're eating for two now.'

She smiles politely and reaches for the serving fork, but as she hesitates, her hand hovering in the air as if it's suspended in ice, the only thought running through my head is, *No, she isn't.*

Within the hour, Thomas has left, and Natasha and Poppy's phones are ringing non-stop. Predictably, Natasha's publicist, Nicole, is going apeshit, as she now has to deal with a barrage of media calls on a matter for which she has no game plan and about which she had no prior knowledge.

'Nicole – chill,' I hear Natasha say, as I help Olga tidy the kitchen so that I can continue testing this afternoon. 'It's fine. The news is out there. It's over.'

I hear loud screeching coming through the receiver. 'Listen, I'm sorry I didn't talk to you first, but it just sort of came out in the middle of the interview. It isn't a big deal.'

More screeching.

'I know it's early. Yes, I know what can happen in the first trimester.' Natasha sighs. 'And if that happens, we'll cross that bridge, okay? I don't see the point in keeping it all a big secret.'

She carries on mollifying Nicole, while Poppy fends off calls from other people in the industry, like Natasha's agent, who is similarly pissed that he is finding out about this news on the Internet. As all of this is going on, I wonder how bad it will be if and when it comes out that Natasha isn't pregnant after all – that this is a big ruse.

Because it is. It has to be. A mere two weeks ago, she was drinking so much Scotch in Nottingham she had a hangover. I guess she could have been pregnant and not known, but when I try to do the math – the timing of her period, the birth control – it doesn't add up. She doesn't have any symptoms – no nausea, no fatigue, no vertigo. She's been bitchy ever since she returned from LA, but that's standard operating procedure. Absolutely nothing has changed, other than her sudden suspicious attitude towards me.

I finish helping Olga clean the kitchen, and then Olga disappears upstairs with Poppy to help Natasha organize and pack for Nottingham. Even though I feel like curling into a ball and hiding in a corner somewhere, I decide to press on with the recipe development, turning my sights now to a roasted eggplant salad and garlicky white bean dip.

As I search through the walk-in pantry for a few cans

of white beans, I hear Natasha enter the kitchen on her phone.

'Well, maybe if I could ever get a hold of you, you wouldn't have found out through a website.'

I freeze, staying out of sight in the pantry, as Natasha continues to talk on the phone.

'So?' She pauses. 'What difference does that make? We can figure that out later. I don't understand why you're freaking out about this. No one will know.'

I can barely breathe as I eavesdrop on her conversation. She has to be talking to Hugh.

'I thought this is what you wanted. I thought you said a family would be great for your career.' She huffs. 'Well, maybe you should have been clearer.' She listens as he says something at the other end. 'Why should I have to clear it with you first? You don't clear everything with me . . . Like what? Oh, I don't know, maybe like taking my ghostwriter with you to Nottingham.' I hear her open the refrigerator and close it again. 'You think I care? It looks bad – for both of us.' She takes a sip of something. 'So? We'll figure it out. And if we have to lose the baby, we lose the baby. People will understand. Miscarriages happen. They'll have sympathy for me – for *us*.'

Her voice fades as she leaves the room, and I emerge from the pantry, my hands shaking as they clasp two cans of white beans, my stomach in knots. I place the cans on the counter and slide into one of the kitchen chairs, and then I hold my head in my hands and start crying because, at this point, I'm not sure what else to do.

## Chapter 41

I'm trapped. *We*'re trapped. I could barely envision a future for Hugh and me when he was simply a Member of Parliament married to a movie star. But now he's a Member of Parliament married to a *pregnant* movie star, and even if that pregnancy is faker than their marriage, the public doesn't know that. If Natasha has her way, they never will.

I call Hugh's cell phone as soon as I get home from work that evening. I hadn't wanted to call him, for fear of leaving a paper trail, but at this point, I'm more worried about the future of my career and love life and the potential for both to implode.

Unfortunately, the call goes straight to voicemail. I guess I shouldn't be surprised. The press is probably hounding him after Natasha's announcement. I leave a brief but frantic message: 'Hi. It's me. Call me as soon as you get this.'

I contemplate calling his Nottingham office, too, but decide that's asking for trouble – a decision I increasingly regret when he doesn't call me back. Did he not get my message? Or does he not want to talk to me?

I check my email obsessively all evening, hoping for a quick note from Hugh to indicate he at least received my message. But there's nothing. That means I'll have to wait until tomorrow to talk to him – assuming I don't lose my mind first.

Before I go to bed, I check my email one last time. My pulse quickens when I see there is a new one in my inbox. But, to my disappointment, it isn't from Hugh. It's from my brother.

hey, the mouse thing kind of backfired, haha, long story, but what do you think about snakes?

*

The next morning, I arrive at Natasha's house to find a mob of paparazzi loitering out front, all of them hoping to snap a shot of Natasha's non-existent 'bump'. I hunch my shoulders and push my way through the crowd, and one of her security guards escorts me through the front gate. Cameras and flashes click in rapid succession as the gate opens and closes, but there is nothing to shoot, other than me and the guard.

'How long have they been out there?' I ask.

'Since yesterday,' the guard says. 'Bit silly, really. She snuck out early this morning. She's already in Nottingham. Not sure what they're hoping to see.'

Olga lets me in at the side entrance, seeming a little on

edge. 'All the cameras – *oy*. It haven't been like this since they move in.'

'Shouldn't someone tell them Natasha's not here? Or that she isn't coming back for a while?'

'Meh. If they too stupid to figure it out, they can wait.' She heads for the island and rearranges a bouquet of white lilies. 'Oh, but I buy new brand of tahini on Edgware Road. Supposed to be best kind – special sesame seeds or something.'

I dump my bag on a chair. 'Thanks. Sounds delicious.'

'I go pick up dry cleaning now. You need anything else?'

'No, I think I'm okay. But thank you.'

She grabs her purse and leaves through the servants' entrance, and as soon as I'm sure she's gone, I grab my phone and try Hugh's cell again. He picks up after two rings.

'Kelly?' He speaks in a low whisper.

'It's me.'

'Oh, thank God,' he says. 'I've been going mad. I wanted to call you yesterday, but my office was swamped with reporters.'

'What is going on? What is this?'

'I don't know. Natasha arrived early this morning, and we're speaking later. It's a mess. I'm so sorry.'

'There's no way she could be pregnant, right?'

'Of course not.'

'Then what are you going to do?'

'I don't know. But I'll fix this. I promise.'

'How?'

'I just…will, okay? Give me time.'

'*Mr Ballantine?*'

387

Someone calls to him in the background, and he muffles the receiver. 'Mr Brandt – hi. I'll be there in one minute.' He redirects his voice into the phone. 'Listen, I have to go. But I'll call you once I've had a long talk with Natasha. Okay?'

'Okay.'

There is a brief silence on the other end. 'I love you, Kelly. Whatever happens, I want you to know that.'

And although I know he means those words to reassure me – words I've longed to hear him say – they don't. Today they do the opposite.

Five days pass without my hearing from Hugh – or Natasha, for that matter. Poppy informs me they decided to take a quick trip to the Scottish Highlands to escape the paparazzi, meaning I have been on my own, with only Poppy to advise me. I hate the idea of Hugh and Natasha in some far-flung place. What are they doing up there? This is the longest period of time they've spent in each other's presence since I arrived and possibly in years. Picturing them together makes me blind with jealousy. I can't focus on anything else – not my work, not my appearance, not my weekly chores. All I can think about is Natasha reeling Hugh in with her manipulative schemes.

If ever I needed a friend in London, it's now. But Jess Walters is on an exploratory trip to Sweden for work, and Poppy has made it abundantly clear that she is Natasha's surrogate, not my pal. Harry hasn't called me since I bailed on our last date, so he's out – and even if he weren't, the last thing he'd want to hear is that I've been sleeping with someone else instead of dating him. Meg has been at her grandparents' cottage on Saginaw Bay for the past week and is incommunicado, and I haven't kept up with the rest of my high-school and college friends enough to warrant calling them from England. Obviously I can't call Sam about this, given that I broke his heart and haven't spoken with him in months. I could call my dad or Stevie, but doing so would only make me more frustrated than I already am.

I suppose the person I want to speak with most is my mom. For all her faults, for all of the missed school plays and embarrassing outfits, she was always there with a hug when I needed it. She didn't always say exactly the right thing or have the perfect solution, but sometimes I didn't need words or answers. I just needed love, the unconditional kind that only a mother knows how to give, even when she didn't know how to provide much else. I miss her. And somehow, fearing Hugh is slipping through my fingers, I feel as if I'm losing her all over again.

When I feel lost and out of control like this, there are only two things that can ground me: cooking and writing. So, as the week slips by, I buy a box of spaghetti, some ham and a few other ingredients, including salad cream. Then on Friday evening, as I blast 'Dancing Queen' on my computer, I whip up a batch of spaghetti salad. And then I sit in front of my computer, a massive bowl beside it, and I write.

Two hours later, I stare at the essay in front of me. The thousand words came pouring out in gushes – about my mom and her spaghetti salad, about love and loss, about forgiveness and regret. Like my mom, the recipe isn't perfect, but the flaws are what make it great. It isn't *haute cuisine*. It isn't meant to be. It's a salad made of spaghetti and Miracle Whip, and I love it for what it is. And I love my mom for who she was – for every one of her flaws, in all of their messy glory, the ones I couldn't fully accept until she was gone. I wish I'd told her that when she was alive. I hope she somehow knew.

Rereading my words, I can't believe how real and raw they are, how true they feel. I've spent so many years writing as other people – as François or Natasha, as anyone other than me – that I almost forgot who I was, that I had a voice, too. I'd perfected the art of being a ghost, but now it's my mother's ghost who has breathed life into my writing, reminding me of who I am and what I want.

I send the essay to Meg with a quick note:

Let me know if this is of interest. Might resonate with a Michigan audience. Also, we need to talk. Everything is falling apart.

As soon as Meg returns to Ann Arbor on Sunday afternoon, she calls me for a video chat. I answer after one ring, and within seconds, her face appears on my screen, her freckled, sun-kissed cheeks a familiar and much-needed tonic.

'I don't think I've ever been so happy to see your face,' I say.

'Ditto. My grandparents live in the Stone Age and don't have Internet or decent cell service. I've been going through Kelly withdrawal.'

'You haven't missed much. Just me losing my mind.'

'Before we talk about all of that – and we *must* – I have

to say, that essay? Holy shit, Kelly. It's the best thing you've ever written. I cried. Like, five times.'

'Really?'

'Okay, fine, six times. Seriously. It's going on the website first thing tomorrow.'

'Tomorrow? Don't you have to clear it with your boss?'

'Technically, yes, but he's going to love it. Anyone with a pulse will love it. It's poignant and honest and just ... Wow.'

'Thanks, that means a lot. Especially since I don't feel so awesome lately.'

'Yeah, okay, so what is going *on*? I saw the news on People.com before I left, but I couldn't get online up in Bumblefuck. How can Natasha be *pregnant*?'

'She isn't.'

'What do you mean? She's lying?'

'Yeah. I think so.'

'How do you know?'

'Because she and Hugh don't have sex. And she got her period less than a month ago. *And* she's on birth control. Or, at least, she was.'

'What?'

'During my first week, I found her assistant rooting through her trash to keep the paparazzi from seeing one of her prescriptions. I assumed it was for diet pills or pain-killers, but when I saw the name, it was some combination of oestrogen and progesterone – the same two I take for my pill.'

'That was when? May?'

'Yeah.'

She scratches her head. 'That is definitely suspicious. But

391

not conclusive. It only takes one time, and the pill isn't fail-safe.'

'True, but that seems like a long shot – especially since the guy she is sleeping with lives in Paris. Not only would the timing with her cycle have to be perfect, but then her pill would also have to fail. Seems highly unlikely.'

'True.' Her expression turns serious. 'What does this mean for you, then?'

'I wish I knew. I talked to Hugh more than a week ago, but he hadn't had the big talk with Natasha. He said he'd call me once they did, but now he's in fucking Scotland, and I haven't heard a peep.'

'You're kidding.'

'Nope. My guess is that between Natasha and the paparazzi, he hasn't had a second to breathe. But still. I'm going crazy.'

'Maybe you could email TMZ or *People* – give them proof she isn't actually preggo, tell them about her lover.'

'No, I can't. I signed a non-disclosure agreement.'

'Oh. Can't you break it?'

'Not unless I want Natasha's lawyers to come after me for all I'm worth.'

'Which is what, at this point? A hundred bucks?'

'More than that, thank you. Though compared to how much money she has, it might as well be.'

Meg bites her thumbnail. 'Okay, so…What are you going to do?'

I consider her question, the same question I've asked myself over the past week. What *can* I do? Anything? I've run various scenarios through my mind, but in the end, I always come back to the same conclusion.

'I have to wait,' I say. 'And hope for the best.'

She rests her chin on her palm and gives me a pitying smile because we both know if that's the best plan I've got I'm probably doomed.

## Chapter 42

The next morning, before I leave for work, my stomach seizes when I find a note in my inbox from Hugh:

Kelly –
I'll call you tonight. Sorry for not contacting you sooner – everything has been complete madness.
Hugh

The email is abrupt – sterile, even – which makes sense, given who he is and what we've done and what would happen if anyone hacked his account. But if he was going to email at all, why didn't he do so sooner? And why is he planning to call me and not see me in person? Is he still in Scotland? Is Natasha with him?

When I arrive at Natasha's, Olga greets me at the servants' entrance, her auburn hair glinting with flecks of copper. I have a dozen questions to ask her about Natasha and Hugh, but with Olga, I've learned to start off with pleasantries rather than dive straight into the nitty-gritty.

'Good morning,' I say. 'How was your weekend?'

She heads inside and makes for the sink. 'Okay. Busy.'

'Did you do anything special?'

'Special? No. Was a weekend like any weekend.'

No matter how many times I've tried to probe Olga for information – about herself, about Natasha, about Hugh – she never gives me anything. I've tried to ask if she's married, has children, siblings, likes England, but she always counters my questions with stiff, succinct replies, none of which gives me any insight into who she is and what she's really like. Is she Russian or Ukrainian? ('Yes.') How long has she worked for Natasha? ('A few years.') How long has she been in England? ('A few more years.') The only interesting information she has ever provided has come unprompted, like when she told me Hugh 'liked hodgepodge', and even then, she only gives me enough to whet my appetite.

'Have Natasha and Mr Ballantine returned?' I ask, deciding to get straight to the point.

'Miss Natasha, yes. Mr Ballantine, he return to Nottingham for couple more days.'

I rest my bag on a chair, my stomach in knots. 'So they didn't come back together?'

'How are they coming back together if Mr Ballantine is in Nottingham?'

'Right. Sorry.'

This is good, right? That they're not together? Maybe they've separated. Maybe Hugh settled things, after all.

Though I suppose that still doesn't resolve the matter of my future employment.

I clear my throat. 'Is Natasha in the house, then?'

'I am.'

I whirl around to see Natasha standing in the doorway. She wears a black maxi dress and black sandals, a gold cuff shaped like a snake around her upper arm. Her hair spills over her shoulders in loose waves, and I notice the dress's empire waist carefully disguises her stomach.

'Did you have a nice trip?' I ask, my voice tight.

'I did. It was great to reconnect.'

My stomach churns. *To reconnect?* What does that mean?

She saunters to the island, across from where I'm standing, and presses her hands against the cool surface. 'Olga, maybe you should leave the two of us. Kelly and I have a lot to discuss.' Her eyes flit to Olga. 'About the book,' she adds.

'I go shopping anyway,' Olga says. She looks at me. 'You need more ingredients?'

'I could actually use some—'

'She's fine,' Natasha says. 'Why don't you get going?'

Olga slips out of the kitchen, and Natasha and I stand in silence, staring at each other.

'So, what did you want to discuss?' I start to say.

She keeps her eyes fixed on mine. 'You know exactly what I want to discuss.'

I swallow hard. 'Do I?'

'Cut the bullshit. Your little ingénue act – it's pathetic.'

Her words sock me like a punch in the gut. As much as I hate lying to her face, as much as I've been dying to tell her the truth, to have it out once and for all in a big, messy fight, I'm not sure I'm ready for this. The steely look in her eyes, the tightness of her jaw – she'll crush me.

'Okay. Fine,' I say, the courage building inside me. I can do this. I have to. 'Let's cut the bullshit, then.' My eyes drift to her cabinets. 'Maybe we should talk over a glass of wine. Unless that would be bad for the baby.'

I wait for her to take the bait, but she just stares at me.

'There is a baby, right? You wouldn't make something like that up. Only a crazy person would do that. Only someone who was truly horrible, all the way to her core.'

She clenches her jaw. 'You have no idea what you're talking about.'

'Yes, I do. And you know it.'

'Watch yourself.'

'Why? So you can steamroll me, like you steamroll everyone? You don't even love him.'

'You have no idea how I feel. About anything.'

'I know your marriage is one of convenience. That you sleep in separate bedrooms. That you're having an affair with a guy named Jacques.'

'And I suppose that makes you an expert on my love life.'

'No, but it means I know you don't have Hugh's interests at heart.'

'What do you know about his interests? You think you can parachute in, five years into our marriage, and decide you understand how or why any of this works? You think a month or two of screwing means you know more about him than I do?'

'I know he doesn't love you. I know he never did.'

'Well, la-di-da. Here's a newsflash: it takes more than love to make a relationship work.'

'But you can't really make a relationship work without it, can you?'

'You can if you want to.'

'Only if both people do. And Hugh doesn't. Not any more.'

'Is that so? Then tell me, why did he just spend more than a week with me, discussing our future?'

'Because you created a phantom pregnancy without consulting him? Because he's trying to do damage control?'

'Ah, I see. Is that what you keep telling yourself?'

My face grows hot. 'It kills you that he'd choose me over you.'

She throws her head back and cackles. 'Is that what you think? That he'd choose you? Christ, you're even more naïve than I thought.'

'He loves me,' I say. 'He said so.'

'You know what else he loves? His career. And how do you think you fit in with that? Let me answer for you. You don't.'

My hands are shaking. 'What about you? You're having an affair with some French guy named Jacques. How do you think that will play with Hugh's constituency? Let me answer for *you*. Not well.'

'Jacques and I are through.'

The blood rushes to my cheeks. 'What?'

'We called it off. It's over. I'm going to focus on my marriage.'

'What marriage? You mean your business relationship?'

'It is what it is.'

'Do you even care about him at all?'

'What business is it of yours?'

My chest tightens. 'Because *I* care about him. I love him.'

'Aw, isn't that sweet? Well, guess what? Your little schoolgirl crush is a fucking fantasy. Love isn't some silly crush. Love is complicated and layered and a hell of a lot deeper than a sex-driven fling. Wake up and join the rest of us in the real world.'

'The real world? Is that where people play house for publicity's sake? Where people care more about what *OK!* magazine might say about them than how they actually feel?'

She smacks her hand against the counter with force. 'Don't you dare pretend you know what it's like to be me. To have the paparazzi hound you day and night. To have them splash the gory details of your break-up across the web for everyone to see. To have them revel in your heartbreak. And to have them waiting – drooling – for someone to break your heart again. You don't have a fucking clue.'

'So, what, you protect yourself by marrying someone you don't care about and ruin his life, too?'

'I'm not ruining his life.'

'You've lied about being pregnant to trap him in a marriage. That's even worse than not loving someone. It's cruel. It's the opposite of love.'

'Wrong. The opposite of love is indifference. And I am not indifferent.'

'Then what are you?'

She stares at me, her expression cold and hard as ice. 'Winning.'

She stands firmly in place, watching me closely as I try not to react, my breath so shallow I'm afraid I might faint.

'You haven't won yet,' I say. 'This isn't over.'

She glowers at me, her face like stone. 'Oh yes it is.'

She turns around and walks towards the hall. When she reaches the doorway, she rests her hand on the frame and gives me one last probing look.

'Oh, and in case you were wondering,' she says, 'you're fired.'

## Chapter 43

Fired? *Fired?* But that means…Oh, my God. I have to talk to Hugh. Immediately.

I grab my belongings off the kitchen chair, then race down the street to Belsize Park tube station. I pull the phone from my bag and call Hugh. It goes straight to voicemail.

'Hugh – hi. It's me. Kelly. We need to talk. I spoke to Natasha earlier, and…Could you just call me? Soon? I know you said you'd call tonight, but I need to talk to you now. I thought about coming up to Nottingham, but I realized that would be stupid, especially with all the press, and…Anyway, just call when you get this, okay? I'm going crazy.'

I barely recognize the neediness in my voice, the clinginess of my words. Who have I become?

I hurry home, and as soon as I enter my flat, my phone

rings. My heart leaps, but it quickly sinks when I discover Hugh isn't calling. It's Poppy.

'I've just spoken to Natasha,' she says. 'I'll need you to hand over any notes or documents related to the cookbook, along with your phone and any other items we provided for you.'

'Okay.'

'And of course you'll need to leave your flat.'

'What?'

'Well, I suppose technically you don't need to *leave*, but Natasha certainly won't be paying for it any more.'

I'm about to ask how much the rent is, to see if I could pay it on my own, when I remember something. 'Larry still hasn't paid me for the work I've done so far.'

Poppy snorts. 'You aren't actually asking for money, are you? After what you've done?'

'I worked really hard on those recipes. Her cookbook wouldn't exist if it weren't for me.'

'Do you honestly think no one else could do your job? Don't flatter yourself. She'll find someone else.'

'She still owes me for the work I've done so far.'

'That's Larry's domain. Take it up with him.'

I clench my fist. 'Fine. Whatever. I'll get another job here in the meantime.'

'Here? Oh, I don't think so.'

'What's that supposed to mean?'

'Darling, Natasha knows everyone in London. And, right now, you are the last person she would ever recommend.'

'Then I'll go back to America.'

'Good. As of today, you have only thirty days left on your visa anyway.'

I start. 'What?'

'Your visa was contingent on your working for Natasha, and now that you aren't, you have thirty days to leave the country or find another job here – which, as we've discussed, you won't. So it sounds to me like you'd better start packing.'

She hangs up and, her strident voice still echoing in my ear, I wait for my life to implode.

I never appreciated how long a minute could feel. Sixty achingly long seconds, each beat dragging its heels to the next. And an hour – oh, God, an hour feels like a year. Which means waiting eight hours for Hugh to call feels like eight years, and by then I'm exhausted.

He calls just after six, and the phone has barely rung once by the time I pick up.

'Kelly – hi. I'm so sorry, I only just got your message.'

'What the hell is going on? You haven't called in more than a week.'

'I know. I tried – several times – but Natasha has made it impossible for me to contact you.'

'I talked to her this morning,' I say.

'You did? Where?'

'In your kitchen.' A lump forms in my throat. 'She knows about us. And she made it sound as if you'd reconciled.'

'She what?'

'She made it sound like you weren't going to leave her. Like, ever.'

He lets out a deep sigh. 'Jesus. Listen, I'm heading back to London late tonight. Let's meet tomorrow to talk about all of this. I can be at your flat for breakfast. Okay?'

'Why can't we talk about it now?'

'Because I love you, and I want to talk to you about this in person.'

The words echo in my head: he loves me. Does he? If so, then why isn't he saying, *I'm leaving Natasha*? Why do we need to talk about this in person?

'Can't you at least tell me whether you're leaving her or not?' I ask. 'It's a simple question.'

'It isn't simple at all. It is, in fact, the opposite of simple.'

'But can't you just—'

'*Mr Ballantine, someone from Crabtree Farm Primary School is here to see you. Shall I let him in?*'

He muffles the receiver. 'Yes – just a moment.' He directs his voice back into the phone. 'Sorry – between Natasha's bombshell and this education bill coming to a head, I haven't had a moment's peace. I'm still at the office. But I will see you first thing tomorrow. I promise.'

'But—'

'*Mr Ballantine?*'

'Coming!' He clears his throat. 'Sorry, I have to go. But tomorrow. Breakfast. I'll see you then,' he says, and then he hangs up.

When I wake up the next morning, I rush to the bathroom to shower and make myself presentable for Hugh. I haven't seen him in more than two weeks, and even though I'm completely rattled by the events of the past week and a half, I still want to look good, more for my own self-esteem than anything else.

I flick on the shower, expecting the weak stream of

water to which I have become accustomed, but nothing happens. Instead, the showerhead heaves forward and back with a loud whine, like an angry donkey – *hee-haw, hee-haw, hee-haw*. I flick off the faucet, then switch it back on, and as I do, I hear something rattle behind the tiled wall. The sound gets louder and louder until – BOOM! – the showerhead bursts from the wall and a surge of water explodes through a gaping hole in the tiles. I panic as water gushes into my tub and onto the floor, soaking me and pretty much everything within a five-foot radius.

I fumble with the tap and finally manage to turn it off. I shiver as I scan the puddles on the floor and catch my reflection in the mirror. I am drenched. My hair clings to my face and neck, and my nightshirt is now transparent. Perfect. This is exactly what I need.

I throw on a fresh T-shirt and sweatpants, pull my hair into a high ponytail, and head down the hall to Tom's office. He sits at his desk and seems to be playing some sort of game on his computer. I knock on the doorframe, and he jumps.

'Good morning,' he says, clicking furiously with his mouse to close whatever application he'd been using. 'Sorry – you caught me by surprise.'

'My shower broke.'

'Oh dear. Is it not running?'

'It's running – all over my bathroom. Something happened with the water pressure, and the showerhead burst off the wall. There's water everywhere, and I can't shower until it's fixed.'

'Hmm. I see.' He leafs through a Rolodex on his desk.

'I'll call the plumber. Hopefully he'll be able to come this afternoon.'

'This afternoon?' I glance at his clock. 'Is there any chance he'd be able to come sooner? Like…within the next half-hour?'

'Possibly. Will you be at home?'

'Yes. All day.'

'Ah, a day off?'

'No, actually…' I decide against regaling Tom with my personal and professional saga. 'Long story,' I say. 'I'll be around.'

'Great. I'll put a call in to the plumber, and I'll pop by in a few to let you know what he says.'

'Great. Thanks.'

'Bugger me – first locking yourself out, now a problem with your shower. You've had quite a time of it here, haven't you?'

'Trust me,' I say, 'you don't know the half of it.'

When I get back to my flat, I pull myself together as best as I can without showering. Even if the plumber is able to come soon, I have no idea how long it will take him to fix the faucet, and by the time he's finished, it may be too late for me to wash up. So I clean myself with a washcloth, spray my wrists and neck with perfume, and do my best to tame my stringy locks. Once I've applied a bit of makeup, I head for the kitchen, put on a pot of coffee and pull out a loaf of bread to make toast. Under normal circumstances, I would throw together something special for breakfast with Hugh – pancakes or an omelette – but at the moment, I don't have much of an appetite. And, anyway, this rendezvous isn't about food.

As I wait for Tom to update me about the plumber and for Hugh to arrive, I flip open my laptop. There is an email from Meg with the subject line 'Check this out.' At first, I assume her account has been hacked and the link is some sort of virus, but then I notice the link has the address 'michiganradio.org'. I click it and am taken to the essay I sent her, which now has 107 comments and has been reposted and shared on a dozen other sites. I tentatively glance at the comments, knowing I may instantly regret doing so, but to my surprise, they are nearly all positive. People love the piece. The piece I wrote. About *me*.

Before I can contemplate what this means – for me, for my career – Tom knocks on my door, as promised. I flip my laptop shut, smooth my navy sundress, and rush to the door. But when I open it, it isn't Tom at all. It's Hugh.

'Oh – hi,' I stammer, barely able to breathe as my eyes land on his. After not seeing him for more than two weeks, I wondered if the image I'd created in my head wouldn't live up to the man himself. But standing before me in his crisp white shirt and charcoal pants, he looks even better than I remembered.

'Sorry,' I say. 'I didn't realize you'd be here this early. I thought you were the building manager.'

'You almost sound disappointed.'

'No, no – I mean, I do need someone to fix my shower, but that can wait.'

He glances over my shoulder. 'May I?'

'Oh – right. Of course. Come in.'

God, why am I acting like such a moron? Why am I so flustered? It's as if I've forgotten how to act around him, as if the events of the past few weeks have somehow sent us back to the beginning.

I let him in and close the door. We stand in my entryway for a few awkward moments, and then I gesture towards my table.

'I put on a pot of coffee, and there's—'

He grabs my face and kisses me, his lips pressing against mine with intensity. My body dissolves into his, and all I want is to stay like this for ever, for him never to leave, for me never to let go. But just as I start to unbutton his shirt, he pulls away.

'No,' he says.

A lump rises in my throat. 'No?'

He walks over to my couch and collapses, holding his head in his hands. 'I'm sorry. God, I'm so sorry.'

'Why? Please – tell me what's going on.'

He looks up at me, his eyes pink. 'Everything just sort of…spun out of control.'

'What did? What were you doing in Scotland?'

'Escaping the paps. Trying to sort out this mess. Talking to Natasha.'

I sit next to him on the couch. 'About what?'

'Our marriage. Our future.'

'Your *future*? I thought you were getting divorced.'

'I thought so, too. But then…'

'Then what?'

'Then she told everyone she was pregnant.'

I sink back into the couch. I have so many questions, so many things to tell him – about my conversation with Natasha, about how much he means to me – but there is too much to say, and I don't know where to begin.

'Does that really change anything?' I ask.

'It changes everything.'

'How? Do you suddenly love her? Does a fake pregnancy erase your feelings for me?'

'Of course not. But the way it appears to the public…' He rubs his temples. 'If I have any hope of climbing the ranks within the party, I can't leave my pregnant wife – certainly not for a woman who worked for her.'

'But she isn't even pregnant!'

'The public doesn't know that.'

'Okay. Well, what if they did? Doesn't that change things?'

'Yes – for both of us. If she goes down for a horrible lie that I knew about, I go down with her.'

'So what happens when there's no baby, huh? What happens then? She fakes a miscarriage?'

'Possibly.'

'What do you mean, "possibly"? Of course that's what she'll do. Because then everyone will feel really sorry for her, and she'll be the centre of attention, which is what she loves anyway.'

'Okay, and if that's the case, am I really supposed to then leave my wife, who has had a very public miscarriage?'

'Fake miscarriage.'

'Whatever. As far as the public is concerned, it's real.'

'So tell them it isn't.'

'I can't.'

I clench my fists. '*Why not?*'

'Because that isn't how the real world works, Kelly! I have a career. A reputation. And telling everyone my wife is a liar doesn't just affect her life, it affects mine as well.'

'Is that what she told you?'

'She didn't have to tell me. It's the truth.'

'What about all those things you said to me? About not being able to keep up this charade any more. About wanting to be with me.'

'I meant them. I still mean them.'

'Really? Then why the fuck are you staying married to her?'

He takes a deep breath. 'Because I can't leave her. Okay? I wish I could, but I can't. She may be difficult and malicious, but she is the person I agreed to marry, and even if that was for professional reasons, it's the choice I made.'

'But I thought you wanted a family. Not a fake one – a real one.'

'I do. And I still might have one.'

'With whom?'

'Natasha.'

The blood rushes to my face. '*What?*'

'She is my wife. Do you understand? Legally, she is my wife.'

'But she doesn't have to be.'

'Yes, but as you've said, I'm not getting any younger. Neither is she, for that matter. And to make up for this hideous lie, she agreed that maybe we would consider trying for real.'

My eyes fill with tears, my fists clenched. 'No. You can't be serious. No.'

'It isn't what I want, but it's the only way I could see out of this mess.'

Tears stream down my face. 'You're an asshole, you know that?'

'Kelly…'

I punch him in the chest with my fists, again and again, choking on my sobs as the salty tears run over my lips. 'I hate you. I fucking *hate* you!'

He grabs my hands and holds them tight as I try to wrest them from his grip. 'Well, I fucking love you. Okay? Do you hear me? I love you.'

'No, you don't. You're full of shit.'

'I do love you. I understand why you wouldn't believe me, but I do.'

The words slice me down the middle, and my heart throbs. 'If you love me, then…'

But I can't finish the sentence. If you love me what? You'll leave your movie-star wife? You'll give up your dreams? You'll trade in everything you've worked for your *entire life* so that you can run off with a cookbook ghostwriter?

'If you love me,' I say, 'then why are you staying with a woman who plans to trash my entire career?'

'She won't.'

'Oh yes she will.'

'No, she won't. That was one of my conditions for not leaving. I told her if she says so much as one nasty word about you to anyone – a chef, a stylist, anyone – I would destroy her.'

'Whatever. It doesn't even matter any more. I'm planning to go out on my own anyway. I don't need your help – or Natasha's.'

'Good.'

'Good?'

'Yes, bloody *good*. I told you – you're unbelievably

411

talented. And not because you do great work for other people. Because of who you are. If I were to find out five years from now that, on top of letting you slip through my fingers, you were still doing grunt work for people like Natasha, I wouldn't just be disappointed in myself, I'd be disappointed in both of us.'

My lip quivers as I study his face: his blue-green eyes, his soft lips, his chiselled cheekbones. God, I wish I could hate him. But I can't. As hard as I try, I can't.

'Don't cry,' he says. 'Please.'

I wipe the tears away with the back of my hand. 'I just…I wish things were different. That we could be together, or at least try.'

He casts his eyes at the floor. 'So do I.'

'No, you don't.'

He looks up. 'Yes, I do.'

He leans forward, rests his hand on my cheek, and presses his lips against mine. His kisses are soft now, slow and sad, like a goodbye. He pulls away, his hand still on my face.

'One day, when I look back on all of this, letting you slip away will be one of my great regrets.'

Tears run down my cheeks and over his hand, and as he kisses me one last time, all I can think is, *But not quite great enough.*

## Chapter 44

If you'd asked me before today whether I'd ever had my heart broken, I would have considered the question and, after a lengthy pause, said, 'Yes. Definitely.' I lost my mother. Is there a heartbreak greater than losing a parent?

But there is a difference, however nuanced, between losing someone by circumstance and losing someone by choice. It's not that losing Hugh is a greater loss than losing my mother. It's that the million little heartbreaks that led up to my mom's death – the screwed-up birthday parties, the missed school plays, the disappointing Christmases – prepared me, on some level, for that final loss. With my mom, it was like ripping a bandage off at an excruciatingly slow pace, feeling the sting of each hair as it was torn from my skin until, suddenly, the bandage was gone. I got used to that feeling, the searing prickle on my skin, and now that it's disappeared, I even miss it. But with Hugh, it's like yanking the bandage off in one painful tug. The experience will probably leave me with less pain in the end, but for now, I feel bruised, raw and, on top of it all, entirely expendable.

I go to bed at seven o'clock and don't get up until three the next day. There are dozens of things I need to do – figuring out how and when I'm flying back to the States, for example, or sorting out my career before it collapses – but the weight of the conversation with Hugh bears down on me and prevents me doing anything useful.

My appetite has vanished, and the prospect of searching for flights makes me want to cry, so instead I grab a glass of water and my laptop and head back to bed. When I open my email account, I notice that my brother is online. Part of me would rather walk on broken glass than discuss another of his harebrained ideas, but I decide I could use a distraction that bears no resemblance to my current reality. I ping him with an instant message:

Kelly Madigan: Hey, you there?
Steve M.: hey yeah how are u?
Kelly Madigan: Not so great. Wanna video chat?
Steve M.: ok sure

I log on for a call, and Stevie's face appears on my screen. His light brown hair sticks out in every direction, the stubble on his face about a day away from a full-blown beard.

'Did you just wake up?' I ask.

'No, but apparently you did…'

I catch a glimpse of myself in the corner of my screen.

Oh, God. I look like a rabid wildebeest in a pink terrycloth robe.

'It's been a rough twenty-four hours,' I say.

'Why? What happened?'

'I don't even want to talk about it.'

'Are they making you eat weird shit? Mike said his uncle went a few years ago, and they made him eat pig's blood or something.'

'He probably meant black pudding.'

'They put blood in their pudding? Sick.'

'No, it isn't pudding like Jell-O. It's...' I take a deep breath. 'Never mind. That isn't why I wanted to talk.'

'Then why did you?'

'To hear your voice, I guess. To see your face. And to hear more about this plan involving...snakes?'

'Oh, right.' He rubs his hands together. 'Are you ready?'

'I don't know. Am I?'

'It's pretty sweet. I think you'll be impressed.'

'Okay.'

'So, like I said, the mouse thing sort of backfired.'

'How? What did you do?' I lean towards the screen. 'Did you put mice in my bed?'

'No. Well, not exactly.' He waves me off. 'It's a long story.'

'I have time.'

'Okay, but consider yourself warned.' He takes a deep breath. 'I decided live mice might be a problem, since they could infest Dad's house, even after we got rid of Irene. But then dead mice might kind of smell, and I wasn't sure if they had diseases and stuff. So—'

My phone rings, interrupting him. It's Poppy. I

415

contemplate ignoring her call but, considering I still have loose ends to tie up regarding Natasha's book and my possible expulsion from the country, I decide it's worth answering.

'Hey, Stevie? Sorry to cut you off, but I have to take this call. Can we pick this up later?'

'We don't have to pick it up at all. Like I said, I'm moving on to Plan B.'

'Which involves snakes?'

'Maybe.'

'Isn't there a better way to get rid of Irene? Something that doesn't involve pests or vermin?'

'Listen, you asked me to come up with something, and this is what I came up with.'

'I know. But there must be a better way. Couldn't you talk to Dad?'

He shrugs. 'I tried. Or sorta tried. But the thing is...he actually seems happy. Happier than he did a month or two ago, at least.'

'Yeah, but is that because of Irene?'

'I kind of think it is. I hate to say it, but I think she's been...good for him.'

I glance at my phone and see I've missed Poppy's call. Crap.

'Shoot – I have to call this person back. Can we talk later?'

'Sure. Although I'll be out this afternoon. I have to swing by Washtenaw before work.'

'Washtenaw?' I ask, referring to the community college Stevie started at. He never finished his course. 'I thought you dropped out.'

'I'm registering for the fall session. I realized I only need a few credits to graduate, so after talking to you last month, I figured…might as well.'

'Stevie, that's great. I'm really proud of you.'

'Don't be proud until I actually finish.'

'I'm proud of you for trying. Sometimes that takes the most courage.'

'Listen to you, all philosophical and shit. You should, like, write a book or something.'

'I wouldn't go that far.'

'I'm not kidding. I saw that thing you wrote about Mom. It was…pretty awesome, Kel.'

'Really? You read it?'

'I know how, believe it or not.'

'All I meant was…I didn't think reading public-radio websites was your thing.'

'It isn't. But everyone around here has seen it. You kind of said all the stuff I feel about Mom, too. Only you said it better.'

'Well…thanks.'

'You should write more stuff like that.'

'About Mom?'

'About you. I'm sure you have some stories to tell about the work you've done for other people. And the way you write – you make people feel stuff, you know? Like, real stuff.'

'As opposed to not real stuff.'

'Hey, I'm trying to give you a compliment, okay? You'd better take it. This doesn't exactly happen every day.'

I smile. 'You're right. Thank you.'

'You bet I'm right. Now, don't you have an important call to make?'

I look at the missed call on my phone from Poppy. 'I do,' I say. 'But you know what? It's not half as important as this one.'

I called Poppy back later that afternoon, and in a brief exchange, we agreed to meet on Friday morning at the Starbucks next to my flat so that I could hand over my notes and recipes.

Now as I wait at one of the tables, I close my eyes and picture Hugh's face the way I saw it last. I wish I could erase him from my mind, as if he never existed – as if *we* never existed together – but I can't, and no matter how hard I try, I doubt I ever will.

'Are you asleep?'

I open my eyes and find Poppy towering over me. She is wearing a form-fitting coral shift dress with cap sleeves and a square neckline, and her hair is drawn into a high ponytail.

'Sorry,' I say, shaking myself out of my daydream. 'I was thinking about something.'

'Or some*one*.' She extends an open palm. 'Do you have the notes?'

I reach for the manila folder on the table in front of me. 'Everything is in here. Most of the notes are handwritten, but I printed a few things off my laptop. I hope my handwriting isn't too illegible.'

She takes the folder from my hands and flicks through a few pages. 'Good God.'

'It isn't that bad!'

She slams the folder shut. 'It is. But I'm sure your successor will be able to decipher something from it.'

'Natasha has already chosen a successor?'

'Not yet. She's deciding between three candidates. Given how behind we are, she needs someone quick and professional – who, incidentally, won't sleep with her husband. It won't surprise you to hear she's only looking at men this time.'

'Ah.' Part of me feels strangely comforted by that. At least Hugh won't have a fling with one of her other ghost-writers, as if that's even something he'd do.

'When do you leave for America, then?'

'Not sure. Soon. I'm still trying to sort out my next career move.'

'Good luck with that.'

'I don't need luck,' I say. 'But thanks.'

'You sound very confident for someone who's just been fired.'

'I'm striking out on my own,' I say. 'I've already sent out a few emails to editors I've worked with on other projects. A couple of agents, too. I don't need Natasha any more. Maybe you do, but I don't.'

Poppy looks as if she's been slapped. 'I don't need her. She needs *me*.'

'To be her lackey . . .' I mumble. Then I catch myself. 'Sorry – that was rude. I know you're just doing your job. And I know it isn't easy.'

She holds her head high. 'It can be quite difficult at times.'

'To be honest, I don't know many people who could put up with all of the shenanigans you tolerate on a daily basis.

You work really hard. And I know Natasha trusts you, which is no small feat.'

'Well…thank you.'

'You're welcome.'

She smooths her ponytail. 'This doesn't make us friends, you know.'

'I know.'

'Good.' She grips the folders in her arms. 'Right. I'm off. I'd say good luck, but I'm not sure I'd really mean it.'

'That's okay. You can just say goodbye.'

'You know, it would be a lot easier to hate you if you weren't so bloody…nice.'

I hold back a smile. 'Who said life was easy?'

She rolls her eyes. '*Goodbye*,' she says, and then she walks out of the door.

When I get back to my apartment that afternoon, I find an email in my inbox from one of the literary agents I contacted in New York. I sent her the piece I'd written for Meg, along with a pitch for a memoir about my experiences growing up in Michigan and working behind the scenes for some major players in the culinary world.

*Kelly,*
*I like what you have here. I'm not sure if there's a*
*book in this or not, but there's a lot to work with.*
*Let's talk. You free next week?*
*Alanna*

My fingers tingle, the next chapter of my life peeking

through like a small green shoot. I rest my fingers on the keyboard and take a deep breath.

*Alanna,*
*I'm free whenever you'd like to talk. How's Monday?*
*Kelly*

Then I click 'send', excited for what the future might bring.

## Chapter 45

'Tom?'

He jumps as I knock on the doorframe and peers over the computer screen. 'Blimey, you startled me.'

'Sorry. I seem to be good at that.'

'Not to worry. Shower finally fixed, then?'

'Yep. More than a week later. And just in time for me to leave.'

'Very sorry to hear about your departure. Are you flying back to America this evening?'

'I'm making a little detour first and heading home next week.'

'Ah. Lovely.' His eyes flit to the suitcases at my side. 'Taking all of that on your "detour"?'

'No. That's why I'm here. I was wondering…Would you mind storing these in your office for the next five days? I'd ship them, but when I calculated what it would cost, I realized I'd be better off burning everything and buying new stuff at home.'

He looks at the luggage, then at me, then at the luggage again, as if he's contemplating whether or not he can ask me to burn my own belongings.

'I suppose you could leave them here. A bit unconventional but…' He waves me toward his desk. 'Come along.'

I wheel the two suitcases behind his desk, and as I do, Tom clicks manically on his keyboard.

'Bloody Windows!' He frantically presses 'escape', and I peer at his screen, which is open to a photo of someone dressed as a furry Teddy bear in a bikini. He gives a sideways glance. 'I…What in God's name is this? Bill Gates's idea of a joke?'

He keeps pounding on the escape key, and I avert my eyes and head for the door. 'I'll stop by next Tuesday to pick up my bags,' I say, though I'm now having second thoughts about leaving any of my possessions with him.

'Jolly good,' he says. He stops clicking when I reach the threshold. 'Incidentally, where are you heading on your little detour? Somewhere nice?'

I look over my shoulder and smile. 'Paris.'

Before I leave for St Pancras station, I call my dad. Ever since Stevie and I spoke last week, I haven't been able to shake the idea that I'd been selfish in trying to evict Irene O'Malley. Sure, she was my mom's arch nemesis and is a supremely annoying individual, but if she makes my dad happy, well, how bad can she be, really? And who am I to say they shouldn't spend time together?

He picks up on the second ring, his voice more cheerful

than it's been in weeks, though, given it's my dad, 'cheerful' might be overstating it.

'So what's the word?' he says. 'Heading back to the Motherland already?'

'I'm taking a quick side trip to Paris first, but I'll be home next week.'

'What the heck happened? I thought things were good over there. Couldn't take any more fish and chips?'

'Something like that…'

'So what's next?'

'I'm working on a book proposal.'

'A book? Like a cookbook?'

'Sort of. More like a memoir with recipes.'

'Whose memoir?'

'Mine.'

'*Yours?*' I try not to bristle at my father's blatant shock. 'You're only twenty-eight. What the heck do you have to write about?'

'It's about me and Mom and growing up in Ypsi, and what it's like to be a cookbook ghostwriter.'

My dad hums, as if he is the great arbiter of memoir proposals. 'I guess it could be interesting,' he says. 'Does anyone but your friends and family actually want to read about that?'

'My agent seems to think so.'

'Your agent?' My dad whistles. 'Well, ex*cuuuuse* me.'

'It's not as fancy as it sounds.'

'Really? Because it sounds pretty impressive. Then again, most of the stuff you do sounds impressive to me.'

This is possibly the nicest thing my dad has said to me in the past twenty years. 'Thanks, Dad. That means a lot.'

'When would this book come out?'

'I have to sell it first. After I finish the proposal, my agent is going to pitch it to a few editors, and we'll see. Hopefully one of them will want to publish it.'

'You're saying you don't have a job *or* a book deal?'

'Correct.'

'Then how are you affording a trip to Paris? Last I checked, that wasn't exactly the cheapest destination...'

'I made enough money from this job to pay for a quick trip. I'm only staying five days.'

'Must have paid well, huh?'

'Well enough.'

Larry's deposits finally came through two days ago, after he resolved the series of problems, including lost paperwork and routing-number typos. Since Natasha fired me, I worried I'd never see a penny from her but, to my relief, she agreed to pay me for the work I'd completed. Whether this was her idea or Hugh's influence – or possibly another screw-up by Larry – I'll never know, but my bank account is now a lot fuller than it was three months ago. I'll never get the full $200,000 stipulated in the contract but, considering the circumstances, I'm not complaining.

'You planning to write this book from Ypsi, then?'

'Not sure. That's where I'll probably finish the proposal, but after that we'll see. Maybe I'll move near Meg in Ann Arbor. Or maybe I'll go someplace totally different, like Portland or New Orleans or Boston.'

'Keeping your options open, eh?'

'Something like that.'

'Good for you. Your mom would have liked that.'

I smile at the mention of my mom, the words in her letter

replaying in my mind. She was right: I needed to leave the Midwest, at least for a little while. What she probably didn't realize was that doing so would make me appreciate what I'd left behind.

'Speaking of Mom, I wanted to apologize for giving you such a hard time about Irene O'Malley. I spoke with Stevie, and he said you seem happy lately.'

'Happy's a bit strong…'

'Happier, then.'

'Yeah, I guess that's true. But don't worry. Irene isn't sleeping in your bed any more.'

My stomach turns as I flash back to Stevie's email about the snakes. 'Oh? Why not?'

'Well, it's your bed, and I figured you might be coming back at some point. And, anyway, you didn't seem too thrilled about the idea.'

'I was kind of getting used to it.'

'Really? Because it sure didn't sound that way last time we talked.'

'I guess I was worried she was taking advantage of you.'

'Listen, I'm no dummy. I thought she might be, too. But you know what? I didn't care. I missed the companionship. Having somebody in the house. I hadn't lived alone for almost forty years, Kelly. I either had roommates or your mom, and when I didn't have either…well, it was weird. Being all by myself with my thoughts – I didn't like it. Not one bit.'

'Then it's good she was there for you.'

'It was. And I realized…well, I kinda like her. She's not so bad. She's actually kinda nice to have around.' He catches himself. 'God, your mom is probably rolling in her grave.'

'I wouldn't rule it out.'

He sighs. 'The thing is, Irene makes me feel good. Better than I've felt in a long time. It's not like I'm going to marry her or anything. She's just keeping me company. Your mom was the love of my life, and she always will be. Full stop. But Mom's been gone four months now, and I know her better than anyone. She may have hated the idea of me and Irene spending time together, but that's because she loved me and wanted me for herself. Well, she's gone now, Kelly. And she's not coming back. And sometimes we don't have to listen to voices from beyond the grave. Sometimes we have to listen to the voices in our hearts.'

His words echo in my ears, and my eyes fill with tears. This is the most profound thing my father has said since…well, ever, as far as I can recall, and whether that's down to Irene or my mother's ghost or some secret depths he's managed to plumb, I'm glad for it. I brush away the tears with the back of my hand, wondering if my heart still has a voice, and if it does, if I still have the courage to hear it.

'So where is she sleeping now, if she's not in my bed?'

'At her own place. She still comes by to check on me a fair amount, and she's signed up for a massage class, so that should work out real well for me. She has remarkably strong hands, and when she works them the right way—'

'That'll do, thank you,' I say, cutting him off.

'Suit yourself.'

I glance at my watch. 'Hey, Dad? I hate to do this, but if I don't leave in the next two minutes, I'm going to miss my train.'

'Then by all means…'

'I'll email you from Paris, and I'll call from Heathrow before my flight.'

427

'Okey-dokey. Don't let me hold back the Madigan World Traveller.'

I laugh. 'You sound good, Dad. Really good.'

'I sound how I sound.'

'Well, whatever you're doing, keep it up.'

'Couldn't stop if I tried.'

'Good. I love you.'

'Love you, too. Oh, but real quick before you go – I'm considering getting a pet. A dog. Maybe a black Lab or something like that. What do you think?'

A grin crosses my face as I remember the words in my mom's letter. 'I think it's a great idea.'

'Yeah? Okay, good. Then it's settled. You can tell your brother to take his crazy ideas and stick them where the sun don't shine.'

'Crazy ideas?'

'About pets.'

'What about them?'

He sighs into the phone, as if merely speaking the idea out loud is too ridiculous, even for him. 'I don't know,' he says. 'Something about snakes...'

As I wait on the platform at St Pancras, I glance up at the arched glass roof, which is traversed by wrought-iron beams and rises some hundred feet from the ground. Light pours in, drenching me in the shimmering evening sun, and as people rush around me, I close my eyes and soak up the noise bouncing off the rafters.

'Now boarding, the nineteen oh one train to Paris Gare du Nord...'

I snap out of my trance and push through the open

428

doors, taking a window seat in the second car from the front. I watch throngs of busy travellers scurry along the platform and wonder where they're heading. I decide the man in the tailored navy suit is rushing home to see his family after a busy day of meetings in Paris, and the teenage girls running for my train are about to visit France for the first time. I've always loved creating stories for other people – it's what I've always done, it's what I'm good at – but now, as I sit on the train, I wonder what story I'm creating for myself. Who am *I*? Where am I headed?

'This seat taken?'

I look up, and my eyes land on a stocky young man with thick brown hair and black-rimmed glasses. 'Nope. All yours.'

He hesitates for a moment, gripping his bag in his hand. 'It's...Kelly, isn't it?'

I hold my breath as I try to place his round face and broad shoulders. 'Sorry...do I know you?'

He reaches out his hand. 'James. We met at the Blind Pig last month. With your friend Jess?'

'Oh – right, of course. I'm sorry. A lot has happened since that night.'

'No worries. You spent most of the time chatting to my mate, Harry, so I'm not surprised you don't remember me.'

My cheeks flush at the mention of Harry's name. Oh, God. What must James think of me? What must Harry think of me? I never did hear from him.

James gestures at the aisle seat. 'You're sure you don't mind if I sit here?'

'Not at all.'

I scoot closer to the window, as if to make room, even

though there is plenty of space between us. He plops into the seat and pulls a well-worn book from his bag.

'Harry and I were actually supposed to meet up a few times,' I say, 'but I kept having to cancel because my boss was a little crazy.'

'Maybe you'll have better luck in Paris, then.'

'Sorry?'

'In Paris. I'm meeting up with Harry and some other mates from uni. Sort of a send-off before Harry moves to the States at the end of the summer.'

'He got the fellowship at Harvard?'

James looks surprised. 'How did you know about that?'

'We talked about it at the Blind Pig. He wasn't sure he'd get it – or that he'd take it.'

'Well, he did, and he is.'

'That's amazing. Tell him I say congrats.'

'Tell him yourself. I'm sure he'd love to see you.' He leans in conspiratorially. 'He'd kill me for telling you this, but he was really disappointed when you kept cancelling. He figured you weren't interested.'

'No – really, it wasn't that at all. My boss kept changing her plans, and then life sort of…spiralled out of control. But I'd love to meet up with him – with all of you. I'll be on my own.'

'Brilliant. I'll let him know. You have his number?'

'Unless he's changed it.'

'Nope. Same as always.' He grins. 'And we all thought he turned you off with talk of trade subsidies or globalization.'

'No – at least, not yet.'

James laughs. 'He always was a bit of a swot. But a lovable one.'

'What's a swot?'

'Think Hermione Granger. Number-one student. Eager to please. Loves learning for learning's sake.'

'In that case, I think I might be a bit of a swot, too.'

'Then maybe this really is a match made in Heaven.'

I smile. 'Maybe it is.'

'All aboard!'

Our heads snap up as the last passengers hurry to their seats. The doors close, and the train lurches forward, gaining speed as it pulls out of the station. We chug past the crowd on the platform, the faces blurring together as the engine accelerates towards Paris, towards the future, towards the unknown. James takes a deep breath and raises his eyebrows expectantly as the car fills with the hum of the wheels against the track. 'Here's to adventure, eh?'

My eyes linger on his and, for a moment, I feel as if my mother is on the train with me, her presence so full and real that I half expect to turn around and see her sitting in the seat behind me. *Adventure*. I'd thought that was what the past three months had been about – England, Natasha, Hugh – but maybe it's this. Maybe my adventure is now. Maybe this is just the beginning. And maybe it doesn't have to end. A chill races up my spine as the train whooshes down the track, pressing on at great speed.

'To adventure,' I say, and though I can't be sure, I swear I hear someone behind me humming 'Dancing Queen'.

# *Recipes*

Cup measures are US cup size (8 fluid ounces). All other measurements are US imperial. A Tala Cook's Measure will help you calculate the correct quantity if you don't have US cups. You will find conversion charts on the Internet.

## Spaghetti Salad
Serves 10–12

This recipe was given to me by my friend, Marie, who grew up in Ypsilanti. The original recipe calls for 6 teaspoons of 'Accent seasoning salt', which is just monosodium glutamate (MSG), and some may have trouble finding it. If you can't or don't want to use it, just season with additional salt to taste.

1 lb vermicelli/thin spaghetti
1 large green pepper, diced
3 stalks celery, diced
1 large sweet onion, diced
1 cup diced Swiss cheese
1 cup diced ham
8 teaspoons sour cream
2 cups Miracle Whip
4 teaspoons sugar
8 teaspoons apple cider vinegar
1 teaspoon salt
1 teaspoon pepper
6 teaspoons Accent seasoning salt

Cook the vermicelli according to the package instructions, until *al dente*. Drain. Combine the pasta with the green pepper, celery, onion, cheese and ham. Toss together.

In a separate bowl, mix together the sour cream, Miracle Whip, sugar, apple cider vinegar, salt, pepper and Accent (if using). Add the dressing to the pasta and vegetables, stir it in, and refrigerate at least three hours before serving.

## Banana Bread
Makes 1 loaf

This isn't the prettiest banana bread, but it might be the tastiest. I compared and tweaked many recipes until I came up with this one. It develops a lovely crunchy crust, which disappears upon storing, but the flavour only improves. Use the ripest bananas you can find – the blacker the better.

1 ½ cups plain flour
1 teaspoon baking powder
1 teaspoon baking soda
½ teaspoon salt
6 tablespoons unsalted butter, at room temperature
½ cup caster sugar
½ cup light brown sugar
3 eggs
1⅓ cups mashed ripe banana (about 3–4)
⅓ cup full-fat Greek yogurt
1 teaspoon vanilla

Preheat the oven to 325°F. Grease a 9" × 5" loaf pan and line the bottom with a piece of parchment paper long enough to drape over the sides.

In a small bowl, whisk together the flour, baking powder, baking soda and salt.

In a large bowl, using an electric mixer, beat the butter with the sugars until fluffy. Add the eggs one at a time, beating well after each addition. Add the mashed banana, yogurt and vanilla and mix until combined. Pour in the dry ingredients and mix, on low speed, just until the dry ingredients disappear.

Pour the batter into the pan and bake for 60–70 minutes, until the top is browned and a toothpick inserted into the centre comes out clean. Let the loaf cool in the pan on a rack for 10 minutes, then run a knife around the edges to loosen it. Using the parchment to help you, lift the banana bread from the pan and transfer to a wire rack to cool completely. Store for up to 3 days.

## Chocolate Mousse
Serves 10 or more

My mom has been making a version of this mousse for years, and everyone always loves it. She usually pours it into a springform pan lined with sponge ladyfingers, so that it's more like a charlotte, but I've also served it as a traditional mousse, and people go crazy for it.

1 lb 61–70 per cent cocoa solids chocolate, chopped
3 ounces unsalted butter, softened
3 eggs, separated, at room temperature
½ cup sifted icing sugar
2 tablespoons dark rum
2 tablespoons crème de cacao
1 teaspoon instant coffee granules
2 cups double cream

Melt the chocolate and butter together in a heatproof bowl, either set over a pot of simmering water or in the microwave. Once the chocolate is completely melted and smooth, remove it from the heat and set it aside.

Whisk the eggs yolks with the sugar, rum, crème de cacao and coffee in a very large mixing bowl. Stir in the chocolate, adding a little at first, then the rest.

Whip the cream in a large bowl until stiff. Gently but thoroughly fold the whipped cream into the chocolate mixture, adding a small amount first to lighten the mixture, then the rest.

Beat the egg whites in a medium bowl until soft peaks form. Fold the egg whites into the chocolate cream. Refrigerate overnight. Serve in bowls or goblets.

## Sesame Chicken
Serves 4

This is my grandmother's famous sesame chicken. Every time I smell it cooking or take a bite, I think of her. You can easily double the recipe.

4 bone-in, skin-on chicken breasts
½ teaspoon paprika
½ teaspoon garlic powder
lemon pepper (or freshly ground black pepper, if lemon
    pepper is unavailable)
sea salt
1 tablespoon sesame seeds
½ cup plain flour
table salt
sunflower or rapeseed oil

Season the chicken breasts evenly with the paprika and garlic powder, the lemon pepper (or black pepper) and sea salt, to taste, being sure to rub under the skin as well. Sprinkle the sesame seeds over the top and press them down so that they stick. Place the chicken on a dish, cover, and refrigerate at least 6 hours.

Preheat the oven to 425°F. Line a large baking pan with foil and pour in the oil to a depth of about ⅛ inch to cover the bottom. Place the pan in the oven until the oil sizzles when you drop some flour into it.

Place the flour in a shallow dish and season with a little salt and pepper. Dredge the chicken breasts in the flour mixture, covering them completely on both sides and tapping off the excess.

Place the chicken in the pan, skin side down. Return the pan to the oven and reduce the temperature to 400°F. Bake for 30 minutes, then turn the chicken over and continue to cook for 20 minutes more, or until golden brown.

Drain on paper towels and serve.

## Dried Apricot Canapés with Herbed Goat Cheese and Serrano Ham
Serves 8–10

If you can't find serrano ham, you could easily substitute prosciutto, or even speck for a smoky twist.

2 slices serrano ham
4 ounces goat cheese, at room temperature
2 teaspoons milk
4 teaspoons minced chives
40 dried, ready to eat apricots

Preheat the oven to 375°F. Line a baking sheet with parchment paper and place the slices of serrano ham on top. Bake for 15 minutes, until it has darkened. Remove with tongs and drain on paper towels: it will become crisp as it cools. Crumble into large shards.

In a small bowl, beat the goat cheese and milk together until fluffy. Mix in the chives.

Spread a small amount of the herbed goat cheese on top of each apricot and top each one with a shard of crisp serrano ham.

## Sweet Potato Fries
Serves 3–4 (or 2, if you're really hungry...)

The key to crisp oven fries is not crowding the pan. Use two pans if you need to – there should be plenty of space between the fries.

2 large sweet potatoes
¼ cup cornflour
1 teaspoon salt
¼ cup olive oil

Preheat the oven to 425°F. Line one or two baking sheets with parchment paper.

Peel the sweet potatoes and cut them into ½-inch-wide batons. Soak them in a large bowl of cold water for at least 30 minutes and up to half a day.

Mix the cornflour and salt together in a plastic bag.

Drain the fries and pat them dry with paper towels (you don't want them too wet, or the cornflour will get soggy: you need just enough moisture for the cornflour to stick).

Dump the fries into the bag and shake vigorously to coat them with the cornflour mixture.

Before you place the fries on the baking sheets, drop them into a sieve and shake off the excess cornflour. Then put them on the baking sheets, making sure there is enough space between them.

Drizzle olive oil over the fries and toss to coat them evenly. Bake for 15 minutes. Flip them with a spatula and bake for 10–15 minutes longer, until they are crispy.

# *Acknowledgements*

As always, a big thank you to my editors, Esi Sogah at Kensington and Dominic Wakeford at Little, Brown. Working with the two of you is such a joy. And thanks to the rest of my publishing team: Jane Nutter, Vida Engstrand, Kristine Noble and Steven Zacharius at Kensington, and Grace Vincent, James Gurbutt and the entire team at Little, Brown. And a massive thank you to Hazel Orme – you are, truly, the best copy editor on the planet.

Thanks to Scott Miller and Sylvie Rosokoff at Trident for your continued hard work. I am so lucky to have both of you in my corner.

I couldn't have written this book without the help of the cookbook ghostwriters who were kind enough to answer my phone calls and emails and respond to my many questions. You know who you are, and I am forever grateful.

I am also hugely grateful to Marie Hughes Chough for

giving me a primer on growing up in Ypsilanti. Your detailed accounts of Ypsi life were beyond helpful. And thank you for your mom's spaghetti salad recipe – a crucial part of the book!

This novel would still be a messy draft on my computer if it weren't for the help of my early readers. Thanks to Sophie McKenzie for your British insights, and to Mandi Schweitzer for writing a note that transformed the book.

For the first time, I let my mom read a draft of this book, and I'm so glad I did. Thanks, mom, for your useful advice and unconditional support – and know that I will be calling on you again in the future! And thanks to my dad for continuing to spread the word about my books. You are a great publicist and an even greater dad.

Thanks to my brother, Brian, for continuing to make me laugh. Maybe one day I'll be as funny in writing as you are in person.

A huge thank you to Alice Pooran – I never would have made my deadline if it hadn't been for your help.

And finally to Roger and Alex: thank you both for inspiring me to be a better writer, wife, mother and person. You have utterly transformed my life, and I love you.